THE HIBBING HURT

a novel

by pat mcgauley

For the literary gentlemen of the 'Greater Mesaba' book club, past and present.

Copyright pending: 8/28/05
Manufactured in the United States of America. PJM Publishing.

ISBN: 0-9724209-3-2
First Edition, October 2005

Cover photograph from Aubin's Portrait Studio,
Hibbing, MN 55746.

Minnesota author, Pat McGauley, is a former Hibbing High School teacher. Born in Duluth, McGauley grew up in Hoyt Lakes, graduated from Winona State University (BS) and the University of Minnesota (MA). Former mineworker and historian, McGauley has lived in Hibbing for the past forty years.

Other novels and stories by Pat McGauley:

'Mesabi Series' Trilogy

To Bless or To Blame	(2002)
A Blessing or a Curse	(2003)
Blest Those Who Sorrow	(2004)

Children's Stories

Mazral and Derisa: An Easter Story	(2004)
Santa The King	(2004)

This story, the Hibbing Hurt, was conceived three years ago. From a rough draft to finished book became a lengthy endeavor. In February of 2005, I passed the story to my friends of the G.M.M.B.C. (Greater Mesabi Men's Book Club) for their critical review. I want to thank the following 'book scholars' for their remarkable insights and critique: Rich Dinter, Ed Beckers, Jim Huber, Charlie Grant, Roger Saccoman, Craig Holgate, and Colin Issacson. My friend Andy Miller also scrutinized the story.

Norma Grant and Faith Marston did the tedious text editing. Shirley Burritt typed the preliminary manuscript, and Shawn Nevalainen did the technical manuscript formatting and cover prep.

I am grateful to the staffs of the Hibbing Public Library, Hibbing Historical Society, and Ironworld Research Center for their always kind assistance.

We do, as the lyrics of a sixties Beatles classic suggest, "...Get by with a little help from our friends..." My sincerest thanks to all of you. And, to you—my readers— for your encouragement and support.

My intention was to remain in Hibbing until after my old friend's funeral; then return to pressing matters at home. But an unexpected opportunity to meet Kevin Moran presented itself. In that the Moran family had been an integral part of my writing life since the early 1980's, I could hardly pass on the luncheon invitation.

Lingering those few additional days would also provide occasion to further browse around the community I had written so much about in previous novels. Days quickly became a week. Then something unexpected happened to dramatically change my plans.

That something was a story! A story with pathos, depth, and an emotional tug beyond anything my creative gifts might have conjured. And, adding further dimension to the intrigue, I found myself caught in the middle of every unfolding detail—day-by-day, and week-by-week—until mid-December.

A young Hibbing man had mysteriously disappeared! Adding to my personal anguish, the ill-fated episode stabbed deeply into the hearts and minds of those very people I had come to know so intimately while researching my earlier books.

When a small town experiences an incident as heinous as this, the delicate fabric of life is shattered like a hammer striking glass. Such is especially so when the undertones are blatantly racial. Since its inception in the late 1880's, Hibbing had always prided itself as being an exemplar of the great American *melting pot*. But sadly, some elements of that timeworn perception were made of an ice that never quite melted.

So, during those months, I watched the players of the evolving drama through the eyes of a journalist. I listened to the street talk and engaged locals in discussions about the crime which had became more widely discussed than the '56 Presidential elections. On two occasions I had lunch with Kevin Moran at his grandiose Androy Hotel. Being as close as he was to all that was happening, the lawyer-businessman talked candidly about politics and sports, while remaining circumspect about matters sensitive to the ongoing investigation. He did, however, conclude one of our conversations with a heartfelt observation: *"Like myself, all of Hibbing is hurting these days!"*

Early one morning in October, I had a cup of coffee in the Androy Coffee Shop with Kevin's son, Officer Pack Moran. The introspective young man was pleasant but noticeably cool toward me. He knew who I was and why I had remained in Hibbing. "Don't believe what you read in the papers or hear on the street," he said— biting off each word for emphasis. His green eyes were riveting, his rare smile enigmatic. I had the feeling that my inner motivations were being probed and measured against some yardstick of his own definition. Pack had a subtle remoteness that I had rarely experienced before. Unlike his amiable father, he made me feel discomfited and defensive.

Much later, when the sordid details had been sorted out and properly concluded, I realized that—of all the people involved— Pack Moran would capture center stage in what would soon become this story. When typing my last words, I considered something profound that Pack had told me before I left Hibbing in December..."*There are no heroes in your story..."*

1/ PACK MORAN
September 1956

Amidst the bustle of early morning activity in the hotel lobby, none of the staff on duty, nor any of the many lingering guests, noticed the delivery. Perhaps the distraction caused when a young man bumped a waiter, spilling a tray of coffee, had something to do with the collective disregard. With covert facility, another man slipped an unstamped envelope into the assortment of mail already stuffed inside a specific box an arm's length from the mahogany registration counter. Below the rectangular cubicle was a brass nameplate identifying the Androy Hotel's esteemed owner, Kevin Moran.

~

From a crest on the cemetery's western hillside, twenty-six year old Pack Moran watched the somber funeral scene unfolding below. The Hibbing police officer was on duty this September morning. Shielding his eyes from the sun's shimmering glare, his focus riveted upon the tall, auburn-haired man. "Hang in there, Dad..." he said under his breath. Pack could sense the restrained emotion in Kevin Moran's downcast focus upon the dark hole only feet away from where his father was standing. "It's almost over now, Dad," he mumbled a conclusion to his thought.

Although Pack had not known Claude Atkinson very well, he was well aware of the strong bond between the late newspaper man and his father. His understanding that the deceased journalist had been both a surrogate father and mentor to Kevin was a sobering reality.

He watched with a heavy heart of his own.

The father-son bond between Pack and Kevin Moran had been forged by years of sensitive life-sharing conversations. To this day, the two men were able to open their thoughts and souls to each other.

On countless occasions, Pack had been told about how his father had grown up with adoptive parents and had never known about his biological father. Perhaps that reality, more than anything else, was the reason for Kevin's need to be so deeply involved in the life of his oldest son.

Pack wished he could read his father's thoughts at this moment.

Kevin Moran pondered the obscure and transient reality of life. He imagined our time on earth as a river on its course to a far distant sea of conclusion. Some rivers meandered along, flowing almost peacefully across the lay of the land without any discernible turbulence. Others, however, roiled in restless tumult over ragged outcroppings, tumbling ever downward while sweeping away every obstruction. Although his own life of nearly fifty years had been marked by a little of each extreme, recent times had been relatively comfortable and placid. Yet his musings were stirred this morning-his easy river churned uncomfortably. Inside the breast pocket of his expensive black suit coat, the letter he concealed diffused a troubling heat. He would deal with the matter later; after this trying ordeal had unfolded itself.

The trace of a smile etched his handsome features as his eyes averted the hole and regarded his lovely wife, Angela, who was deep in thoughts of her own at his side. His devoted wife, and the mother of their three children, was his most trusted confidante and friend. Sensing his glance, she gave his elbow a knowing squeeze.

Kevin and Angela Moran were standing among those gathered in the front row of the graveside farewell. The river that had been the life of Claude Atkinson had run its course. As Kevin contemplated the man and the meaning of this ceremony, a lump formed in his throat. Christian burial rites were intended to nurture one's belief in an omnipotent God, to bolster a concept of life eternal, as well as to inspire a sense of solace and peace. But to Kevin, in these moments of remembrance, the observance seemed far more painful than comforting.

While kneeling beside the finality of Claude's casket during wake visitations the night before, Kevin's emotions had been drained in their fullest measure. The funeral ceremony at First Lutheran Church earlier that morning nurtured the progress of his healing. But now, in the solemnity of this cemetery, his every emotion became unsettled again—like a scab being torn from a wound.

Following the burial, a community reception was scheduled. There, with the sharing of good fellowship, the subdued laughter of old memories, and plates filled with various ethnic foods, the final chapter in a book that had been Claude Atkinson's wonderful life would be concluded.

Pack watched his father's gaze move from the earthen void to a passing bank of clouds above. His father always found mystical images in clouds, and had often told his son that clouds allowed him to interpret things suspended in a realm between earth and heaven. Pack mused on that concept as his own eyes tried, without discernible success, to read something in the floating billows.

Kevin looked down for a final moment, blessed himself with a sign of the cross, placed a hand on Angela's shoulder and drew her to his side.

Pack Moran was Patrick Anthony Claude Moran. His parents had named him after an old priest friend, Father Pat Foley, his grandfather Tony Zoretek, and Claude Atkinson, his father's departed friend. Three strong men were embodied in a name he had struggled to become comfortable with over the years. Despite the circumstances, Pack could not keep a smile from his lips over a fleeting memory from his childhood. He remembered that time when he seriously began to dislike the name Patrick—back in the fifth grade when everyone called him Pat. There had been a girl in his class named Patty Murray. Patty was his first crush and 'Pat and Patty' sounded stupid when the ten-year-old mulled it over in his thoughts back then. Patrick was determined to change that!

"I don't want to be called Patrick, or even Pat, anymore, Dad," he informed his father one evening after finishing his homework (and a note he had just finished writing to Patty, offering to help her with a difficult science project). "I hate my name!"

"What's wrong with Patrick, Son? He was a great Irish saint, you know. And Father Foley is a saint in his own right."

Patrick tried to explain his awkward circumstance without divulging his feelings for Patty Murray. "Pat could be a girl's name, Dad. It's not really...what's the word—maskalin? And I don't want to be called Tony or Claude, either."

Understanding his son's perceived dilemma, Kevin gave the matter some thought. Combining the first letter of the three names provided an unusual, but certainly masculine, nickname. "How about Pack?" (Kevin had added a k for an emphasis to his proposal). "Pack Moran! What do you think about that, son?"

At school the following day, Patrick shared his new nickname with his pals, Tim Sullivan and Andy Brandt—as well as with Patty Murray. The two boys merely shrugged at the notion, but his pretty, red-haired 'girlfriend' confided that Pack sounded just great! In her next breath, however, Patty informed Pack that she got his note—but was already getting help with her science project from Benny Robinson. "He's so smart...and, so cute, too." In the first few hours of his cleverly masculine nickname, Pack had failed to sufficiently impress that one person in the world he most wanted to affect.

But from that day on, Patrick became *Pack* to almost everybody. Everybody except his mother who was appalled, insisting that he come up with something more appropriate. "It makes me think of cigarettes!" Angela had told him in a sharp tone of indignation. "My son—a *package* of cigarettes!" Despite her protest, however, the Pack moniker stuck with the lad. To this day, only his mother unfailingly called him Patrick.

While in junior high school, Pack joined two of his father's friends from St. Paul on a fishing excursion at Timo's Lake east of Hibbing. Kiernan McGinnis and Duane Locher were retired cops. While listening to the men's colorful police stories, and realizing his father's deep respect of the two men, Pack developed a lucid picture of what he wanted to become some day. After the experience, he asked his dad, "Do you have to be really tough to be a policeman?" Kevin smiled at the notion. "Not really. Being courageous and fair-minded are much more important. And wanting to help people, of course."

Sturdily framed like his father, but a few inches shorter, Pack had been an all-conference athlete in both hockey and baseball for the Hibbing High School Bluejackets. As a freshman puckster he took a high stick from an Eveleth defenseman, which left a one-inch scar on his square chin. The gash was his 'badge' of emerging manhood— almost like an exclamation mark behind the name Pack. When stationed in Pusan as an Army M.P. for two years during the Korean Conflict, he was called 'Packo' by his partner Carlos Vasquel and the other GI's in his unit. While breaking up a fracas in his barracks, he added a second scar—this one over his right eye. Back in Hibbing after his military stint, he became Officer Pack Moran on the local police force. As a policeman, he was fair-minded and helpful to those in need- but he was tenacious, too! His intolerance of those who 'stepped over the line' had earned him the reputation of being a tough cop.

Pack spotted his younger sister huddling behind the Johnsons and Moores who were among the group of mourners near a far edge of the cemetery gathering. Mary Rebecca Moran was 'Maribec' to all who knew her—even her mother. He cursed audibly under his breath, "What the hell is she doing!" Circling behind and down the hillside he approached his sister unseen. "Put out that damn cigarette, Maribec! For God's sake, you know you're not supposed to be smoking while a funeral is going on."

Mary drew a deep final drag and tossed the butt off to the side. "You're not my damn father, Pack. You wanna give me a ticket or something...Officer?" She glowered at her brother. "I didn't want to be here for this thing anyhow. Mom and Dad said 'if I didn't come they'd be disappointed'. Jeeze. This funeral stuff gives me the creeps."

"Is that why you're hiding back here where no one can see you?"

Maribec gave him a sharp scowl without reply. Pulling out a small bag of Sen Sen from her purse and pouring a handful in her mouth she squinted at the sharp burn on her tongue. "How much longer is that minister going to be droning on, for God's sake? He's been talking all this morbid religious stuff for half an hour already. I've got a lot better things to do than to hang around here."

"Have you no respect? Claude was one of Dad's best friends. Why do you have to be so negative all the time?"

Turning away, Pack's attention returned to the graveside where the clergyman was pronouncing a final blessing over the simple mahogany casket. In moments the crowd would begin to disperse. "I'm going to visit with Dad for a few minutes. He called me early this morning. There's something—a letter, I think—that he wants to tell me about. Why don't you join Mom and Grampa before they leave?"

As the service concluded, Pack watched his parents' small talk with friends standing nearby. He waited a moment. When his dad gave his mother a quick parting kiss, he returned his gaze to Maribec who was driving the heel of her shoe into the soft turf. "Looks like Mom's going to get a ride with Grampa. Maybe you'd better catch up with them. I'm going to hang around here for a few minutes. See what's on Dad's mind."

"I'm not going to any reception, Pack. If they won't drop me off at my apartment, I'll walk back to town." Maribec gave her brother a quick frown, "And don't think for a minute that I'm going to take a ride with you in that squad car." She spotted Annie Rebrovich, a nurse from the hospital, and waved in her direction. "I've found a ride—see ya later officer. Have a good day and arrest someone."

As the minister gestured for family members to proceed toward the idling hearse, Kevin met Angela's dark eyes; "I'd like to wander around the cemetery for a few minutes, Angie. I don't get out here to pay my respects often enough. Could you catch a ride with Dad?" He gestured toward the Zoretek's who were visiting with the widow Dinter and her family.

Kevin wandered across the freshly mown, fragrant slopes toward a cluster of pine trees. A matching pair of headstones marked the burial sites of two of his dearest friends. Throughout most of his life, Senia Arola had been 'Aunty Senia' to Kevin. Originally from Finland, Senia had made her life in Hibbing for nearly fifty years. Next to her grave was that of Steven Skorich. Soft-spoken, compassionate Steven. Like many of Hibbing's early settlers, Steven came from Slovenia and had worked in the iron ore mines. He and Senia were closer than most husbands and wives, but never chose to get married. Steven died while hunting during the Armistice Day blizzard of 1940.

Walking farther down the hillside past the headstones of Lars Udahl and Norman Dinter, Kevin stopped at the grave of Rudy Zoretek, the younger brother of his father-in-law, Tony. Rudy had been killed in an automobile accident near Chisholm in 1950. Life could be so very short for some, he realized. And unfulfilled. It was much too brief for those like Rudy—and enriched with many years for others like Claude Atkinson. But, trying to comprehend God's plan for every soul was far too overwhelming for him.

2/ FATHER AND SON

Watching his father from a tree-shadowed distance was his son. He wanted to respect Kevin's moments of reflection. A lump formed in Pack's throat Pack when he saw his father crying. Dad had always been as solid as a rock. This was a side of the strong-willed man that the son had rarely seen. Kevin was standing near Rudy's grave and Pack could well understand his father's unabashed grief. When Kevin began to turn away, rubbing his eyes with a coat sleeve, Pack called out in a strained voice that easily carried the distance between them. "Hey, Dad...you okay?"

Without trace of embarrassment, Kevin replied in a tone hoarse with emotion, "Just a very sad day, Son." Recovering his composure and forcing a thin smile, he added; "Lots of memories resting here. I'm fine now."

Kevin pulled sunglasses from his breast pocket as Pack walked in his direction. His son looked smart in the dressy navy blue uniform with its brass buttons and shiny sergeant's badge. The young man had many of Angie's features: dark hair and olive complexion, wide set eyes, narrow nose. Yet, no one would doubt he was Kevin's son with his broad shoulders and square jaw. Pack was Kevin and Angela's first born. Daughter Mary followed Patrick four years later. And Steven Peter, the youngest of the Moran children, was a sixteen-year-old sophomore at Hibbing High School. His three children centered Kevin's life and gave him satisfaction beyond measure. All were very different. Pack was an achiever and pragmatist, Maribec his opposite in both regards, and Steven something of both. While Pack was athletically inclined like Kevin, and Maribec creative like her mother, Steven had interests similar to his schoolteacher uncle, Marco Zoretek. The teenager's life was focused almost exclusively on playing his piano and listening to rock and roll music.

Kevin realized that his family's wealth inspired high expectations in the minds of both him and Angela. Yet both were in agreement that the college degrees and professional careers which so many parents push their children to achieve were far less important than insuring opportunities for their happiness. Neither parent had ever suggested that their children do anything they didn't determine to do for themselves. "My ambitions and motivations are mine—not yours," Kevin once told his son. "Just be yourself!" was Angela's constant reminder.

Pack had finished a year of college before enlisting in the military. It was his decision to make. And it was not a decision made without considerable thought and foresight. He was determined to become a policeman and the army offered the regimen of discipline and training he needed.

Mary Rebecca, strikingly attractive, dark-haired, and small-framed like her mother, possessed her mother's artistic inclinations as well. The twenty-two year old had chosen to become a nurse and had lived on her own since graduating without distinction from high school. Angela would describe her daughter as being more spirited than Pack and, unlike her older brother, a nonconformist in nearly every manner of dress and demeanor. To the degree that Pack had clearly defined ambitions, to Maribec life was to be experienced without the structure of any predetermined goals.

Steven Moran's young life read like a roadmap. He was destined to become a musician. Of that reality neither Kevin nor Angela had any doubt. So nurturing his passions and fantasies was never an issue.

Stepping close and embracing his father, Pack struggled to keep his own emotions in check. "Lots of memories out here, for sure, Dad. Rudy was—well, he was really special to all of us." Eyes cast upon the granite gravestone, Pack remembered the accident as if it were only yesterday and realized that he might well have been a part of that late July tragedy.

It had been a Saturday night after a championship softball game in Chisholm. Pack played on the same team as Rudy, and all the guys were celebrating winning the tournament over a keg of beer. Underage at the time, Pack sipped Coca Colas despite the teasing he endured from others who were also too young to be drinking. Before Rudy left the party, he hollered at Pack to join himself and Cory Debevek along with two other players to ride back to Hibbing. Although Cory was probably too drunk to drive, nobody raised any objections when he took the wheel. Rudy was in the passenger seat when Cory's Plymouth left the highway minutes later. Only Rudy, from among the four men, was killed.

"I almost caught a ride with Cory that night, Dad. Almost! Thank God I...well, I hung around the party a while longer."

Releasing from Pack's bear-like hug, Kevin placed his two hands on his son's wide shoulders. "Thank God is right! Like Rudy, we never know when our time might come. I guess I'm a fatalist about those things, but sometimes I can't help thinking about predestination." Kevin frowned over his observation, letting the concept drop without further elaboration.

"Dad...something wrong?"

"What...?"

"You just had the strangest look on your face, that's all."

"Oh, just morbid thoughts, I guess," Kevin forced a weak smile. "Cemetery thoughts." Gesturing his hand over the green landscape, "No place like a graveyard to remind a person of his ultimate mortality."

Pack frowned at his father's unusual melancholy without comment.

Sensing his son's concern, Kevin lightened up. "Enough of this. I've made my rounds, said my prayers...Let's get ourselves over to Claude's reception. We don't want Mom to be stuck there all by herself."

"She'll be fine, Dad. You know that. And I won't be able to..." Pack peered into his father's reddened eyes. "Wasn't there some letter you wanted to tell me about this morning?"

Kevin remembered his earlier phone call to Pack, and the troubling envelope tucked into his suit coat pocket. For the past several minutes of private reverie, he'd forgotten. Linking his arm with his son and beginning to walk in the direction of his car, Kevin said, "Thanks for reminding me. I've got something I want to show you." He withdrew the unmarked envelope and handed it to Pack. "It had to have been slipped in with my regular mail this morning. I have no idea what to make of it. But, it's vulgar, and...here, read it for yourself."

The scrawled note had only two capitalized words, 'NIGGER LOVER'.

"What the hell is this about? NIGGER LOVER?"

"I found it with the mail in my box. Someone at the hotel must have put it there because it didn't come through regular postal delivery."

Pack could feel the chilling hatred in the words. "You think it was someone at the hotel? Why...?" He met his father's eyes, "This has something to do with Gary Zench, doesn't it?"

"It must. Who else could it be, Pack?"

Gary Zench was a childhood friend of Kevin's when the two boys were growing up in a West Duluth neighborhood. Gary was a mulatto—his mother a Negro. It wasn't until Kevin was nine or ten that he realized his friend was different. That difference, however, only strengthened his friendship with the impoverished, father-abused, and wayward boy. By his late teens, Gary had dropped out of school and gotten himself in trouble with the police. After three years in the St. Cloud Reformatory (while Kevin was in college) Gary was paroled. Kevin convinced his unfortunate friend to come to Hibbing and finish his schooling.

Gary was bright and motivated to make something of his ravaged life. With Kevin's financial support and a small scholarship, he graduated with a degree in accounting from a Duluth business college. Following his graduation and marriage to Nora Pratt, Gary had rejoined Kevin in Hibbing and eventually became a manager at the Androy Hotel. The Negro couple had two children and lived in a tidy, three-bedroom home on a corner lot in the fashionable new Greenhaven development. The Zenches' were the only black family in Hibbing.

"Damn cowardly! And threatening as well." Pack said.

"Damned racist! And, yes, I take it as a threat," Kevin added. "I don't really know what to do about it. Have the police heard of any racial issues going on in town, Pack? This really caught me by surprise."

"Nothing to my knowledge, Dad. But this integration stuff down South is all over the news these days. Even so, your letter is the first anti-Negro thing I've heard about in Hibbing." Pack shrugged his shoulders; "I can pass it along to Chief Lawrence at the station if you think that will do any good.

"Maybe we should keep this between the two of us for now. You know as well as I that your boss is—"

"Incompetent?"

"Maybe indecisive is a better word, Pack."

Pack nodded. "How about Gary? Shouldn't you mention something to him about it?"

"I don't think so. Whoever wrote this garbage didn't make any specific threats toward Gary. And it was delivered to me—not him. Anyhow, I don't think my friend needs to worry over this."

"That may well be. But, keep your eyes open at the hotel, okay? If anything else comes up...well, just keep me posted. Meanwhile, I'll do some digging around on my own."

Kevin nodded without reply. He remembered overhearing racial jokes in the hotel coffee shop the day before. Ian Roberts, a retired mining official, was at a table with some of the Androy's morning regulars. Ian's comment brought a round of laughs: "The sheriff down in Biloxi said it was the worst suicide he'd ever seen. The nigger had stabbed himself sixty times with a butcher knife!"

Kevin pondered the fleeting memory. What could possibly explain bigotry in an isolated, out of the mainstream place like Hibbing?

"Thanks for letting me know about this harassment, Dad. We'll get to the bottom of it, I'm sure." Pack pulled his navy cap down over his eyes. "If you don't mind, I'm gonna run now. My regrets to the Atkinson family, but I can't make it to the reception."

Pack checked his wristwatch as he approached his squad car parked at the south end of the cemetery. It was eleven forty-five. He had spent more than half an hour in the cemetery. Like his father in so many ways, Pack felt an arcane attraction for these green acres.

During his first years on the force, when Pack patrolled on the night shift, he'd swing his squad through the quiet cemetery lanes. On many occasions Pack would focus his spotlight on the parked cars of teenagers who found the secluded location ideal for making out. After creating enough discomfort to hastily evacuate the parkers, he would often pull over to the veteran's burial plot off Highway 169 and spend a few prayerful minutes. With his flashlight, Pack would wander through the rows of white crosses marking Hibbing's fallen warriors. Among them were twelve young men who were Korean Conflict casualties. Men he'd known from high school or while in military service himself.

~

As he drove toward First Avenue, Kevin Moran's thoughts were scattered. Along with memories of Claude Atkinson and other friends, the strange note came back to mind. He ruminated on prejudice and hatred and his friend, Gary Zench, on his employees at the hotel, and on what he might do about the 'NIGGER LOVER' allegation? Pack was probably right—there had been no threats in the note. Yet the implication stirred an irritation inside.

Distracted by the crush of emotion, Kevin turned on his radio to catch the last few minutes of Rick Bourgoyne's 'Morning Show' on KHNG. His radio personality friend would probably be doing his sports report on the popular program. Kevin had grown up with sports and remained an ardent baseball fan.

3/ RADIO MAN

Rick Bourgoyne might never comprehend a most profound irony buried within the complex texture of his life. He had been born in the Rood Hospital of old North Hibbing on Thursday, October 24, 1918, at 6:42 in the evening. His parents had told him many times that he was most fortunate to be alive. Hibbing, and much of the United States, was experiencing the heart-wrench of a terrible pandemic influenza at the time. Of the hundreds who contracted the dreaded flu in Hibbing, forty-two people died. Among these was Mary Zoretek, the young and vivacious wife of Tony Zoretek. Mary had spiked a fever early in the morning of October 24th and passed from life at precisely 6:42 that night. At the moment of Mary Zoretek's last breath, Richard Bourgoyne breathed the very first breath of his life.

Within the fabric of some African cultures, there is a spiritual perception of this surreal occurrence. From every death comes new life. It is believed, therefore, that one's life journey is destined to complete the affairs of the person who has passed. The concept is a metaphysical justification and a rationale for death. Without any awareness of these primitive belief patterns, Rick Bourgoyne would never discern his mystical connection with the unknown woman who died at the moment of his birth thirty-eight years before. Rick's closest friend, Marco Zoretek, however, happened to be Mary's only son!

Rick's adult life had been a search for his niche in the scheme of things. After graduating from Hibbing High School somewhere in the middle of his class, and without motivation to do much of anything, he made his way to St. Paul. There, he tried some college, found a bartending job, tried—and failed—to 'find himself'. Facing the inevitable draft, Rick enlisted in the Navy, became a medic, and toured bloody Tarawa. In '45, the discharged veteran drifted to San Francisco.

While living in the Bay City, Rick Bourgoyne took a job in radio broadcasting at a small offbeat jazz radio station. He loved being a KBAY disc jockey but soon tired of the formatted music venue he was required to play. Feeling his need to improvise and ad lib being stifled, he quit. Idle time stirred homesickness and the lack of a paycheck churned a familiar restlessness. With few 'good-byes', he left California for Minnesota's thriving Twin Cities metro area. Maverick WDGY radio, was becoming the hottest station in The Cities, and Rick was hired to fill a late-night disc jockey slot and promised an ideal format—"You can do your own thing just so long as you don't offend our sponsors."

Renting a flat in 'Dinky Town', near the University campus, Rick found himself in the center of college fraternity party life. Despite the constant vitality of the neighborhood, he ended up spending most of his weekends and all of his vacation time on the Iron Range. Upon returning to Minneapolis after every quiet respite at home, Rick would ponder why his life had become so curiously centered in relatively isolated Hibbing. The attraction was always a puzzle.

When his father Edgar died suddenly of a heart attack in the winter of '52, Rick decided to make Hibbing his permanent home again. Some inscrutable magnetism drew him back to the place of his birth. It wasn't climate or career or romance—but it was something. Something he could never quite explain.

Radio broadcasting remained his career passion and KHNG of Hibbing was highly impressed with Rick's large-market professional experience. The station created an opening for him. Maureen Loiselle, the KHNG manager, agreed to allow Rick to be innovative, play his own kind of music, and mix dialogue with discs. In the early morning hours, Rick did the standard venue of music, news, sports, and weather.

Within a year, Rick's popularity with local listeners had given him local celebrity as "Ramblin' Rick". His dialogue was freewheeling and, as he put it..."from the hip!" His formula of provocative commentary mixed with quick humor and blended with a dash of audacity rarely failed to charm his audience.

In the first minutes of his Tuesday morning's program, Rick paid tribute to the respected newsman, Claude Atkinson. "My family grew up with Claude's Mesaba Ore newspaper and those timely editorials he was famous for. Let me tell any of you folks who might never have met the man or read his paper, he was the greatest! Mr. Atkinson, Hibbing's going to miss ya."

The headline story that morning amplified yet another in the tragic series of chapters which characterized this turbulent time in American history. The anti-integration pressure on Southern all-white schools was spawning a contemptible violence in one community after another. Today's focus was on Clinton, Tennessee, where nine Negro students were attempting to enroll at the local high school under the supervision of more than six hundred national guardsmen and ten tanks. Nearly eight hundred white students stayed home. In the riot the night before at nearby Oliver Springs, there had been gunfire, and dynamite blasts.

"What's wrong down there?" Rick's voice had a hard edge as he leaned over the microphone. "They just don't get the damn message! We're one country, one people...those days of 'separate but equal' treatment are gone folks." Rick realized he would get another reprimand as soon as the word damn left his mouth. The station manager had warned him more than once about the use of 'hells' and 'damns'.

Rick continued. "My heart goes out to those nine kids in Clinton. Can you imagine going to school surrounded by militia and tanks, and being jeered and spat upon by people who hate you? Hate you because your skin color happens to be black! I wish I had the guts to do what those kids are doing down there this morning. Let me tell you—that's gotta be a terrible thing for a child to experience. It's their high school."

He swallowed a profanity and continued without a losing a breath. "They want a decent education and they know damn well they're not going to get one at an all-Negro school." Another unconscious slip. "No. I just can't stomach racism! If we can't live together in harmony we're headed down a dead-end street. I can see it coming, folks...there's gonna be some violence one of these days. I mean really bad stuff! Racial madness like we haven't seen before. Negroes aren't going to tolerate this kind of unlawful, and unjustifiable, abuse much longer. Mark my words, the days of peaceful resistance to segregation are numbered."

Rick Bourgoyne realized the subject was getting him overwrought and that he needed a break from the Clinton integration story. The issue was sensitive and gut-wrenching, divisive and explosive.

With the approach of fall, politics and the national election were popular topics, so he steered his commentary in that direction. "Also in the national news this morning, President Eisenhower has a challenging agenda for the day. Ike will tee-off for eighteen holes of golf at ten-forty and dine with Mammie at six. Those of you who worry about the health of our Prez' ought to be more concerned with his golf score." Rick forced a laugh with his stab at humor. "Democrats. What would America do with Adlai? The guy is single and doesn't golf!" Hibbingites and the Iron Rangers were predominantly Democrats and Rick enjoyed being on the 'wrong' side of political controversies from time to time.

He glanced at his notes, then the wall clock, and realized he had less than a minute before doing ninety seconds of his sponsor's commercials. Near his elbow was a page of corny doctor-patient jokes relating to old-timer's ailments. "So the doctor told Millie— 'The check you gave me for your last visit came back.' Said Millie, in that sharp tone of hers—'So did my arthritis!' "

Rick gave his joke the inane laugh it deserved. "Now—moving right along to those who make my bad jokes possible. Micka Furniture has just announced its annual Fall Days Sale. Yes, folks, that new twenty-one inch General Electric television set you've wanted for your living room entertainment is now priced at only $149.88. The drastically reduced price is only good through this weekend...so hurry on down to Micka's Furniture before they're all gone!" Then in his 'folksy' voice, Rick added, "When you stop in, say hello to Abe Zimmerman—tell 'em 'King Rick' at KHNG sent ya." Montgomery Wards promoted their school clothing sale, the Red Owl grocery store offered double Green Stamps throughout this week, and the Lybba theater was showing High Society featuring Bing Crosby, Grace Kelly, and Frank Sinatra.

Burgoyne's program format was loosely structured. Usually he opened with national stories before moving on to state and local events. He kept a list of commercials he needed to get on air and often improvised the sponsor's message between breaks in the topics he'd chosen to cover. Throughout the Morning Show's two hours, his phone line was open to comments from listeners. Rick checked off the ads he'd just completed on the notepad at his elbow. Weather forecasts were interspersed throughout the program. To Northern Minnesotans, weather was always critical. Any unpredicted frost in early September might kill ripening tomato plants and Rick didn't want to be roundly criticized for not properly warning the local gardeners. Bad weather was the reporter's problem—Mother Nature never took the blame.

Rick reminded his audience that Hibbing's schools would begin classes on Thursday, as would schools in neighboring Chisholm and Keewatin. "Watch out for school buses and children in the streets...!"

He took a call from the Cobb Cook Elementary School principal, Robert Dietrich. The two men talked at length about school district policies. Then a parent, new to the community, phoned about bus schedules, pickup locations and class times.

Rick glanced toward the wall clock. Time was flying this morning. "You're listening to Rick Bourgoyne and the 'Morning Show' on the 'KING' of local radio, KHNG! It's a beauty out there this morning, and it's going to stay unusually mild through the week."

As he usually did, Rick gave a quick review of the evening's television shows. "Don't miss the 'Sixty-Four Thousand Dollar Question' at eight!" he insisted.

Over the next forty-five minutes, Rick did some TV and weather analysis, some bad jokes and trivia, and defended rock and roll music to an irate mother who thought her child was possessed of the devil for listening to such "shrill sounds and suggestive lyrics..." A high school girl called to request that KHNG play more Elvis Presley records, and another parent phoned to complain that if the station played any more Elvis, "I'll turn my radio to WEBC in Duluth!" Enjoying the lively banter, Rick blurted his favorite Rhett Butler line: "Frankly, ma'am, I don't give a damn!"

It was approaching 11:30, time for his next ninety-second commercial break. Looking up from his microphone, Rick noticed Maureen Loiselle at the window peering into his small studio. Maury was the station manager, and Rick sensed by the expression on her face that she was not happy. The scribbled note she held up to the glass confirmed his suspicions...'Watch Your Language!' it read. Rick gave her a thumbs-up and a quick smile.

Rick and Maury had been working through a contentious relationship both in and outside of the studio during the three years they had been dating. The Hibbing-transplanted single mother was good-looking, bright, and an independent-thinking woman. He covered the microphone and mouthed, "I love you." Maury shook her head and sent an amused smile of her own through the glass.

The last half hour of his program was his favorite segment. Sports! To claim that Hibbingites were addicted to sports stories would be an understatement. Many of his listeners tuned onto KHNG only to catch the last half hour of the 'Morning Show' program. As he was about to go to a Piggly Wiggly commercial, his telephone rang. The ad could wait a minute. Maybe somebody had the answer to a trivia question.

"Rick Bourgoyne here, what's on your mind this morning?" Hearing no response, Rick tried again, "What's—?"

The voice on the other end of the line was garbled. It sounded to Rick like the caller had put something over the speaker of his phone. *"Ya like niggers so much then ya otta..."* Immediately...a clunk!

"Wha—?" Rick was flustered. "Caller?" He knew the connection was already gone. Rick's thoughts raced for a moment. Otta what? He tried to complete the caller's thoughts. Otta...live in the South, sleep with one? For a brief moment there was dead air in KHNG land. Two faces raced across his memory. Lucas Jackson and 'Big Jimmy' Kidd. Lucas had cradled Rick like a baby in his arms when Rick thought he was going to die on Tarawa. 'Big Jimmy', a towering former UCLA lineman, had taught him more about the radio business while they worked together at KBAY than any three people since. Both were men he loved. Both were Negroes.

The pause was noticeable. "Well, folks. We've got crazies out there." Rick would dismiss the aborted comment for the moment and get on with his commercial. "After a word or two about this week's specials at your convenient Piggly Wiggly store, the 'KING of Hibbing radio' will move along to this morning's sports. Don't move the dial. At Piggly you'll find bargains..."

Distracted, Rick reeled off three ads before reading the major league baseball scores from the Duluth Tribune's sports page spread across his desktop. Without his usual enthusiasm, he commented briefly on the pennant races, and the Yankee's growing lead in the American League. "The 'Mick' hit one out yesterday..."

4/ GARY ZENCH

Leaving the cemetery for the Atkinson funeral reception, Kevin Moran swung north into the First Avenue traffic. Turning up the volume of his radio, he detected an edge to Rick's voice. Bourgoyne was speaking about one of the biggest local sports stories of the year. "Congratulations again to our Victory Bar softball team and their

State Class 'A' championship! Great job, guys!" Rick briefly reviewed the course of events leading to the title in words that flowed as if from a scripted page. Lacking any sense of spontaneity, Rick's inflections seemed stuck in a distracted monotone. "From here our locals will play in the regionals next weekend in Fargo. Then, let's hope, the National Tournament out in sunny San Diego."

Two other sports stories were lightly touched: Local favorite Johnny Magina had won the Labor Day Northwest Golf Tournament at the Mesaba Country Club; and, Coach Herm Frickey's Hibbing High School 'Bluejacket' football squad would open their season at home under the Cheever Field lights on Friday against Ely.

"This is Rick Bourgoyne saying good-bye for Tuesday's Good Morning Show...hope to have you on board again in twenty-two hours. All of you out there have a great day—I'm going to try to do the same myself!"

Kevin checked his watch. It was five before noon. Rick had signed off five minutes early! Something wasn't right! His friend had hardly touched on the softball championship. "What's going on Rick?" he mumbled to himself. Both Kevin and Rick were avid softball players in the Hibbing Rec. League. Their team had even beaten the Victory Bar crew once during the past season. Victory's ace wasn't pitching that night, but never the less...the brevity of Rick's report perplexed him. Where were the typical bragging and cajoling his friend was famous for?

Softball had largely taken the limelight from baseball with local athletes and spectators alike. Iron Range community leagues were popular and highly-competitive tournaments scheduled almost every weekend during the short summer months. Kevin sponsored and managed the Androy team while playing right field whenever he found an opportunity. At forty-nine Kevin Moran could still hit the ball with authority, but fast-pitch softball was mostly a speed game. He often joked that he ran as hard as anybody, but didn't get there as fast.

Rick Bourgoyne was a steady third baseman on the Androy team, Pack caught, and Gary's son, Jerry Zench, was easily the best shortstop in the league. Kevin's team seemed to be only one solid strikeout pitcher away from being on par with the Victory Bar team. Kevin's thoughts returned to the missing five minutes of the Morning Show. Maureen Loiselle filled the void with improvised school safety reminders and a repeat of the local forecast. Still puzzling, he turned off the radio and found a place to park in the crowded lot to the East of the Memorial arena. The Atkinson reception, it appeared, had attracted half of Hibbing's population. Maybe Rick had slipped away for the gathering?

Gary Zench listened to the Bourgoyne program on his Zenith while doing the Androy Hotel's payroll work. Although Gary was certain he knew the answer to one of Rick's trivia questions he would wait until the program's end before venturing a call the station.

Gary was a competent business manager. Two years older than his friend Kevin, he was an accomplished tennis player and early morning jogger along his neighborhood's streets. Gary was tall and slender, with hair turned premature gray. "The emotional strain of working for you...and being a Negro up here," he often chided Kevin.

Stress formed lines in Gary's face. The *Duluth News Tribune's* morning report of events in Clinton, Tennessee was a weight he could not leave on the Howard Street sidewalk before coming to work. The Atkinson funeral had been penciled on his calendar but he chose to stay in his office instead of attending. The South had been in turmoil since the Supreme Court's Brown ruling two years before. When would all of this racial strife end, Gary wondered? Or, would it ever go away? Was it only a matter of time before the hatred struck home?

The Zenches were the only Negro family in Hibbing. It wasn't easy living here. Every day either Gary, his wife Nora, or one of his two children experienced some mild manner of racial bias—mostly subtle incidents which each of them had come to accept. Despite the petty episodes of prejudice, the Zenches generally considered themselves lucky to be away from the overt discrimination so widespread in other parts of the country. His twenty-four year old son, Jerry, seemed well-adjusted and earned good wages at the Scranton mine where he worked as an ore production truck driver. A gifted athlete, Jerry had earned three letter awards in football, basketball and baseball while in high school. He had been an all-conference selection in basketball and baseball for his senior year achievements.

For daughter, Naomi, a seventeen year old senior in high school, life was much more difficult. The diffident youth had always struggled with her grades in school and had few friends. For Naomi, school was to be endured and quickly escaped after the last bell. She planned to "get out of Hibbing for good!" after she graduated. If things went as she planned, Naomi would go into a nurses training program and find a job in Minneapolis. The large city would offer far more opportunities for a single Negro woman, and give her a change to meet a colored man. Such would be an impossible expectation in Hibbing.

When Gary heard the Morning Show caller's venomous remark, he almost dropped his pencil. *"Ya like niggers then ya otta..."* His ears perked at Rick Bourgoyne's audible gasp at the racial comment. 'Niggers', the slur would never go away, Gary realized. But, he'd never heard the word on the radio before. Maybe, he contemplated with a painful frown, the troubles of the Southern integration movement were finally here. Here in Hibbing. Here in remote, snow-white, Northern Minnesota! "Let go of it, Gary! He reprimanded himself. "Let it pass." Fortunately the radio episode was brief and his bimonthly payroll work pressing.

~

In his hotel office that afternoon, Kevin troubled over the note he had found sloughed in with his morning's mail. He was unaware of the second incident—the racist caller's comment on Rick's radio show earlier that morning—had no idea that a pot was beginning to boil.

The innocuous envelope must have come from someone employed in his hotel, or...? 'NIGGER LOVER', the two words burned in his thoughts.

Kevin put his feet up on his wide oak desk, and reclined in the plush leather chair with hands tucked behind the back of his neck. Closing his eyes against stress, he tried to think of some way he might be able to resolve the episode nagging at his thoughts. However vague, the note was something tangible and his legal training ought to give him some insight. There had to be a way to track the handwriting down. But, how? Within minutes the germ of an idea struck him. He might be able to identify the scrawled words if he did something covertly clever enough. Especially if the perpetrator was someone working at his hotel. He would need to be discreet, but...Yes! "I'll run it by Gary."

Kevin pushed away from his desk and tossed his suit jacket toward a nearby chair. Long strides carried him down the hall to Gary's accounting office. The door was open and Kevin walked in, plopped himself down on a wooden chair across the desk from his hotel manager, and gave his old friend a familiar smile. "What are you up to, Gary? Looks like I caught you working." Kevin provoked.

"About six-two, boss, and I heard you coming. I ain't workin', only shuffling papers to look busy." Gary's wit was standard fare between the two men. "What's on your mind, Kevin? Thought you were planning get in a round of golf at the club after the funeral. It's a great day to be outside."

"I'm out of luck, it's women's league on Tuesday afternoons—maybe I'll get in eighteen tomorrow." Kevin's eyes narrowed on his manager. Gary had aged noticeably these past few years, seemed thinner, more introverted. The humor was still there...but his demeanor wasn't quite the same. And, Kevin was certain; the furrows on Gary's broad forehead were related to something stressful. He ventured an inquiry, "You feeling okay, Gary?"

"Behind on some things, that's all. What's on your mind?"

Kevin leaned over his elbows on the edge of Gary's desk. "Let me run an idea by you. Tell me what you think about it."

Conjuring a weak smile, Gary tried to lighten up. "If it's a pay raise for your accountant, I'm totally in favor..."

"You're already overpaid, my friend." Kevin laughed easily. "Maybe a little pay boost for one of our employees, though. I'm thinking more in terms of a bonus. Here's my idea...I got the notion from something I read in Business Week a while back. Has to do with employee involvement and morale."

Kevin explained a plan whereby all hotel employees would be given an opportunity to submit one 'new idea' to improve hotel operations and make the working environment better for the staff. "We'd give each employee a blank sheet of paper and have them write out their idea. Keep it open-ended so they could input on what we should do—or, maybe what we're not doing very well. We wouldn't have to require any names. Maybe they'd be more willing to voice their gripes anonymously. A fifty-dollar bonus for the best idea might perk their interest. How about it?"

For a moment Kevin thought Gary's thoughts were somewhere else. He waited for a response, rolled up the sleeves on his white shirt.

"Sounds good to me." Gary's words, like his gaze, seemed remote. A long minute passed between them. "I wouldn't expect you to get any names from those who have complaints. We both know we've got quite a few people here who aren't very happy with their jobs these days—or their pay. Especially the laundry workers and the kitchen staff. The housekeepers got a pay raise in June, but a lot of them are already grousing." Gary knew the hotel personnel and their problems better than anyone.

"Do you think it might get people thinking more positively? I mean, we're asking for their input and offering to pay for suggestions that they give us. And, we will follow-up."

"How about a first, second, and third award? That might give the staff a little more incentive to participate."

Kevin nodded, "Good idea. Let's get this off the ground tomorrow. I'll have Elsie type up a simple form our staff can use for their comments. Then, we'll ask that everybody get the form back to her desk by 3:00 Friday afternoon. That gives them two days."

After returning to his own office, Kevin decided to give Rick Bourgoyne a call at the station. He would remind the radio man about the team's practice that night and try to find out why his friend had cut short the Morning Show.

Rick was gone for the day. "Said he wanted a few hours off and was out the door, Mr. Moran. Don't know where he's gone, didn't say," the KHNG secretary said. "Miss Loiselle is looking for him, too. But I'll leave a message that you called, sir."

Rick found a parking place just south of the Androy on the East side of City Hall across from the attractive new, glass-fronted library building. The police department was on the second floor of the red-bricked municipal building, a smaller architectural replica of Faneuil Hall in Boston. He was hoping to find Pack Moran in the office, but if necessary, he'd talk to Chief Donald Lawrence. Over the years, Rick had lost all respect for the Chief and swallowed hard on the prospect of having his frustration fall on deaf ears. After a softball game earlier in the summer, Rick overheard Lawrence refer to Jerry Zench as a spearchucker! Lawrence got some laughs from his pals over the slur, and a hard glare from Rick. The chief was a bigot in Bourgoyne's mind. But, Rick might be forced to swallow his contempt; Lawrence was the top law enforcement officer in Hibbing.

As it turned out, Pack was not in—Lawrence was.

"I had a little episode on my program this morning, Chief. Thought I should report it and see if something can be done..."

Lawrence interrupted, "The nigger comment? I heard about it. Heard it got you a little rattled," the lawman leaned back in his cushioned swivel chair. "Wish I could help, but there's nothing illegal about using the word nigger, I'm afraid. If I heard right about the caller's comment, there was nothing threatening—to you or anybody else." Lawrence shrugged. He had been listening to the program that morning but wouldn't admit it to Bourgoyne.

"You heard it right. No threats or anything like that, I guess. Just a cruel racial slur being shared with a few thousand people. Kids listen to my show, you know. It's just not appropriate."

Lawrence measured Bourgoyne with level eyes. He had never been impressed by the popular radio personality—considered him a wise guy. The chief, a large man with a bulbous nose and squinting eyes, had a small sense of humor. And, being neither articulate nor well educated, he was jealous of people who were clever with words. "Some folks might be offended by a comment about the President's playing golf today, Mr. Bourgoyne. Maybe even some of the kids that you claim listen to you on the radio. They might think disrespectfully of General Eisenhower, don't you agree?"

Rick felt a heat rise from his stomach, caught himself short of blurting a profanity. As expected, Lawrence was taking an adversarial posture. He would avoid getting into an argument with the cop. "Is there any way the radio station can have their phone calls traced? I mean, what if that caller had made make some kind of personal threat?"

"That's hypothetical, Bourgoyne. Fact is, he didn't." Lawrence seemed pleased with his multi-syllable word and sent a smug grin across his desk.

Rick bit his tongue without comment.

Enjoying his status advantage of the moment, Lawrence forced a tight laugh, leaned forward and clasped his large hands tightly together. "We've got a situation here that you ought to know something about—being a radio show host, and all. It's called the First Amendment. In this country you can say pretty much whatever you want, and whenever you want to say it. Ain't that right? People gave their lives for that right, Mr. Bourgoyne. You know that as well as I do." Lawrence shrugged his wide shoulders dismissingly. "Is this something your boss, Loiselle, wanted you to see me about? Or, are you here on your own, Bourgoyne?"

"On my own. I'm pissed, Lawrence."

"I can see that. Well, hypothetically speaking (the impressive word, used for the second time, rolled easily off his tongue), if a caller had threatened you, or some Negro in this community, we'd investigate the incident as best we could. I'm sure we'd find lots of suspects in this town." Lawrence's comment was barb-wired.

The Police Chief would play his cards close to the vest and refrain from saying anything about the note Pack Moran had brought to his attention less than an hour ago. Lawrence had told his young sergeant he'd "Check it out" then stuffed the envelope in the bottom desk drawer when Pack left his office. So there was a troublemaker out there. Better a racist than a rapist, he reasoned. "You want someone arrested for using the nigger word, Mr. Bourgoyne?"

Rick did not reply. This conversation was going nowhere.

"Would you want to tell your radio audience that their calls were being monitored by the police? That they had better be very careful about anything they say? I don't think so."

Rick stood up from his chair. "I can't argue that. Thanks for your time."

~

Back at his car, Rick decided to give Pack a call later that night. Pack was easily the best cop on the force. Yet, maybe, he'd rather talk with his closest friend, Marco Zoretek first. Marco was his most dependable sounding board. At five, he would be having dinner with Maureen Loiselle. She'd have questions about his taking off early and probably be pissed at him. But, maybe Maury would surprise him. Knowing his sensitive nature, maybe she'd empathize with his frustration. For the moment, however, Rick just needed to get away for a while. He'd drive out to Dupont Lake, park his car somewhere in the shade, and if he was lucky, listen to the call of loons. He needed to think things out. The presence of water always seemed to have a calming effect on him. Maybe the tranquil little lake and some fresh air would soothe his troubled thoughts.

The faces of Lucas Jackson and 'Big Jimmy' Kidd passed through his mind for the second time that day. Estranged by too many years and too many miles, Rick felt pangs of guilt. He hadn't kept in touch with either man. What were his old friends thinking about all the racial violence in the news these days? Were they parents? Did they have children in segregated black schools? Would they be passive observers—taking inferior treatment in stride?

No. Rick cursed himself for the notion. He had known both men too well. Neither would ever tolerate any form of discrimination against another human being. Although by nature sensitive, each had an inner strength and righteousness of character, which he had always admired. Rick made a mental note to reestablish a connection with his old friends. A perturbing sense of shame tugged his conscience.

5/ ANGELA'S ARTWORKS

Angela Moran became more strikingly beautiful with the passing of years. She was forty-five, still youthfully slender, with the golden tan of one who spent much of the summer outdoors. Angie wore her dark hair long and, more often than not, in the popular ponytail style. Although not a vain woman, Angie was pleased with how her features came together—the deep-set oval eyes, full mouth, and narrow nose. Pack often teased his mother that his softball buddies had thought she was his girlfriend the first time they saw the two of them together. Daughter Mary said her friends thought she looked more like her sister than her mother. Angela was flattered.

The beauty of Angela Moran was in her disposition even more than her appearance. She loved life to its fullest. And, her husband was her greatest treasure. She believed that the security of Kevin's love enabled her to radiate far more luminously than she might ever be able to on her own. Their relationship had evolved into a dependency of independent spirits. Together they were complete.

~

Although seldom brought to mind, there had been a tragic episode in Angela's life nearly eighteen years before. To her family, the incident which claimed international notoriety in 1938, was simply referred to as her missing time. In basic psychological terms, Angela had been diagnosed as having a condition her Mayo Clinic doctors referred to as a post-trauma amnesic syndrome. The recurring health issue stemmed from an automobile accident Angela had experienced as a teenager. For the past fifteen years, Angie's health issue had been monitored by the Rochester specialists and her local physician. There had not been any significant reoccurrences of those once dreaded 'blackouts' since 1938.

~

These days, when Angie wasn't working in her downtown art studio, 'Shades of White', she might be found riding horses across the vast Moran property south of Hibbing. The Maple Hill mansion, built by Kevin's father, had been home since shortly after her marriage in March of 1931.

In the summer months she enjoyed landscaping and tending to her lush flower gardens. Kevin had helped her build a rock garden in a shaded area to the west of their back deck. Angie's sun plot of bee balm, dahlias, and day lilies covered much of their back yard space. During the long winters, Angela became absorbed with her painting. Winter's isolation provided her with forceful inspiration. In her upstairs studio she spent many early morning hours at her easel while attending to her art business two or three afternoons each week. Angela had purchased the quaint studio from her old mentor, a French artist and dear friend named Jacque Grojean, some twenty years ago.

Angie Moran had become an accomplished artist. Some of her oil landscapes had sold for more than two thousand dollars at art fairs in Minneapolis and Chicago. Her finest works were winter scenes, and Northern Minnesota provided her with solitary months of contrasting whites and opportunities to experience the beauty of snow. Two of her works, Birch Ice and Winter Wisps, had achieved national attention and she had been profiled in Artist's Easel Magazine on several occasions.

Angela had taught herself to harmonize her colors in abstract conceptions of winter's wondrous majesty. Her vivid imagery was almost sensual, the silence of snow could be heard, the softness felt. A single birch tree might be obscured within a snowy landscape from one perspective, and virtually leap from the canvas in another. She had developed a unique mastery in shades of white.

The Maple Hill property where she and Kevin lived had grown to more than one hundred sixty acres over the years. The wooded sanctuary was virgin and pristine. The hill below their mansion sloped sharply in places, gradually in others, to a large pasture below. In the southern corner of the land, a creek wound its way to a small pond surrounded by huge White Pines. The dramatic contrasts of the property provided Angela with an artistic workshop as well as an inspiration to find new meanings in the changing faces nature provided.

~

"Are these for me?" Angela opened the wrappings and inhaled the rich fragrance. "Or Clara?" Clara Motter had been the Moran's nanny and housemaid for more years than they could remember. The bouquet was too fresh to have been left over from the Atkinson funeral.

Stooping to give her a kiss, Kevin smiled, "Or myself? Could be I needed something to lift my spirits, sweetheart." Kevin had brought Angela a bouquet of roses for no special reason when he arrived home about seven that Wednesday evening. "No. Actually, I realized it's been weeks since I've given you flowers. If you'll get them in a vase, I'll get us both a glass of wine."

"Fair enough. Hmm, why am I suspicious, Kevin? Something going on I should know about?"

"Nothing that can't wait until after dinner. And what's that wonderful smell? Lasagna?"

"Just thrown together, I'm afraid. Give Steven a holler, will you? As usual he's in his bedroom. Still trying to figure out that saxophone his grampa got him at Crippa's, I think. I wish he spent more time outside."

After dinner and small talk about the new school year, Steven was excused from the table and retired to his upstairs bedroom. It was nearly nine o'clock and the teenager wanted to listen to a new Little Richard album he'd borrowed from a friend. After kissing their son goodnight, Kevin and Angie left the dishes on the counter so they could lounge in their spacious living room overlooking the western slope of hillside. It was an evening ritual for the two of them to have a highball, or glass of wine together and share the experiences of their day before going to bed.

Angela could read her husband's thoughts like a familiar book. "Tell me about it, Kev. Are you missing Claude tonight, or is something else bothering you?"

"Something else, dear." Kevin regarded his lovely wife sitting on the sofa with her feet tucked under her bottom. Typically casual, Angie was wearing one of his white cotton shirts over Levi blue jeans. He loved the soft flow of her dark hair splayed on her delicate shoulders.

Taking her hand in his, he smiled. "Claude's in a much better place tonight, sweetheart. No, I've found peace with all that." Kevin was anxious to share the disturbing 'something else'. Years before he had painfully learned that keeping secrets from Angie only complicated them—secrets were like poison.

"This morning before the funeral I found something in the hotel mail on my desk, Angie. A blank envelope with a note inside." Kevin explained its contents in every detail that might be given to two words. "I gave the note to Pack at the cemetery, asked him to pass it along to Lawrence when he got to the station."

Angie squeezed his hand. "The note was referring to Gary, wasn't it? Did you talk to him about it?"

"No, I just couldn't do that. Maybe nothing will come of it anyhow."

"You think it came from one of your staff?" Angie knew a hotel with so many employees always had personnel issues of one kind or another. And, she knew without saying as much, the depth of her husband's affection for Gary Zench. "Is there anything you can do, Kev?"

Kevin explained the 'bonus' idea he'd improvised that afternoon. "I didn't tell Gary anything about my ulterior motives. He thinks the idea is a pretty good one, though. Long overdue he said."

"My husband the detective." Angie snuggled under Kevin's arm. "That's pretty Sherlockian if I do say so myself. When you get the forms back I'd like to help you analyze the writing. I might be pretty good at that. Artists have an acute sense for detail, you know."

"Probably a lot better than I'd be, sweetheart. We should be getting them back on Friday. Maybe Pack can come over and help us out." Kevin gave Angie a soft kiss on the forehead, drawing in the fragrance of her hair. "I don't know why I've let this note get me so upset. I've had a knot in my stomach all day."

"I'll see if I can help you forget about it when we get upstairs." Angie ran her fingers across Kevin's thigh. "Anything else your wife can take care of for you?"

Kevin smiled. "If I've already got a promise, then—there is one other thing bothering me. It might sound awfully trivial, Angie, but..."

"You've got your promise. So, what's the other trivial thing?"

"I can't get hold of Rick Bourgoyne. I've tried the station and his home phone all afternoon. He even skipped our practice." Kevin went on to explain the abrupt conclusion of Rick's radio show that morning and his concern. "Probably nothing worth worrying about, Angie."

"I wasn't listening this morning. Took advantage of the weather and went riding over along the northeast ridge. There's some fence work that we'll need to take care of one of these days. Did you try calling Marco or Maureen?"

Kevin shook his head, met her eyes; "Probably nothing—trivial, like I said. How about you, Angie. Anything on your mind tonight?"

"Only Maribec. I worry about our daughter, Kevin. We didn't get so much as a phone call over the Labor Day weekend. I saw her at the cemetery, toward the back of the crowd. But she didn't show at the reception...and I don't know how she got back to town. It was like she disappeared. Have you heard anything...?"

Kevin rubbed at stubble on his chin. "I saw her riding with Maury Loiselle's daughter, Maddie, in that dented-up Nash of hers the other day. I waved but Maribec didn't see me. I'll make a point of stopping by the hospital tomorrow. Maybe she'll be able to join me for lunch one day this week."

~

When Rick Bourgoyne arrived at Maury's house across from the high school, on the corner of Ninth and Twenty-first, his girlfriend was drumming her fingers on the kitchen table. Rick was nearly an hour late. Maury glared as he approached, folding her arms across her chest in obvious frustration. "Dinner was ready at five. Now everything's ruined!" The sliced potatoes in the cold frying pan were charred; the pork chops wrapped in foil were overdone. "You've got some explaining to do, Rick. Where have you been all day? You left the studio early and left me holding the bag with five minutes to kill. And not so much as a good-bye before you were out the door."

Rick hung his head without reply. Their two-year relationship had blown hot and cold. Maury was a spirited and high-strung businesswoman, Rick a lackadaisical introvert. Crossing the bridge between being lovers and being in a committed relationship had proven difficult. The two of them were just recovering from a three-month separation as it was. Rick fought the urge to head back out the door. Being agitated over the day's events already, he didn't want to justify himself nor argue over dinner plans gone awry.

"Well?"

After a long pause, Rick decided to attempt at reconciliation and mumbled an apology of sorts. "Sorry, Maury. I've had a lousy day. Okay? A really shitty day."

"That's it? You had a shitty day? So? You and half the world. Where have you been?"

"Out at Dupont Lake. Thinking, I guess. The show this morning really upset me."

Maury stood up from the table, took a step in his direction. "Are you mad about the 'bad words' note I held in the window?" She knew that Rick's crude language on The Morning Show, although distasteful to a few listeners, was something that endeared him to most of his large daily audience. The 'damns' and 'hells' were a part of his shtick. "I have to remind you, Rick. It's my business and I damn well don't want to lose any sponsors. And, you ought to know by now that I'm mostly teasing."

But Rick was still too uptight to even crack a smile. "You're the boss, Maureen."

"Maureen? Come on, Rick...What's eating you?"

"Weren't you listening to the program?"

"Most of it. I'm running around half the time."

Rick cursed, "You didn't hear that god-damned caller, Maury? The racist?"

Maury's blank expression brought a glare.

"Some asshole called in and..." He hung his head and kicked at the back of his shoe distractedly. "God, I hate it when someone uses the word nigger! It just turns my guts." Rick explained the incident. "So, I went to the police station this afternoon, talked to that pompous ass, Lawrence. That fuckin' bigot didn't give me the time of day. Started giving me some First Amendment bullshit—like I needed a high school civics lesson."

"So that's it."

"Yeah. So dock me five minutes pay if you want. I really don't give a damn."

"My, my, aren't you wound-up tonight? And such vulgarity!" Maury scolded as lightly as she dared, then appeased, "I'm sorry. I had no idea, Rick."

Maury knew his sensitivities and impulses better than anybody. She puzzled. "Why would you see Lawrence anyway? You hate the guy. And feelings are mutual from what I understand."

"Pack wasn't in the station at the time. But, I did talk to him before I came over here. That's why I'm late if it makes any difference. Told him I was skipping practice." Rick shook his head. "Maybe Pack can find out something. It could be that people in this town are getting edgy over all the school integration stuff in the news. I don't know."

"Lots of people have quit watching the evening news on TV. The whole country's going to hell," Maury added her insight with a shrug

and an indignant footnote—"Liberty and justice for all!. What bull—
!"

Rick nodded. Maury had strong feelings of her own about this
and most social issues. Glancing at his watch, then at the table
setting, he remembered his call to Marco Zoretek after talking with
Pack. He had promised Marco that he'd stop by around seven—an
hour from now. Maury would be pissed when he told her.

Maury had lost her appetite, "What do you think that crazy meant
by 'ya otta...?' Any ideas?" she asked, noticing Rick's quick
wristwatch check, but choosing to disregard it. She'd let Rick get to
the bottom of his frustration without mentioning supper again.

"It's got something to do with the Zenches—who else could it
be?" Rick played softball with Jerry Zench, and often had a beer with
Jerry's father after a game. "They're really nice people, Maury. Mind
their own business, go to church on Sunday, keep their yard
groomed. I don't understand where that crazy bigot's coming from."
Rick shrugged, sighed. "It must be awfully tough being the only
Negroes in this town."

'This town' was something that Maureen Loiselle would never
really understand or feel connected with. She had always felt like an
outsider. Some of the locals referred to those who were not born and
raised in Hibbing as 'pack sackers'. The reference was blatantly
derogatory. She found most people pleasant, but socially cool. Most
Hibbingites seemed to have a hundred relatives and grandparents
who came from the Old Country. Locals held a deep pride in their
ethnicity. Maury had no relatives here and only a vague sense of her
own family's roots. Consequently, Maureen Loiselle didn't seem to
melt in the fabled melting pot of the Iron Range culture.

Born Maureen Collins, she was originally from the West Duluth
neighborhood of Norton Park. Her father bought into the radio
business after the war and soon owned stations in Duluth, Superior,
and Hibbing. Maury had managed Hibbing's KHNG for her father
over the past five years.

Being an Iron Range native son, Rick never really understood
Maury's feelings about Hibbing. Jokingly, he once suggested that

she change her name to something with an 'ich' at the end if she felt so much like an outsider. She failed to find any humor in his suggestion.

"Why do the Zenches live here? If I were a Negro, this is the last place on earth I'd choose to live. And that poor girl, what's her name—Naomi? How can she stand it? The only black face in a high school of more than a thousand kids. No dates, no social life whatsoever, and everybody doing a double-take when she walks down the hall. God, that must be miserable." Maury couldn't imagine.

Her brow furrowing at the social reality, Maury continued her diatribe. "Her brother Jerry was an athlete in high school. It wasn't so bad for him. Everybody loves a ballplayer, no matter what color they are. That's the way it is. Guys have it made in school. Sports, music...they've got every opportunity to get beyond the color thing. To get beyond anything for that matter."

"I won't argue that. It's a lot easier for a guy." Sitting down, Rick took off his silver-framed glasses, placed them on the table next to his empty plate, and massaged his temples. Rick Bourgoyne was not a handsome man. His blond hair was thinning on top of a head that almost seemed too large for his bony shoulders. He wore a beard to fill out his narrow jaw line, and often wore turtlenecks to bulk the transition from his sunken chest. But his deep, green eyes were almost magnetic. "Let's eat those chops, hon. I don't care if they're cold and overdone. Then I'll give you a hand with the dishes."

"When you offer to help with the cleanup, and call me 'hon', I know something's fishy. You've got other plans for the evening, don't you? I though we'd watch the 'Sixty Four Thousand Dollar Question' on TV tonight. But, I have the feeling that you're not planning to hang around."

"Yeah, I'll watch some TV with you, but...I told Marco..."

Maury shook her head, her amorous thoughts dissipating, "So I play second fiddle tonight?" Turning toward the stovetop to retrieve the pork chops, she mumbled her resignation. "I'll warm them in the oven for you...and take care of the dishes myself."

Stepping behind her and brushing a kiss into her cinnamon hair, Rick tried to recover. "Tomorrow night, hon. I'll take you to the Lybba for that new Frank Sinatra movie." Although he was unable to see her face, Rick knew she was hurt. Her upset was justified. "Maybe even some shrimp at the Androy." He offered to sweeten the ante. "And, there's the football game on Friday night."

"Whoopee, a football game!" Maury laughed her sarcasm. But the Sinatra movie, High Society, was something she really wanted to see. "I guess I'll have to settle on two dates for the one I'm giving up." If all she was going to get was another hour or so of his time, she'd rather have a cigarette and a whiskey-coke with Rick. "Dinner at the Androy tomorrow, and the movie afterwards? The ballgame on Friday. Is there anything else you're going to throw into the deal?"

Rick winked. "I'll stay late and watch some TV after the game."

6/ MARCO'S WORLD OF MUSIC

Marco Zoretek did not own a television set. He did, however, have a state of the art high fidelity sound system in his living room. From his threadbare recliner he could spend hours absorbed in the rich sounds of the Boston Pops orchestral renditions of Beethoven, Rachmaninov, or Mozart. Classical music was his passion and Tchaikovsky easily his favorite composer.

Marco was Angela Moran's younger brother, now forty-three and never married, and the music appreciation teacher at Hibbing High School. A popular teacher with his students, he had an ability to relate to every taste in music—even the newly popular rock and roll that infatuated this generation of teenagers. Mr. Zoretek, or 'Mr. Z.' to most of his students, was tall, conspicuously overweight, and wore his unkempt sideburns down his long square jaw. There was nothing in his meager wardrobe to adequately disguise a stomach that hung over the belt of his forty-three inch waist trousers. His suits were mostly threadbare, shirts frayed at the collar, ties stained. But Mr. Z. was good-natured and always without pretensions. A lion's share of his monthly income went into his assortment of music equipment, and trips to the Twin Cities for concerts.

Rick Bourgoyne might never be able to explain how he'd become drawn to Marco Zoretek after returning to Hibbing years before. The two men were as different as apples and oranges. Marco had no interest in politics, didn't know the difference between the Yankees and the Knickerbockers, and wouldn't cross the street for a ball game if hot dogs were being given away free. Five years older than Rick, Marco lived in a little one-bedroom house on West Fourth where he spent most of his time involved in his music or reading biographies. During the school term, a clock could be set by his daily routine.

Marco's refrigerator, however, was always well stocked with Schmitz Beer and his cupboards with Old Dutch potato chips. Perhaps, the attraction between the two men was more that of opposites than anything else. But Marco was an insightful man and a good listener. Rick always felt better when he shared his personal issues with his congenial and nonjudgmental friend.

"I don't know why it's got me so damned flustered!" Rick said after a deep swallow from his bottle of beer. "I've never personalized this race stuff, I guess. It's always been so far removed from my life here in Hibbing. Back in the service, and later in San Francisco, I had some great Negro friends." From his lotus position on the carpeted floor, he back-rested his head on the frayed cushion of the sofa. "I've been thinking about them a lot lately. With us back then it was never anything about color or race. Lucas and Big Jimmy were just people in my life that I really enjoyed being around." Rick paused significantly, his thoughts wandering to those dust-covered times.

Marco simply nodded. Rick had told him about these old friends on other occasions.

"Since coming back to Hibbing, it's like prejudice and discrimination are somebody else's problem. Something blowing up in another part of the country. Not my issue, not in my back yard."

Rick plucked at his beard. "But it is here and it is now—and it isn't somebody else's problem, Marco. I can't help thinking of Jerry Zench. He's a buddy of mine. We're together most of the summer with practices and ballgames. And Jerry's dad, too. When we were talking earlier tonight, Maury mentioned the Zench girl, Naomi. You must see her at the high school now and then—don't you?"

Marco nodded without reply. He'd let Rick get all his feelings on the table while emptying his first bottle of Schmidt and opening another he'd set near his elbow on the end table. The cannons in Tchaikovsky's 1812 Overture were pounding through the low volume setting in the background of their conversation. His eyes closed imperceptibly at the dramatically resonant soundtrack.

Rick's emotions put a sharp edge to his words, "I actually felt violated when that son-of-a-bitch called in. Do you think I should say something on the air tomorrow? Maybe challenge that bigot to have some guts and finish the comment he started before hanging up on me. I'd really like to confront the asshole...but, on the radio? Maybe that would incite things even more. What do you think?"

For the most part, Rick had answered his own questions without Marco's insights throughout a dialogue that rambled for nearly twenty minutes. Looking over the top of his eyeglasses, he sought Marco's response. "I might do it anyhow. Say something clever to provoke another call—'If you've got any guts...come on the air with me, Mr. Anonymous. I could hang up the phone on him if things got too sticky. Yeah, just leave him hanging. I doubt if that imbecile has any support in this town, anyway. God, Hibbing's about as tolerant as any place can be. People here aren't going to stand for..."

Marco winced. He believed his friend was often sadly mistaken on the reality of local culture. He knew the Zenches well and liked them. They were good friends of his sister Angie, and Kevin. When the Morans had summer cookouts or other family occasions, the Negro family was always invited. His nephew, Pack, and Jerry Zench had grown up together. Naomi Zench had been in his beginning music class as a sophomore, two years ago. Although the girl had some musical aptitude, she lacked any volition to take up an instrument and participate in the band. Naomi Zench, he believed, was a loner of her own making.

"Have you heard anything I've said, or are you too absorbed in that annoying classical crap of yours?" Rick shot his question across the space between them.

"Every word, Rick. And, the music is relaxing." Marco's smile was one of amusement. "But, I think you're dead wrong about our so-called tolerant community of Hibbing—to use your own word. There's a hellava lot more prejudice here than you seem to realize. I wish I had a dollar for every time I've heard the word nigger spoken in the hallways of our high school. I asked a student once why he used the word. The kid gave me a strange look as if I were from the boondocks. 'What's wrong with nigger, Mr. Zoretek', he asked me? 'My dad uses the word all the time. He was in the war with some niggers; told me they were a lot different from us—and never to trust them. Not under no circumstances'."

"You're kidding me?" Rick shook his head in disbelief.

Putting his heavy legs on the ottoman and leaning back in his chair, Marco fingered his sideburns. "I wish I were. Rick, kids get their racial attitudes from their parents. You know that. Just like their politics. And nearly everything else they believe to be facts of life. Almost every kid in high school claims to be a Democrat. They can't give me one good reason why they are, or give me any rationale for their hatred of Republicans. That's just the way it is. Two out of three adults in Hibbing would vote for a jackass if he were a Democrat. You know politics better than I do, but don't think for a minute that you can argue that point."

Marco drained his bottle. "And if any kid picks up the idea at home that Negroes are lazy, stupid, and dishonest...well, that's what they're going to believe. And that's why they're going to call Negroes niggers. I'm not ever going to change that. Neither are you, Rick."

Rick shook his head. "Then you're telling me that there's a lot of prejudice in this town? I mean, like...well, you don't really believe most people up here are bigoted, do you?"

"Yes, I do. I think most people are. Few would ever admit it...but—"

"But I grew up here, just like you did, Marco. A Serbian family lived two doors down from us and a Finnish family across the street next to the Edlesteins and Kolars. It was a great neighborhood. Where you lived in Brooklyn must have been the same."

"Take off your rose-colored glasses, Rick. I learned in sixth grade that there were Bohunks, Dagos—some kids called them Wops—and Finns and Krauts and Oles...it goes on and on. I was a Mick. And Jewish kids were Kikes. I can remember asking my father what a 'mackerel snapper' was. And God, how I hated Ash Wednesday when my forehead got those black smudges—then everybody knew I was a Catholic. We all got along well enough but we always knew we were different." Marco reminded his friend of how things were in Hibbing back then. "Believe me, Rick, things haven't changed much."

"Now that you mention it...I guess my mother always asked if a new friend of mine was Catholic. And we always called Cory Depelo 'Dago'. But, that was years ago," Rick said.

"Like I just said, not much has changed." Marco smiled, "And I still hate that badge of ashes!"

Rick laughed along with his friend, "So do I." Shrugging his shoulders, he added, "What if most folks in Hibbing weren't Catholics? How much worse would it be then?"

With his observation, Rick thought once again of the Zench family.

In the two hours at Marco's, Rick was so absorbed in his own issues of the moment, that he had failed to get in-touch with his friend's activities of the day. Teacher workshops had been going on since Monday. Marco, however, rarely allowed his feelings to be bruised over his friend's self-absorption. "Sometimes I can't help thinking that you're schizophrenic, Rick. On the radio you sound like an all-together guy—witty, intelligent, perceptive. Then, in the real world outside...well, you're a rather gloomy myopic."

Rick laughed at the analysis. "At least I play ball and have a heartbeat part of the time. You...you on the other hand, are about as lively as a clam. Do you even get a blood pressure reading?"

"As content as a clam, my friend. And yes, thanks for asking, perfectly normal blood pressure. Of course, in two days that will all change."

Rick felt ashamed, "I'm sorry, Marco. How do things look for classes on Thursday?"

7/ THE MORNING SHOW

Two men sat in a blue '49 Chevrolet parked along the south curb of Howard Street deeply shadowed from the four-storied Androy Hotel in the distance. It was nearly ten in the morning and their radio was tuned to KHNG.

"A big 'how-are-ya today' from KHNG to all our listeners out there in our fair city of Hibbing and surrounding 'suburbs' of Kelly Lake, Leetonia, Kitzville and Kerr Location. And to our audience in Chisholm, Keewatin and Nashwauk. Your host as always is Rick Bourgoyne, the King of Iron Range airwaves, and this is the Morning Show coming to you from our dungeon studios in the Androy basement on this lovely Wednesday morning!!" Rick's opening line was always delivered in a distinctive, high-pitched voice. "Stick around for a couple of hours; we're going to have a great time talkin' all kind'sa things together."

~

"I wonder if Bourgoyne's expecting another call," the baseball-capped man in the passenger seat said with a twisted smile. "I think we got him pretty rattled yesterday."

"I wonder if we rattled old moneybags, Moran, too. I'll wager next week's paycheck that cool Kevin ran to old man Zench after he found our note in the mail. Let those nigger lovers scratch their heads about who done it for a while." The second man's voice was edged with the venom of hatred.

"Maybe we'll see a 'for sale' sign in Zench's yard before winter," commented the mustached man slouched behind the steering wheel. "Good riddance to bad rubbish I always say," he added while using a matchbook to pick at a piece of bacon stuck in his teeth.

~

Rick started off his program with the weather. "Another picture perfect day coming our way this Wednesday, September fifth. From Hoyt Lakes over on the Eastern Mesabi to Grand Rapids in the west, it's going to be sunshine! Seventy degree sunshine, folks. Not a cloud between the Iowa border and Manitoba. Tonight we'll drop just under fifty...and more of these same mild temps running into the weekend.

"Let me remind you to get your kids to bed early tonight because summer vacation is finally over. Finished. Kaput. Washed-up and down the drain." Rick made a swooshing sound that came off poorly. Giving himself a quick laugh, he continued his thought. "Tomorrow should be a 'parent's holiday'—not only here in Hibbing but throughout the country. Our local schools will open their doors to all those summer-weary kids and begin an exciting new school year in the morning. Yes, you heard it right—exciting! Be sure to consult this afternoon's Daily Tribune for school bus routes and class schedules."

Rick gripped the microphone on his narrow studio desktop. "Remember the phone lines are always open on the Morning Show so give me a call any time. One qualification, however, I don't want any complaints from students who may be listening. I know you can't wait to put on those new school clothes, get all those wonderful new textbooks, and begin learning all those amazing things your teachers will have in store for you."

Rick swallowed hard. His next words would be a sharp turn from his cheery school reminder, but a sleepless night of rehashing Tuesday's show had set his mind. "And, to yesterday's caller—give me a ring and tell me what 'I otta do...' I'm curious." His voice was tight. "Yes, friends, we live in a wonderful country where we can speak openly about what's on our minds. Without fear of reprisal. And, a country that believes in the equality of all people, regardless of religion or color. That's what makes us so great. Something else that makes us the envy of the rest of the world is our courage. Courage to stand up for what we believe in...only a damn coward would hide behind our freedoms and take potshots at people who look or think differently from them."

Rick paused for effect. "Anyone who thinks differently—well, I'm sitting here next to the KHNG phone waiting to hear what you've got to say."

∼

"Hot damn," the man with the mustache pounded the steering wheel. "We really got the 'King' shook up, don't we? Did ya know yer a coward for hatin' niggers? Yep, yer just a fuckin' American coward." He poked his friend in the ribs.

"I'd just love to turn his crank again this morning," rejoined the other man.

"Nah. I've got another note to plant before we hit Bourgoyne's nerve again. Just a matter of decidin' which of them niggers to send it to. Whatta ya think?"

"How about the hotshot shortstop? He thinks he's so fuckin' cool. Yeah, Jerry Zench otta hear from us sometime this week."

"Yeah, then we'll get to that fat-assed Zench girl later."

8/ STEVEN AND BOBBY

Friday bloomed with the northern Minnesota splendor promised on Rick Burgoyne's Morning Show. The pleasant weather of August had lingered into the first week of September. Yet the feeling of autumn seemed to have settled upon a community which had begun to settle into the lolling effects of school routine. Hibbing experienced a metamorphosis when summer vacation ended. The entire town became noticeably subdued, a hollow echo of its former self. Idled playgrounds and ball fields slipped into a lifeless mode. Downtown sidewalks, free from the clutter of bicycles, seemed wider and more composed. Neighborhoods, like deflated balloons, were sapped of the August vitality. A sense of public normalcy and efficiency, compromised for three months, once again rooted city life. As it always had, the advent of a new school year focused people's thoughts on the academics and activities of its esteemed Hibbing High School.

Behind the brick-faced facades of Hibbing's several public and parochial schools, however, a pandemonium roiled on the second day of classes. From kindergarten to the twelfth grade, students of every age were beset with a myriad of challenges: new teachers to become familiar with, new schedules to memorize, new faces to ponder in rows of classroom desks—everything about the first week of school was newness!

For Marco Zoretek, a new school term was always exhilarating. As it was throughout the entire education system, the veteran music teacher would need to cope with new experiences. Mr. Z had new names and faces to connect, along with new lesson concepts he would implement during the first semester. And, this year Marco had a new corduroy sports jacket with leather patched elbows. His new teaching schedule would provide him with a unique experience and long-anticipated opportunity. His musically gifted nephew, Steven Moran, had been assigned to his second period music appreciation class.

Marco noticed that Steven had chosen a desk across from a well-dressed, seemingly shy, Jewish boy named Robert Zimmerman. The teacher could tell by the pre-bell conversation between the two boys that they were already friends.

After Friday's second period class, Steven lingered self-consciously at the door. "When I answered that question...I almost called you 'Uncle Marco' instead of Mr. Zoretek. I'm going to have to be careful" Then he paused, "But it sure is awkward having my uncle for a teacher."

Marco smiled his amusement. "It's going to be fun Stevie. Don't worry about making any slip-ups, most kids know that I'm your uncle anyhow. Oh...I wanted to mention that I picked up my first Elvis album last week. I'll have to admit I'm enjoying it quite a bit."

"Wait 'til you hear some Little Richard and Chuck Berry, Unc— there I go again! Sorry."

"Bring some of your rock and roll records over to the house one of these days, Stevie. I'll listen to your wilder stuff if you'll sit back and listen to some mellow classical arrangements from my collection."

In five minutes, Rick Burgoyne's Friday episode of the Morning Show would go on the air. The top national news story made him sick to his stomach. More school integration violence in the tumultuous South. Today's story centered in Sturgis, Kentucky, and a coal-mining town of about five thousand people. A mining town,

Rick thought to himself. Was Sturgis anything like Hibbing, he wondered? Negro students had attended their first day of school in Sturgis yesterday, under the supervision of more than 200 Kentucky militiamen with machine guns, and had to be protected from an angry white mob estimated in the hundreds. This morning, however, the Negro students had not reported to their Sturgis school classes. Parents of these children promised, however, that their sons and daughters would return on Monday. Governor A. B. Chandler had a 'martial law' order ready to execute for the expected recurrence of violence next week.

Thursday night in Sturgis had been relatively calm. National Guardsmen with riot guns and bayonets reported no unusual problems while more than a thousand local residents congregated in the streets and parks listening to pro-segregationists make threatening speeches. In a related story, school officials and militia in Mansfield, Texas, were bracing for the same kind of violence as had been occurring in Clinton, Sturgis, and other locations throughout the South.

Rick felt a throb at his temples. His heart wanted to speak sharply against the racists and segregationists, but his head told him to soft peddle the divisive issue. At the same time, he sensed that his tormenter from Tuesday morning was probably listening to a radio somewhere out there in KHNG land. The 'on air' light flashed and Rick cleared his dry throat one last time. The scribbled notes at his elbow, if he followed the agenda, were rife with light topics, jokes for the Goldies, trivia, and sports.

Lots of sports this Friday morning.

~

Friday night.

While Hibbing High School's Bluejacket football team was trouncing the visiting Ely Timberwolves, Rick Bourgoyne felt relaxed for the first time all week. His radio show had been uneventful that day—even dull for a Friday morning.

Maury was in good spirits this crisp evening and actually seemed to be enjoying the football game. Their relationship had been relatively calm over the past few days. Reaching for her gloved hand he smiled, "I love you, boss". The expression was a favorite of Rick's and always brought a chuckle from Maury. "I've really enjoyed our time together this week—since Wednesday, I should say."

He gave her a wink, "I've been charming haven't I?"

"Maybe pleasant company is a better way to put it."

"Have I mentioned that you're the best looking woman in the grandstand."

"Where are you going with such flattery?" Her voice coy and flirtatious; "Remember, my romantic man, Maddie's still not in her own apartment yet." She gave his hand a squeeze. Maury's daughter was looking for her own place but dragging her feet.

Rick frowned, "Maddie's twenty-two, Maury. She knows about us. We don't have to sneak around like she's an impressionable eight year old."

"You're probably right. Okay. A sleepover...but we'll park your car in the garage overnight. I think she's at a party tonight anyway. I'm guessing she'll end up crashing at Maribec Moran's apartment."

Rather than waste his time watching a football game, Steven Moran chose listening to Gene Vincent songs at his friend Bobby's house just a block south of noisy Cheever Field on car-clogged Seventh Avenue. Bobby Zimmerman had several 'groovy' records, many that Stevie hadn't heard before. The sophomore pals mixed listening with jamming. Bobby, Stevie had come to realize, was almost as good as he on the downstairs rec room piano where they pounded out their version of 'Tutti Frutti' and 'Maybellene' together. While Stevie played the notes precisely across the ivories, Bobby preferred to ad-lib to the rhythm in his own discordant and flairful fashion.

Stevie noticed something else about his friend. An intensity. When the two of them listened to music, Steven's mind often wandered to the hallways at school, a girl who had caught his attention at band practice, a nice-looking car, things he wanted to do, places he wanted to go. All kinds of things. With Bobby it was different. Bobby seemed to have almost total concentration on words and tones and beats. His focus was absorbed at a different level.

Bobby wore his dark hair longer than most kids at school, combed it up toward the top, and always wore his shirts buttoned up to his neck. "James Dean is my hero", he told Stevie when they talked about movies, and the red jacket he always wore gave him a 'rebel' feeling. In school, however, Bobby was always well-dressed in stylish sweaters and slacks. Among their classmates, Stevie and Bob were probably the best dressers.

"I like your Uncle Marco, Stevie. I can already tell he really knows his music...I mean, really! Johnny Bucklen and Leroy Hoikkala told me he can play every instrument in the band." He mused for a long minute before adding, "Wish I could do that."

Steven saw that Bobby had a faraway look as he spoke. He'd seen the expression before, wondered what his friend was thinking. Usually outgoing and expressive, there were times when Bobby was pensive. Steven considered saying something but didn't.

"Someday I'm going to be a big time musician. Guitar, piano...I'm going to be the best at both."

"Maybe someday you will. Uncle Marco can probably teach you anything you want to learn. We'll have to drop over and visit him one of these days. He told me that he's got that new Elvis album." Steven considered the casual invitation he'd offered. Would his uncle enjoy having the two of them over? Or, was he out of line with his suggestion? Wincing, he continued, "I'll have to ask him. You wouldn't believe the sound system he's put together. And he's got the most beautiful Gibson acoustic guitar I've ever seen, too. Maybe he'd let us pick..."

Bobby nodded, "That would be really cool."

The two boys listened to 'Bo Diddly' on the phonograph.

"I know who your dad is." Bobby commented when the tune was over. "He owns the Androy, doesn't he?"

"Yep. And your dad has the appliance store down the block from the hotel, right? We got our TV set there." Steven thought about things they had in common. "I suppose most kids think we're rich because our parents own businesses. Don't you think that sometimes?"

Bobby shrugged, "It's not something I want to do with my life. Run a business in Hibbing with my father, I mean. I'd be bored to death! I'm going to the Cities when I graduate. That's where everything's happening: Minneapolis!"

To Steven, Minneapolis seemed a world away. "The Cities, huh? I've been there a couple of times with my parents. Really big, I mean—tall buildings, lots of people, traffic..."

"It's big time. Lots of bands and bars where you can play your music if ya want to. And, babes."

Steven could only stay at Bobby Zimmerman's house until nine. His brother Pack was going to pick him up there and give him a ride home. As the two boys stood on the front porch waiting for Pack, they could hear the crowd cheering under the bright stadium lights down the street.

Following the roar of what must have been a home team touchdown, Steven, who was a full head taller than Bobby, asked his friend, "Did you ever play any sports?"

"Summer cub league baseball. Bowling. I was on the Gutter Balls team last year. We were pretty good. That's about all the sports I've ever gotten into."

"I don't care much about athletic stuff either. My dad was pretty good at sports, I guess—and my brother Pack, too. They both still play softball on the same team. I go down to Bennett Park and watch their games sometimes. Kinda boring. I bring a book along."

"There he is now." Bobby gestured toward the '53 Ford pulling up to the curb on Seventh Avenue. "If you're not doing anything tomorrow afternoon, we could go down to Crippa's Music Store and hang around. I'll give you a call, okay?"

"Who's your friend, Stevie?" Being a local cop, Pack had a pretty good idea about which local kids were troublemakers and wanted to keep close tabs on his little brother's pals.

"Just a kid from school. He's not much into sports. We both like music, though. He's in my second hour class with Uncle Marco."

"Okay. He's in your class and likes music. But what's his name?"

When Steven told him, Pack only shrugged with indifference.

It took about ten minutes to drive south from the city out to the Moran's house on Maple Hill. Pack had promised his parents that after picking up his little brother he'd help them out with some kind of project his father was working on. Pack had Friday night off and nothing better to do for an hour or so. Later, he would cruise Howard Street. His newly-waxed Ford with its chrome moon hubcaps was a head-turner.

~

Kevin and Angela had reviewed all fifty-two pages of 'employee suggestions' by the time Pack and Steven arrived shortly after nine. Steven said a quick 'goodnight' to his parents, gave his mom a light kiss on the cheek, and headed upstairs with a small stack of 45's he had borrowed from Bobby.

Pack regarded his parents sitting at the dining room table pondering two separate stacks of papers. He set down the bottle of Coca-Cola he'd pulled out of the fridge and pulled up a chair. "What's going on?"

Kevin explained the hotel employee's suggestion project to his son. "So your mom and I have been reading through every one of these. More than half of them are signed and have some pretty good ideas. The pile over here is just a waste of paper," he pushed the stack to the side. "But these..."

"We found three that raise some suspicion, Patrick." Angela would never use her son's nickname.

"More than some suspicion, honey. We've got a real problem here." Kevin frowned. "Take a look at this for yourself, Pack."

Pack took the unsigned page and scanned the two capitalized sentences written with a dull pencil.

'THE HOTEL SHOOD HAVE SEPRATE ROOMS
FOR PEOPLE THAT ARE NEGRO. WE SHOOD
NOT LET THEM IN THE BAR AND MAKE OTHER
PEOPLE UNCOMFERIBLE.'

"Well, whoever wrote this one didn't use the word, nigger. But all the words are capitalized just as they were in the original note. I wish I had it with me right now. But if I remember right, this is not the same writing." Pack observed. "Save it though, Dad. We can compare later."

Angela slid the second page in front of Patrick. "How about this one?"

'what is this for. nobody listens to nothing around here. if you want to make things better get rid of that Zench. he is no good for nothin at all here.'

Pack scratched his head. "I don't think so, Mom. It's a personalized gripe, but it's not exactly racist. He's just pis—I mean, he's got some problem with Mr. Zench."

Angela glared at her son's near slip, cleared her throat.

"Sorry."

"It's the only one that mentions Gary from all of the fifty-two we've read." Kevin said in a flat tone.

"How many employees do you have at the hotel, Dad? Pack wanted to know.

"Eighty-two. About sixty are full time, I think. Gary would know for sure. We delivered these simple forms to all of them, even the part-time people. So, thirty didn't send anything back to Elsie, and twenty-four were unsigned." Kevin said.

"Where's the third one?" Pack held out his hand to his mother. He read the typewritten page:

> *we had a nigger at the hotel last summer pissed in his bed. my dog dont piss his bed. so my dogs smarter then a nigger is. hibbing is not a place for niggers to come. i should say negroe but i dont care.*

"What do you think about that one, Patrick?"

Pack considered his mother's question. Rubbing his index finger along his nose (a mannerism of serious thought since childhood). "If, in fact, someone did wet their bed at the hotel, who would know about it? The housekeepers and maybe the laundry?" Pack shifted his gaze from his mother to his father.

"But the laundry wouldn't know what room the sheets came from. Or who occupied the room on any given night. Everything's thrown all together and carted downstairs." Kevin said with narrowed eyes. "I don't know what to think."

"How many of these forms were returned typewritten?" Pack was staring at the last note.

"Only three, I think."

"Is there any way you can tell if this last one was done with a hotel typewriter?"

Kevin smiled at his police sergeant son's question. "I checked that, Pack. The answer is no. The others were signed and came from my secretary, Elsie Hopkins, and from Doris Tarnowski in supply."

"So, where does all of this leave you, Dad? This last one is clever. Using a typewriter wouldn't give anybody handwriting clues. Also, there's the excuse for using nigger. How are the two of you going to narrow anything down?" Pack looked from his dad to his mom and back again.

Kevin shrugged, "It's a start, I guess. Don't really know. If another note shows up and it's typewritten...maybe then we can make a trace. And we do have the first one written out in capital letters. At least it gives us some kind of base to work from."

"Have the police come up with anything?" Angela asked.

"Not much they can do about the note. Rick Bourgoyne talked to Chief Lawrence about the radio caller on Tuesday morning. Nothing for us to follow on that matter either. Not that it surprises me, but Lawrence hasn't said anything all week. And, whoever it was that harassed Rick—well, he's a needle in the old haystack."

Kevin looked puzzled. "What's that all about? Did Rick get some kind of note, too?"

Pack explained the radio episode to his parents. "I talked to Rick the next morning. He was really p-pouring mad about that."

His mother missed it.

"Hate to be rude, but—" Pushing himself away from the table and finishing his bottle of Coke, Pack was anxious to head back into town. It was Friday night and he had tomorrow off. "Good luck with finding your winning suggestions. I don't think any of the three I read are worth a reward," he humored. "That's going to be up to you and Mr. Zench."

"A dead-end street, Pack? Kevin asked as he stood.

"Maybe not. Don't throw anything away, Dad."

Angela touched Kevin's elbow, "Are you going to show these to Gary?" Her gesture pulled the tablecloth, spilling some coffee into her saucer.

"Not right now, Angie. Hopefully this whole episode will blow over and there'll be no need."

Pack was standing, hands thrust deeply into his trouser pockets. The kitchen clock swept close to ten. "See you both Sunday. You making pot roast, Mom?"

Angie nodded, "Give your mother a kiss before you go, Patrick. You've got to learn to be more affectionate if you're ever going to get yourself a girl friend. And, don't slouch. Be conscious of your posture."

Pack straightened his shoulders. "Girls notice that, huh. Thanks, Ma." He smiled, gave a light kiss on her cheek.

9/ MALCONTENTED MARIBEC MORAN

Pack did have a girl in mind when he left Maple Hill for town. He lit a Lucky Strike, checked himself in the rearview mirror, tuned up his radio, and slung his arm out the open window. Maddie Loiselle was Maribec's best friend and the daughter of Rick Bourgoyne's girlfriend. There were some natural connections. Although Rick knew that Pack found Maddie attractive, Pack was certain his sister didn't have any idea about his interest. Pack and Maribec were not close. To his way of thinking, his rebellious sister was the kind of girl Pack would tell Steven to stay away from. He wondered, were both Maddie and Maribec on the wild side?

Watching his speed as he came over a crest on First Avenue, Pack felt the cool breeze under the rolled t-shirt of his left arm and regarded the star-speckled sky. Sometimes he wished he wasn't so damned uptight and obsessed with 'living-by-the-rules'. When was the last time he let his hair down and had a good time? He couldn't remember.

"Count your blessings, Pack," he mumbled and smiled inwardly as he downshifted to second. Even if he felt alone at times—like tonight—he had a lot going for him. Great parents, good job, nice little house, friends-things a lot of men his age might envy. Still—he waved at Larry Messner leaning against the front fender of his chopped and customized '49 Chevy—still, he felt a hole in his life. Being a private person by nature, when there was pain—he swallowed it without betraying emotion.

Friday night. Alone. Nothing to do. "Yeah, just count your blessings!" he repeated as if there was a need to convince himself that he had his life together.

Pack cruised Howard Street for the second time, then turned off the main drag up First Avenue to Twenty-Fifth. Teenage girls were strolling the sidewalks after the football game, hoping to pick up a ride from one of the guys whose cars were the trolling-bait in a traditional small town routine. Getting 'picked-up' was a weekend night ritual for the younger generation of Hibbing's high schoolers. Their curfew was eleven. Pack never hustled the 'jailbait' (a reference used by the older guys) walking the streets, and felt self-conscious about being a conspicuous participant in the girl-pickup traffic. He was a policeman in this town and everybody knew it. If he wanted to find a girl that way, he'd go over to Virginia—thirty miles east—and cruise Chestnut Street. Lots of Hibbing guys did just that on a Friday or Saturday night.

What Pack really wanted to find out, however, was where Maddie Loiselle and his sister might be hanging out tonight. There were a few parties he'd heard about earlier in the day. He decided to check out one at Randy Tobin's apartment on east Twenty-Third. Pack's softball teammate was having some guys over tonight, and wherever Randy was, there would be girls. He hoped everybody at Randy's would be twenty-one (the legal age for drinking). Being a cop had proven to be a big liability in Pack's deficient social life.

There were several cars parked on both sides of the street in front of Randy's place. Two of them he recognized. Dave Dahlberg's navy-blue Ford Crestliner and Maddie's unmistakable Nash Rambler. From the street he could hear the blare of loud music from the open upstairs window. If Randy didn't turn down the racket, there would probably be some irate neighbors calling the police department. Maybe he shouldn't go in after all. He turned off the engine and sat for a few minutes. Checking his wristwatch under the streetlamp's glow he noticed it was already after ten. Once again, Pack felt more like a policeman than a single guy out to have a good time.

What to do? He drummed his steering wheel, lit another cigarette.

Within a few minutes his decision was made for him. Dave Dahlberg came out the front door of the two-story, apartment-converted house supporting the limp form of Pack's sister. Maribec was obviously drunk. "I'm fine for chrissakes, Davy...you don't have to carry me to yer car. Just gimme a ride home...and keep your hands off my tits."

"I ain't tryin' to feel ya up, dammit."

Pack tossed his cigarette and, leaping from his car, hustled over to the couple as they were stepping from the front porch to the sidewalk. "I can take her home, Dave. Looks like you've probably been drinking a little too much yourself."

"What the hell are you doing here, Pack?" Maribec pushed herself away from Dahlberg and teetered noticeably. Squinting, Maribec's voice raised sharply, "I can damn well go where I want to. And I ain't going home at ten o'clock. You go home, yourself. Just leave me alone, will ya." Taking a step toward her brother, she put her hands on her hips and mocked, "Or are you arresting me, Officer Moran?"

"Just doing you a favor, Sis." He regarded Dahlberg, "Who'd Maribec come with, Dave? I see Maddie's car across the street..."

Dahlberg didn't answer.

"None of your business," Maribec said.

"Hey, man, I ain't been drinkin' much. Do like your sister said and leave us alone. I can drive as good as you can. So butt-out, I'm takin' her back to her place."

"Sorry, pal. Why don't you just go back upstairs and tell Maddie that I'm taking Maribec with me." Pack moved closer to his sister, put his arm around her waist. "Let's go, Maribec. We'll fix up some coffee at your apartment."

"Just a God-damned minute, Moran. Maybe ya didn't hear me." Dahlberg put a firm grip on Pack's shoulder. "I'm with your sister tonight."

Pack could smell the acrid beer on Dahlberg's breath as the taller man leaned closer toward him. "Another time maybe, Davy. But not tonight."

"Fuck you, not tonight!"

Maribec wasn't too drunk to realize that the two men were dangerously close to going at each other right in the street. "Take it easy, you guys. I'll go with Pack, Davy. Gimme a call tomorrow why don'cha?"

Dahlberg seethed without reply.

After Pack had ushered Maribec into the front passenger seat and closed the door, he met Dahlberg's glare. "Take it easy, Dave...and, tell Randy to turn down the volume upstairs. Someone's going to call the police on you guys."

"I could give a shit about the cops, Moran." His fists were clenched at his side, his tone confrontational. "Why don't you go on up and turn down the music yerself? Just get me outta the way first." Dahlberg stepped closer to Pack, gestured for Pack to take a shot at his chin, "C'mon, tough guy."

Pack could put Dahlberg on the ground in ten seconds if he wanted to, but thought better of the idea. With a tight smile and conciliatory voice, Pack would end the episode. "Say hi to Randy for me, and Maddie, too. But, turn down the music, Davy, I don't want you guys getting into any trouble. Okay?"

Pack wished he could go upstairs and rescue Maddie from the drinking party. She was foolish not to realize the potential trouble she might be getting herself into. Maddie was a Hibbing elementary school teacher and this was no place for her to be.

Back at Maribec's apartment, Pack brewed a pot of coffee while his sister showered. It was only eleven, but his Friday night was already pretty much shot. Still looking strung-out, with untoweled mascara smudges around her eyes, Maribec pulled her robe tie about her waist and slipped onto a chair across from her brother at the kitchen table. She smiled weakly, "Thanks, Pack. I didn't really want to be with Dave tonight. He's a pig when he's been drinking." She drew a deep sigh, "So am I, I guess. Sorry about the scene I caused you...and, thanks for not kicking the shit out of Dahlberg." She lit a cigarette, poured a cup, sipped; "And thanks for making the coffee, too."

Pack measured his sister with sympathetic eyes. "Why do you do this crap to yourself, Maribec? And, God, the language you use! If Mom heard what comes out of your mouth, she'd..." Reaching across the formica tabletop he found his sister's cold hands, let his mother's anticipated 'wash your mouth' drop. "You're getting a reputation,

Sis. This is a small town and everything you do reflects on our parents, you know that. We're Morans, and—" The rest of his comment seemed almost redundant. His twenty-two year old sister had always been a free spirit. In a way, Pack resented that reality...and, in another way, he was jealous.

Maribec glared. "You don't have to remind me of my name, Pack. It's like a shadow over everything I do. You want to know something; I almost resent being the daughter of the hoity-toity Morans. Sometimes I think they're too perfect to be believable."

Pack let go of her hands, sat back in his chair. There were times when he had similar feelings. But he knew some things that his sister did not. This, however, was not a good time to detail past trials and tribulations that both Kevin and Angela had experienced. Did Maribec know that her mother was a rebellious teenager? That her father had been arrested for underage consumption while a student at the U.? That he was conceived out of wedlock? All that Pack could say was, "Let's not blame Mom and Dad for who we are. Okay? We're pretty damn lucky."

Like her mother, Maribec liked horses and being outdoors whenever possible. While Angela was an accomplished painter, she enjoyed photography, and had a knack for taking unusual pictures. Some of her black and whites were on display in her mother's art studio. And, she liked writing poetry in notebooks which she stored on a shelf in her bedroom closet. Her poems were something she never spoke about. Unlike Angela, Maribec was reclusive, apathetic, and too easily depressed. At times, she would spend an entire weekend in her apartment listening to music or writing dark poetry about being alone in a world she didn't understand. If being a Moran was something her brother was proud of, she had always had problems with her name and the expectations that it carried. Maribec believed she had failed her parents by not going on to a four-year college and making more of her life. In high school, she was on the honor roll without much effort and qualified for almost any college in the country. But, Maribec chose to stay in Hibbing.

"You really do care about me, don't you, Pack? Even if you don't like me most of the time—you do care. God, I'm sorry. I've got to get my life together. Nobody knows that more than I do." With the second cup of coffee her thinking and speech were noticeably improving.

"Damn right I care about you. So do Mom and Dad. Why do you shut us out all the time?"

Maribec hung her head. "I haven't been out to the house in two weeks. I'm sure they've called, but sometimes I don't even pick up the phone when it rings. I just get so down sometimes, Pack. Then the weekend comes and I just want to go out and—"

Pack gave her hand a squeeze. He let her vent without any more brotherly advise. "You hungry, Sis? Why don't you throw on some jeans and we'll run down to Sammy's and get a pizza. I was out looking for a girl tonight and I found one that's pretty special. What do you say?"

10/ 'NIGGER COON'

When Jerry Zench returned to his apartment building on the southern edge of Bennett Park, it was eleven-thirty. He had just finished an afternoon shift at the Scranton Mine and could still taste the iron ore in his mouth. Driving a production truck in the mine pits was a lousy job, especially when the weather was as dry as it had been. Sometimes the road dust was so thick it choked in the throat and even a wad of Juicy Fruit couldn't moisten his mouth. As he unlocked the door he noticed an envelope tucked under the floor mat. Had Maddie stopped by? He hoped not. Once inside the room, Jerry flipped on the light switch, tossed his jacket toward a kitchen chair, and tore open the blank envelope.

'GO BACK TO THE JUNGLE YOU COME FROM NIGGER COON HOTSHOT.'

Jerry's jaw dropped. "What the hell is th—?" He reread the pencil written line scribbled in capital letters across the center of the page. Who would write such hate? Jerry fought back tears as he walked into his small living room. Who? Someone had been in the building between two-thirty this afternoon when he left for the Scranton and now—and it wasn't Maddie Loiselle. Nigger! Coon! Hotshot! The three words pounded in his head. Why?

Jerry peered absently at the door. Widowed, Mrs. Rummel lived in the apartment across from him, but she would be sleeping now. Dewey Bartz, down the hall, was an imbecile on some county assistance program. What would he know? But someone must have been seen...someone? He cupped his face in his hands and cried. "Why, God...?"

Seldom had Jerry Zench felt so alone, isolated. He wanted to scream his anger, unload his pain on someone. He felt threatened, violated, vulnerable. It was approaching midnight. His parents had long since retired and he wouldn't wake them up. Who to talk with? His buddies—the softball guys? Some of them would still be up. Pack. Bourgoyne. Tobin. Dahlberg. Of those on his team, Pack Moran was the one he trusted the most. Although he sometimes hung out with Randy Tobin and Dave Dahlberg, they were...What? No, he didn't really like either of them. Rick Bourgoyne was older, a decent enough guy. Among his coworkers at the Scranton, only Jake Markie ever said much more than hello. On the job, Jerry remained to himself most of the time.

No, Jerry decided, he wouldn't make any late-night phone calls. What would he say to any of his friends, anyhow? That someone out there hated him?

The last name that came to his thoughts was Maddie Loiselle. What they had done together was terribly wrong. Both of them knew it.. Beautiful, blonde-haired Maddie. If anybody ever learned about them, God...But, he hadn't seen or heard from Maddie in nearly a month. It would be best if they never saw each other again.

Jerry decided to try and sleep it off. He'd call his dad in the morning. His father was an early riser—maybe the two of them could go out to breakfast. And talk. His dad, he believed, was possessed of Solomon's wisdom and the goodness of Jesus himself.

~

Gary Zench was delighted by the breakfast invitation from his son. Although it was only six-fifteen, he'd already showered and was reading the morning paper over a cup of coffee in the kitchen. "Great idea," he said with enthusiasm. "Just you and me, Jerry? I can wake your mother. She'd love..."

Despite having the day off, Gary would dress on this Saturday morning as he did every other morning; wearing a crisp white shirt and tie. The silk burgundy stripe from his closet rack complimented his gray tweed sports jacket. As he was leaving his Greenhaven bungalow to meet his son, the telephone rang again. "Kevin!"

"I knew you'd already be up, Gary. How about joining me for lunch?"

Gary smiled at his sudden popularity wondering if something was going on that he didn't know about. His birthday was months away. "Meet you around noon—at the Androy."

Gary chose a booth in the back of the Sportsmen's Cafe— wondering about the early-morning white patrons at the counter who watched him pass without any apparent interest. How many of them had heard Rick's radio programs this week? Had Bourgoyne stirred the pot too much? With the caller's slur and all the national troubles, were any of them thinking differently of him today than they might have a few weeks ago? He felt strangely conspicuous this morning.

Gary always selected a rear location when dining in a local restaurant. Subservient behavior in public places was not required, but he chose not to be distracting to other patrons. The message of humility in Luke's gospel, "sit in the lowest place", seemed appropriate. Gary had lived with that subtle reminder all of his years in Hibbing and hardly gave the matter a second thought anymore.

The waitress brought a decanter of coffee along with a breakfast menu. The table was already set with two place mats and cups. Gary knew instinctively, as a father does, that something was wrong in his son's world. Something Jerry didn't want his mother to know about. Several of the mines were cutting back production as was common practice in the fall. Perhaps a layoff was coming at the Scranton? Whatever, Jerry usually slept late when he didn't have to get up for work. His watch read six forty-five. What else could it be?

Jerry arrived a few minutes later and spotted his father in a corner booth. "Hey, Dad. Thanks for coming." Jerry gripped his father's large hand, smiled tightly. Just the touch of his brown skin brought a needed sense of comfort and communion. He held the handshake longer than usual. Jerry's father was a handsome man—warm, perceptive, and intelligent. The most beautiful human being in the world.

"I thought you were working the afternoon shift. You're not sleeping in, so you must really miss your old man." Gary laughed easily as his son sat down across from him, then poured him a cup of coffee.

"Haven't seen you all week, Dad. It's too nice to stay in bed this morning anyway." Jerry said. The September morning was gorgeous.

"Your father knows better than that. I remember when cannons wouldn't wake you on a Saturday morning. What's up, son? Something's on your mind." He noticed that Jerry's eyes were red and guessed his son had not slept well, or had been crying...or both. "Spill it out to dad."

Jerry had anticipated a few minutes of small talk, but that wasn't going to happen. He withdrew the folded envelope in his shirt pocket and set it on the table in front of him. "Yeah, somethin's on my mind, Dad. I hate to bother you with it...but it probably concerns all of us. The family, I mean." His voice choked with his emotion as he slid the envelope toward his father. "This was under my door when I got home from work last night."

Gary's stomach tightened. "Something bad?"

"Something scary."

Gary opened the envelope slowly, pausing significantly when he'd finished glancing at the note. He couldn't suppress the gasp. "My good God in heaven!" escaped his thick lips. In all his Hibbing years, he had not seen so much hatred expressed in a single, boldly scrawled line.

Jerry watched his father's eyes without saying a word.

The waitress stopped at their table. Both ordered the ham and eggs with hash browns and toast. As Jerry tucked the menus behind the napkin dispenser, his father stared at the envelope resting under his hands.

When agitated or confused, Gary unconsciously rubbed at his temples with long fingers, as if to conjure a thought that might loosen the right words. His mouth, however, was suddenly dry and his words were stuck somewhere between his brain and tongue. Looking at his son, he drew a deep sigh. "This—" Gary swallowed hard. "This breaks my heart, Son." His eyes scanned the page another time. "You're right—it does concern us all." Gary mumbled..."GO BACK TO THE JUNGLE..." Who could write such venom? "NIGGER COON..."

"I have no idea where this came from, dad. I asked Mrs. Rummel if she'd seen anybody in the hallway yesterday before I left the apartment this morning. She hadn't."

"Who else might have?"

Jerry shrugged. "There's nobody I know who could be that pissed at me...Sorry, Dad. I mean I haven't done anything to—"

Gary rubbed his temples thoughtfully. "You have no idea whatsoever?"

"None. And I don't know who to talk to. I'll probably talk to Pack. He's probably the only person I trust enough, you know."

"Yes, you might do that, Jerry." He pressed his mind for some idea of what to do. "Talk to Dewey Bartz when you get a chance.

He's just down the hall, maybe—? You never know. Sometimes it's those who you least expect..." Gary couldn't finish the thought.

Sparkie's an idiot, Dad." He forced a weak smile.

"Keep your voice down."

The waitress was approaching with their order. Verna set down their plates, refilled their cups, asked if there was anything else she could get them.

Jerry picked up where they had left off moments before. "Okay, I'll ask him if he saw anybody yesterday." He placated his father despite believing the effort would be a waste of time.

A long silence passed between the two men as they dabbled at the food. After a few tasteless bites both pushed their plates to the side.

"I think that what's going on down South has some people in Hibbing awfully pissed off...Sorry, son—it's your word, but I have nothing better." Gary tried to smile at his vulgarity. "Have you heard anything about the radio caller last week?"

Jerry had not, so his father explained. "I got a call the other day, from your softball teammate, Rick Bourgoyne. He was really offended by the racist comment and wanted to assure me that it was a crank. I appreciated the gesture and told him so."

"Rick's a decent guy. A lot more sensitive than most people probably realize. What did he have to say?"

"Not much. Said he brought the matter to the police."

"Did he say if he talked to Pack at the department?"

"Pack was out, he talked with Chief Lawrence." Gary remembered.

"Lawrence?" Jerry shook his head. "Nothing will come of it then."

~

Mary Rebecca Moran was up earlier than usual for a Saturday morning. She had a mild hangover, and the pizza (along with countless cups of coffee) had not allowed her much sleep the night before. It turned out to be a great night considering how everything started. She had enjoyed being with her older brother more than at any time she could remember. The two of them talked until nearly three in the morning. The usually hard-shelled cop let down his guard allowing the concerned brother to manifest himself for the first time in her memory. Pack didn't lecture her as she probably deserved. And he listened more than he spoke. He even confessed his own loneliness and frustrations over being a policeman in Hibbing...and being a Moran. "When your parents own businesses in town and live in a mansion, it puts us in a fishbowl. We're the kids of Kevin and Angela Moran: Not just Maribec or Pack! Sometimes I resent that."

"People are measured by their money, or a perception of their money, in a small, middle-class town. That's just the way it is, Pack." Maribec had said. "Mom and Dad are the greatest, but they're rich. And that's a pretty big but around here."

They talked about Maribec's friends, especially Maddie Loiselle. Pack seemed unusually interested in Maddie. "Randy Tobin is trying to 'put the make' on her." Maribec told him. "But she has no interest in him at all. She even told him that his mustache looked like a grease smudge."

Pack laughed, pressed his sister for a little more information. "Who does she like?"

Maribec divulged a secret she'd sworn never to breathe a word about. "She's been out with Jerry Zench a couple times...but nobody besides the two of them—and me—know anything about it. God, could you imagine what people around here would say about that? She'd probably lose her teaching job. Maddie's got lots on her mind, Pack. She's not happy here. Lately she talks a lot about her father, and...living with her mom hasn't been easy."

Maribec realized that she was probably divulging more than she ought to and let the matter drop abruptly. She remembered steering their conversation back to family relations. "How about if I join you for some of Mom's pot roast on Sunday?" She asked. "I've been kinda shutting them out lately."

~

Kevin could sense the tension in Gary's demeanor as he watched his friend make his way through the tables in the Androy dining room. Usually affable, Gary would stop briefly at each table and say a quick 'hello' to whoever was dining in the elegant room. Today, however, Gary walked brusquely past people he knew with obvious disregard.. One of them being Doctor Perpich who was Gary's dentist and had been recently elected to the school board. Perpich looked surprised when his patient passed by the table without any acknowledgment.

Gary's handshake was brief, clammy. His eyes almost brooding. Even his friend's silk tie uncharacteristically loosened at his collar. "What's wrong, Gary?" were the first three words out of Kevin's mouth. "Having a bad day?"

In the four hours since having breakfast with his son, Gary had done some serious soul-searching. His kind of people were not wanted in Hibbing, he concluded. After returning home and showing Jerry's note to his wife Nora, the two of them cried together. "I'm tempted to put a 'for sale' sign in the front yard and get us the hell out of here!" Gary had fumed. "I won't tolerate this kind of abuse. First the guy on the radio, now this!" He crumpled the note in his fist.

Nora tried to calm him, "Where in God's creation are you going to find a job like the one at the Androy, sweetheart. We're in our fifties, the house is paid for...Naomi's still in high school. We can't just uproot ourselves over a couple of stupid racist episodes. We've lived with prejudices in Hibbing for years. Nobody's ever done us any harm, Gary. Let's just try to forget this...this—" Nora didn't have the words to express what the crumpled note was.

"This is hate, Nora. There's no other word—hate! Trying to ignore petty prejudice is one thing, but this is far worse. What if something were to happen to Jerry, or Naomi? Me or you, for that matter."

Nora nodded without reply. The note frightened her more than she would admit.

"Should I tell Kevin about this, Nora? We're having lunch together today."

"He's your best friend—maybe, your only friend, Gary. Yes, by all means. 'Something' shared is half as heavy," my ma always said."

The wisdom of Nora's mother always brought a smile to Gary's face. "You're right. If I can't tell Kevin..."

~

"A bad day? Good God, it's been more like a bad week, Kevin." Gary slipped out of his reverie, giving Kevin a wan smile. "A hellava week."

Kevin saw his friend's stress in the deep furrows lining his brow, the furtive glances around the room, and the focus on his tightly folded hands on the table. Gary was a straightforward, eye-contact man. Their friendship was long in years and deep in trust.

Kevin was feeling guilty. He hadn't told Gary about the reason behind their employee survey. A lie of omission he was resolved to remedy. He was further resolved not to sugar coat his concerns. Folded in his jacket pocket were the three racist responses. There would be no secrets between the two men. Gary would never tolerate anything less than straight talk, and was among the most perceptive people he'd ever known.. Kevin would not be surprised if his hotel manager already recognized the employee questionnaire as a sham.

"I need to apologize to you for something I've done behind your back, Gary." Kevin's statement narrowed Gary's eyes, engaged his attention. "The real purpose of our hotel survey..." He explained his concerns about the note he had received on the previous Tuesday morning. "All it said was NIGGER LOVER, in bold capital letters."

Gary regarded his friend with doleful eyes. His dearest friend had been threatened because of him. He looked away for a moment, searched his tormented mind for something to say; then pulled his handkerchief from the back pocket of his trousers. A tear was escaping the corner of his eye. "Kevin, I'm truly sorry...you don't deserve—"

"Cut that nonsense, Gary. This is not about my deserving anything. We've got a problem here! To me, it's a big problem—and the two of us are going to get to the bottom of it."

Gary's composure returned. Leaning forward on his elbows and meeting Kevin's eyes he said, "There's more to this than you realize, Kevin. My son got a note last night—must have been slipped under his door while he was at work. It was like yours: all capitals, pencil-written, in a plain white envelope. It's crumpled a bit but I've brought it along with me to show you."

Kevin read the line of hate scrawled across the white page. "It's the same handwriting, Gary. I'd bet on it. Identical! I gave my note to Pack on Tuesday, asked him to check it out for me."

"Then it's probably in Lawrence's desk drawer right now. I don't expect he's going to do anything about it. Rick Bourgoyne's already talked to the 'Chief' about that radio caller. He thinks Lawrence might be the biggest racist in town." Gary leveled intelligent eyes on Kevin. "So, we've got the caller's slur...and now two notes to work with."

"And we've got these..." Kevin withdrew the three survey pages and handed them to Gary. "From our employees at the hotel—unsigned, of course."

Gary showed no emotion as he carefully read through each of them. The second sheet was specific, "...if you want to make things better get rid of Zench. he is no good for nothing around here..."

"What do you think, my friend?" Kevin asked.

"I'm not at all surprised. When you first mentioned this survey of yours, I knew you'd get some of this kind of feedback. I could probably give you the names of five or six people who might have singled me out as a problem here at the hotel. And another twenty who don't like Negroes."

Kevin nodded at the reality. "Unfortunately, that might be the way it is right now...but, let me tell you, if I find out I'll sure as hell—"

"Come on Kevin, you can't do that. You know that as well as I do. You can't do anything about nigger-haters. There's no law that prohibits prejudice. Not unless, or until someone does something."

"What? We sit on our hands until we have an incident? Until maybe someone in your family gets hurt?"

"Or your family, Kevin! You got the same kind of message that Jerry did—in the same white, non-addressed envelope."

11/ SPILLED PAINT

Pack spotted Rick's '53 Ford Fairlane in the Loiselle driveway as he drove down Ninth Avenue past the castle-like Hibbing High School building. He downshifted as he approached the intersection. Maddie's Nash Rambler was parked on the side street. It was ten-thirty in the morning and he was tempted to stop by Maureen's for a cup of coffee. Would it be an intrusion, he wondered? Rick was a good friend of his, but he didn't know Maury well enough to drop in.

Although the inspiring Saturday morning sunshine lifted his spirits, he couldn't get last night's conversation with Maribec out of his thoughts. Maddie remained a mysterious attraction, a challenge. What was he going to do about his feelings? With the softball season over, the weekends were a void to fill with other things. Since rising early and contemplating the day, he had come up empty of ideas on what to do with the day ahead—fishing or golf were possibilities, but...

He pulled near the curb but didn't stop. "What the hell," he tried to convince himself. Maybe Rick and Maury would see through his intentions? Obviously, Maddie, had made it home last night. Or, could she have dropped off her car after the party and spent the night at Randy Tobins? From what Maribec had told him, however, that wasn't likely. Would she be up? Hung over? Had she heard about the little episode with Dahlberg in the street outside? Probably. Was she the only girl at the apartment after Maribec left? Questions without answers!

He continued down to Howard Street, turned left toward the Androy, and caught a red light at Shapiro's Drug Store across from the hotel. Hibbing's downtown Saturday morning traffic was coming to life, he noticed. The front doors to Ace Hardware were open to the sidewalk. Customers would be shopping for weekend fix-up supplies—plumbing, electrical, painting. It was going to be an ideal day for anything out of doors. Further down the block, both Feldman's and Penney's had clothing sales. Crippa's Music already had the younger crowd loitering inside.

Pack tuned up the volume on an Elvis song airing on his radio. "Don't be cruel to a heart that's true...Baby it's just you..." Pack was neutral on Elvis, but liked this song. He took a left at the signal lights on Third and drove south to Twenty-third, then east back toward Cheever Field on the high school property. Blessed Sacrament Catholic Church, and the Assumption School dominated the block to his right. Pack had gone to the Catholic school through his eighth grade. Every time he saw the parochial school, bittersweet memories of stern nuns and rigid discipline were conjured.

At Ninth Avenue, he made the same left turn as he had only a few minutes before. As he approached Loiselle's on his second swing by, he spotted Rick and Maury standing by the Chevy having a cigarette. Pack pulled his Ford over, turning down his radio and switching off the ignition at the curb.

Rick waved, gesturing for Pack to join them. "Hey, Pack...what ya up to buddy?" Rick said as Pack slammed his car door and walked toward him. "Wish we had a ball game today. It's just like June out here."

"Is that all you guys ever think about—sports?" Maury's voice was teasing. "Can't you think of something...useful to do on a day like this." She looked at the wood trim on her stuccoed, Hathaway-style house and pointed toward the peeled paint. "I've been after Rick all summer to do some scraping for me, Pack. I'd gladly do the painting myself, but the scraping...!"

Rick shrugged his shoulders without reply. He had done his eaves only weeks before and didn't mind painting so long as it was outdoors. Inside was another matter entirely.

Pack sensed an opportunity. "I don't mind the scraping so much. Have you got extension ladders, Maury? Tell you what, you grill some burgers and get a case of beer...I'll bet me and Rick could do some serious work around here today."

"Thanks, buddy!" Rick regarded the trim Maury was pointing toward. It was a job he had promised to do. "What the hell. You serious, Pack—you'll pitch in and help us with this project?"

"Just a matter of changing into some painting clothes. The two of us could probably get the whole house done in a day. Burgers and beer, what do you say, Maury?"

"I'll run down to Ace and have paint here in half an hour. And, I'll make all the burgers you guys can put away. Maybe Maddie will help us out, I can wake her up right now if you're really serious." Maury looked from Pack to Rick.

Rick had spent the night. She hated to have him over when Maddie was home, but...She regarded Rick. Short, thinning hair, unkempt beard—her man wasn't handsome by any definition. But, Maury loved him. Pack, just under six feet, had his father's good looks. Rugged good looks. A square jaw, thick auburn hair, wide shoulders. Pack Moran exuded cop—even in jeans and a sleeve-rolled t-shirt.

"Pack, I think you've just hooked me into something I wasn't planning on doing today. Fate! If I hadn't stepped outside for a cigarette just now, you'd have driven right on by the house and none of this project stuff would be happening."

Pack smiled to himself. Fate was right! If it hadn't been for that cigarette? "Smoking, is no good for ya, Rick. How many times have I told you to quit? Pack, a sometimes smoker himself, laughed. "Meet you both back here in half an hour."

From her bedroom window, Maddie saw the three of them talking by Rick's car. Pack Moran was leaning on the front fender. Pack? What was he doing in her mom's yard? Must be something to do with Rick. Or, was it police related stuff? Remembering the night before, she wished that she'd have been the one to take Maribec outside Tobin's apartment. Dave Dahlberg had told her that Pack was being an asshole and was taking his sister home. Dave had been pissed and was bragging that he'd backed Pack down in the street outside. "Id'a kicked his ass," Dahlberg said after returning upstairs in a huff. Maddie remembered laughing out loud at his boast. "Yeah, you and Randy together, maybe."

Maribec's older brother was good-looking. Maddie remembered having a crush on him after high school, but didn't think she had a chance. Pack was four years older and just back from Korea. And he was a Moran, besides. The Morans had money. Despite Maribec's casual disregard of her family and independent life style, her best friend was still a Moran. That reality was a teasing thing between the two women.

Sometimes Maddie wondered, though. This past summer at ballgames, she had caught Pack looking at her a couple of times with that interested look that a guy can give a girl. She had asked Maribec about Pack on several occasions..."Who's your brother dating? What's Pack up to these days? Why don't you ask your brother if he wants to join us for a beer?" But Maribec never said much about Pack's life or interests. The two of them, she gathered, were not very close. So, Maddie let her interest slide.

Maddie was tall, slender, and strikingly attractive. When she and Maribec entered a room, the two girls always turned some heads. Maddie had naturally blonde hair and blue eyes like her mother. Unusual considering Maury was mostly French. Her father was Scottish. "A scoundrel Scot," Maury had claimed more than once. His name, McDougal, like his role in her life, had vanished years ago. The last she had heard about Sean McDougal, he lived in California. Somewhere in the Sacramento area. Maddie had been seven years old at the time, and never had an opportunity to get her father's side of the divorce story. Maury had told her little more than that Sean liked women—all women! He could no more be monogamous than he could be sober. Women and booze were the only two words ever used to characterize a man she had not seen in fifteen years—but still missed terribly—more often that she would ever admit to anyone. Her father was not someone she and her mother talked about—hadn't for years.

Pulling open her window, she leaned over the sill, "Hey, Pack!" The neckline of her nightgown was open and cleavage showed. Glancing down at her breasts, Maddie decided against buttoning herself.

Surprised by the greeting, Pack shaded his eyes against the sun with his hand, looked up toward the voice he know was Maddie's. He waved, trying to think of something clever to say. He didn't know her well enough to have any idea about her sense of humor.

"Hmm, looks like a conspiracy going on down there. What's going on? And what time is it, anyhow?" She tousled her long hair, yawned.

"Maddie. I've got a proposition for you." As soon as the words were out they sounded stupid, but Pack's line of thought had to continue. "You help us out with your mom's house project and I'll buy you a burger and a beer.

Maddie puzzled, her eyes intent on Pack below, and modestly fixed her nightgown. A proposition? A future date? "What's on your mind? Sounds like work and I'm not feeling too well this morning. Fluish." Pack would probably know the reason. More than likely,

Maribec had told him that she was with Randy Tobin last night. She wanted to tell him that wasn't the case. That she thought Randy was a jerk. Whatever Pack might have heard, she considered that fate had provided an opportunity for her to get to know Pack a little better.

"So, what would I be getting myself into?"

"We're going to paint the trim on your house. The three of us— we could use some help." Pack's eyes had focused by now. Maddie looked good for just getting out of bed. Her blonde hair was all over the place and she hadn't made up her face, but she was damn attractive none-the-less. Pack, wondering if she saw him staring, noticed her quick adjustment to the neckline of her soft blue nightgown. He flushed. "What do you say, Maddie?"

Maddie could only imagine how terrible she looked. "Mother! Did you rope these guys into this?" Then to Rick, "Or, was it your idea 'Radio Man'?" The nickname was something Maddie often used. She liked Rick a lot, found him easy to be around, but had doubts that he and her mother were right for each other. Rick wasn't the kind of guy her fastidious and all-too-serious mother should be attracted to.

"Don't blame your mother, or me. The project was this guy's idea." Rick put his arm around Pack's shoulders. "Apparently he's got nothing going on in his sorry life—wants to go around making other people's day off miserable."

Laughing, Maddie slashed her finger across her throat and pointed at Pack. "So there was a conspiracy going on out here. And Pack's the culprit, huh? Okay. I'll pitch in...but not for another hour or so. I need a shower, fix myself a bit, and get something to eat first." Maddie pulled down the window. What was this all about, she wondered? Pack was going to buy her a bottle of beer and a burger? Was he serious? Rick and Pack were softball buddies, but...whatever? She would find out before the end of this day. The prospect brought a smile to her lips.

Later in the afternoon, while Pack was descending the ladder with a bucket of paint in his hand, Maddie stepped over to brace the flimsy wooden device. When Pack looked down to check the distance between himself and the ground below, the paint can tilted. Before he could rebalance himself or warn Maddie, still several feet below, it was too late! Disaster! Maddie, doused with a half-gallon of white paint, plopped bottom-first onto the grass. When she saw the inevitable and tried to scream her alarm, the spillage splashed over her face in a drench of ooze.

Pack virtually leapt the last few feet to the ground. "God, I'm sorry, Maddie ! What can I say? The bucket just—"

Rick howled at the sight. Maury couldn't contain her own laughter. "Aren't you a sight to behold? I wish I had a camera." Maury giggled her delight.

Pack felt like a klutz. What kind of apology could he make for this mess? He grabbed a rag he'd tucked in his back pocket to daub at her face and remove some of the paint dripping down her chin and neck and all over the front of her bib overalls. Her beautiful hair hung in sticky white braids plastered across her forehead and cheeks. "Let me get some of this..."

The humor of the moment and her foolish circumstance took a long minute to hit Maddie. Dropping the brush she was holding she bent over in uncontrolled laughter herself. She could only imagine what she must look like covered with the thick paint. "This is a hell of a way to treat a woman, Moran. You ought to be arrested for...assault with intent to do bodily harm—whatever that is?" She could feel the ooze of paint between her breasts. Scooping a handful of paint from below her open shirt, Maddie laughed, "No use in crying over spilled paint, I guess." She got up on one knee. "All is forgiven."

Pack, leaning over her in obvious embarrassment, groped for something to say without laughing himself. Nothing came to mind.

"Just help me to my feet and...let me share some of our mess." She put one hand behind his head and scrunched the cupped hand in his face—smearing a white swath across his chin and mouth.

Pack dropped to his knees, then rolled over in hilarity. Now they were even, or almost even. Without her noticing, he slipped his hand into the overturned paint can. "Let me help you up," he offered.

When she clasped his hand, she let out a shriek, pulled her hand away and rubbed the paint on the leg of Pack's bluejeans. "This was all planned. I know it. You two guys."

Maddie did have a sense of humor after all. A damn good sense of humor at that! Her reaction endeared him more than ever before. "You can do anything to me Maddie, but don't...please, don't tell the police about this."

"And don't blame me, Maddie. I should have warned you that this guy is a natural screw-up." Rick made his contribution to the comedy of the moment.

Maury stood by in speechless amusement.

That evening, Maddie reflected on the events of her day, often laughing out loud over the spilled paint incident. She hadn't enjoyed a Saturday more than this one in months. Pack was a fun guy to be around—not the rigid and aloof policeman she had imagined he would be. He loved to laugh, even at himself. And she found a different perspective on Rick Bourgoyne as well. Up until now she didn't know what her mother saw in the man. Pack, however, had opened windows to Rick's personality and charm that enabled Maddie to better understand Maury's attraction. Both men were much more than the self-absorbed softball 'jocks' of her imagination. They were sensitive, even tender during fleeting moments of the eclectic conversations which ranged from police work to teaching to the radio business. Each of the four had opportunity to talk about themselves, their feelings and frustrations. Rick was intelligent, but Pack could respond to any topic he raised with equal insight. They hardly mentioned sports in the hours spent in the backyard while barbecuing and socializing. Sports probably gave them both a necessary outlet to their innate masculine aggressions, yet there was far more depth to their character.

Pack had lots of questions about school, kids, and teaching which enabled Maddie to share her care-giving passions with the men. His inquiries generated some mother-daughter dialogue that had been too long repressed in the separate lives of the two independent women. The conversation had been marvelous and stimulating...until!

Without realizing he had done so, Rick had touched a sensitive chord in Maddie when voicing his frustration over the racist caller earlier in the week. Pack, she sensed, was keeping something bothersome within unspoken thoughts while Rick vented his angst. For quite a while, Pack seemed lost in some painful reverie. His eyes, far away and unfocused, betrayed that private something—whatever it was.

Rick, feeling the effects of too many beers, began slurring some words and using vulgarities. Inadvertently, Rick revealed a confidence that he and Pack had shared. "Just between us, Pack's dad got a racist note at the hotel on the same morning," he divulged. "Used the nigger word just like the caller did."

Attention switched to Pack for some response but he only shifted nervously in the lawn chair, frowned. "We're looking into it," was his only comment. The subject died almost immediately.

Throwing back her comforter and sliding under the sheets, Maddie propped a second pillow under her head. Rick's venting about the racial issue had noticeably disturbed Pack. She knew that Jerry Zench was a good friend of both men. Yet, neither mentioned Jerry's name at any time. What did Pack know? Had Maribec betrayed a confidence? Pack and his sister had been together the night before...

Maddie's thoughts drifted from Pack to Jerry as she tossed in her bed. Sleep was going to be difficult she could tell. What were her feelings toward Jerry? Had they been little more than a fleeting sexual attraction? Yes, Jerry was about as different as a man could be in Hibbing. Handsome, athletic, modest—but, mostly different! He was a brooder, hard to draw out, and repressing what Maddie believed to be a deep-seated resentment. Being a Negro among whites must be tough. Racial feelings were an unspoken void between them on the three occasions they had been together.

Maddie first met Jerry Zench at the Homer Bar after a softball game she and Maribec attended back in early June. They were at a table with several of the other Androy players—Randy Tobin, Dave Dahlberg, and Ian Roberts (JR to everyone). Jerry was the hero of the moment having hit a triple to score the winning run that night. With the personal attention being directed his way most of the evening, Jerry was modestly charming and amiable. Maddie, sitting next to him at the time, bought him a bottle of Hamms, then toasted..."To the best shortstop in the league."

Jerry smiled at the recognition, putting his arm across the back of Maddie's chair. "Thanks...for the beer, and the compliment," was all he said. But his hand gripped her shoulder for a brief moment. Maddie remembered the feeling of his touch—a strangely exciting feeling!

Maddie went to the next two games but didn't see Jerry afterwards. Then, on a Tuesday night, the ball game was interrupted by a sudden downpour. As the players raced from the field toward their parked cars, Jerry called to Maddie, "Hop inside, you're getting drenched." He held open his car door for her while trying to shield her from the rain with his softball glove held over her head. In Jerry's car, the two of them talked superficially about the game, the storm, and other small talk she couldn't remember. But she remembered Jerry's smile, expressive eyes, and sensual lips. For reasons she would never quite understand, Maddie wanted to experience kissing those lips, feeling his lithe body on hers.

When the rain let up, Maddie excused herself and self-consciously rushed from Jerry's car to her Nash parked nearby. The incident embarrassed and excited her in near equal measure. Later she tried to come to grips with 'what would people say?' Like her best friend, Maribec, Maddie had some rebel in her blood.

About a month ago (August tenth, she remembered exactly) Maddie did something impulsive. She put a letter under Jerry's apartment door. I want to see you again, Jerry. Where can we be alone together? Call me at my mother's house. She works during the day. She added a p.s.: What's your apartment like inside? I'm curious. She signed the note simply, M. L.

On the following night she slept with Jerry in his apartment. He said it was "his first time..." and Maddie was quite certain it was. Afterward, she felt a consuming guilt over the whole experience and resolved never to do it again. This could never work, regardless of their feelings. This was Hibbing.

After more than an hour, Maddie slipped into a fitful slumber. As often happens, those in your thoughts before falling asleep are manifest in your dreams. The nightmare she had that night would never be remembered.

12/ 'LEFTY' ROSNAU

Police chief Don Lawrence was having a whiskey-seven with Hibbing Lieutenant Lefty (Leonard) Rosnau at Checco's Bar. The two officers were good friends both on and off the job.

Down the bar were Randy Tobin and Dave Dahlberg. "Say Chief, one of yer cops is a wise-ass, if ya don't mind my tellin' ya."

Lawrence turned his head, "What's your problem, Dahlberg?"

"Last night, Pack Moran was picking up his drunk sister over at Tobin's place an he downright assaulted me." Dahlberg fabricated Pack's behavior and exaggerated the comments exchanged between them. "An he wasn't on duty or nothin'. Just lookin' for trouble when there ain't none. Otta leave folks alone."

"File a complaint then, Dahlberg." Lawrence aborted the conversation. Dahlberg and Tobin were jerks. Moran, though the Chief didn't care much for him personally, was a good cop. Dahlberg must have instigated whatever happened. Shifting his shoulders and leaning toward Rosnau, "What were we talking about, Lefty?"

Rosnau frowned, "I wouldn't be so quick to dismiss what Dahlberg said. Those Morans thinks they're somethin'. It wouldn't surprise me one bit if what Dahlberg said was true. Pack likes to push people around."

Lawrence knew that Rosnau and Moran were not close. "I told you about the note Pack gave me last week, didn't I, Lefty? The one his father got in his hotel mail?"

"The nigger thing? Yeah, what's the big deal? I don't have any problem with niggers—so long as they stay in their place! Know what I mean?"

Looking away from Rosnau's eyes, Lawrence found his reflection in the mirror behind the bar. Despite some prejudices, the word nigger made him uncomfortable. He wouldn't, however, acknowledge that, "The Zenches aren't bad people for being Negroes. They keep pretty much to themselves far as I can tell."

"I wonder about that Zench kid, sometimes. The ballplayer. What's his name, Jerry? Anyhow, he likes to hang around with the other guys after games—over at the Homer Bar. Sits at the same table as some white girls, even talks to 'em like they're friends. Moran's sister is one of them—and that teacher, Loiselle. Now that kind of makes me sick." Lefty shook his head, fingering his narrow mustache. "Just not the way things are supposed to be, Don. Niggers otta know their place, that's my feeling."

"Is that so? You've seen them? You'd think that Zench would keep more to himself," Lawrence commented over his drink. "Watching that sort of thing might upset me a little, too. Not much we can do about it, though."

"I know I've told you this before, Don, but if I ever heard about a nigger monkyin' around with one of our white girls...Well, I think I'd do the same damn thing they do down South. I'd castrate the son-of-a-bitch!"

"That's pretty strong talk, Lefty." Lawrence felt awkward about what else to say. "You're talking more like a vigilante than a cop. You ever do something like that and you'd be history around here."

"You'd suspend your best friend, Don? C'mon, I'd be doing this town a service." He laughed at the notion, "Some things the law can't protect the people from."

Lawrence wondered if Rosnau was really serious. Was he being too uptight with his companion? Slapping Rosnau on the back he tried levity. "I'd suspend you for...at least a week, Lefty. And recommend the suspension coincide with the opening of deer season."

"Don't give me any ideas, Don. Opening of deer season, huh? That's what you said, ain't it." Lefty Rosnau gave a belly laugh, then ordered two more drinks. "Give those two guys whatever they're drinkin'." He told the bartender, gesturing toward Tobin and Dahlberg.

Lawrence wished he hadn't said what he just had. Sometimes he simply wanted to make a joke and an 'old buddy' impression on his subordinates. He tried to recover. "Best to just let sleeping dogs lie if they're not giving us any trouble. I mean, we wouldn't want any of the crazy stuff going on down in Tennessee to happen up here."

Rosnau sensed his friend was backing away from the issue he had raised about Zench's social behaviors—down-playing the matter. He reiterated a previous comment. "Me neither, I guess...so long as they don't have the balls to mess with our women—things will get along fine up here."

Unlike his drinking partner, Lefty Rosnau's hatred ran deep in the marrow of his bones. A justified hatred, the forty-four year old cop believed. And, his hate was not exclusive to niggers—Rosnau hated Injuns and Japs, as well as Catholics and Jews.

Ironically, perhaps, young Leonard was an altar boy of twelve when he first found justification for hating another human being. After confession one Saturday afternoon, Father Flambeau approached the youngster on the playground. "Come over here, Leonard," the priest had said. "I want you to understand the seriousness of something that's been troubling you."

That 'troubling something' concerned his confession of "being impure with himself...five times in the two weeks since his last confession."

In no uncertain terms, the priest told the youngster that he "would go to hell if he didn't respect his penis and control his sinful thoughts." Humiliated and shamed over the trauma of that experience, Leonard would never again kneel at the communion rail of Flambeau's, or any other Catholic church.

While in the military during the Second Word War, Leonard had many white friends from places like Alabama, Georgia, and Mississippi. These were the guys who really knew about niggers! He also had a DI by the name of Stienberg—a Jew who was easy for all the GI's to hate.

As an aspiring young officer on the Madison, Wisconsin, police force, Leonard Rosnau's hatred received another boost. In line for a promotion to Sergeant, he was passed over—a Negro officer named Leroy Jefferson was given the position. "We've got to show the coloreds in town that we care about them, Len...I'm sorry, you probably deserved the job." He was told this by a police board commissioner "just between us" after the decision was publicly announced. Leonard quit the Madison force and moved to Hibbing (where his wife was originally from) the following week.

The education and experiences of Leonard Rosnau had conditioned him to hate.

Hibbing was predominantly Catholic, had a large and prosperous Jewish community, and one Negro family. So, Rosnau spurned going to church, always shopped at non-Jewish stores, and kept his eyes upon the affairs of the Zench family.

13/ STAFF INTERVIEWS

After two days of 'thinking things over' and further discussing his fears with Nora, Gary Zench was determined to suggest to Kevin that they abandon the project the two of them had been working on. It was a gray Tuesday morning outside—and in his heart. A meeting on the survey responses had been scheduled for ten.

Wearing his stress like a like wrinkled shirt, Gary closed the door to Kevin's office behind him. "Before we go any further with these employee letters, I've got to level with you, boss." He swallowed hard, "I've had a change of heart."

Kevin regarded his friend, "Sit down and tell me what's bothering you."

"I'd rather stand." Gary thrust his hands in his trouser pockets and walked to the window overlooking Howard Street. He stood for a long minute. "I think we're making a big mistake," he said with his back turned on Kevin and his shoulders sagged by the weight of his words. "We've just got to let sleeping dogs lie. Some things are best left alone."

"What?"

"You heard me. I don't want us making a mountain out of what's been going on."

"Please look at me when your talking, Gary. Making a mountain?"

Gary turned, met Kevin's gaze. "You've got to understand something. Naomi's a senior in high school and...after she graduates we can decide what to do. Until then, I don't want to have any part in a witch hunt."

"A witch hunt?"

"Sorry, but that's how I see it. If we start leaning on our employees this whole ugly thing's going to blow up in our faces, Kevin. I don't want that to happen. I'm just not willing to take the risk of inciting any more hate."

"Since when have you ever backed away from something tough, Gary? I'm confused."

"Since now. And, there's nothing to be confused about. I tell you, this is not a good idea." Gary sat down, folded his large hands in his lap.

Kevin could read the fear in Gary's eyes and demeanor. The two men had rarely disagreed over their many years of friendship and Kevin was at a loss as to how to confront the issue. "I'd never try to force you into any situation you're not comfortable with, Gary. If you don't want to be involved, that's fine."

For a long moment a pall of stress hung like a curtain between them. Gary, eyes downcast, fidgeted nervously with his hands. Kevin contemplated his next words carefully.

"You can close your eyes and bide your time until Naomi graduates if you want to, but I'm not going to. This is my hotel, Gary—and I got the goddamn note from someone that might work here." His words had a sharp edge. "So, maybe it isn't all about you. Maybe it's my problem as much as it is yours." Kevin stood, "Sorry you feel the way you do." He would not press the issue any further. "I'm sure you've got better things to do..."

Gary shifted in his chair, "Sit down, Kevin. And please spare me the lecture." He realized that he'd misjudged his friend's resolve. Kevin was right and he was wrong. It was time to be honest with his feelings. "This whole business scares the hell out of me. I'm looking over my shoulder all the time, Kevin. Wondering?" He paused, "I just don't know what to do—I can't live this way. None of us can."

Kevin saw the beginning of tears in the corners of Gary's eyes. Leaning against the edge of his desk, he smiled a warm empathy. "Finally the truth! For a while I didn't know where you were coming from, Gary. Yes, hate is a damn scary thing—scares me, too."

Gary dabbed his crisp white handkerchief to his eyes. "So...I guess we'd better get back to what we've started. Right, boss?" His smile was weak but hopeful.

"That's why we're here, my friend." The two of them had spent hours going over the survey materials with particular focus and conjecture on the three pages which most clearly expressed the prejudice they were planning to follow-up on. "I think we both agree that Carl Wicklund and Phil Nash are our prime candidates here at the hotel. Neither one of them signed a survey sheet and Elsie remembers both of them turning one in to her office last Friday. I want to talk with each of them."

Gary nodded agreement with reservation. "What are you going to say to them? I think you're a racist—or, ask them if they really hate niggers?"

"Just let me handle that. And I mean me, with a capital M. I don't want you to be involved in any confrontations—that's my job. But, I'm open to any ideas you might have."

Gary mused, rubbing his large hands over his knees. "Use me. I mean, maybe you could try..." Gary explained his proposal. He suggested that Kevin talk to Wicklund and Nash "in confidence, of course" about some shoddy management practices. "Explain to both men that you are considering some management changes. Tell them that you're not very pleased with how I do things around here."

Kevin liked the idea, but—"Almost everybody here knows we are pretty good friends."

"We can have a highly conspicuous falling out, Kevin. Something that will get everybody talking. I could make some major mistake with this week's payroll. Get everybody riled up. Then you reprimand me in front of staff...say something like 'you've been much too careless lately, Zench'. Use my last name."

The two men considered the strategy along with others for another hour. When they were finished, Kevin gave Gary a hug. "Now, you just quit looking over your shoulder and go about things at the hotel as you normally do." Giving Gary a slap on the back, he added, "And, trust me—you know we're a helluva lot smarter than they are."

Gary shook his head, "Kevin, I've trusted you all my life...that's never going to change." Then he frowned, "But don't get yourself involved too deeply. I don't want anything happening to you."

"Don't worry about me."

At the door, Gary hesitated, "You've got the softball banquet tonight, don't you?"

Kevin nodded.

"I'd appreciate if you...well, don't say anything to Jerry about what's going on here at the hotel when you see him tonight, Kevin. He's got enough on his mind."

"Just between the two of us, my friend."

Kevin dictated a simple memorandum to Elsie:

Employees:

I want to thank the entire Androy staff for participating in our 'Suggestion Survey'. There were many very good ideas, and many valid criticisms, as well. In order to determine the prize winners, I will personally interview some of the top entries. By Friday, I will make an announcement of the winning entries. Thank you again for sharing your views.

Sincerely
Kevin Moran

Kevin's first interview (a much softer word than interrogation) was with Carl Wicklund. The Androy bartender was twenty-seven and had gone through school with his son, Patrick. Carl and Pack, although teammates in hockey and football, had never been buddies. Wicklund was a square, powerfully-built man with crew cut blond hair and a pug nose. His full, brown mustache almost contradicted the military-style haircut.

With Carl, Kevin would be blunt. He hoped to put the dullard on the defensive right away. "I've read your unsigned survey comments from last week, Carl." If Wicklund denied submitting a questionnaire, he'd be caught in a lie. Elsie had assured Kevin that the bartender had given her the paper on Friday afternoon.

"Yeah. Okay. So what? Don't tell me I won somthin." Carl gave a twisted smile. "Yeah. Like lots of guys, I din't sign it, Mr. Moran." He emphasized the Mr. Moran to give the impression of being respectful. "Least that's what I hear. Maybe even half. "

Kevin stared into Carl's narrow eyes without comment. Let him talk.

"How would ya know mine from anyone else's?" Averting Kevin's eyes he swabbed the bartop with a terrycloth rag. "I thought the whole idea was bullshit, anyhow."

"You may think so, Carl, but others took it seriously."

"Yeah. Maybe the 'ass-kissers'." His tone belligerent. Recovering, Carl looked up, "Sorry...I'm jus' givin' an opinion, ya know."

Kevin would put Wicklund more at ease. "I know all the ass-kissers as you call them, Carl. We've got a few for sure. But, naturally they all signed their questionnaires."

"Suppose they would."

"Carl, nobody's job is in any jeopardy over this. I want to assure you of that. And, I agree, everyone's entitled to their opinion about things. That's why I wanted to give you folks the opportunity to remain anonymous. Right?"

Wicklund tossed the rag into a nearby sink. "Then I ain't gotta say nothin', do I, Mr. Moran? Cause I don't wanna. If ya saw some things ya din't like, ya ain't gonna prove nothin'. Right?" A smug grin of self-assurance creased his broad face. "Right?" he repeated. Pausing for a significant moment, Carl added his clincher. "I din't even hanrite mine anyhow. Jus' like lots of people, I used a typewriter."

Carl was not bright enough to recognize his admission. "Yes, there were several typed responses, Carl," Kevin fabricated. He knew all that he wanted to know already. "Before I leave, what was your idea, Carl? You can tell me in confidence, if you'd like. Maybe it's worth a few bucks."

Carl felt the warm glow of vindication. With a laugh, "I learnt in the army not ta volunteer nothin' ya don' hafta. Ya ever serve yer country, Mr. Moran? Ya get to know lots about different kind'sa people in the army. Some ya like, some ya don't. Know what I'm sayin'?"

Phil Nash had been employed at the Androy for fifteen years, most of them as the hotel's afternoon shift desk clerk. Nash had thick white hair. narrow nose, and a flushed face. Phil was fifty and twice divorced. Most importantly, from the desk he was an arm's length away from the hotel mailboxes.

Often when he finished his shift, Nash would spend a couple of hours at the Androy bar before going home, usually chatting with his younger friend, Carl Wicklund. Kevin would not draw any unwarranted conclusions from their acquaintance. Unlike the bartender, however, Nash was a courteous and articulate man whose work routines were always meticulous.

Kevin's relationship with Phil Nash had been amicable but distant. He would use an entirely different approach with his desk clerk than he had with Wicklund earlier. "Sorry you didn't win our little employee contest, Phil. You might have had a pretty good idea—but then forgotten to sign your name."

"What do you mean, sir? I signed my name on the bottom of the page. I'm certain of it." He lied. "I'm always careful about those things. Perhaps you should check again, sir."

"What was your idea, Phil? I'm sure I'd remember."

"Oh, well...let me see." His delicate finger found the side of his nose. "I had several ideas, sir. All of them quite positive. I just can't seem to recall which one I actually submitted to Elsie."

"I've got them all in my desk drawer upstairs. Should we go through them, Phil? You would surely know which one was yours." Kevin looked levelly into Nash's moist, red-rimmed eyes—magnified by the thick glasses set tightly on the bridge of his nose.

Nervously, Nash looked beyond Kevin's intent gaze. "Maybe you're right. I must have forgotten to sign mine. Last Friday was busy as you remember. It's not like me..."

Kevin could see the slightest trace of perspiration on Nash's high forehead. "Let me get them out. It would only take a minute or two—as I remember, your handwriting is quite distinctive."

"I typewrote mine, sir. I'm positive." He checked his wristwatch nervously, hoping for a distraction. Any distraction.

Of the three typewritten pages in the batch of fifty-two, two of them came from secretarial employees—Elsie and Doris—and were typed on Androy office machines. The third was the disturbing racist reference which suggested a bed-pissing incident and stated...Hibbing is not a place for niggers to come. I should say negroe but I don't care.

Kevin puzzled over Phil's unexpected admission. Both Wicklund and Nash now claimed to have typed their survey responses. One of them was a liar. Both were legitimate suspects. But—who was the third? "Well, there were so many typed suggestions that it might take more than a few minutes and I know you're a busy man, Phil. Maybe another time, okay?"

"Certainly."

"Too bad you can't remember what idea you submitted, Phil. If I can figure things out, I'll let you know."

"Thank you, sir." Nash's relief was an audible sigh.

~

Jerry Zench ran into Dewey Bartz on his way out the door to the softball banquet being held at the Androy that evening. "Sparky, I've been meaning to talk to you. Can you remember back...last Friday?"

"Ya—ya." Sparky always responded to questions and comments alike—Ya—ya.

Jerry smiled at the town imbecile. "Did you happen to see anybody in the hallway by my apartment on Friday?"

Dewey nodded with typical enthusiasm. "Ya—ya."

"Could you tell me who that was?"

"Ya—ya. Mizzuz Rummmo."

Frustrated, Jerry asked, "Anybody other than Mrs. Rummel?"

"Ya—ya."

"Who?"

Sparky gave Jerry an enigmatic grin. "Yer friends, Jerrree."

"My friends?"

"Ya-ya. Softball."

"Guys from my team?"

"Ya-ya. Yer team."

"But you don't remember their names?"

"Ya-ya." He nodded his large head. "Know everbuddies name, Jerrry. Last Friday—seven forty-five on my watch here...they dint see me tho cuz I was peeking through my door at 'em. Always peek when I hear somthin', Jerrry. Even you. I seeze lotza things."

"Who were they?"

Sparky told him the names of the two men. "Ya-ya. That's who wuz here."

14/ MADDIE LOISELLE
Wednesday, September 12th

Maddie Loiselle was disturbed by the note in her mailbox at the Cobb Cook Elementary School. The principal, Mr. Robert Dietrich, wanted her to stop by his office for an after-school conference. Throughout that afternoon she stewed over the meeting. Agitated, she abandoned her lesson plan for story time and gave her first-graders an improvised cut and paste project from a stack of Life magazines she kept in reserve. "Find pictures that will tell us about any three things you did this past summer. And please be very careful with the scissors."

"Miss Loiselle, I'm afraid we have something highly unpleasant to discuss this afternoon." Dietrich's tone was stern. His narrow forehead furrowed over bulging, frog-like green eyes. "In fact, two matters of considerable gravity have come to my attention."

Maddie had not been behind the closed doors of the principle's office since her job interview more than a year before. The atmosphere was intimidating. "Yes, sir," were the only words she could say.

"As a single female teacher in this community, you realize that our district holds your behavior to the highest moral standards. I believe I made that crystal clear when we first met, Miss Loiselle. You do remember?"

Maddie nodded.

"At that time I was most candid about the employment of women for teaching positions. You might even remember that the staff vacancy was due to an unexpected pregnancy. With the school term only weeks away, I was in a real bind." Dietrich, avoiding eye contact, continued. "Anyhow, I stressed the importance of what I term, 'social discretion'. I even suggested, as I always do, that if ever you wanted to have a glass of wine or whatever liquor—publicly, that is—you should consider traveling to Virginia or Duluth. Some place far enough from Hibbing where the parents of your children would not be witnesses to such reprehensible activity."

Maddie nodded, remembering the put-down vividly. "Yes, sir." Her heart was sinking into the bowels of her stomach. She had been reported to Dietrich for being at Tobin's party on Friday night.

"Well, it seems, Miss Loiselle, that the Hendersons—I believe you have little Nellie in your first grade class—called the superintendent of schools on—" Dietrich shuffled the papers in front of him, pinching his small chin as he did so. "—Yes, on Monday morning it was. They reported seeing you leave the residence of a Mr. Tobin on Twenty-Third Street, somewhere around midnight." He emphasized midnight and shook his head in obvious irritation. "The Henderson's claimed there was loud rock and roll music playing, and suggested that some drinking had been going on there."

"Yes, sir."

"Are you acknowledging this complaint, Miss Loiselle?"

"Yes, sir. I mean, yes...I was at Tobin's apartment on Friday evening. And, yes there was some music, and the adult gentlemen were drinking, sir."

Dietrich shook his head in mock disgust.

Maddie remembered Maribec's urging her to leave the party around nine o'clock when she did. Why had she been so stupid? Tobin, Dahlberg, and JR Roberts were all jerks. Maddie tried to make eye contact with the principal but failed. Dietrich's eyes kept shifting away, from papers to desk phone, and clock to wall calendar. If he was uncomfortable, he was also enjoying his authority.

"You know, Miss Loiselle, there must be a presumption of 'guilt by association' in matters like this. Do you understand? Looking up momentarily, a smirk crossed his thin lips. So far the woman could say little more than "Yes, sir". Within the next few minutes he would have her resignation. Dietrich already had a male teacher in mind for her first grade teaching position. He could hardly contain his eagerness to drop the second bomb on his unsuspecting victim. But, first things first. "I asked if you understood what I was saying, young lady—I mean, Miss Loiselle. Perhaps young lady is no longer an appropriate reference."

Maddie made a mental note of the comment, chose not to throw it back in his face. Bite your tongue for now, she told herself. "Yes, sir. Did the Henderson's claim that I had been drinking?" Her voice strained.

"That, it would seem to me, is quite irrelevant, Miss Loiselle."

"I see." But, Maddie did not see. "Guilt by association, is that what you are alleging, Mr. Dietrich?"

"Quite precisely. I must, of course, suspend you for this incident until the school board has had an opportunity to review the complaint and take any further action. Do you understand?"

"Yes, sir...Will I have an opportunity to speak to the board at that meeting?"

"Well, it is a public meeting, but—are you sure you want to..."

Maddie nodded, swallowed hard: "Oh, yes, sir! I wouldn't want to miss the Inquisition you have in mind. Oh, yes. I'll have something to say."

Dietrich gasped at the audacity of her words.

"Now, if that is all, I would like to be excused." Maddie pushed back her chair and began to stand.

"Please sit down, Miss Loiselle. As I said earlier...there is a second matter that has come to my attention today. Perhaps this will change your mind about wanting to appear before the school board for—how did you so insolently put it—the Inquisition."

Maddie frowned, sat back down on the uncomfortable wooden chair. "Yes, sir? What's that?"

"This letter, or whatever one might consider it, came in the morning mail today. Granted it is unsigned, but it certainly raises some even more serious moral questions." Dietrich slid the opened envelope across his desk for Maddie to read. "Go ahead and see for yourself."

Maddie checked the envelope before extracting the letter. It was typed and addressed simply to 'Principal, Cobb Cook School, Hibbing, Minnesota'. The blurry Hibbing postmark read September 10—Monday of this week. Inside was one typewritten line:

> Loiselle sleeps with niggers at nite and teeches kids
> at day.

Maddie's jaw dropped. "This—!" Her throat constricted. "This is totally—" Totally what? Her thoughts were in turmoil! How could she defend herself against this terrible accusation—this despicable truth? "I will not comment on this letter, Mr. Dietrich." She summoned every ounce of resolve to avoid a break down—every fiber of her emotion strained. She must not allow this pompous man see her cry.

"Unless you can unequivocally deny this allegation, I will expect a letter of resignation before you leave this building tonight, Miss Loiselle."

Maddie had contained herself and tempered her words long enough. "There will be no such letter! And, further...I have endured quite enough for one afternoon, Mr. Dietrich." She stood, "Now. Please excuse me. I will expect to see you at the next school board meeting. In the meantime, you might want to use discretion in speaking of these damnable allegations. If I learn that you have spoken to any faculty, parents, or...anybody during my suspension— well...you'd better be careful. You've already put yourself in a compromising situation with your arrogant and bullying behavior. Sir!"

Dietrich's jaw dropped as the spirited young woman stormed from the room, slamming the door behind her. Why was he perspiring? Obviously, there would be no letter of resignation, which would enable the superintendent to quickly dispose of the matter. Should he have discussed the issue with Superintendent Mitchell before issuing the arbitrary suspension? Surely he had 'gone by the book'. Surely Mitchell would support everything he'd done. What should he do now? Dietrich eyed the desk phone. Yes, he'd explain to Mitchell exactly what that obnoxious bitch had done. And, he'd tell Mitchell about her threats. Who did Loiselle think she was anyhow?

Devastated, Maddie left the building without returning to her classroom to turn off the lights or collect her wrap. Confused and frightened, she wondered to whom she might confide her dilemma. Certainly not Randy Tobin—nor Jerry Zench either! If only she knew Pack a little better. He would have some knowledge about the law and a person's rights. And his father was an attorney. No, she would talk to Maribec and make an indirect connection to the other Morans.

But first she would have to tell Maury. Maddie was certain that her mother's business retained a lawyer. Maybe for the first time in years, she needed her mother's support.

Rick's car was in the driveway. Entering the kitchen Maddie found her mother and Rick talking over cups of black leftover coffee.

She immediately broke down in tears. "I've been ruined!" she blurted from the depth of shattered emotions. "Ruined and slandered! Dietrich has suspended me from school. What am I going to do, Mom?" Heavy sobs shook through her body, her knees weakened, and she slipped onto the kitchen floor, crying uncontrollably.

Maury leaped from her chair and knelt beside her daughter. Wrapping an arm around her shoulder and putting her hand under Maddie's chin, she implored. "What happened, sweetheart? Tell your mom. Ruined? What happened at school?"

Rick joined mother and daughter on the floor hoping to offer solace of his own. "Maddie, try to calm down. Tell us what happened. We can help."

Within minutes Maddie had regained her composure. She described her meeting with Dietrich, recalling every 'he said' and 'she said' as carefully as her memory would allow. While explaining, she broke down several times, only to continue through the traumatic episode in halting breaths. "So, that's it. What am I going to do now? This whole mess is going to the school board...and I told Dietrich I was going to be there to defend myself." Rubbing at her eyes with the back of her hand, she added; "I was at Tobin's house last Friday night. Maribec went with me. I admitted that to Dietrich. But I didn't get drunk or anything."

"So what? That's your own business! God, I can't believe all this."

Rick was fuming. Without saying so, however, he was much more disturbed by the content of the anonymous note sent to Dietrich. A pattern of racism was unfolding around him. 'Sleeping with niggers!' was what Maddie had told them. Once again his softball friend Jerry Zench came to mind.

As Maury helped her daughter to her feet, Rick took the young woman's elbow. "I'll talk to Rudy tomorrow about the Henderson's party complaint" he volunteered, almost wishing he didn't have the softball banquet that night. "He's fair and pretty liberal-minded about school policies." (Rudy was twenty-nine year old Rudy Perpich, the young dentist recently elected as a School Board

Director. Rudy was a good friend of Rick's). "He'll listen and steer us in the right direction."

Maddie gave Rick a hug, "Thanks. That would help a lot."

Rick met her red-rimmed eyes, "The racial thing...well, that's the work of some crazy out there. Somehow, we've got to find that son-of—"

"I'll get in touch with Jack Fena tonight," Maury offered. "My attorney will have some idea about what we can do. Don't worry your pretty little head, sweetheart. That 'single female teacher' stuff is bullshit! God Almighty, go to Duluth for a glass of wine! That's sexual discrimination—that's small town crap!" Maury was tempted to vent another tirade about Hibbing's close-mindedness. In any respectable community this would not be happening. But Maury checked herself. Rick was overly sensitive to criticism about his beloved birthplace. And, she had to admit, there were some decent people living here. She glanced at Rick, smiled..."I won't retract what I said about small-town crap."

"That's fine—but, I wouldn't be a bit surprised if female teachers in Duluth have the same ridiculous contracts as here. And this is 1956 for God's sake!"

15/ BANQUET BUST

Kevin Moran thoroughly enjoyed the end-of-the-season banquet he hosted for his Androy softball team. For tonight's gathering in the hotel's posh and spacious Georgian Room he was going all-out to recognize their achievements. His Androy team had placed second in the competitive Rec League and had even beaten the eventual Minnesota state championship Victory Bar nine once during the season.

Pack showed up early to help his father with the last minute details. "Prime rib, Dad? I'm impressed. What would we be eating tonight if we'd won the title?" Pack walked through the dining room his father had reserved for the occasion, noting the small individual trophies at each place setting. "This is a nice touch, Dad—the trophies, I mean. The guys ought to really appreciate the gesture."

"The fellas gave up a lot of evenings and weekends for the team. They deserve a gourmet meal along with a small token of recognition." Kevin, however, spoke listlessly—as if his thoughts were somewhere else. His meetings with Wicklund and Nash still lingered like a bad taste in his mouth.

The players began arriving a few minutes before seven. Kevin had set up a wet bar in the corner of the large room and everybody gravitated toward the Schmidt Beer kegs. Randy Tobin, Dave Dahlberg, and JR Roberts all came together. Then Rick Bourgoyne and Milt Senich—the Androy's veteran pitcher. Eight other players straggled in one or two at a time and, by seven-fifteen, everybody but Jerry Zench had arrived. Pack kept his eye on the door. His friend had a day shift on this Thursday, and Jerry was never late for anything.

Everybody found their places. Two long tables were arranged at right angles to the podium where Kevin would make a few comments before their meal was served. Kevin noticed that one chair remained empty. "Where's Jerry?" He asked Pack over the murmur of several conversations.

Pack frowned, "We can wait a few more minutes before getting..."

"Maybe we otta call the national guard to make sure this meetin' of ours gets integrated, Kevin." The comment from Randy Tobin brought a chuckle from Dahlberg and Roberts seated on either side of Tobin. "That's what they're doin' everyplace else these days."

Incensed, Rick stood up from his chair. "What the fuck's that supposed to mean, Tobin? It's not funny—just keep that racist bullshit to yourself."

"Wow, aren't we sensitive, Mr. Radioman? I was just kiddin' for chrissakes," Tobin elbowed Dahlberg in the ribs with a small laugh.

"Looks like we got us a nigger lover, here, Dave," Tobin said loud enough for all to hear.

Kevin's jaw dropped at two words in the shot leveled at Rick.

Enraged, Rick charged Randy Tobin. "I'll bust your face for that, you son-of-a-bitch, Tobin!"

Bewildered by the outburst, Kevin raced from the podium to separate the two men. Pack was already on his feet and grabbed Rick before he could get to Tobin. "Cool it, Rick!"

"C'mon Bourgoyne—start somethin', you asshole! You ain't big enough to mess—"

Kevin had Tobin by the shirt, spun him around so the two men were face to face. "If I ever hear that word in my hotel again, I will personally put you out on the sidewalk, Randy. If you think that's amusing...you're sick! All three of you." Kevin eyes locked with Dahlberg sitting at the table, then Roberts. "I've got half a mind to..."

Pack had his father's elbow, "Dad, Jerry's at the door!" All eyes in the room shifted toward Jerry Zench who had just entered the room. In the heat of the argument, apparently nobody had seen him come into the room. Pack wondered how much of the fracas Jerry had witnessed.

Regaining his composure, Kevin sought to diffuse the keyed-up situation, "Jerry where have you been? We were ready to get going without you." Jerry's wide eyes belied his awareness of the tension in the room.

"The militia outside the hotel slowed me up, Kevin." Jerry said. Everybody knew he'd heard the conversation. "It's their job to prevent us niggers from integrating places like this."

"Jerry, I'm sorry! Just some inappropriate humor." Kevin gripped Tobin's shoulder as hard as he could. "Randy here's going to give you and everybody else in this room an apology. Right now—aren't you?" He glared at Tobin.

Wincing from the pain of Kevin's grip, Randy jerked himself free. "I ain't apologizing for nothin'! Let's get the hell outta here, guys. Let'm have their little inegrashin meetin' all to themselves."

Dahlberg and Roberts stood up beside their friend. Locking with Kevin's eyes, Dahlberg leaned into the older man's face. "Yeah, I'm with ya, Randy. Kevin, you better look for some new ball players for next year's team. We're done! We ain't playin' with no—" He let the sentence drop for fear that Kevin would put him on the floor if he said the nigger word.

As he passed Pack only inches away, Dahlberg gave him a nudge with his shoulder. "We still gotta finish what we started at Tobin's the other night, 'copper'."

Pack's fists clenched at his side. But he swallowed "anytime".

Tobin followed Dahlberg's steps toward the door, with Roberts following right behind. Tobin stopped to face Rick Bourgoyne at Pack's elbow. "We'll finish our business, too. Outside, right now if ya wanna."

"The Radioman's chicken-shit, Randy." Roberts said, nudging join his two friends doorward. "We'll be around any time, Rick."

The dining room door was ajar. Jerry Zench was gone. The evening was ruined.

What might have been a jovial evening reliving the exploits of the past season became an abbreviated meal of subdued conversations. By eight, Robby Johnson, Eddie Baratto, and the others at the table with Milt Senich, began filtering toward the door. Feeble 'thank you's' followed from another table. The party rapidly disintegrated.

Kevin, along with Pack and Rick, lingered after the last of their teammates were gone. "I've enjoyed myself at funerals more than I did tonight," Kevin grumbled. "If I hadn't over-reacted...maybe...?"

"If you hadn't stepped in, Dad—I would have," Pack said.

"Need any help with the clean-up, Kevin?" Rick asked, hoping his offer would be declined. It was still early enough to phone Rudy Perpich—maybe even visit briefly with the School Board Director about Maddie's issue. Part of him wanted to hang around and talk with Pack about the day's events, but seeing Perpich was a promise and a priority right now.

"Nah. Thanks for the offer, Rick. Let's all just go home and call it a night. A miserable night, at that!" Kevin forced a smile.

At the door, Rick turned. "Need to talk to you about something, Pack. Let's be in touch tomorrow."

Pack nodded, "Sounds good. Give me a call when you're free."

When Rick was gone, Pack put a hand on his father's shoulder. "The guys really liked the trophies, and the prime ribs were out of this world."

"Pack, will you swing by Jerry's and drop off his trophy...give him our apologies." The gold memento rested beside an empty plate on a nearby table

"Sure. I promised Mom I'd pick up Steven at Marco's, too."

Jerry Zench's car was not parked in front of his Bennett Park apartment building and the lights upstairs were off. Pack headed to Marco's house. He would catch up with Jerry tomorrow.

16/ PLAY THE GIBSON

Although Wednesday was a school night, Steven Moran had his parents' permission to visit his Uncle Marco in town. Pack would pick him up after the softball banquet, somewhere around nine.

Steven and Bobby Zimmerman met outside the Lybba Theater just before seven. The two boys walked the few blocks south to Marco's house. They had spent much of Saturday together hanging out at Crippa's Music shop in the morning, then wandering over to Mal-Rads on First Avenue for cokes and fries. Bobby chain-smoked cigarettes. Stevie, hoping he might impress the girls hanging around the cafe, lit up a Lucky Strike from Bobby's pack. It tasted horrible! Anyone watching him try to inhale could tell he hadn't smoked before. Stevie turned red when Bobby poked fun at his coughing.

Later, they went to the Minor's Club in the Memorial Building for a few hours—played some ping-pong, listened to the jukebox, watched girls. Bobby's mother, Beatty, came in. She was one of the volunteer parents at the teen hangout. "I hate it when she's here," Bobby said. "Let's bug."

There were times that Saturday when Stevie felt as if hanging around with Bobby Zimmerman might get him in trouble with his parents and/or his brother, Pack. His friend smoked, used vulgar language a lot, and wore a chip on his shoulder. Bobby berated everything and everybody in Hibbing as 'square and boring'. But, his companion held a subtle magnetism, too—a quiet kind of arrogance. And neither of them had many close friends.

Always sloppily dressed, Marco was wearing his oversized and stained U of M sweatshirt, cut-off khaki shorts, and unbuckled leather sandals. After opening bottles of Coke for his visitors, he poured himself a mug of tar-black coffee. The revered teacher presided over a clutter of magazines and album jackets across the living room floor.

"For the first couple of weeks I just review the basics—probably kinda boring for astute musicians like you guys, right?" Marco opened the dialogue. "Well, rest assured, you'll be getting a lot deeper into music theory later. I think that's what's going to get you both fired up."

Bobby stared wide-eyed at the huge speakers on the floor near Mr. Z's high-fidelity sound system. The rich classical sounds wafted through the room, soft enough to allow conversation, but with enough volume to amplify the precise, exquisite sound of every instrument in the orchestra. The mesmerized teenager had never heard such sound clarity before. His eyes focused on the Gibson acoustic guitar in the corner of the room. "I play guitar, Mr. Z," Bobby said.

"I've heard that. You're with Fabrow's jazz quartet, aren't you? I'll have to see you guys some time. You playing the guitar in the group?"

Bobby's disappointment was obvious. "Not yet. I'm stuck playing piano for now."

"Nothing wrong with that." Marco said. "Gotta have some piano."

"I guess not. But when I get my own band—then."

"He's pretty wild on the keyboard, Uncle Marco." Stevie, joined the conversation. "We were playing together over at Bobby's house last Friday night. I couldn't keep up with him most of the time."

Marco looked puzzled. For his age, his nephew was quite accomplished on the piano. "I'm sure you could hold your own, Steven."

"Do you give guitar lessons, Mr. Z?" Bobby interrupted. "I've gotta learn a few more chords to go with what I've taught myself already." His eyes darted from Marco to the Gibson which had riveted his attention the moment he saw it. Bobby's cheap Sears Silvertone paled in comparison.

Marco sensed Robert's fascination. Anybody who knew guitars would drool over his '52 Gibson J-200, advertised as 'King of the Flattops'! "Give it a try, Robert. Let me hear some pick and strum," he gestured toward the Gibson in the corner.

Stevie smiled at his uncle's unexpected invitation. "Go ahead, Bobby," Stevie encouraged.

Bobby rested the blonde Gibson on his thigh and fretted a G chord with his left hand. The instrument was in perfect tune. Fascinated by the tone quality, Bobby did a quick C and a D chord, followed by another G. The three were all he knew. Alternately humming and singing, Bobby did a medley of familiar Hank Williams songs he knew by heart. Eyes closed, he became totally absorbed in the sounds—and in himself.

After a few minutes, Bobby stopped playing, running his pick over the strings in dramatic flare. "What do you think, Mr. Z?" A satisfied smile begged a compliment.

Marco recognized potential more than skill. If Robert had the passion for music that Steven did, he could teach the Zimmerman boy to make a guitar virtually sing. Marco acknowledged the boy's need for some recognition. "I picked out your three chords right away, the basic majors—not too bad for a sixteen-year-old. Pretty good in fact. And the improvising you did perked things up." He took the guitar from Bobby and returned to his chair. "Listen to what this Gibson can do for a few minutes. I'm not going to show-off, but this instrument is magical. You probably know that already."

Marco moved his fingers skillfully over the frets in clean major chords, the same chords Bobby had used minutes before. The difference was day and night. Then Marco added new dimensions to his picking and strumming, fingers moving rapidly up and down the neck of the Gibson.

Stevie and Bobby sat wide-eyed as Marco made the Gibson trill. After only a few minutes, Marco did an arrangement that brought the two boys to the edge of their chairs. Finishing his little demonstration, Marco had a wide, infectious smile on his face. When he strummed the Gibson, he could virtually lose himself within an oblivion of heady tones.

"What did you just do...right at the end, Mr. Z? I couldn't believe what I was hearing!" Bobby asked with unbridled enthusiasm. "What was that?"

"It's called a 'walking base line', Robert. I'm glad you picked it up."

"I've just got to learn that! I must. It's exactly the thing I've been wanting to do. Can you teach me?" Bobby pleaded.

"First things first. If you really want to play the guitar with skill, you've got to master some minor chords. I'll teach you the E and the A, along with the B7. It's going to take you some time and practice, but if you've got the patience and desire, I think you'll be making some pretty decent music by the end of the year," Marco said.

17/ GIRL TALK

As Maribec Moran sorted through some newly developed black and white photographs she heard her kitchen phone ring. On the other end of the line, Maddie was crying. "I've got to talk to you, Maribec. Some real shit is going on with me. Can I come over tonight?" Maribec's wall clock read seven forty-five. "About nine would be perfect, Maddie." Thinking of her evening's project—she cursed herself. "I didn't even ask Maddie what was wrong." Her friend had already hung up. "Damn it!"

Maribec, a hobby photographer, was impressed with a few of the prints, but most of them would probably be thrown away. One of them she appraised at arm's length. Smiling her satisfaction she said "Wow! This one turned out great!" The photo had been taken while riding horses with her mother the previous Sunday afternoon. The two of them had split from her dad and Pack and ridden to the southwest corner of the large Moran property by themselves. Angela had dismounted near a pine tree with boughs overhanging a gurgling creek which roiled into a small pond. Maribec watched as her mother knelt, picking a handful of pine needles and examining them with unusual interest. Something about the needles seemed to fascinate Angela, enveloping her in what seemed to Maribec a momentary daydream.

Without her mother's awareness, Maribec had focused the zoom lens on her Kodak camera and snapped a few quick shots. Later, on the ride back to the barn, she asked her mother about the episode near the pond. All Angie said was "old memories, Sweetheart." Maribec didn't probe but had a feeling that the site was a special place in her mother's past.

Maribec regarded the photograph, chewing on her cuticles as she often did when concentrating on something. The shot was a close-up of Angela's hands tenderly holding an array of pine needles. The camera had captured the moment perfectly. A beam of afternoon sun had pierced through the branch overhang, creating a slight sparkle on Angela's diamond wedding ring. "Perfect!" Maribec complimented herself. "I'm going to have this photograph enlarged and framed—it ought to be an ideal Christmas gift for Mom."

~

"No apologies necessary, Rick, it's not late at all," the tall man said. Taking his visitor's jacket and gesturing to come in, he added, "Lola and I always enjoy company."

Rudy and Lola Perpich sat together on their living room sofa while listening to their friend, Rick Bourgoyne, explain the incident at Maddie's school. The husband and wife were inseparable and, Rick considered, looked almost like siblings with their dark hair and handsome features. Rick welcomed Lola's presence. Her perspective on the school district policy regarding female teachers would certainly influence her husband.

After Rick finished recounting the episode, Rudy leaned forward on the sofa. "Won't happen, Rick!" the school board director exclaimed in his typically high-pitched voice. Clasping his large hands over one knee, he elaborated. "This matter won't get on the board's agenda. I can almost guarantee that! If we've got these kinds of double-standards in our district policy—and believe me I'm going to find out—they're going to be eliminated!" Removing his dark-rimmed glasses, Rudy leveled his eyes on Rick. "I'll talk with Dietrich...and John Slattery in the super's office, first thing tomorrow."

"Maddie will be relieved when I tell her," Rick said.

"You tell Miss Loiselle not to worry about anything."

The three of them talked about the Iron Range 'melting pot' of ethnic minorities. Being the son of an immigrant father from Croatia, it was always a favorite topic of Rudy's.

Perpich stood and offered his hand to Rick. "I'll be in touch with you tomorrow." Smiling he took his wife's hand, Rick's elbow, and escorted his guest to the door.

~

Maureen Loiselle sat at her dining room table with Jack Fena, a forceful young Hibbing attorney. Maddie poured coffee and joined them.

"Tell me everything, Maddie. Try to include all the details you can remember. The 'he saids' and the 'I saids' are important. I'll be asking you some questions and writing everything down." Fena placed his legal pad on the table next to his tattered brief case.

Maddie explained the Dietrich meeting in lucid detail, answering every question the attorney raised.

"So what do you think, Jack? Can Maddie be suspended for being at a party where some allegedly loud music was being played and a few young adults were having a drink?" Maury asked.

"As of today, she probably could. I'll research the district policies and Maddie's contract in the morning. I agree it's discriminatory, but Dietrich was probably doing what he felt he should under the circumstances. You see, the administrators are just puppets of the superintendent. The super pulls their strings, and the board of education tells the super what to do. That's the system." Fena continued, "But when a parent calls with a complaint, from top to bottom they all seem to panic. The political reality of all this usually puts the teacher on the defensive."

Maury nodded knowingly, "Parents elect the board members."

"I know it's wrong. Teachers deserve a hellava lot more respect and support than they ever get from the administration."

Maddie shook her head. "That's what scares me, Mr. Fena. If it comes down to a parent accusing a teacher of something...?"

Fena shrugged without reply.

"But, what about this suspension? And the school board meeting? Will Maddie lose her job over this?" Maury was still deeply stressed.

Fena laughed confidently, took Maury's hand, "If I can't get this matter cleared up before Friday, fire me!"

~

Maddie had a much better grip on her situation when she arrived at Maribec's later that evening.

Three cups of coffee into her recounting of the day's events, Maddie was feeling as drained as a trial witness. "Mom and Rick were just wonderful, Maribec. They didn't push or probe or make any judgments. All they wanted to do was help me get out of this mess."

"Are you planning to tell Jerry about the letter?"

Maddie sat back in the sofa, ran her fingers through her long blonde hair, and drew a sigh. "I've got to, don't I? Someone must have seen me when I visited his apartment that night." She wondered who that might be. Maddie had been so careful...and, Jerry wouldn't have said anything about their being together. "Not right now, though. I'm going to wait and see what happens with the school board first."

"I think you should. At least give him a call—it's his problem, too." Maribec said.

But Maddie didn't want to resolve that issue at the moment. For the past several days, Maribec's brother had been consuming her thoughts. Whenever she thought of Pack, a smile creased her face. The spilled paint episode of last Saturday and their time together memorable. "Maribec, I've got to ask you something. You've got to be perfectly honest with me." She swallowed hard before continuing, "Did you tell Pack about Jerry and me?"

Pack had told Maribec about his feelings toward Maddie. Her brother's interest in Maddie was supposed to remain a confidence between the two siblings for right now.

Maribec regarded Maddie for a long minute. "I guess I did—I'm sorry. Pack and I talked for hours last Friday night, about everything. We were here until about eleven and at Sammy's Pizza until they closed after one. He asked about you several times and...I let it slip out, Maddie."

"What did he say?" Maddie said with more interest than disappointment.

"Nothing that I can remember. Jerry's one of Pack's best friends, you know. He didn't really have any reaction to what I told him—I think I was surprised that he didn't ask for details. But if it bothered him, do you think Pack wouldn't have been over at your place helping you guys paint the next day."

Maddie nodded without reply. That made sense.

Maribec's telephone rang. The caller brought a wink from Maribec. She covered the receiver and whispered, "Speak of the devil."

After a few minutes, Maddie leaned into Maribec's ear and whispered, "Tell Pack I'm here. Maybe—?"

"I'm being rude to my guest, Pack. Can I call you back later? Yes, it's Maddie. Maribec smiled toward her friend as she held the phone between them. "Pack wants to say hello."

Maddie tried to collect her thoughts. She wished she knew Pack better—wished she could trust sharing her turmoil of the moment.

Pack on the other end of the line sensed a tightness in Maddie's tone. If they knew each other better he'd probably probe. If they knew each other better he'd share his frustration of the evening with her. Maybe later—maybe he'd call her tomorrow.

~

Kevin found Gary at his desk reviewing narrow-lined hotel ledgers under his reading glasses. "What are you up to, Gary?"

"Just a fraction under six feet this morning, boss." He offered his friend an easy smile along with his standard reply to Kevin's standard question. "Same as yesterday...and the day before, and the day—"

"Have you talked to Jerry since last night?"

Gary puzzled, shook his head. Why do you ask?"

Kevin tool a chair, sat down, and explained what happened at last night's banquet. "Another incident, Gary. I felt just terrible for your son. He must have heard everything that was said."

"So he just took off?"

"Yes. And Pack called me later to tell me that he had swung by Jerry's place. Jerry wasn't home yet."

Gary's downcast eyes told of the pain he felt. "I'll call him tonight. Poor kid...that must have been tough. Just hope he didn't go after those guys. He's a hard-nosed kid but he certainly can't handle all three of those ass—"

"I'm sure Jerry knows that he's got some damn good friends. If it ever comes down to..." Kevin let the thought of further confrontation drop. If Pack went looking for a fight, he might lose his job with the police force. And, Rick? Rick was not someone who ought to look for a fight with any of those guys.

Gary's stomach was a knot of agitation. What was happening around here? What had his son ever done to be singled out and harassed by his friends? No, it was his skin color—no more and no less. "Thanks for telling me about the incident, Kevin. I'm sure all this racial stuff has been hard on you as well. I'll bet you wonder sometimes if you did the right thing by bringing your old buddy up to Hibbing years ago."

He tried to laugh at the irony. "Just this morning, Gary, I thought about that very thing. And, despite what's going on these days, I'd do it again. You're like the brother I never had, Gary. You know that."

18/ "THAT TERRIBLE 'F' WORD..."

Deeply troubled, Robert Dietrich returned home after school on Wednesday and headed straight for his liquor cabinet without so much as a fleeting hello to his wife. He poured himself a straight-up whiskey.

The elementary school principal was a weak man. His decision to suspend Miss Loiselle had given him a splitting headache. He wanted to believe he'd made the right decision, but doubts plagued like an abscessed tooth. When Miss Loiselle left his office, Dietrich called James Mitchell to inform the Superintendent of the action he'd taken. But Mitchell's support seemed lukewarm at best. His supervisor was harshly critical of Robert for not discussing the matter with him before taking the action he did. "I like to know what's going on before it happens, Robert. You don't suspend a faculty member without letting the Superintendent know all the facts first. Suspension is a serious matter!"

Robert was adamant—he'd followed district policy. But Mitchell was nervous about factual credibility. "The Hendersons called my office to report an incident, but I haven't had time to properly follow up yet. Details are sketchy and the Henderson's have a history of being nuisance callers."

Contrite, Robert had inquired about the provocative letter.

"To my way of thinking an anonymous letter has no credibility. I'll want to talk with Lawrence about that before we go any further." What upset Mitchell the most was what might happen next. "So, Loiselle told you that she would be showing up at the school board meeting?"

"She had a very hostile attitude—quite disrespectful, if you ask me, sir. Yes she did. And she stormed right out of my office without even returning to her classroom to pick up her coat. What should I do with her coat, Mr. Mitchell?"

Mitchell exploded on the other end of the line. "Her coat? Did I hear you correctly—her coat? Good God, Dietrich, get your head out of your ass!"

Robert's apology was feebler than his promise to have someone return the coat. Mitchell only sighed—then exploded again.

"Do you have any idea who Miss Loiselle's mother is, Dietrich?"

"I don't think so. Should I, sir?"

"You ought to, she's damn well-connected to this town. Maureen Loiselle runs the radio station. I'm going to get some heat over this—and so will you! Damn it, Dietrich, why didn't you call me before..."

The superintendent had called him Dietrich several times—not the customary Robert. The surname references were very unsettling.

"What's the matter, honey?" Iris watched her husband swallow his whiskey, then pour a second one. "A bad day at school?"

"Fucking female teachers!"

"Robert!" Iris startled, her mouth agape. "I've never heard you use that terrible F-word in this house before!"

"That terrible F-word is female!" He blurted his anger. "Education is a man's business, Iris. I've always believed that. If women aren't out getting themselves pregnant, they're out fooling around. And I've got to deal with the consequences." Robert added another splash to his whiskey and felt a soothing warmth as he drained the glass.

Through his third drink, Robert explained what had happened that afternoon. "So, now Mitchell's got his ass in a bundle!"

Iris listened attentively, interrupting her husband only to reassure him that he'd acted responsibly. "Mitchell just doesn't appreciate the stress of running a school. You do such a wonderful job, my dear. Everybody respects you."

It was after six. Iris' tuna casserole was scorched. "I'm not hungry anyway," Robert glowered. "I'm going next door for a few minutes, talk to Leonard. You can give my portion of that crap on the stove to the dog."

Devastated with guilt over the spoiled meal and Robert's angry outburst, Iris dabbed at her tears as the door slammed behind her husband. When Robert got this overwrought, there was nothing she could do to settle him down. Sometimes his bad moods would last for several silent days. Robert was a brooder. Then Iris remembered the framed photograph she had seen in Angela Moran's little art shop days before. She made a mental note to stop by in the morning and purchase the artwork for Robert. Maybe a little unexpected gift would lift her husband's spirits. "Poor Robert," she sighed as she took the hot dish from the stove, "such terrible stress he has at the school!"

Leonard was Lefty Rosnau. The police officer was working on a furniture- staining project in his garage. The pungent fumes of varnish made Robert even more lightheaded. "Got anything to drink, neighbor?"

Lefty held the bottle of beer he was sipping, "Got a few more in the fridge. Help yourself."

"You must have a bottle in the house. I need more than a beer right now."

"Looks like you've got a good start already, Bob. Just a minute, I'll grab the Old Crow." Lefty went inside and returned in a minute with a bottle and a tall glass. "Drink up." The police lieutenant wouldn't ask his friend what was bothering him. He knew from long association that it wouldn't be long before Bob started dumping his problems.

One deep swallow of whiskey and Robert was already explaining his dilemma. Every lamentable detail tumbled from his full, flaccid lips like vomit after a bender.

"Tell me more about that letter. Sleeping with niggers? A white teacher sleeping with niggers?" Lefty repeated leaning back against the workbench and downing his bottle of beer in one angry swallow. "She otta be hung for that! I ain't got no tolerance for that shit! And, the nigger—he's gonna get himself castrated!" The cop did not say 'otta be castrated'! Rosnau was livid. "You know Goddamn well who the nigger is, don't ya, Bob?"

Dietrich was feeling the mild oblivion of booze. "Not too hardda figger out, is it, Lefty?" Robert's speech was slurred. "The Zench kid. Alweeze knew he was a trubble maker."

Leonard Rosnau didn't reply to the obvious. Something drastic would have to be done—and soon. "Ya did the right thing, Bob. Matter of fact, if it had been me, I'd a fired the bitch on the spot. Don't worry, lots of people in this town feel the same as I do. It ain't prejudice so much as it's protectin' ourselves from mixin' good white blood with jungle bunnies. Know what I mean?"

Uplifted, Robert found himself nodding agreement. Maybe Lefty had a better grasp of things around here. 'Lots of people'...'protecting ourselves'...perhaps the cop had it right. For a moment, Robert imagined himself being praised by the school board, parents of the children, and all the righteous folks in Hibbing for having the courage to protect their community's values. If a respected police official felt this strongly about the matter, so would most other people. For the first time in hours, he felt vindicated. "You really think moze people feel the same as we do, Lefty? We've gotta protect ourselves?"

By nine o'clock that evening, Lefty Rosnau was sitting in the Androy bar talking with Carl Wicklund. The burly bartender shook his head, "What we gonna do about it, Lefty? That coon was here at the hotel just a couple of hours ago. Moran's softball banquet was goin' on. He din't stay long, tho. I think some of the boys let Zench know what's what around here." Wicklund gave a wink.

"Ball players?" Lefty asked.

Wicklund nodded. "Tobin and Dahlberg. Roberts was one of 'em, too. The three left together—a few minutes after the nigger did."

Rosnau remembered buying drinks for Tobin and Dahlberg the previous weekend but didn't know Roberts very well. He checked his watch, "I'm gonna see if I can find those guys—have a little talk about things. D'ya think they're of the same...persuasion, as we are, Carl?"

"I'd bet on it, Lefty. Don't know 'xactly what happened at that softball thing, but from the look on Moran's face aftawards, it wasn't nothin' pleasant." Wicklund remembered the conversation with his boss the day before. "Moran was buggin' me yesterday about some survey he's been doin'. Then today he's tellin' people that his nigger boy really fucked somethin' up at the hotel. Thought they was good friends."

"Oh, they are, Carl. Moran's a NIGGER LOVER, from way back." Rosnau emphasized the two words. "We both know that. Maybe his softball boys do too."

"Another one, Lefty? On the house."

Rosnau's mind was turning at high speed. "Not right now. Lots of things to get done tonight." Only two other patrons were in the lounge. "What time you done here? Need your help with somethin', Carl."

~

Thursday.

Maddie Loiselle's mixed emotions would not let her sleep. It had been a good news—bad news day!

Being home from school had put her in a funk. How could people just hang around a house all day without getting bored out of their mind? Maybe that was the allure of the popular soaps on television— escape! As she lay in bed, with her head propped upon an extra pillow trying to concentrate on a Steinbeck novel she was reading, Maddie reflected on the good news.

Earlier that evening, she had received an unexpected phone call from Robert Dietrich. The school principal was profusely apologetic. "I must confess that I was out of line, Miss Loiselle. Only allegations, that's all they were...and I overreacted, I'm afraid. I want to assure you, Miss Loiselle, that you are a valued employee of our district—and a wonderful classroom teacher. I wish we had more faculty like you to nurture our children."

Maddie was dumbfounded. "Yes, sir."

"I've talked with Superintendent Mitchell, and he agrees, that you can take tomorrow off without any loss in pay. I've already arranged for tomorrow's substitute you see, but I'll be looking for you on Monday morning as usual. I'm sure your children will be happy to have you back. You have such a marvelous rapport with them." The principal swallowed noticeably. "Once again, I truly apologize for any discomfort I might have caused you, Miss Loiselle. I hope this can be the end of an unpleasant matter...with no hard feelings between us."

"Then, there won't be any school board meeting about the allegations, Mr. Dietrich?" Maddie wondered if she was hearing everything correctly. Dietrich was almost drooling his praises and apologies.

"Absolutely not! Our district might even reevaluate some of our, er, gender policies in light of this incident. In reviewing things, I must admit—in confidence, of course, Miss Loiselle—the administration might even have been somewhat discriminatory toward our female teachers in the past. I, for one, am strongly opposed to any...ummm, double standards."

When Maddie had hung up and shouted an ecstatic "hurray" into the empty room the phone rang again. Maury and Rick were bowling at the downtown alleys and wouldn't be back for another hour, so she was home alone. Sometimes Maddie would just let the phone ring without picking it up, and play a mind game with who might have called. If the phone didn't ring again within two or three minutes, it probably wasn't anything important anyway. She let it ring seven times without picking up the receiver, and then waited. Within a minute, there was another ring.

"Maddie, Pack calling. I just heard about what happened at school yesterday. Rick kinda filled me in—I hope you don't mind. Thought I'd call and find out how you're doing."

"Thanks for calling, Pack. No...I don't mind at all. Rick's been great and...it's really thoughtful of you to care."

"I do. So does Maribec. She called from work this morning, too. I wish one of them had said something last night." He wanted to say 'I wish you had'. "You've got good friends, Maddie." He wanted to say 'I'm one of them'. "That Dietrich is some kind of jerk. Have you heard anything since yesterday?"

"Oh, yeah." Maddie explained her call from the principal only minutes before.

"Wonderful. Then your mom and Rick must have found some sympathetic ears last night." Pack hesitated. "I mean Perpich and Fena must have gone to bat for you with Mitchell." By mentioning the two men's names, Maddie would know that he had some idea about what probably happened.

"They must have, as you so aptly put it, had 'sympathetic ears'."
A twinge of stress tightened in her stomach. Did Pack know about the letter as well as the party? No, she tried to assure herself. "Thank God for Perpich and Fena. Pack, I wish you could have heard Dietrich stumbling over his apologies. It was almost humorous, and so full of bull...bologna as well. He hates female teachers, everybody at Cobb Cook knows that!" Maddie chuckled.

"That doesn't surprise me."

There was an awkward pause of several seconds. Pack checked his pre-scripted notes. After his words of concern (which were written much better than he'd expressed them) he wanted to ask Maddie for a date tomorrow night. Dinner someplace, or coffee or cokes, or maybe a movie—anything she might want to do. Pack wished he could be more specific. What were Maddie's interests? Maribec had suggested bowling but Pack had a 190 average and didn't want to show her up or fake his ability by deliberately making a lousy score. Maddie would see right through it. That might ruin the evening. Asking a girl out was absolute hell, and Pack had never been good at coming up with impressive lines.

He swallowed hard in a throat gone suddenly dry. "Maddie, I think I owe you something for the paint job I did on your face last weekend, and thought I might be able to make it up to you...you know."

Another significant pause. His pitch sounded juvenile. "...You know. Maybe take you out to dinner tomorrow night, or whatever you'd like. Or, Saturday." He wasn't giving much advance notice. "Maybe Saturday would be better—but, whatever."

The moment's pause seemed liked minutes. Pack picked up the thread, "Anyplace but the Androy, my dad, you know..." he was self-conscious about dining at his father's hotel despite the excellent cuisine. He always got special attention from the people there. Often the waitress would comp the bill. If that happened, it would make him feel cheap and might embarrass Maddie.

"Why not tomorrow night? And the Androy would be perfect, Pack. It's the best food in town, and the atmosphere—well, it's the Androy!" Maddie sighed the last three words as if the hotel were the Ritz. "And, being your dad owns the place, we might even get a free meal. There's nothing wrong with that is there?"

Now Pack really felt stupid. He had asked Maddie out to dinner and ruled out the finest place in town in the same breath. "No, not at all. I just thought..."

Maddie, sensing Pack's distraction, helped him out, "Great! Dinner at the Androy tomorrow night. I'd love that, Pack. But you don't 'owe me' because of the paint thing last Saturday. That was hilarious! I haven't laughed so hard in months."

Should he apologize for suggesting he 'owed her' something? No, just go with the flow. "I'm glad you found humor in it, Maddie. I can't tell you how embarrassed..." He made a stab at humor. "You didn't report me to the police afterwards, did you?"

Maddie laughed, "You must remember, I promised I wouldn't do that, Pack. Anyhow, I don't want anything to do with Chief Donald Lawrence. He's a jerk in my book." Ooops, Maddie bit her tongue.

Were Pack and the Chief good friends? If so, he'd probably be offended. How might she recover from her careless slip? Getting to know someone you really cared about was pure hell, she thought.

"I couldn't agree more, Maddie. Let's just keep it between us, though. Unfortunately, he is my boss."

"Whew, I was worried I might have said something very wrong."

"Even if I liked the guy, Maddie, it wouldn't bother me a bit if you didn't. I could even respect that. Having different views on things..." As Pack completed his thought about how healthy it was to 'agree to disagree' he realized he might be sounding like a jerk himself.

"That was sensitive, Pack. I appreciate that quality in a guy. I think people who agree about everything are pretty dull."

Pack gave another sigh of relief.

"Will you allow me to have a glass of wine tomorrow night?" She alluded to the drinking issue with Dietrich.

He laughed easily for the first time. "That would be great. Let's share a bottle, Maddie. I even hope there are lots of people there to watch us enjoying ourselves." Pack was feeling relaxed now, Maddie was so easy to converse with. "Wouldn't it be something if Superintendent Mitchell sent us a drink...as part of the school district's apology program. I think he and his wife are Friday night regulars at the Androy."

The conversation left them both smiling long minutes after their phones had been hung up. It left them puzzled as well. Neither had made any reference to the letter. Would they do so on Friday?

Maddie's smile faded with the thought. Gary Zench came to mind.

Pack's good feelings faded too. He hadn't said anything about the banquet last night. Gary Zench entered his thoughts again.

~

Tossing and turning, shifting from one side of the bed to the other, Maddie's thoughts wandered from Pack to Jerry Zench. Her period had been due on Tuesday, and she was never late! Rubbing slender fingers over her flat stomach, Maddie agonized over possibilities. How could she have let her physical attraction to Jerry go so far? She knew from the start there could never be anything between her and Jerry—not in this time and place. And what was Jerry thinking? He was neither color-blind nor stupid. If they had been seen together at his place that night it would be much harder on him than her. In the narrow minds of many, a Negro man with a white woman spelled rape!

Someone must have seen them!

The thought of the racist letter delivered to Dietrich caused her to toss from her back onto her stomach. Had Maribec told Pack about the letter? If he knew, would he have called her tonight for a date? What would John Q. Public think of the allegations in that letter? Her reputation would be ruined in Hibbing. She'd have to resign for sure—and leave town. Even those who didn't believe the allegation would wonder...And, worst of all, what if she was pregnant? Her eyes moistened, "Please God, don't let me be pregnant. I can deal with anything else, but...please."

19/ GOSSIP

Angela Moran spent most Thursdays at her quaint downtown art studio, Shades of White. Sitting at the easel in the back of her shop, she stared at a blank canvas without inspiration. Her thoughts wandered back to a conversation with Kevin the night before. He was still deeply troubled about what was going on. The banquet fiasco really bothered him. The depth of Kevin's feelings had always impressed and attracted her. Her husband put others before himself. Always! He was a man of substance and goodness and loyalty. She thought of the Zenches, too—the years of friendship and trust between them.

In her reverie of the moment, Angela resolved to show Kevin how very much she loved him. Tonight. Maybe a bottle of red wine, some candles, the new silk sheets, her black negligee—Good God, it had been a while and she was feeling warm already!

Angela heard the shop door open and let her daydream of the moment melt away.

"Yoo hoo, anybody home?" The woman's shrill voice was familiar. Angela groaned under her breath.

"Yoo hoo." Iris Dietrich waved her gloves from the doorway.

"Good morning, Iris." Angela tried to be enthusiastic—knew she'd failed. "How are you this morning?"

"Oh, how we needed the rain, Angela." Iris referred to last night's downpour.

"Indeed we did." Angela preferred to discuss weather to whatever else Iris had on her mind. Mrs. Dietrich was a notorious gossip. "It's been terribly dry for weeks..."

Iris interrupted, "I need something for Robert, my dear. Something to cheer him up a bit. He's under so much stress with the opening of school, you know how that is. My poor husband always gets himself stuck in the middle of things, you know. It's one thing to run a school efficiently, you know, but what's happening in this town is just...so stressful!"

Angie was curious where Iris was going with her thoughts, but decided against encouraging the latest gossip. "What can I help you with this morning, Iris? Something for your husband?"

"Why, yes, I saw that photograph over there as I was passing by a few days ago." The rotund, matronly woman gestured toward the front window. "Robert played hockey as a boy, you know. If it weren't for Boy Scouts and school activities, I'm sure he would have been quite good, you know. He's such a marvelous skater. To this day, Robert loves to whisk about the ice rink behind his school."

Angela knew the photograph that Iris was inquiring about. It was something that Maribec had done last winter. The black and white print captured a small boy chasing a puck with his hockey stick thrust out in front of him. The ice rink in the picture was located on the Cobb Cook School grounds in the west side of Hibbing. Maribec's photo perfectly captured the boy's determination. The bent-ankled youngster would score a goal and win the game of his imagination! Maribec's blurred background effects were a marvelous contrast to the purposeful lad skating by himself on this cold winter's day. "My daughter took that shot. You can tell it's the rink near your husband's school."

"I could recognize the building right away. That's what caught my attention, you know. It could almost be my Robert when he was a boy."

Angela took down the photo for Iris to examine more closely. The first thing Iris did was check the back for a price tag. Finding the cost, she smiled her satisfaction; probably more at the ten dollar sticker than the photograph. "I'm sure you've already heard about that teacher in Robert's school, Miss Loiselle? She's been suspended, thank goodness. Some young women in our town these days! What was the word Robert used?...'Immoral'—yes, that's what he said. They just have no respect for common decency."

"Maddie Loiselle?" Angela blurted.

"Yes, Maddie is the name. Anyhow, the woman was drunk and disorderly, staggering down the streets last weekend. Creating quite a scene for all of Hibbing to see. Fortunately, I heard that Gladys Henderson reported the episode to the Superintendent."

"I'm sorry, Iris. I find what you're saying very hard to believe. Why Maddie and my daughter—"

Iris wasn't listening. "But that's not all. Not by any means. Now, don't breathe a word, but Robert's gotten letters from several people about..." Iris leaned closer to Angela's ear as if other people might be listening. "About those Negroes in town. Of course, Robert believes it's that wild Zench boy. Anyhow, all the letters say that the Loiselle woman—how can I say it ladylike...you know, spends her nights with that Negro!"

Angela's jaw dropped. "Your husband told you these things?"

"As I said, so much stress for Robert to deal with. Why, yes—of course. My poor husband has total responsibility for his school, the teachers, and protecting the children from corruption. Such a job! I think he would have been within his rights to fire that harlot on the spot. I told him so. But, these days...there will probably have to be a school board hearing. Then she and her lawyer will deny everything. You know how that goes. Her mother, another free spirit if you ask me, probably has an attorney hired already. Poor Robert—maybe your daughter's picture will lift his spirits."

~

At nearly the same time that Maddie and Pack were having their phone conversation, Robert Dietrich was visiting with Leonard Rosnau in his neighbor's garage again. Dietrich had just finished the apology to Miss Loiselle that Mitchell had insisted he make. "I was crucified, Lefty! Perpich called me at home even before I was out the door to school this morning. He wanted to stop by the school and have a visit about the Loiselle suspension—at seven o'clock! Then Mitchell called me at Cobb Cook. I no more than got off the phone with my boss and that arrogant lawyer, Fena, was all over my ass. My phone was ringing off the hook, for God's sake."

Rosnau offered a sympathetic smile but said nothing. His thoughts were consumed with his private plans of retribution. He would need to be careful to keep a lid on what was happening.

Dietrich took a deep swallow of Old Crow. "At one this afternoon I had a meeting in John Slattery's office at the high school. Slattery kinda runs the school district's show, you know. We all respect him a lot—knows more local history than anybody I know. And the guy's some kind of policy genius. He'd already made language amendments to the teacher's contract. Mitchell rubber-stamps everything John proposes, and Rudy said he'd steer the changes through the school board next Tuesday. God, everything happened so fast!"

Lefty spoke for the first time. "You were forced to apologize to that Loiselle bitch, Bob?"

Dietrich nodded, downing the remains in his glass and pouring another. "Loiselle will be back in school on Monday—that was the order I got. 'Not a word to anyone about this incident', Perpich insisted. Not a word! Perpich was emphatic about that. When I got home I told my wife to keep her big mouth shut." A frown creased his forehead. His wife had given him a strange expression when he told her. Iris had been out shopping downtown that morning.

"She thought a stupid picture was going to make me feel better."

Rosnau puzzled. "What ya talking about, Bob?"

Dietrich shrugged, "Nothing. Iris talks too much, you know. Makes me nervous, that's all."

"Yeah. My woman's the same. What about the nigger letter, Bob? That's what I want to know about."

"Mitchell's got it now. He told me in no uncertain terms that if I ever breathed a word about the letter he'd have my ass over a barrel."

Rosnau laughed at Mitchell's threat. "Don't let them nigger-loving assholes get to ya, Bob, They're out of touch with reality. Like we talked last night, even folks up here won't tolerate niggers messing with white women. Just wait—you'll see."

"Yeah, maybe—but what if she didn't do it? I mean, what if that letter was all bullshit just to stir things up around here? You know, with all the school integration stuff going on these days, maybe someone just wants to get Zench or something."

"I think that whoever wrote that letter knows exactly what's going on. Furthermore, that person ought to get a community service award. We can't just sit back and do nothing about racial contamination. And we won't, Bob." Rosnau's voice rose, "Sure as

I'm standing here right now, we won't. Me and some guys already talked about it last night, and—." Rosnau realized he'd better be careful about what he said.

"You told someone else about the letter?" Dietrich's voice betrayed his panic. "It was supposed to be between the two of us, Lefty. I thought you knew that." Robert Dietrich could almost picture in his mind what Mitchell would do to him if word leaked out. "Holy Jesus...I wish you'd have kept this under your hat. It's going to be my ass if any of this gets out."

"You'll be a hero, Bob. Mark my words, when justice has been served, you're going to be applauded for what you've done." Rosnau could have framed his comment in the present tense. "Mark my words, Bob," he repeated.

20/ "YA—YA"

Every town in America has its unique personification of Dewey Bartz. The fabled and maligned 'village idiots'—dimwitted and ostensibly aimless, they wander the streets with little more than a vague awareness of what's going on. Connected is the perception that they are oblivious to the countless jokes and ridicule their presence inspires. So, the enlightened citizenry pass them by with condescending smiles and well-wishes. The Deweys' of this world come in varied shapes and sizes, have a peculiar oddness in both appearance and demeanor, and are perceived as being as harmless as they are imbecilic. To some, the idiot evokes a sympathy or sadness, to others smug perceptions of self-worth. To all who pass him, there is usually an unspoken gratitude: "Thank God I have my faculties."

Sympathy, however, is misplaced. If one could only look into their souls, they might find qualities woefully lacking in their own lives. Peace, contentment, happiness...There may even be a measure of truth in the adage that 'ignorance is bliss'. Yet that very ignorance of our reasonable assumptions could well be an illusion. More often than not, the idiot of public derision is often remarkably intelligent. And, bliss...?

Deward Arlen Bartz, known to most as Dewey or Sparky or Sweep, was probably forty-something, but no one quite knew for certain. Whether he was born in Hibbing or came from some other place was one of many "who-cares". It seemed to most that Dewey had always walked the Hibbing streets doing odd jobs for local merchants, hustling nickels and dimes and quarters along with free meals, while smiling pleasantly at everybody who passed him by. In good weather and bad, seven days a week, Dewey wandered up and down Howard Street and First Avenue in an almost predictable pattern. In the summer he swept the sidewalks in front of the shops; in winter he shoveled the sidewalk snow. He might take a note and thirty cents to the tobacco shop for a merchant's needed pack of cigarettes; or run a letter to the post office for anyone too busy to do it for themselves; or pick up a lunch order at a cafe for those tied to their shop while serving customers. Everybody was so busy that the menial tasks were passed along to that someone who had 'nothing better to do'. That was Dewey Bartz.

At the end of the day, Dewey would carefully count his coins, emptying them one at a time from his bulging pocket. Sometimes there was a dollar bill or two which he kept tucked in his left stocking. Mr. Moran at the hotel always gave Dewey a dollar bill. If he missed a day for some reason, he would give Dewey two dollars the next day. The Androy sidewalk was his first chore of every day. Then, he'd cross the street and clean the Sportsmen's Cafe front walkway. His coffee was always free at the popular cafe, as well as a bowl of soup and crackers whenever he plopped himself on a stool at the counter. Dewey was careful to respect his privilege and eat no more than three meals a week in any of the cafes that provided him with a free lunch or dinner. (He kept a careful count in his memory).

At the Sunrise Bakery he'd get a donut and a dime at midmorning. Feldman's Department Store gave him a quarter every day and a new pair of gloves when his old ones were worn out. Mrs. Moran always had a Hershey bar under the counter of her shop to go with a fifty-cent piece. In Dewey's thoughts, Mrs. Moran was like a fairy tale princess. The most 'booteeful' woman in the world. Some merchants paid him fifty cents every Friday. Friday was his big money day!

Short and squat, Dewey covered his red, cowlicked hair with an old Yankee baseball cap. Conspicuously soiled, visor creased in half, and a size too large, Dewey went nowhere without the cap pulled down over one of his ears. His days were filled with a thousand smiles, and the "Ya-ya's" which accompanied each, to everybody he met. To most, "Ya-ya" meant yes or no or maybe—depending on the question or comment. Usually the diminutive man was as ignored as a Howard Street lamppost, or mailbox, or fire hydrant. He was, after all, the local idiot.

But, nobody could possibly realize that Dewey's vacant blue eyes saw everything along the streets of Hibbing. And his protruding ears heard everything. He never forgot a name or the specific date of anything that happened. It was uncanny, but Dewey could tell anyone who might ask him the precise day on which the blizzard of three years ago struck, or the exact time when lightning struck the water tower on Bennett Park hill, or even the date when the local high school basketball team last beat Chisholm. But only rarely did anybody ever ask Dewey anything. His 'Ya-ya' was all that anybody ever expected from him. So Dewey Bartz got by with only two words with most people for most of his life.

The favorite person in Dewey's small world was Mr. Moran at the hotel. Not only did Kevin (he'd never call him by his first name) give him a dollar every day, but he would take the time to talk with Dewey. Whenever he met Mr. Moran outside the Androy, Dewey Bartz would actually have a conversation—sharing news and expressing ideas in complete sentences. Mr. Moran was the one person who made Dewey feel like a regular person.

It always seemed to Dewey that Mr. Moran arrived at his hotel precisely when he was involved with the sweeping or snow shoveling. Or, was it the other way around? His day would not be complete if he didn't see Mr. Moran the first thing every morning. Often, especially if the weather was bad, Mr. Moran would invite Dewey into the plush Androy lobby just to sit and chat. "How did you do yesterday, Deward?" (Mr. Moran always called him by his proper first name and he liked that).

"I got six dollars and twenty cents, Mr. Moran," Deward might say. If asked, he could break the amount down to the exact number of nickels and quarters he'd been paid at every business, just for Mr. Moran's information.

"I hope you're saving your money, Deward," Mr. Moran would often warn—following with words of advice: "I wish you would put your money in the bank where it's safe." (Yet, never once did Kevin suggest that he would do it for him).

"Don worry 'bout that Mr. Moran, ain't nobody gonna rob me," Dewey would assure.

One day Mr. Moran gave Deward a bright new summer jacket printed with Androy Hotel in bold letters across the back. It was the same jacket he'd given to his softball team players. The only time Deward wore the green nylon jacket was when he attended games at Bennett Park across the street from his apartment building. The jacket was his most prized possession.

Kevin's care for Deward Bartz went beyond his conversations, and his dollars bills, and his genuine affection for the little man. Few people were aware of a promise Kevin had made to Deward's mother, Ardis, before she died from tuberculosis nearly twenty years before. Kevin was the attorney she had chosen to draft her will. Upon liquidation, her estate would amount to less than five hundred dollars. "Will that be enough to take care to Deward, Mr. Moran?" she asked.

"For the rest of his life, Ardis," Kevin assured.

And, like fishes and loaves of bread, the money had been taking care of Deward's rent, utilities, and medical bills ever since.

On this damp Thursday morning, Kevin invited Deward Bartz to join him in the lobby. He reached into his pocket for a dollar bill and asked Lillian at the desk to bring them both a cup of coffee— reminding her to put lots of sugar and cream in Deward's cup.

"How did you do yesterday, Deward?" Kevin inquired.

"Only three dollas fitty cents fer jobs, Mr. Moran. Rained in da afternoon...'member? But Jerrey Zense givz me a dolla last night so dat makes it okay after all."

Kevin puzzled, "Gary Zench?"

"Yez he did. Wannid to know sompin 'bout las' Friday nite an' I tol' 'em." Deward recounted their brief conversation in the hallway of the apartment building.

~

Friday.

Standing at his front door, Gary Zench watched the sheets of gray rain sweeping across his asphalt driveway. He'd need his raincoat. The much-needed morning downpour added freshness to the September morning's air. With all the books in good order, Gary could take his time today. His Friday agenda was light. After a special luncheon for the three recipients of Kevin's Suggestions Survey project of the previous week, he might have to look for work to do. The winning proposals included ideas for improving the Androy's lobby lighting so as to make "a guest's first impression a bright and inviting experience..."...another, "adding upholstered booths to replace several tables along the interior wall of the coffee shop..." and a third for "renovating the bathrooms in all 160 rooms installing vanity fixtures and glass shower enclosures..." Gary's preliminary estimate on the costs for accomplishing all three proposals was over ninety thousand dollars, but Kevin believed all were long overdue improvements. Gary chuckled to himself as he peered at the streams of water rushing down Inner Drive outside. Kevin was paying his three hotel employees a bonus for providing him with ideas on how to spend a fortune.

As Gary reached for his raincoat in the foyer closet, the telephone rang. His watch read seven-ten. Who...? The caller identified himself as Stanley Lolich, a foreman at the Scranton Mine. Gary's first thought was that of any parent—his son had been injured on the job.

"Mr. Zench, we're wondering if Jerry is sick or something? He hasn't called in," Lolich informed. "He didn't show up for his day shift yesterday and he's not here this morning. It's not like Jerry."

"No, it isn't, Mr. Lolich. Let me call his apartment and see what's going on." Gary hadn't talked with his son since breakfast last Saturday.

"We've been trying for two days, sir. Would you go over and check for us?"

Jerry's car was parked in the street where he always left it. The doors were locked.

Mrs. Rummel opened Jerry's door with her master key. "No, I haven't seen Jerry in a couple of days, Mr. Zench," she said. "And his car hasn't moved that I can remember."

Inside the apartment everything was orderly—bed made, clothes on hangers in the closet, and no dirty dishes on the kitchen counter. Even the carpet appeared vacuumed. Gary checked the hall closet for Jerry's old leather-strapped suitcase, then found it stored under the bed.

"I don't know what to think, Mrs. Rummel. If Jerry was going somewhere for a couple of days, he'd surely pack his suitcase. In the bathroom his son's Gillette razor, toothbrush, Ipana toothpaste, and Mennen aftershave lotion were resting on the vanity. "It looks to me like he just didn't come home after—" Gary remembered the incident Kevin had told him about at Wednesday's softball banquet. He hadn't gone to work Thursday...?

"Can you remember when you last saw my son, Mrs. Rummel?"

"I didn't really see him, Mr. Zench, but I heard him talking with Dewey out here in the hallway last...let me think...last Wednesday night, somewhere's around seven o'clock."

Back at the hotel, Gary phoned Lolich at the Scranton Mine and explained the situation. "I'll let you know as soon as I learn anything—and, please let me know if you hear from Jerry." Seeing Kevin's office door was open, Gary headed down the hall and walked in. "Something's wrong, Kevin. Very wrong!" Gary's voice betrayed his emotions of the moment. "Jerry's missing."

After explaining the sequence of events to Kevin, Gary asked, "Do you think I should phone the police?"

"Have you talked with Nora yet?"

"No. I'm going to run home later. Don't want to tell her about this over the phone."

"Do you want me to go with you?"

"Won't be necessary. Maybe you could cover for me at our Suggestions Survey luncheon if I'm not back by noon. I'm going to do some looking around on my own." But where, he wondered?

"I want to help, Gary. We're in this together," Kevin said.

"If I don't find out anything in the next few hours...maybe you can go with me to the police department."

When Gary was gone, Kevin found Deward Bartz sweeping the sidewalk in front of Ace Hardware across the street. The squat little man was drenched. Despite rain dribbling off his hat brim and pants soaked up to his knees, a vacant smile creased his round face like a ball of sun in a sea of gray.

Kevin called, "Deward" and gestured. "Come in out of the rain for a few minutes. Let's have some breakfast together." Remembering that Jerry Zench had given Deward a dollar the other day, Kevin was curious about what the two men talked about. Over bacon and eggs in the Androy coffee shop, he listened as Deward recounted the events of the previous Tuesday night. "I tol' Jerrey what I seen in the hall." Deward explained. "But he dint come back that nite, Mr. Moran. I always heer his door cuz I don sleep relly good, ya no."

With dread matching the dismal morning, Gary contemplated how he would explain their son's disappearance to Nora. His wife was ironing and listening to the KHNG Morning Show when he came into the kitchen. "We've got to talk, Nora. Something bad is going on."

Nora remained dry-eyed as Gary explained the incident at the softball banquet. As always, he found strength in Nora's calm. "I think I've always known we would be tested by God, Gary. He will be our rock and our refuge."

Gary sobbed, and Nora consoled. "We must be strong and place our faith in Jesus. Hold my hands...we'll pray together." As they prayed, Gary found his first moments of peace.

When they had made their last petitions, Nora stood. "You go out and find our son, Gary. I'm going over to the high school to pick up Naomi. She needs to know."

Gary skipped the employee recognition luncheon at the Androy to make some phone calls to Jerry's friends and coworkers. He began with Pack Moran and Rick Bourgoyne. Both offered to help in any way they could.

"I'm going to do some looking around, Mr. Zench. Jerry is like a brother," Pack told him. Rick was supportive as well, "I'll try something on the air near the end of my program."

Gary listened to KHNG as he drove from the house to the hotel. Rick was humming along with Fats Domino's Blueberry Hill. "Speaking of 'though we're apart'...I haven't heard from my friend Jerry in a couple of days. If you're out there listening, buddy—give me a call. Maybe we can go out and lose some golf balls this weekend."

Gary smiled to himself, "Thanks God for blessing my son with such wonderful friends. And, have mercy on his enemies."

Gary had missed the employee recognition luncheon at the Androy but found Kevin in his office. "Will you join me for a trip across the street?" Across the street from the hotel was the Hibbing Police Station. "I guess I'd better let Lawrence know that Jerry's missing. I've already talked with Pack and Rick—Kevin, your son is a wonderful man. I think you know that, though."

Kevin smiled, placed his hand on Gary's shoulder, "We've both got wonderful sons, Gary. Let's go."

Donald Lawrence made Kevin and Gary wait outside his office for ten long minutes. He hoped to convey an impression that the Hibbing Police Chief was a busy public servant. While they waited, Lawrence finished the morning paper's crossword puzzle.

Lawrence gave Kevin a warm, first name greeting while offering his handshake and inviting the businessman to sit in the more comfortable of two chairs by his desk. To Gary he offered a cool "Good afternoon, Mr. Zench," and the straight-backed wooden chair. Kevin, however, slipped in front of Gary and took the flimsy chair for himself. Lawrence puzzled, wondered if the gesture was a deliberate snub of an obvious hospitality.

Gary began explaining the events of the past several days. He was an articulate man and stuck to the facts, his emotions carefully restrained. "Since the Wednesday banquet episode, nobody has seen Jerry. And he's never missed work before, Mr. Lawrence. Not even when he's been sick."

"I can understand your concern. I'll follow-up on this matter right away, Mr. Zench," a modicum of empathy in his tone and expression. "I know the young men you've mentioned, Tobin, Dahlberg, and Roberts. I'll certainly talk with them—" the policeman paused, shrugged. "Have to admit I'm surprised, though.

None of these boys have ever been in any trouble with the police before. Fine young men as far as I know."

Lawrence had neglected to completely shut his office door when escorting the two men into the room. Lefty Rosnau had noticed Moran and Zench waiting for their meeting with Lawrence. When the three of them were seated inside the Chief's office, Lefty winking at the officer behind the counter, put a "be quiet" gesture to his lips. Standing to the side of the partly opened door, he eavesdropped on the conversation.

When it appeared the meeting was over, Rosnau nonchalantly returned to his desk and busied himself with some paperwork. After Moran and Zench had left the office, Rosnau gave Tobin and Dahlberg a call to make them aware of what was going on. Lefty was assured they'd keep their mouths shut. He'd tell Dahlberg to get to Roberts.

Pack cruised over near Bennett Park, spotted Jerry's old Plymouth, and pulled his squad to the curb behind the parked car. As the squad car idled he contemplated what he might possibly find that Mr. Zench hadn't earlier that morning. Maybe just a feeling? Stepping inside the apartment building, Pack first checked the mailbox for #04 (Jerry's apartment number) and noted what appeared to be a few days of uncollected mail. Upstairs he knocked several times while putting his ear against the locked door. Nothing. Pack decided not to interview Mrs. Rummel across the hall and returned to his squad car. Besides Rummel, Sparky Bartz and a divorcee named...Deloris? Deloris Ames—or Alms—something short with an A? Four tenants he might talk to later lived along the narrow second floor hallway.

Pack could not rid himself of a gut instinct. Something bad had happened to Jerry. When talking with Mr. Zench earlier, Gary had told him that he was certain his son had not just taken off somewhere. Pack was of the same mind. Whatever had happened related in some way to the banquet incident two nights before. Considering this to be the best theory, he would need to talk with Tobin, Dahlberg, and JR Roberts. Questioning them wouldn't be a pleasant task. Of the three men, Roberts might be the easiest to approach. JR worked as research assistant at the Lerch Brothers laboratory over on Grant Street just a few blocks away.

As he parked in the lot beside the gray-stuccoed Lerch building, Pack tried to collect his thoughts. Pulling his pocket-sized Spiral notebook from his shirt pocket he regarded the calendar taped inside the front flap. In a few minutes he sketched the events that brought him to JR's place of work. It was conceivable that he was the only person who had all the puzzle pieces. Neither his father nor Gary knew about the anonymous letter to Dietrich. His notes were chronological:

> *-Dad's anonymous note and Rick's radio caller on the morning of Claude's funeral—both Tues, 9/4*
> *-Jerry's letter on Friday, 9/7*
> *-Dietrich letter (re: Maddie) on Wednesday 9/12*
> *-Banquet at Androy on Wednesday 9/12—Jerry last seen*

Today was Friday, 9/14—each of these four separate incidents had occurred in the past ten days.

Pack returned the notebook to his pocket and considered what line of inquiry he might use with JR. Roberts would be upset over a visit from a cop while at work, even if that cop was his softball teammate. He contemplated possible outcomes. Pack would rely on his knack for reading faces, expressions, and demeanor—make an effort to keep matters light, even apologetic.

~

"Hey, JR, just passing through the neighborhood and thought I'd stop by for a minute." Pack took JR's tentative hand with a firm shake. "I'm still feeling lousy about the other night. I can't help thinking that maybe I should apologize to you and the guys if I behaved out of line. God, it turned into a miserable night after you three took off. Our little celebration ended up being a big flop."

"Rick started it all. That asshole's so uptight all the time...can't even take a little joke." JR had picked his scapegoat for the fiasco.

"Keep it down, JR," Pack said. The busy lobby, with people passing by and telephones ringing in the background, was less than ideal for conversation.

"Yeah, I guess you're right. But we're all supposed to be buddies. It shouldn't have turned out the way it did," Pack said. A knot in his stomach was growing over his 'old buddy' role-playing. Rick had every justification for his reaction to Tobin's remarks. Pack studied JR's eyes, looking for something—anything? "Anyhow, I was just hoping you guys weren't serious about quitting the team. I don't know where we'd find players to replace you."

"We're fucking done, Pack! Nothing against you—or even your dad, I guess." JR's tone was sharp at first, then almost apologetic.

"Mostly Rick? Or is it Jerry Zench?"

"Both. One's a hothead and the other's a—" JR caught himself. "Zench is a fuckin' showboat. Always out there for himself, ya know. That goddam 'I'm an all-star' attitude crap. He's not a team player like the rest of us guys."

A secretary nearby looked up from her desk at JR's profanity. Both men noticed and smiled apologetically in her direction.

Pack would be more subtle, change his tactics. Arguing over players, he realized, would accomplish nothing. "Maybe you're right about Jerry—and Rick flies off the handle sometimes. Anyhow, maybe you and me could talk to them, JR—maybe clear the air a little."

JR frowned, said nothing.

"Where did you guys head off to when you left the hotel?" With the unexpected question, Pack could almost feel a reaction from JR. His eyes narrowed perceptibly. When JR rubbed the side of his nose absently Pack perceived a lie was coming.

"Down to the Homer. Why?"

Pack tried to finesse around JR's 'why'. "I went looking for you guys later. Wanted to try and patch things up if I could." He lied. "I looked for Jerry, too. Did you run into him anywhere?"

JR's left eye fluttered at Pack's question. Then a sinister smile played across his thin lips. "Ya couldn't have looked very hard for us, Pack. Should'a known we'd be at the Homer. That's where we always go."

"I went to Checco's, thought that's where Randy and Dave usually play pinball." Pack tried to recover.

"If I'd told ya we were at Checco's, you'd tell me you looked at the Homer, right, Pack? I think you're trying to play detective with your old buddy. That's what I think."

"Why should I be playing detective, JR?"

JR stepped back to create a little more space between them. He was about Pack's size, but carried fewer pounds on his slight frame. Pack's question struck a nerve. "How should I know? The 'where were you' shit is cop talk. Interrogation. I'm not stupid, Moran. What's the deal?"

Pack noted that he was Moran now. "I hope you're not bullshitting me, Roberts." Pack reciprocated a surname. "Where you were on Wednesday night might become very important." Pack swallowed hard. "As you probably know, being as perceptive as you are, I didn't come here to apologize for anything. You guys were out of line." He felt heat in his stomach. "And damn lucky you got out when you did."

"Fuck you."

Pack realized his last comment was uncalled for. Get control, he warned himself. Enough skirting the issue. "Jerry Zench is missing, Roberts. Probably since Tuesday night."

JR leveled a cold stare at Pack. "So what? How does that concern me? I ain't seen him since he tucked his tail between his legs and took off." Roberts turned abruptly to return to his lab. After two steps, he turned and shot Pack a menacing glare. "What you getting at, Moran? Go talk to somebody else; I've had enough of this shit."

If Roberts reported this conversation to Chief Lawrence, Pack would find himself in hot water. He hadn't been authorized to interrogate anybody about the Zench matter. He swore under his breath. He'd probably find out more about what had happened to Jerry if he were not a police officer. And he was too close to the situation to be objective.

Pack checked his watch. He had some end-of-the-week filing to take care of back at the station. In another hour it would be four o'clock—then he could call it a day, call it a week.

Thoughts of the weekend had become thoughts of Maddie Loiselle. A smile creased Pack's face. Tonight he had a dinner date at the Androy. How much of what was going on would he share with Maddie? He remembered promising a bottle of wine. Questions lingered in the back of his thoughts. What was her connection to Jerry all about? Would Maddie want to tell him? Should he ask? Did she know that he knew?

Inside the upstairs police headquarters, Pack almost ran into Lieutenant Rosnau as he waved to Marinsek at the front desk. "Sorry, Lefty, I wasn't look—"

"Where you been all afternoon, Moran? You have your radio off?"

Rosnau had never been pleasant toward Pack. More than once Rosnau had ragged on him about being a lowly cop when his father had so much money.

"Sorry, again. Guess I had it off for the past hour or so. Did I miss something I should have—" Pack met the cold blue stare of Rosnau's eyes.

"I otta write you up. You know the goddamn regulations, Sergeant. No, fortunately for you, it's been quiet all afternoon. Where were you, taking a nap somewhere?"—he baited, knowing exactly where Pack had been that afternoon.

Pack tried to smile, "Just cruising, Lieutenant. You're right, it's been quiet all day. If something criminal was going on in Hibbing, we sure didn't hear about it, did we?"

At his desk, Pack gave his father a quick call to find out if Kevin had heard anything more about Jerry, and to inquire about how Mr. Zench was handling things. Kevin told his son that he and Gary had been by the station earlier that afternoon and talked with Lawrence. "We told the Chief about the episode on Wednesday and gave him some names to check into. Gary kept everything matter-of-fact—but, he's really hurting."

"I wish I could do something, Dad. Don't expect much help from Lawrence," Pack whispered into his phone.

"I don't, son. Neither does Gary. What are we going to do? I'm damn worried. I can't help thinking there's been foul play. Someone's got to start asking some tough questions, and damn soon!"

22/ MOSQUITOS

When consciousness returned, Jerry Zench retched.

His next sensation was the splitting ache in the back of his head, followed by throbs of pain raking through every joint in his body. Cramped and bound in a natal position, there was no way for him to massage the places that hurt—his hands were tied tightly behind his back. Another tooth-clacking bump tossed his body against the cold metal wall of the black compartment surrounding him. The side of his face smeared into the pool of warm vomit. As his thoughts began to clear, he realized that he was in the trunk of a moving car. He had no memory of how long he might have been here or where he was going.

All that Jerry could remember was getting out of his car in front of his Bennett Park apartment, closing the door, and...then voices— then the crushing blow to the back of his head. But they were only a vague blur in his strained memory of the moment. Where had he been? What was the time? Dust from the rough dirt road choked in his throat as the car sped to wherever it was going. Another jarring bump sent pain shooting through his shoulders, elbows, knees and hips. His breathing was labored, lungs throbbing against bruised or broken ribs. He'd been brutally beaten up.

Wednesday night! Jerry's memory jogged—that was it...! He had just returned from a drive out toward Dupont Lake. He had needed a place and time where he could reconcile his troubled feelings. The memory of an ugly scene at the Androy raged in his thoughts. Jerry's world had been in a downward spiral since the racist note tucked under his door on Friday night. Not even his father's gentle words could soften the outrage he felt. Then, Tobin's comments. His life was being pushed toward the edge.

While driving out to Dupont Lake, Jerry replayed the hatred in his mind. It must have been somewhere around ten when he returned to his place. In moonless dark he had parked under the huge elm tree on the boulevard. Then...

Jerry could feel the sudden swerve as the automobile turned to the left at high speed. Minutes passed. Soon the car was slowing down, another left turn, and the scratching of brush against the side panels.

A minute crawled by before the car stopped abruptly, causing him to scrape his face on the cold rubber of a spare tire near his chin. Unfamiliar voices outside—two men, he was certain. A key in the trunk lock squeaked, and then the blinding beam of a flashlight. Before Jerry's eyes could focus on anything, one of the men wrapped an oily rag around his head, covering his eyes. Hands tightly gripped his aching shoulders as he was yanked to an awkward sitting position in the trunk space. "Get yer nigger ass outta the trunk," an angry voice demanded.

Before Jerry could respond, both men were dragging him over the rear bumper. He tried to get his feet under himself, but his legs were too weak to support his weight. Helpless with bound hands, he fell shoulder first onto the rough road where sharp gravel tore his shirt to the flesh.

The two men jerked him to his feet, supporting his weight with hands gripped under his armpits as they dragged him away from the car. The sound of a rust-hinged screen door opening caught his ears, then the smell of a musty room. Rancid cigarette smoke combined with spilled beer, and old cooking grease pierced his nostrils. Neither man spoke again. Only indiscernible grunts—"The chair—" Two words from the second man, another unfamiliar voice to ponder. Jerry was forced onto a wooden-backed chair. Rope, like a hangman's noose, was looped around his neck, then wrapped more securely around his biceps and waist. Then his legs and feet were bound. The flimsy chair was pushed into a corner—his shoulders felt two converging walls. Then, a heavy trunk of some kind was being lodged against his knees, pinning him more deeply into the corner.

After a long minute, Jerry heard the door slam, followed by the creaky screen door. Were they leaving him here? He strained to hear more—the sound of the car's engine starting, a grind into first gear...then, the sound of his abductor's car fading slowly away down the road.

Where was this place? Jerry's first guess was a hunting shack—probably off some remote township road. There were hundreds of them he knew. How far from Hibbing? How long had he been unconscious? He had no way of knowing. Why had they beaten him? Abducted him? Why were they leaving him here—without water, or food? What were they planning to do with him when they got back? Would they be back? Why hadn't they just killed him earlier? Ransom? Who were they anyhow? He replayed the voices in his mind—nothing connected.

The night sounds abounded...crickets chirping, an owl's eerie hoot in the distance, wind rustling through tree branches.

Then, the mosquitoes began to swarm.

23/ AN ETHNIC COMMUNITY

Since its origin in the late nineteenth century, Hibbing had always been an ethnic community with nationality divisions defining the social milieu of most human relationships. The Slovenian Lodge, Kaleva Society, and Sons of Italy (to mention but a few organizations) served to bond generations of Austrians, Finns, and Italians, keeping their unique traditions alive in the face of an all-pervasive American culture. Being born into Hibbing society, one would almost naturally absorb the many ethnic stereotypes—Bohunks are...Dagos are...Finns are...and would develop an inevitable tolerance for the myriad of differences among the various nationalities. Those who moved into the community from another place often had the sense of being outsiders and sometimes felt themselves to be intruders upon an established social order, an order in which they had no legitimate history and which had, in subtle mien, closed its doors on them. The heart and spirit of Hibbing had always belonged to those with established and legitimized ethnic roots.

~

The community of Hibbing was attempting to cope with tragedy. The disappearance of Jerry Zench, nearly three weeks ago, had become widely discussed in barbershop chairs, beauty salons, grocery story aisles, ball field bleachers, and coffee shops throughout the city. Conversations ranged from casual street chit chat..."He must have taken off somewhere...", "Always thought the boy had outgrown what Hibbing had to offer...", "Too bad, the Zenches seem like nice enough folks..." to more serious theories..."Heard there's been some Klan activity up here...", "This integration business has everybody on edge...", "I ain't prejudiced, you know, but Negro folks..." If most people had any idea about what had probably happened, the consensus seemed to be that the young man had skipped out of town without telling his parents or anybody else, and needlessly upset the normally untroubled composure of the entire community.

Everybody knew that such events happened from time to time—runaway kids with their pregnancy issues or school frustrations or irresolvable problems with parents who were too old-fashioned or too strict or just "didn't understand them". But this current misfortune was unique and more deeply troubling. The disappearance of Jerry Zench was big news. Jerry was the son of Hibbing's only Negro family—a family without legitimate roots in their community.

'Hibbing Negro Missing' was an imperious banner on the *Minneapolis Tribune*; 'Racial Tension on Iron Range' reported a *St. Paul Pioneer Press* headline. The *Duluth News Tribune* revisited the story of the three Negroes who were lynched by an angry mob in June of 1920. (Parallels between predominantly white Duluth and Hibbing were drawn in the article). The Zench story was a racial story—and the eyes of Minnesota were focused on Hibbing. News of the hate note preceding the disappearance leaked within days. Mayor R.B. Tibbits became the reluctant spokesman of alleged progress being made in the Hibbing police investigation. Tibbits was noticeably frustrated by the media attention.

~

Chief Donald Lawrence followed up on the information provided by Jerry's father and Kevin Moran. In a timely manner, he interviewed the three young men who had made 'comments' at a recent softball banquet. Lieutenant Leonard Rosnau assisted in the interrogation process. The official police report simply concluded: "The three men were socializing at the Homer Bar on the night in question before returning to their respective residences about midnight. Their stories have been corroborated by patrons of the tavern, close friends, and family members." Day after day, disgruntled Mayor Tibbits offered the same report to a doggingly persistent press: "No new leads in the Zench matter. The investigation," he always assured, "remains ongoing."

Kevin Moran followed the events carefully, but from a distance, while struggling with his conscience over the degree of his involvement. He had not reported the 'NIGGER LOVER' note he had received nor told the authorities anything about his recent hotel survey. Being an attorney by training, he realized an indictment for withholding vital information and obstructing the investigatory process could result. Yet Kevin rationalized that divulging any of his personal suspicions might only muddy the waters. It was his belief that if Jerry's life was in jeopardy, the first few days were the most critical, and that he probably already knew more than the police investigators. Although holding little optimism that the Lawrence probe would turn up anything of consequence, Kevin allowed the police adequate space to discover leads of their own. When he did become more conspicuously involved, he would do so with far more energy and resolve than Lawrence had demonstrated. And Kevin would hire an outside investigator to assist him with the task. Sadly, however, that task might center on finding Jerry's body.

Further, Superintendent Mitchell had not disclosed the letter addressed to Robert Dietrich at the Cobb Cook School weeks before. That matter had been conveniently swept under the rug and deemed a 'crank'—unworthy of any public scrutiny. But Mitchell was nervous nevertheless. On more than one occasion, his assistant, John Slattery, had advised him to fully disclose the matter.

The anonymous caller to Rick Bourgoyne's Morning Show, however, was already a matter of public knowledge. The police conceded that there might be a connection between the caller's comment and the Zench note. "We get people from out of town in Hibbing every day," Lawrence rationalized to a Daily Tribune reporter. "Who's to say that the perpetrator wasn't someone from the

Cities or from anywhere else in the country for that matter. Racial issues have had this entire country on edge ever since those school integration tensions became big news."

24/ PACK AND MADDIE

Pack remembered returning to work on that Monday morning three weeks ago. (Jerry had been missing since Wednesday—five days previous). Upon his arrival at the police station, Lefty Rosnau summoned Pack into his corner office. Chief Lawrence was already sitting at Rosnau's desk.

"What in hell do you think you're doing, Moran?" Lawrence shot a cold stare with his question. "Rosnau got a call from Ian Roberts complaining that his son, JR, had been harassed by a police officer while at work last Friday. Is that a fact, Sergeant Moran?"

Pack's jaw set tightly. What could he say? "Well, sir, JR might have mistakenly construed..."

"On who's authority are you intimidating citizens, Moran? Rosnau added his question. The familiar team approach of interrogation.

"Can I finish what I started to say?" Pack cleared his throat, feeling a dampness in his armpits. He was in trouble!

"Answer the question, Moran. On who's authority?" Rosnau repeated.

Pack waited a moment before responding. Collecting some measure of composure, he met Rosnau's glare with one of his own. "It's not what JR, or his father, might have led you to believe, sir. I stopped by to apologize to Ian regarding a personal incident between us. We're old friends and teammates. Anyhow, he became obnoxious and..."

Lawrence interrupted again, "We are aware of the incident at your banquet and the comments you made to young Roberts. You're supposed to make social apologies on your own time and out of uniform, officer. You damn well know that by now. When a Hibbing policeman, a sergeant no less, enters a place of business and begins asking questions about a missing person—that smells of official! It's not 'sorry about our argument' bullshit!"

"You're right, sir." Pack would not talk his way out of this rehearsed 'two-against-one' confrontation. Despite hierarchal authority, Pack knew that Lawrence was more politician than policeman. Rosnau, on the other hand, was a clever manipulator. More than likely, when it came to police work, the lieutenant pulled the chief's strings. Pack forced a weak smile in Lawrence's direction. "I'm sorry. I'll apologize to Mr. Roberts if you think that's appropriate. I was probably out of line."

"Yes you were—and, yes you will, sergeant! This incident will go in your personnel files. Furthermore, if you do any more 'investigating'—and that's damn well what you were doing—relative to this Zench affair, you will be suspended from the force. Understand? I want everything to begin and end with the lieutenant in this matter. Rosnau is calling the shots! He's in complete charge of this investigation. Got that?"

"I do, sir." Pack said almost inaudibly, more devastated by the Chief's confidence in Rosnau than his official reprimand. How convenient for a bigot like Rosnau he thought. A fox in the hen house.

Rosnau's smile was a sneer of satisfaction. He had the chief in his pocket and Pack Moran on the defensive.

"What was that, Moran?" Lawrence was agitated.

"I said that I understand, sir." Pack answered in stronger voice nodding at the chief, ignoring Rosnau. "If I hear of anything, I'll pass the information along to the Lieutenant, sir."

Lawrence scowled without reply.

Rosnau narrowed his eyes on Pack. "If I hear of you asking any questions relative to my investigation, Moran—I'll have your ass. And that includes any behavior when you're off duty. Got that? If anybody approaches you regarding this matter, you are to refer them to me." Rosnau enjoyed rubbing salt in a wound.

Pack drew a deep breath. His supervisors had effectively handcuffed him. But his commitment to finding Jerry wasn't going to be diverted by any bureaucratic policy. Although disturbed, he would not allow Rosnau's constraints to thwart what had to be done. "I believe that I've got some vacation time built up, Chief. If I remember correctly, about a month's worth. If it's okay with you, I'll be submitting a request later today, sir."

Lawrence looked at Rosnau, shrugged his shoulders, "Lieutenant?"

Rosnau nodded, smiling faintly through tight lips. "Probably a good idea, Chief. We've got our own work cut out for us these next few days. We can get along fine without Moran." Turning to Pack, "But just don't go fucking around with our investigation. If you're planning on hanging around Hibbing while you're off—well, just don't forget for a minute that we'll be keeping an eye on what you're up to."

"I'm sure you will, sir." Pack got up to leave the office with a parting sarcasm: "Would you like me to report my whereabouts periodically?"

~

During the nearly three weeks of vacation, Pack kept his eyes open and mouth shut. Rosnau's investigation was going nowhere. Each day he drove countless miles along dusty back roads throughout Stuntz, Balkan, Clinton, and Cherry Townships without knowing exactly what he was looking for. Pack found nothing more than abandoned hunting shacks, ramshackle old barns, and wilderness hunting properties often posted with 'No Trespassing' signs.

From a safe distance he also followed the movements of Tobin, Dahlberg, and Roberts, often using an old Ford pickup that belonged to his grampa, Tony Zoretek. On several nights, Maddie joined him while he cruised the streets of Hibbing looking for something— anything!

Lately, Pack and Maddie had been sharing a lot of time together. She was back in school teaching her first graders as if nothing had happened. Most nights, Maddie had an hour or two of lesson planning to get done but was usually finished with her work by seven. This gave the two of them about three hours to spend with each other. By far, the best three hours of Pack's day.

Pack's feelings for Maddie were deepening. There were times during his long, fruitless days when she was all he could think about. 'Unlucky in love' had been his relationship history since high school. When he was a sophomore, Pack had his first date—with a junior cheerleader named Nichole Weaver. Pack fell hard and fast for the pretty brunette, and hurt badly when she dumped him for the high school basketball team's all-conference forward. In his senior year, he dated Pam Paulcich for several months before asking her to the spring prom. After the big dance, however, Pam said she "needed a little space"...and started seeing a junior college guy who played guitar in a popular local band. Pack's calls were never returned and the 'little space' became a chasm. In his year of college at the Duluth campus of the University, there were several short-term relationships. A frustrated student, Pack enlisted in the military and eventually ended up in Korea.

During the four years since his return to Hibbing it had been more of the same—short affairs and still 'unlucky at love'. But Maddie was different from all of the others. This time it wasn't the typical infatuation of a pretty woman. She had substance—intelligence, spirit, and a quick sense of humor. Maddie was fun to be with.

The night before Maddie had told him, "Don't let these dead-ends get you down..." with an added "honey" to make her encouragement even more meaningful. It had been the first time she had called him anything other than Pack. Yet, despite her warmth and affection, Pack sensed that there was something keeping her at a safe distance, some block to their getting to the next level. He struggled with how to chip away at her walls. He knew what had to come out in the open—but, the dialogue hadn't happened. Was he willing to take the risk?

They were driving north past Bennett Park at the time. Maddie, nestled under his right arm, had done the shifting as they passed through the quiet neighborhoods. "Maddie...I've got to ask you something." Pack swallowed the lump in his throat—suffering over his next words. Was this the time and place? Would he regret this moment for the rest of his life? "Something...well, something that's been in the back of my mind for a long time."

"Anything, Pack." Maddie's eyes, however, did not meet his. There was something different in Pack's voice. 'Anything' could be dangerous ground for her—for both of them. Her intuition, rarely wrong, told her that Pack's question could be a defining moment.

"Maddie...can you tell me about you and Jerry?" The words were out! Nothing could bring them back. "Maribec's told me that you were seeing Jerry this summer. If it's something—I mean, under the circumstances right now—if it's something you'd rather not talk about, I'd understand. But—"

Maddie said nothing for a long minute. Pack was the most decent man she had ever met. She didn't want to say anything that might ruin what was happening between them. Yet, she had to be honest. And honesty was a huge risk. In a few days, Maddie's period was due and if she missed this one—she had a major problem! If she was pregnant, Jerry's child was inside her.

"Dear Jesus, get me through this," she said a silent prayer. "I don't want to lose him."

As Pack looped around the east side of the park, Maddie finally spoke. "Let's park the car somewhere and take a walk, Pack. I need to hold your hand, see your eyes...then, I can tell you about Jerry and me."

Quiet minutes later they sat beneath a pine tree gazing at the October night's star-filled sky. The air held an autumnal chill and

Pack draped his jacket over Maddie's shoulders, pulling her close to his side as he did so. Maddie met his eyes, placed her hand on the side of his face, and lifted her mouth to his. A long, warm kiss that she wanted to last forever. But, the question pounded in her temples. She pushed herself away from his embrace. "I suppose the first thing I should tell you is going to be the hardest of all." Tears welled in her eyes. "I'm not a virgin. If that's something more than you want to deal with, then..."

Pack smiled, cupped her chin in his hand, "Then what? Then take you home and say good night, good bye...and let go of the best thing that's ever happened to me?"

Maddie was speechless.

"No, Maddie. I'm not looking for a virgin, and I don't want to know your sexual history. Honestly, that's not a thing for me.

25/ POSTMARKED: MINNEAPOLIS

Following instructions, JR Roberts deposited the envelope in a mailbox on the corner of Lyndale and thirty-sixth south of downtown Minneapolis. JR had traveled to the Twin Cities with his parents for a late September weekend wedding in the nearby suburb of Bloomington. He hardly knew the cousin who was getting married nor his distant relatives, and protested his father's insistence that he attend the event with his family. JR had slipped away from the Friday evening groom's dinner under the pretense of needing to get a package of cigarettes, then drove the few miles into the city to post the letter addressed to Mr. Gary Zench at the Androy Hotel in Hibbing. His instructions were explicit: The letter must have a Minneapolis postmark. Further, JR had been cautioned to handle the letter with gloved hands at all times.

~

Gary Zench was visiting in Kevin's office when the morning mail arrived. Separating his mail from Kevin's parcels, Gary slid several envelopes toward Kevin. "These are yours." Gary kept four letters. "Hmm...Minneapolis?"

Gary stared for a long moment at the postmark, then his typed name and the Androy address. "No return address—who do I know in Minneapolis?" he said absently as he tore open the envelope.

Without paying attention to Gary's musings, Kevin browsed his own mail. Something from the Chamber of Commerce, Rotary Club, Hallocks Clothiers..."Maybe that suit I tried on last week has been altered. Remember? The gray pinstripe just like yours. I just can't bear to have people think that my assistant is better dressed..." Looking up with his comment, Kevin noticed that Gary's eyes had widened. "What—?"

Gary was speechless as he read and reread the single typed line on the page: *I'm living in Minneapolis. Don't try to find me. Jerry.* Feeling a constriction in his throat, Gary tried to speak but no words escaped his mouth. All he could do was stare at the ten words in dumbfounded silence.

"Gary?" Kevin saw that his friend was visibly distraught over the open envelope resting on the desk.

His dark eyes moistening, Gary passed the letter across to Kevin, "Read this."

As Kevin scanned the page his heart dropped.

"I know it's not from Jerry. I can feel it in my gut, Kevin. What in hell is going—" Gary took a deep breath to relax the stab of emotion, when a thought flashed, "Drop it! Kevin, drop the letter!" he exclaimed. "There might be fingerprints!"

Releasing his fingers, Kevin allowed the page to drop on his desk. "God, you're right."

For an anguished moment their eyes locked.

"You're right, Gary. Someone's trying—" Both Kevin and Gary were on the same wavelength. Somebody wanted to divert Gary's attention away from Hibbing—into what would be an almost impossible manhunt in the huge city two hundred miles south. But, who?

"Jerry wouldn't go to Minneapolis. He doesn't know anybody down there that I've ever heard about. He hates cities. This is bogus, Kevin. A cruel ruse. I agree, someone wants us to think—" Gary tried to swallow his thought and failed...to think that Jerry is alive."

Kevin, at a loss for words, ached for the broken man he loved like a brother. For the first time, Gary had said what both of them had tried to repress. There were no words to console. Kevin, needing to feel a bond, simply reached across the desk and laid his hands on those of Gary. He wanted to say that God never gives us a cross that's too heavy—but swallowed the thought. At this moment he had cause for doubt.

Losing his fragile grip on composure, Gary dropped his face onto Kevin's hands and sobbed from the depths of his being.

Squeezing Gary's hands in his, Kevin let him cry.

In a weak voice, Gary mumbled, "We can't give up, Kevin. Maybe we're both wrong. Maybe he had to run. Maybe someone's protecting him down there." But, among all the maybes, Gary could not say...maybe Jerry's alive!

"We won't give up. " Kevin said with as much hope as he could. "Should we let the police know about this?"

Lifting his head and meeting Kevin's eyes Gary nodded. "I guess so. For what good it will do. It's got to be reported."

"I'll go with you. Then, I'm going to try to do something on my own, Gary. I've got some old friends in the Cities who might be able to help." He remembered his college professor, Prentice Garvey, a Negro with wide connections in Minneapolis and St. Paul. Gary had met Prentice years before at a parole hearing in St. Cloud. "I'll call the professor this afternoon, arrange a meeting for Monday. Then we'll go from there. And Pack's still got a few days left on his vacation. He'll want to go with me."

Gary stood, shoulder's drooped, "If you think it's not a waste of time..."

Kevin took him by the elbows, lifted "...Chin up, my friend. If Jerry's down there, we're going to find him. That's a promise."

26/ SCHOOL OFFICIALS

From a window overlooking Fifth Avenue, Chief Lawrence watched the two men cross the street toward the Androy. He felt another curious pang of sympathy for the father of the missing man. At the same time he wondered why Kevin Moran, usually a 'roll up the sleeves' guy, had been so noticeably subdued during their brief meeting. Scratching at his graying head, he wandered back to his office where Rosnau was waiting.

"It's just as I suspected, Chief," Rosnau said. The lieutenant was finishing the notes Lawrence had provided from the meeting with Zench and Moran minutes before. "So, the kid's skipped town. And left us all with egg all over our face. Can't say I'm surprised."

Lawrence mused to himself.

"What's next, Chief?"

"I'll call Chief Pennyman in Minneapolis about the Zench letter. He'll want to check out the Negro neighborhoods down there," Lawrence said.

For three weeks Rosnau had kept his knowledge of the Dietrich letter to himself. He'd expected the school district to come forward once the Zench investigation started, but nothing had happened. To Rosnau's way of thinking there might be some benefit to making that incident public now. In the absence of any new leads, the police department was becoming widely criticized for 'dragging their feet'. The Minneapolis letter, however, combined with the old one addressed to Dietrich at the Cobb Cook School could be a double-whammy. His personal credibility might get a needed boost.

Lawrence interrupted Rosnau's thoughts. "I suppose we ought to let the local press in on this new development, Lefty. If we don't, we're liable to find our ass's in a ringer."

Rosnau nodded without reply.

Lawrence got up to leave. "Anything else we need to take care of?"

Rosnau looked up, "I've had a couple of cops keeping an eye on our officer Moran the past few weeks. Helluva vacation he's been having—hasn't left town that we know of."

Lawrence gave his lieutenant a vacant glance, "His business, I guess."

"I only mentioned that because he's been seeing a lot of that teacher, Loiselle. From what I've heard, the two of them are out riding around town every night.'

Lawrence puzzled, "So—where are you going with this?"

Rosnau confided. "Sorry, but I've kept something to myself, Chief. For two good reasons: I didn't want to get my neighbor in trouble with the school, and, I thought it was Mitchell's business—but..." As Rosnau explained the Dietrich letter and the connection to Moran's girlfriend his small eyes sparked. "The way I figure it, our young sergeant's hanging out with this Loiselle woman, who might have been fucking Zench on the side. What do you think about that? And, we both know that Moran's been acting kind of strange lately. I'm just trying to put two and two together, Chief."

Frowning, Lawrence fingered his chin. "You thinking Moran...?" Pack, despite concerns over his recent behavior, Pack was one of his most distinguished officers. Lawrence's anger with his lieutenant mixed with the possibility of a new angle. "Why in God's name wasn't I informed of this earlier? We've been spinning our wheels for weeks, damn it. You trying to make this your own private investigation, Leonard? You should damn well know that I'm the one who gets all the flack around here. We should have been following up on this with the school weeks ago."

Having been chastised, Rosnau tried to recover an edge. "Moran would sure as hell have a mighty good reason to want to get rid of Zench if that nig—, I mean...if his so-called buddy had been messin' around with Loiselle. Just a theory, mind you, but we don't have any suspects with possible motive right now."

"Pack Moran, huh? As much as I hate to admit, he might have a reason at that. Then, so might, Loiselle. If this theory of yours has any credibility, it's going to tear this town to pieces. We're playing with fire."

Rosnau paused significantly while the Chief pondered the seeds he'd planted. "Chief, I smell motive here—maybe opportunity as well! Who would ever suspect a Hibbing police officer?" Rosnau mentally kicked himself in the ass for not thinking of this angle before now. "I think I'll give our Mr. Moran a call—tell him to stop by the station this afternoon. Ask him a few questions and see what he has to say."

"If you do, Lefty, be careful. He might be your subordinate on the force, but Pack is no lightweight. And he's a Moran—don't forget that." Lawrence stewed a minute. "I'd better phone Mitchell at the school and get a confirmation of that letter. For the first time since Zench took off, I think we've got some leads to follow. Damn! We're going to get to the bottom of this." Before leaving the office, however, Lawrence warned, "No more surprises, Lefty! Keep me informed, damn it! And be careful with Moran."

Lawrence made a mental note of the long pause at the other end of the line. The school superintendent seemed preoccupied with something. Mitchell had been visiting with John Slattery about local tax levies and state school aids when the police chief called. He wasn't supposed to be interrupted. After a moment of small talk, Lawrence asked about the letter. "Excuse me a minute, Don (the two men were Lion's Club members and knew each other on a first name basis), let me close the door." Mitchell covered the mouthpiece and whispered to Slattery, "It's Lawrence, the police know about the Loiselle letter, John. What should I tell him?"

Slattery, a polio victim, shifted in his wheel chair and answered in a hushed tone. "The truth...we found it groundless."

Mitchell explained that Dietrich did in fact receive an anonymous letter weeks ago and confirmed the racial content of the message. "We hardly gave it a second thought, Don. Letters like this don't warrant much attention on our part. We get teacher complaints from people in the community every week. Like I said, they are often malicious and usually groundless, as I said."

"Tell Don we talked with Loiselle and were convinced it was a crank," Slattery scribbled on a notepad.

Lawrence probed his friend, "So you didn't make any connection between Miss Loiselle and the missing Zench boy? He's the only Negro male...you know what I mean?"

After denying having made any connection, Mitchell explained that Miss Loiselle had assured Dietrich that the letter had no substance whatsoever. "We had no reason to doubt the verity of a very respected faculty member. And, there's been nothing since...gosh, since back on—September...twelfth, I guess it was."

There was a pause. Mitchell smiled toward his assistant, believing Lawrence was probably satisfied. But the smile vanished, "Yes, I still have the letter in a file here somewhere." Then, "Yes, I will bring it over to the station myself, Don."

27/ SUSPENDED FROM THE FORCE

With visor down against the glare of western sun, Pack was returning to Hibbing from the east on highway 216 when he spotted the squad car behind him in his rearview mirror. Rosnau was following him, flicking his headlamps. Pack pulled his Ford off to the shoulder of the roadway, turned off the ignition, and walked over to Rosnau's squad idling near his rear bumper. Pack smiled weakly at the man he despised, "Don't tell me I was speeding, officer."

"I've been trying to get in touch with you all afternoon, Pack." Rosnau would be careful, use the 'old buddy' approach. "How's the vacation been treating you?"

Pack stood by Rosnau's squad without expression or reply.

"Hop in. I wanted to fill you in on some new developments. Both Don and me know you've got a personal interest in the case and don't want you to be in the dark."

Pack sidled into the passenger seat next to Rosnau, leaving the door open. He was fully aware that his activities of the past few weeks had been under surveillance. Pack had good friends in the department.

Rosnau gestured at Pack's car. "Where ya been, Pack. Ford looks like it's traveled every road in the county. Never seen a Moran driving a dirty car before." His stab at humor was dismal. "Just kidding."

"Cruising around, that's all. Lots of dust on the back roads."

"Just cruisin'?"

"I've been thinking about getting some property. Maybe building a hunting shack some day."

Rosnau's eyes narrowed at Pack's comment. "Hunting shack, huh?"

"You got it. So, what's going on? Doing a surveillance check on my vacation activities? That's really why you pulled me over, isn't it? I find it hard to believe that you want to keep me briefed on Jerry's case."

"You're wrong about that, Pack. There are some things you should know about." Rosnau began by explaining the letter from Minneapolis. "Chief and I met with Mr. Zench and your father earlier this afternoon."

Pack's face betrayed no emotion. "Doesn't sound like something Jerry would do. He's too close to his family to just take off. Nope, I don't buy it." At the same time he wondered who might want to mislead the police.

Rosnau smiled at Pack's casual observation. He would carefully study the younger man's reaction to the other 'new lead' in the case.

"Well, we'll look into the Minneapolis angle anyway. As they say, can't leave no stones unturned. Oh, and there is something else." He tried to convey an afterthought. "A local school teacher was reported to her principal for having some sexual relationships with Negro males in town. A Miss Loiselle—do you know the woman?"

Pack seethed! "Cheap shot, Rosnau. You damn well know that I've been dating Maddie." Clenching his fists, he checked the urge to grab the officer. "What you're suggesting is bullshit—slander! If you weren't in uniform right now..."

Rosnau saw Pack's hands clench, "Hey, cool it, Moran! I ain't making any accusations. Just letting you know that we've got the letter at the department. Mitchell brought it over this afternoon. It's something we have to look into, that's all."

Pack looked away, the knot in his stomach was intense. That letter, in the hands of Lawrence and Rosnau, would be twisted to suit their purposes. They were desperate. Rosnau would leak the story to the press, call Maddie in for questioning, begin boiling a pot which had become a futile investigation. In a town that fed on rumors, this allegation would ruin Maddie's reputation.

"Be careful, Rosnau. You're getting in over your head."

"I must have struck a nerve. Is that a threat, Moran?" An amused smile creased his face.

"That's just good advice, from one cop to another, Rosnau. No more, no less. You wanted to provoke me—don't deny it. Hell, asking me if I knew Miss Loiselle. Telling me that 'Negro males' were involved. How many male Negroes are there in Hibbing?" Pack looked away for a brief moment, regained his composure, met Rosnau's beady eyes. "Fact is, I've known about the letter for three weeks."

Rosnau smiled at the unexpected admission.

"I'm outta here. The bullshit's getting too deep."

"Before you take off, Moran, you do realize that we'll need to talk with your girlfriend." Rosnau would go for the jugular now. "And, I'm afraid, Pack...I'll need to talk some more with you. If there is anything factual in the allegation contained in the Dietrich letter—well, you would be considered as having a reasonable motive for revenge. You understand that, of course—she's your girlfriend after all."

Pack could not believe what he had just heard.

Rosnau kept the pressure of his offensive. "By your own admission a minute ago, you were aware of the letter in question. Yet, in light of the Zench disappearance, you chose not to bring the allegation to your superiors. In my book that is dereliction of duty, officer."

Pack only glared at the implication.

"Anything to say, Moran?"

"Yes, as a matter of fact, the next time we talk about these allegations will be in the presence of my attorney."

"Fair enough, Mr. Moran. Until you hear otherwise, you are—as of this moment—suspended from the Hibbing police department. I'll expect you to turn in your badge and all your other issue the first thing in the morning."

Pack went directly to the Androy. Although nearly five, he knew his father was likely to be in his office. He swept into the room like an ill wind and yanked a chair to the desk. "Dad, I need a lawyer! Rosnau has just suspended me from the force.

Dumbfounded, Kevin pushed the ledgers he was working on to the side. "What in God's name is going on, son. I've never seen you so angry."

Pack explained the episode.

As Pack detailed what had happened, Kevin could recognize the perverted logic in Rosnau's reasoning. As pathetic as it seemed on the surface, some 'motive' could certainly be drawn from the Dietrich letter. Kevin listened in obvious anguish. Another anonymous letter! How many were there now? His, Jerry's, today's letter from Minneapolis...now the Dietrich letter from weeks ago. Four! In addition to the letters, there were other potential connections—all of them had to be related: the radio caller, the racism in his own hotel, and the banquet incident. The puzzle of

Jerry's disappearance had several pieces. The problem would be finding the missing ones—then putting them all together.

"Have you talked to Maddie, yet?"

Pack shook his head, fought back tears. "What, in God's name, would I tell her, Dad?

"Would you mind if I gave her a call right now, Pack? Not as a potential father-in-law..." he winked to relax the tension. "But as a friend who happens to be a lawyer."

"I'd appreciate that. And, I think Maddie would even more."

Kevin picked up his phone, "I'll hand it over to you after Maddie and I have talked. She's going to need you more than ever, son."

"I hurt more for her than myself, Dad." Pack rubbed at the throb behind his temples, "I really do."

~

Maddie's October period was two days overdue. A second missed period meant...Her headache raged. Maddie resolved to make an appointment with her doctor. Then, what? How would Pack handle a pregnancy? "Oh, God—please don't let this happen to me. Don't let one stupid mistake ruin our relationship. God, I love him." She sobbed her prayer. Maddie wished her mother were home. She needed Maury's advice and support again. Tonight. Her delicate hands moved across her flat stomach, "No...no! Please God."

The ringing phone startled Maddie. She didn't want to answer. Her voice would betray the incredible stress she felt. Yet, maybe it was Pack. She needed his voice- more than anything, she needed his voice.

Her jaw dropped in disbelief. Pack's father was on the line. Mr. Moran! The voice was unmistakable, alluringly masculine, deeper than Pack's, yet almost familiar. Although she had only met Mr. Moran once before—after a softball game—in her mind, he was the most handsome man in Hibbing. She had teased Pack about his father's distinguished good looks several times. Intimidating was the one word that best described her feelings about Mr. Kevin Moran. Yet, Maddie knew well that Pack was closer to his father than to any person in the world.

"Yes, this is Maddie." For a brief moment her headache waned. "No, sir—I mean, Mr. Moran...I'm fine," she forced a small laugh. "Some difficult news?"

As Maddie listened, her headache pulsed in heightened torment behind her eyes. Her knuckles, white with tension, squeezed the phone. The damnable letter was out! Trying to concentrate on Mr. Moran's words became difficult. What was he thinking of her? She felt unclean, unworthy—saw her reputation being ruined. "Yes, I understand, Mr. Moran." He had not asked if the allegation were true. Right or wrong, his feelings seemed supportive of her. "I want you to know that I will do anything I can to help you, Maddie," he said.

"Yes, sir. I understand. Nothing without a lawyer present. Yes. Mr. Fena, he's my mother's attorney. Yes, he knows about the letter."

Despite Kevin's kindness and concern, Maddie felt as if her whole world was crumbling beneath her. What did he really think? Her shame settled like a heavy, gray drape while answering his questions. Then, his consoling voice brought her back, "Maddie, as hard as this may seem right now, try not to worry about this innuendo. I won't tell you it's not going to be difficult, but we're going to take care of it. With your permission, I'd like to contact Jack Fena right away. Is that okay with you?"

"Yes, sir."

"Call me Kevin, please. And, Maddie, keep your chin up. I've got someone here who wants to talk to you. But, before I give up the phone—" Kevin remembered that he and Angie had talked about having some friends out to their place on this weekend. Angie had often expressed her hope to meet Patrick's girlfriend one day soon.

"Mr. Moran—Kevin...?"

He laughed, "I'm sorry. I just got caught up in some thoughts. What I was beginning to say was that Angie and I would love to have you and Pack out to our place on Saturday afternoon. We're going to invite a few friends, barbeque some steaks, do some horseback riding if you'd like."

Pack smiled his enthusiasm at his father's suggestion. "Now, here's Pack. Let him know if that's something you'd enjoy, Maddie."

"I'd love to," Maddie blurted. "I mean, I so want to meet you and Mrs. Moran."

"Well, I know that we both want to meet you, too. Here's my son."

Talking to Kevin had given Maddie an immediate insight into Pack's nature. The unexpected kindness buoyed her spirits. When Pack said "hello" she melted, sobbed.

28/ BOUND AND BLINDFOLDED

Mosquitoes! Incessantly buzzing, biting—behind his ears, on the back of his neck, hands, forearms...every inch of exposed flesh felt their irritating pinch. The small, itchy swells were driving him to the brink of insanity. Helplessly wedged into a corner of the pitch-black space, he screamed for help—hopelessly shouting petitions into the dark unknown until his voice was hoarse, his throat ragged. But the outcries only weakened him, aggravated the growing thirst. His scraped chin and jaw ached from being tossed about the trunk, his shoulder from plunging onto the gravel road outside. Hours passed. The endless hours of misery and desperation.

The following morning's sun lightened the musty smelling room. The rag, still tightly blindfolding him, crossed the bridge of his nose to below his hairline wasn't thick enough to prevent him from realizing the advent of a new day. He tried to wriggle enough so that he might be able to rub the side of his face against the closest wall—only inches he perceived—from his aching right shoulder. But, the constraining bonds had been expertly tied. Any movement he made tightened the noose about his neck causing increased discomfort to his parched throat.

He struggled for hours to gain the few inches he needed. "Relax", he told himself, while trying to develop a rhythm of deep breathing and to focus his thoughts beyond the moment—back to some realm of pleasant memory. "Control your anger," he mumbled—remember...a picnic at Dupont Lake with family, playing catch with Dad, Mom's voice singing over the kitchen stove, helping Naomi with her algebra homework—her satisfaction when she figured a problem for herself. Those thoughts and others brought a smile. And a smile was like a small victory.

He reminded himself again, "Relax. Loosen the tension in every muscle in your body."

Only gradually, he felt the noose about his neck slacken—ever so slightly—yet, even a fraction of an inch helped. With this realization came a noticeable ease—almost like limpness—settling down from his shoulders and through his body; then moving downward through his hips and slowly into his legs. In his struggle, anger and despair were the enemies. Controlled breathing and relaxation were his allies. His only allies! He was slowly beginning to sense his swollen feet...for the first time his brain seemed able to send a weak signal down through his knees and ankles, then to his feet. He imagined nerves transmitting energy from his numbed toes...back to his heels. His left foot seemed capable of responding to the messages gradually filtering their way through his weakened system. Shifting the weight of his left leg onto the ball of his foot he could feel a slight leverage. Relax—he must not get too excited over what was happening. Relax! Refocus! He visualized throwing a perfect strike into his dad's catcher's mitt, hitting a ball over the outfield wall, catching a touchdown pass—sports moments relived. Now—push! The chair lifted—maybe a quarter of an inch. Drop the right shoulder, and lean...easy does it...breath deeply. Shift your weight. He was commanding—push a little harder. Control. A little harder now, don't tense, keep your balance.

The strand of rope over his right shoulder loosened, relaxing the noose just enough. Only a few inches might enable him to touch his forehead against the rough wood of the wall. Enough had been gained. Then, dropping his shoulder, he began to rub his head up and down—gently at first...then harder. Enough slack had been gained.

Forcing the side of his forehead against the wall, he could feel the scraping abrasion on his skin. Harder! More flesh was ripped and a trickle of blood crawled down his face below the blindfold. But the rag was moving—down to his eyebrows. Easy does it, he warned himself, don't overexert. The top of his exposed ear was brushing against the wood now. Hope! He tried to dispel the tight pain in his left foot and leg as he leveraged.

Feeling the exhaustion of his efforts, he returned to his upright position and wriggled his numb foot. The bind of his ankles must have cut off his circulation. But the blindfold was coming off. His face ached more than any other part of his body. As the minutes passed he tried to rejuvenate his strained muscles. In his reserve he knew there was still enough strength—if only he could effectively release it. Taking deep breaths while expanding his chest as much as he possibly could, over and over again, he could feel the bonds slackening across his upper body now. How much time did he have? Would being able to see the inside of his prison give him any advantage? If only he had water. Just a small swallow. He ran a dry tongue over his chapped lips, but it was like sandpaper on wood.

"Now?" He shouted into the stale room, summoning every fiber of strength, he pushed his left side. His face flattened against the wall. Up and down he scrapped, forcing his head and neck to apply an even greater friction. The scab tissue on his chin tore painfully away.

Success at last!

His right eye was becoming uncovered—the cloth band had slipped under his eyebrow. But a corner of the rag remained wedged between his head and ear. Straining at his bonds, he managed to get the side of his nose in contact with the wall. Push harder! He was demanding every ounce of effort his body could give—and his body was responding!

Once the rag had been pulled under his nose, he could finally put his teeth to work.

Despite his consuming exhaustion, he felt a sense of triumph. He could see the room of his captivity for the first time. A double bed occupied the opposite corner. An old wooden table with three flimsy chairs. On the wall to his right, a countertop sink held a rusted hand pump and grungy pots. There was a worn-out sofa to the left. A single bulb hung over the center of the space. A cast iron potbelly stove with a stack of split wood piled nearby was the only other fixture. Rag rugs haphazardly covered places on the rough pine floor. An eleven-point buck's head hung on the wall above the sofa, and two mounted walleye on either side of the trophy deer. His prison was a long-neglected hunting shack.

Throughout that endlessly silent day, he studied every detail of the sparsely furnished room. The trunk that wedged him into the corner was too heavy to move. For hours he tried to chew at the rope across his chest without choking himself on the noose expertly attached to his wrists behind his back.

Hour by hour, the compelling thirst drained his resolve. The water pump at the sink became a fixation. But the thought of water or food, made him nauseous. His next battle would be a greater measure of self-discipline. Don't cry, don't pity, don't despair; he warned himself in desperate breaths.

During the ensuing sleepless night, he thought about death. How much life did he have left in him? Did his captors leave him to starve to death? Or, would thirst kill him first? How terrible would death from dehydration be? At times he prayed—prayers that whoever had brought him here would return and kill him rather than allow him to die this way. But death was becoming a certainty now. Death would be his only escape from this isolated place.

Friday came and went. He had spent every measure of his strength. Despite small accomplishments, he was still too tightly bound to even hope. Lingering on the edge of consciousness, he prayed for God to let him die.

29/ ATTORNEYS

On Thursday, October 4, the *Hibbing Daily Tribune* headlined: 'Zench Reported Alive'. Hibbing Police Chief Donald Lawrence was quoted as saying, "We have been quite positive for some time that the Zench boy was no longer a subject of our jurisdiction. Our investigation has been thorough and the cooperation from local law enforcement agencies across the Range has been commendable." Lawrence was careful not to make any reference to the anonymous letter that had been received by Robert Detrich and which was now in his possession. "The Twin Cities police will be pursuing this matter with all due speed and we expect that young Zench will be located soon," Lawrence added. The interviewing journalist, Neal Beamons, went on to speculate that Gerald Abraham Zench might have been despondent over a racial incident at an Androy Hotel party three weeks before and fled to Minneapolis where he had several Negro friends.

The *Daily Tribune* rested atop a long oak table in the Androy's conference room. Kevin could no longer contain his contempt. "Everybody's going to have the impression that Jerry skipped town. My God, 'Fled to Minneapolis where he has several Negro friends'—the audacity! What kind of two-bit journalism is this? I can't understand how that rumor-monger, Beamons, keeps his job at the Tribune."

Sitting across the table was Jack Fena. On the other side of the attorney were Pack and Rick Bourgoyne. Bernard Bischoff, another lawyer, was sitting at the far end of the table across from Gary Zench. The six men were meeting about Pack's suspension from the police force, and matters relating to the disappearance of Jerry Zench. He thanked everybody for joining him on such short notice.

"I'd like to represent my son, Barney," Kevin said with a shrug and an easy smile, "but I think you're probably in a better position as a neutral party to handle this matter." He gave an overview of the events of the past few days allowing Pack to explain his incident of earlier today with Lieutenant Rosnau. Although they didn't have the Dietrich letter in their possession, Rick was able to relate it's content almost verbatim.

Jack Fena nodded his concurrence with Burgoyne's recall. "I was of the distinct impression that the letter was a dead issue. How did it surface all of a sudden?"

Nobody knew for certain but Pack offered a theory. "I think Rosnau has known about it for some time. He lives next door to Dietrich, and Dietrich has a big mouth."

Kevin vaguely remembered some gossip that Angie had picked up from Iris Dietrich at her shop weeks ago. Angie hadn't gone into any detail because she despised rumors and wouldn't be a party to spreading them. He guessed that what Iris confided that day was probably related to the issue before them right now. If that was the case (and he would find out from Angie later) Pack's theory was probably correct.

Hoping to keep their meeting brief and focused, Kevin turned again to Bischoff. "What do you think, Barney?"

"If Lawrence, or Rosnau for that matter, considers Pack to be a suspect, the matter of a suspension would have to go before the Police Commission. I seriously doubt that the Commission would find the Dietrich letter to be sufficient grounds..." Bischoff paused, looking up from his notes to Fena, "The school people considered the letter to be a crank, am I right on that, Jack? They found no reason to pursue the matter?"

"Absolutely. That's why Mitchell backed away from it when we talked about Miss Loiselle's suspension from the school." He laughed to himself over the irony, "That damn letter's caused two decent people to get suspended from their jobs."

Bischoff said he would talk with Lester Bowman, the long-serving director of the Police Commission. "Les almost always backs Lawrence, but in this matter, he's going to have to look at Pack's commendable record as an officer. He has the authority to reverse the suspension despite what Lawrence might think. And I'd bet he'll do just that. If the school district found the letter groundless, why would the police department give it credibility? Wouldn't make much sense."

Fena put down his ballpoint pen. He had been doodling. Chief Lawrence wore a dunce cap on his tablet page. "My main concern, gentlemen, is Maddie Loiselle. I'll join you in meeting with Bowman, Barney, so as to make certain that Maddie is not harassed by Lawrence and Rosnau like she was by Dietrich."

Throughout the discussion, Gary Zench sat without comment. If Rosnau was so intent on implicating Pack and Maddie, there must be some reason. He'd talk with Kevin privately after the others left. Rosnau had given him negative feelings from their first meeting. Gut feelings were not to be ignored.

Pack informed the attorneys that his vacation ran through Wednesday of next week and that he should not be docked any pay. Then he requested that Bischoff make certain that his suspension, if nullified, did not enter his personnel file. "There was an episode with JR Roberts just before I filed for vacation," he went on to explain the confrontation with his superiors.

After less than forty-five minutes, Rick and the two lawyers left the Androy. Kevin, Pack, and Gary remained. Eager to get to what was eating him, Gary leveled a look at the younger Moran. "What do you know about Rosnau, Pack? Just between us, I don't trust the man as far as I could throw him. I think he's a racist! And, from what Rick has said in the past, so is Lawrence. God, two bigots investigating Jerry's..."

Pack considered. "I think you're right about both of them. I've never gotten along with Rosnau—and Lawrence is more politician than cop."

Kevin interrupted, "What we don't know right now, we're going to find out damn soon." He had been mulling over his plans for the past several days, and the Minneapolis letter made him even more resolved. "I'm going to find a private investigator," he said. "Jerry's not going to be a priority for the Minneapolis police. My old friend, Prentice Garvey has someone in mind. Someone who knows what he's doing."

Pack picked up on his thoughts about Rosnau and Lawrence. "Something just struck me. Rosnau likes guns. I'm told he's got quite a collection at his place. Mostly sporting rifles and the like. He's big on hunting and fishing. Not just big on—I think he lives for deer hunting season. It's all he talks about for weeks before and after. All his trophies. No kids. Few friends that I know about, except for that guy...? You know who I mean, Dad. That crew cut bartender that works for you?"

"Wicklund."

"That's it. I think the two of them are hunting partners. They've got a shack south of town in Silica somewhere."

The reality hit all three men at the same time. A hunting shack!

Silica was largely a wilderness area with a few farms—about fifteen miles south of Hibbing. "Have you been down there in your travels, Pack?" Kevin asked from the edge of his chair. "I know you've covered most of the county these last few weeks."

"Yes I have. But just driving the back roads. Most of the land is posted and I didn't really snoop around where I saw signs."

"I think we could find Rosnau's place easily enough. I'll get some land ownership maps from the County in the morning," Kevin said. "I think the three of us are going to do some back country exploring tomorrow."

30/ THE HUNTING SHACK

On their drive south on highway 73 the next morning, the three men in Kevin's polished, black Cadillac talked about Rosnau, Tobin, Dahlberg, JR Roberts, and Carl Wicklund. Of these five, only the police lieutenant was a new name among the group with apparent racist attitudes.

Kevin told Gary that he and Pack were planning to go to Minneapolis on Sunday afternoon. "I talked again with Prentice Garvey late last night—woke him up, in fact. He remembers you quite well, Gary." Kevin and Gary recalled a parole hearing one afternoon in St. Cloud years before.

"I can't believe it," Pack said. "You were an inmate at the reformatory, Mr. Zench?"

Gary explained his boyhood friendship with Pack's father and his troubled youth. "Your dad and I ran away together once when we were...what was it, Kevin, twelve or thirteen? Hopped a train from the ore docks in West Duluth and went up to Hibbing."

The recall brought laughs from the two older men. "We sure put Tony on the spot that day, didn't we?" Kevin said.

"Not Grampa Tony?" Pack could not comprehend his father and Mr. Zench doing what they had so vividly described. "And Grampa never told your parents about it, Dad?"

"Not to my knowledge," Kevin laughed. "You'll have to ask him yourself. Maybe tomorrow at our place." Excited over the opportunity to have friends out to Maple Hill, Angie had called everybody to extend invitations. "I think all of us could use a little break from all that's been going on."

Turning to Gary, Kevin said, "Angie told me that Nora is looking forward to the get-together. It'll be good for Naomi, too. I think Steven is asking some of his friends to come over so it won't be only us old folks."

"Who else is coming, Dad?"

"Well, besides us and Maddie, Rick and Maureen Loiselle, Grampa Tony and Becca, Uncle Marco, that's about it. Oh, and some of Steven's friends from school."

As the men talked, Gary kept an eye on the land map resting in his lap. "Slow down, Kevin. That's got to be the road we take." Gary's eyes had been peeled for a dirt road exiting the highway on the left.

The gravel back road wound into the forest for nearly four miles through muskeg bogs and tamarack stands. On higher ground were birch and a mix of spruce trees. Kevin slowed the car to a crawl as all of them looked for another road splitting off on the left. Pack had scribbled a map of his own, "should be in this vicinity." Two ruts were all that led off the gravel and into the Rosnau property. About a hundred yards in they found a length of cable strung across the narrow, brush-lined trail. The shiny silver cable looked recently strung from two pine trees standing on either side. Kevin brought the car to a stop, turned off the ignition and stepped out. "Looks new doesn't it?" he said gripping the cable barrier, "We'll go on foot from here. Shouldn't be more than a quarter mile."

The shack rested on a small hilltop clearing just yards away from a tamarack bog. A single, tall poplar tree shaded the sun from the front of the wood-sided cabin. The three men approached slowly, eyes peeled for any unusual markings on the ground. It had rained off and on for the past several days and no trace of any tire tracks or footprints were evident.

The screen door to the shack was padlocked. In the back of the structure was the only window and thick curtains blocked any view of the interior. "Damn it anyhow," Pack cussed. "I wish we could see inside."

Gary gave the lower section of window a lift, felt it move. "It's not locked," he said. The weathered and warped window was stuck in the track however and with all his strength Gary could only open it a few inches. That was enough to get his hands inside and part the tattered curtain. It took a minute to focus inside the one-roomed structure.

Leaning over Gary' shoulder, Kevin asked, "Can you see anything?"

Pack was staring through the small slit as well. "I can, Dad. Looks like a double bed to the left of the front door, a table and some chairs, an old potbelly—that's about it."

"A buck's head mounted on the wall back there," Gary added. "Some walleye, too."

"There's a wooden chest over in the corner," Kevin added.

"Doesn't smell too good in there." Pack pushed away from the opening. "I doubt if anybody's been here for quite some time. I guess we drove out here for nothing."

Gary continued to gaze inside, looking for something, anything! His nostrils sucked in the stagnant air from inside the shack. "I've got a bad feeling about this place," he mumbled. "Can't really explain it, but—" he let the thought drop. He strained to see into the blind spot on the floor below the window frame to no apparent avail. Then, "...Rope! I can see a piece of rope on the floor." His heart skipped a beat. "I've got to get inside and look around. I think there's more than meets the eye."

Kevin , looking about the property behind them, spotted a pile of punky lumber. "Pack, let's see if there's a decent two-by-four in that stack over there," he gestured. "We'll need something to pry with."

They found a six-foot length of wood and dodged it between the bottom of the window and the frame. Pack leveraged his strength until the window loosened—a few inches, then a few more. Within a few minutes he had opened the window enough for Gary's slender body to slip through the space.

Inside, Gary examined the lengthy strand of rope. What else? Looking about, his eyes riveted. On the floor, behind the trunk, was a rag. Picking up the cloth, Gary examined the fabric—stains of blood.

"Did you find something?" Kevin asked from the window.

"Maybe."

Holding the rag to his nose, Gary's stomach knotted. was certain of a familiar smell—a faint but familiar scent. He was certain...Mennen. Immediately he remembered seeing the green bottle of aftershave in Jerry's apartment. His son's smell on this rag! His blood?

Seized with a panic, Gary fought his tears.

"Gary? What's wrong, Gary?" Kevin had pushed his head into the room, "What's that in your hand?" He could see that his friend was crying. "Gary, what's wrong?" he repeated.

~

While the three men were investigating the hunting property, Rosnau was meeting with Chief Lawrence and police commissioner, Lester Bowman. Bowman had already heard from both Fena and Bischoff regarding the Pack Moran suspension. Although normally a 'don't rock the boat' conservative, Bowman sometimes had a short fuse. The phone calls from two Hibbing attorneys had gotten his Friday off on the wrong foot. Bowman leveled a hostile stare at Rosnau. "Are you willing to implicate Moran in the Zench disappearance? If so, are you planning to call him, along with two lawyers, in for questioning? Because if you're only playing a cop's hunch, or floating some clever theory based on an anonymous letter to the school district, you're treading on thin ice. Damn thin ice! As a matter of fact, you're liable to find yourself suspended before we're finished with this business."

Rosnau gave Bowman a defeated look. He had neither the case nor the courage to bring any formal charges against Moran. "All I really want to do is question him, Mr. Bowman. And the Loiselle woman as well. Call it a hunch, if you want, but I'll bet Moran knows something we don't."

Lawrence intervened. "I'm going withdraw the suspension, Lester. But Rosnau's still in charge of this investigation and if he wants to interview anybody, and that includes Pack Moran, I've got to give him the authority to do what needs to be done." The Chief paused, "Zench is probably in the Cities. Maybe Moran or the Loiselle woman knows where."

Bowman seemed satisfied. "Nothing in Moran's personnel file either. That's from Barney Bischoff." The Commissioner shot a hard glance at Rosnau. "Be careful in any questioning you do. I don't want Kevin Moran, or any other lawyers, breathing down my neck. Do we all understand that?" Then to Lawrence, "Kevin probably has more good-will and influence in this town than you and the mayor put together."

Lawrence nodded agreement. He and Kevin had worked together on numerous city projects and always got along well.

Rosnau was thinking to himself. Why maintain an adversarial posture with Pack Moran when it would be advantageous to draw him into the investigation? As an ally, Pack would be obligated to share whatever information he managed to uncover. "I'll patch things up with Pack, myself, gentlemen. After all, we're all on the same team here, aren't we?" He offered an amused smile.

Before calling Pack, however, Rosnau had something else up his sleeve. He knew Neal Beamons at the Tribune. The reporter thrived on rumor and innuendo. On many occasions he had leaked a story and reaped the benefits.

Back in his office, Rosnau dialed the Tribune. "Neal, I've got something for you to kick around—from an unnamed source with the public schools. Anonymous—but credible...okay?" Rosnau continued, "A certain first grade teacher at the Cobb Cook School was allegedly—and I emphasize allegedly—sexually involved with Jerry Zench." He went on to explain that the letter in his possession was not to be mentioned. "Maybe later, Neal. We'll have to see what happens. You've gone out on a limb before with far weaker leads than this one."

In a dark corner of his thoughts of the moment, however, was his memory of what had already happened—nearly three weeks ago. But Rosnau found no lingering guilt in that dark realm. Zench got exactly what he deserved.

31/ DEATH IN THE RAIN

He had little more than a vague sense of the rain outside. The patter against the window must have awakened him from—how long had he been oblivious? The room was cast in an early or late day gray. He had no way of knowing which. The damp chill pervading the room made him shiver convulsively. Then a sudden warmth spread into his groin. He laughed. How could there be any liquid in his dehydrated body? He had thought that his tears had drained him. Yet, there was no embarrassment over the shameless episode. That he had pissed himself was almost funny.

At some level he had resigned himself to an imminent death. What could he do with the time remaining? He was already spent of any vitality, he'd already done all the remembering he was capable of, and his last prayers had been expressed. Now there was nothing left. He began to count—imagining that he could number every last breath his body had remaining. How far could he count? At forty-two, his concentration became muddled. The remembering could not be forced from his last thoughts. The why would never be answered. Never! But...how could any human being do this to another? Such depth of hate was something beyond his comprehension. He tried to let go of the thought. The numbers had given him an oblivion, an escape from the reality of death. How many breaths remained in his spent   body?   He   resumed   his   count— sixteen...seventeen...eighteen...He would make one hundred, then maybe, two hundred.

The damp cold on his thighs and the smell of his urine distracted his counting at...fifty-one? The 'counting to death' plan was not working. The idea was a stupid one to begin with. He shivered. He closed his eyes. It might be best to die while sleeping. Peacefully. Unconsciously.

The sound of an opening door stirred him from his last dream. It took every measure of strength to lift his head, to focus his dry eyes...there were two men. Straining his memory, he found a thread of recognition—the cop's face was familiar. The face, without a name to go with it. A face he'd seen many times but, without a uniform, he couldn't connect a name.

The bulky crew cut man behind the cop was not familiar.

He tried to smile, wanted to say thank you...but he was too weak. His ordeal was finally over. He was being rescued. Thank God he mumbled incoherently.

The cop spoke. But his words seemed directed to the other man—not him. And, that face...that face was—angry?

The other man said, "Looks like our nigger's managed to get the blindfold off."

With a twisted smile, the cop said—"Well, take a good fuckin' look, Zench. It's going to be your last. You fuck a white woman and you pay with your balls."

In that moment he knew. His suffering would soon be over. Whatever these men were going to do to him would be a relief. He was ready to die. He wanted to speak but knew that no words would escape his dry throat. If his swollen mouth could utter any words, those words would be "get it over with."

On the porch outside the shack, beyond the open door, were other voices. Voices muffled by the pound of rainfall. Two men. They were mumbling something about "the body"...his body? He recognized the voices. Stepping toward the middle of the room, the bulky man spoke nervously, "Let's get this over with and get the hell out of here, Lefty."

"Haul the bastard outside, Carl."

There was no fight as he was dragged outside in the headlock of the cop's friend. In the gray late afternoon rain, the other two men stood by a tree. A rope had been slung over a crotch in the limb about ten feet up. The noose dangled in readiness. He knew his fate as certainly as he knew his executioners. His eyes met those of Tobin...then Dahlberg. Both men looked away. Were they ashamed?

"Crissakes, you guys, we're gettin' drenched" Tobin said toward the cop.

"Yeah, c'mon Rosnau, rope's ready." Dahlberg's voice strained.

He closed his eyes for the last time. He had seen everything there was to see on this—this his last day, his last minutes. Under his breath he prayed for a quick death. He prayed for God's forgiveness of everything he'd ever done wrong in his tormented life. He prayed that these four men would suffer even half of what he had. Curiously, he wondered if that was wrong. Right now, that didn't matter. He had made peace with his God long before, surrendered his spirit, and welcomed an end to it all. As he had done a thousand times during these past days of isolation, he forced his thoughts to focus on memories past—on pleasant times with his father, his mother, Naomi.

So deep was his concentration, he was able to block out the events of his last minutes of life. He remembered throwing a ball so hard his father couldn't hold it as his pants were being stripped from his hips; a thick ham salad sandwich with crisp lettuce his mother set on the table as the noose was tightened about his neck...the warm sun on his back as he lay on sandy McCarthy beach when the sharp cut sent pain raging from his groin through his body. The sun, so radiant and so comforting.

The four men wrapped the body in burlap bags, threw it into the trunk of a car, and left the property. Jerry Zench would be transported to a predetermined place far from the hunting shack. It was already dark when the two men dumped their victim in a small ravine beyond a broken line of fencing southwest of Hibbing.

The early October Saturday dawned with unseasonable warmth. The great ball of sun climbed lazily over the thickly wooded eastern skyline like a birthday balloon. Maple Hill was ablaze in a collage of autumnal colors—bright oranges, reds, and ambers given definition by a stately intermixture of lofty pines.

When Angie awoke she found her husband sitting beside her on the bed. A beckoning shaft of sun streamed through the window casting Kevin in a wash of morning radiance. Her nose perked delightfully as the aroma of fresh coffee wafted up from the cup he held out for her. Then the touch of a soft kiss on her forehead. "What time is it, Kevin?" Angie rubbed her sleepy eyes, "I've overslept, haven't I?"

"I just couldn't wake you, sweetheart. Besides, everything that needs doing will get done. Your dad called a few minutes ago to say that he and Becca would be here before ten to help out with the preparations."

Angie ran a parade of thoughts behind her tired eyes. It was going to be a busy day entertaining family and friends. She yawned, sipped at her cup. "Thanks for the coffee, my dear, it's just what I needed. I'm so looking forward to our get-together—especially meeting Maddie." She sat up, propped her pillow, " I love the name Madeline," she smiled. "That's the name I would have picked if we had another daughter. Mary Rebecca and Madeline Marie," she said whimsically. "She's pretty, isn't she?"

Kevin nodded, "And smart and spunky from what Patrick has said. You're going to love her."

"Her mother stopped by the shop yesterday. Maury said that she and Rick would have some wonderful news to share with us all." Angie looked at her diamond, smiled, and wondered. "It's going to be a fun day." Then, placing the cup in her lap and tousling her hair, Angie's forehead wrinkled at another thought. "I only hope we can get Gary and Nora to relax—what they must be going through these days...I just can't imagine."

~

Tony Zoretek had his first mild chest pains on the day before Claude Atkinson's funeral more than a month ago. The antacids he took over the next several days didn't help. Although he kept the discomfort to himself, Tony sensed that Becca knew he wasn't feeling well.

Then, while golfing with Kevin last Monday, he had a sharp pang while walking up the hill to the ninth green at the Mesaba Country Club. He had to stop and catch his breath. The gripping sensation in his chest frightened him for a moment but then went away. Kevin had been playing his ball near the rough on the left side of the fairway and didn't notice Tony's little episode. On the green, however, as Tony's put came up three feet short, Kevin commented, "You look a little flushed, Dad. Are you feeling okay?"

Tony dabbed at the clammy perspiration on his eyebrows, pushed back his cap, "If I can finish with a bogey I'll be fine, Kev," he said dismissively. "I'll get out of this round only owing you two bucks. Not too bad for an old-timer."

In years, Tony might have been an 'old-timer', but deceptively so. At sixty-eight, only his graying hair betrayed his years. Tony was tall and slender, retaining the athletic physique of years before, and might have easily passed for a man in his late forties.

While driving out to Angie and Kevin's place, Tony regarded his wife from the corner of his eye. Becca was scanning the pages of this week's Saturday Evening Post magazine. Dressed in blue jeans and a soft yellow woolen turtleneck sweater, she was still a beautiful woman. Affectionately, Tony placed his hand on Becca's thigh beside him and smiled. A gesture in place of words.

"You didn't sleep very well again last night, honey." Becca frowned and paused significantly. She was a retired doctor and could read symptoms as easily as the magazine in her lap. On several occasions she had commented on her husband's color, his lack of energy, loss of appetite. Only the morning before she watched from the kitchen window as Tony raked leaves in their back yard. There had been pauses to catch his breath, a clammy perspiration afterward, and a noticeable lethargy throughout the remainder of the day.

"What do I have to do to get you to see your doctor, Tony? Just a checkup—perhaps it's only elevated blood pressure and they've got medications for that. Please, just for me."

Tony smiled knowingly. Becca knew more than she would say. "On Monday...I promise. Don't say anything to the kids, though. We're going to have a great day." He gave her thigh a slight squeeze, "I don't want anybody fussing over me."

The southeast corner of the Moran's elegant house overlooked Angie's leaf-mulched and stone-excavated flower gardens from a broad screened porch. During the summer months, the garden was resplendent with colorful blooms, but only a patch of red-orange asters stubbornly resisted nature's call to dormancy. Traces of last night's frost still lingered upon the shaded areas of grass below the rows of maples and Norway pine.

Tony, wearing a light cotton jacket, was perfectly comfortable as the morning's coolness surrendered to the magnificent sun which basked the porch in warmth. The cup of coffee that Kevin brought him was still steaming as the two men relaxed in their high-backed wicker chairs. Kevin sensed Tony's unusually reticent mood and did most of the talking: evoking little more than nods and one-word agreements from the man he loved like a father. Most of what Kevin had to say involved events surrounding the disappearance of Jerry Zench nearly a month ago. "I don't think he's alive, Dad." His reference to Angie's father was a natural one. Throughout his life,

Tony had been the Dad he deeply needed but never had. "And I think that Gary is struggling against the same gut-feeling."

With the perception of years, Tony contemplated Kevin's empathy for his friend's suffering. Gut feeling? Or, heart feeling? To him there was a difference. Gut feelings were despairing, heart feelings hopeful. Tony regarded the younger man who had warmed his heart with that cherished word; Dad. "What does your heart tell you, Son?"

Kevin pondered the question and the man who asked it. Far more than himself, Tony was a spiritual man. His voice choked noticeably, "My heart aches, Dad. Maybe I'm too close to everything that's going on. But I know the family so well, their closeness and compassion for one another. I know that Jerry would never...never run away. He has his father's strength of character. No, Jerry is—" Kevin looked away without expressing the word stuck in his throat.

Tony's smile was one of knowing; a smile like none other in the world. Every good emotion conveyed in the creases of his face, the sparkle in his deep blue eyes. "Take my hands and pray the *Our Father* with me, Kevin."

Just before noon, Maribec was the first to arrive. The women in the kitchen had everything well organized so she made her way to the side porch and her favorite person in the world—Grampa Tony.

Kevin warmed to see them embrace. His daughter's going to her grampa before giving him a hug was expected, even appreciated. At the sight of his granddaughter, Tony's typical animation seemed instantly rejuvenated, and Kevin felt a swell of relief. Tony had been noticeably introspective all morning, and Kevin had wondered about his health without inquiry. After a few moments, Kevin cleared his throat, "Hmmm, what about your father, sweetheart?"

But Tony already had Maribec on his knee, and she had her arm about his neck. For reasons she would explain later, Maribec wanted to savor this moment between just the two of them. Her father could wait. After clinging to her beloved grandfather for another long minute, she gave Tony a kiss on his mouth. "You look just wonderful, Grampa!" she lied.

Pulling a chair to her father's side, Maribec gave him a quick hug and kiss. "Doesn't he, Dad?"

Kevin nodded, "I'm going to let the two of you catch up on things while I check with Angie in the kitchen." His tasks would begin once the others had arrived. The chicken and steaks for the afternoon cookout were marinated and ready for his chef's touch.

The women dismissed his intrusion, so Kevin went to the window overlooking the long driveway. Outside was his son, Steven. Waiting. Stepping outside, he joined the boy.

"I heard a car, Dad."

Sure enough, Marco's unwashed Hudson was pulling toward the house. Not even waiting for the car to come to a halt, Steven was rushing to greet his uncle and the young man with high-combed hair. Bobby Zimmerman, toting his guitar case, was a full head shorter than Steven.

"This must be your friend from school, Steven..."

"Yeah, Bobby."

Marco smiled at his brother-in-law, "Me and the boys have decided to provide some entertainment later this afternoon. They're quite excited about it, Kevin."

"We're going to do some rock and roll, Dad—really groovy stuff. You older folks might not like it too much, though. But Naomi will. And Pack and Maribec, too."

Bobby stood silently with his eyes on Steven's father.

At the door, Angie was quick to welcome her brother and had an open bottle of beer at the ready. "Marco, have you lost some weight?" she asked appraisingly. "You look great." Angie stretched the truth.

"Nah, it's just the black slacks and sweater, Sis," he took the bottle and gave Angie a light kiss on the forehead. He spotted Becca at the counter, "Hey, Mom, you're looking beautiful as always." Marco set down his bottle and gave Becca a big hug. "Where's Dad?"

Marco visited with the women for all of two minutes, draining his beer in three swallows before finding a fresh Hamms in the fridge and heading out to the porch.

33/ NOBODY'S PERFECT

"Pack...will you pull over for a few minutes?" Maddie and Pack were about a mile from Maple Hill. "I'm not sharing something I should be telling you."

He turned west on Lindberg and coasted to a stop on the gravel shoulder. "What's up, Maddie? Nerves?"

"I'm almost sick to my stomach." Maddie took in a deep breath. "I'm only doing this for you, Pack."

"Doing what?"

"Meeting your folks and relatives. They intimidate me."

Although Pack could empathize with what she was feeling he would allow her to explain her apprehension without trying to solace her stress.

Maddie looked away for a long moment. "Maribec and I share a lot of things—girl talk, you know." She looked at Pack, "Don't tell her I told you this...please! We both know that you're a lot closer to your parents than Maribec is but she told me the other day that she— I'll use her exact words—'Sometimes I can't believe them'—she said. I think she'd just finished having an argument with your Mom about not showing up for the Atkinson funeral reception. Anyhow Maribec told your mother 'I'm not perfect like you and Dad. And I'll never be'."

Pack remembered hearing about the episode. "Mom was kinda pissed at Maribec about that." In defense of Angie he was tempted to say that "if she were so perfect she wouldn't get angry" but he let the thought die. Maddie was going somewhere and he'd let her finish.

'Pack, I've told you about my father. Shawn McDougal was a

drunk and a womanizer. Abandoned me and Mom years ago." Maddie's voice choked. "Mom's never gotten over that. Sometimes I think the divorce made her a bitter woman. Until she met Rick—well, Maury's been a bitch! She's channeled her anger into becoming a successful, independent businesswoman."

"She's done well with her life, Maddie."

"Oh, yeah. I won't argue that. What I'm trying to get at...Well, those are my parents—a drunk out in California and a forsaken woman hell-bent on the priority of her career."

"Hmmm. And, then there's Kevin and Angela Moran! So wealthy and so respected and so very all-together in every way. Living up in the opulent Moran mansion atop pristine Maple Hill. Right, Maddie?"

"You're being facetious. But, truth be told—"

Pack took her hands in his. "I know where you're going with this. I want to hear you out, but before you say anything else, I need a kiss."

Maddie was beginning to tear. "I love you, Pack." She kissed him long and clung to his sweater. "I love everything about you—you listen, you perceive...you really care about feelings."

Pack put a finger on a tear that had escaped her eye. "And I love you, too, Madeline Loiselle."

She sniffled, smiled, found her handkerchief in her purse. "Now I'm going to look a mess when I meet your mother, Patrick." (She would try not to forget to call Pack Patrick in front of Angela).

Pack glimpsed the dashboard clock. They were going to be a few minutes late, but their conversation was more important to both of them than being on time. "I'll bet that my sister told you that I am just like my Dad—didn't she?"

Maddie tried to laugh. "As a matter of fact—"

"Stuff your hankie in my mouth if I start getting too wound up. Okay?"

"I'm all ears."

"I hope so, because I'm going to tell you a rather long story—actually a story within a story." Pack squeezed her hands, smiled.

"Two weeks ago, me and Peloquin, one of the cops I work with, were called out to an accident by the airport. A fella named Bussey had hit a deer and totaled his car. Anyhow, Pel said 'the poor guy's really in a bind. No insurance, out of work, kid on the way—really shit-out-of-luck'. Then he said, 'my advise to him would be to see your Dad. Kevin's the only person I know who would be willing to help him out'."

Maddie could picture the dialogue perfectly. Pel's advice might well have been her own to the unfortunate Mr. Bussey. "Well...did the guy talk to your Dad?"

"What do you think?"

"He did, didn't he?"

"Sure he did. To tell you the truth, I actually called him up and suggested he do so."

"You didn't?"

"I did. And I've done things like that before, too."

"Doesn't your Dad get mad?"

"Not usually. He can always say 'no'. And I don't send every down-and-outer over to Kevin's office."

"I hope not."

Pack laughed. "The question I raise is why, Maddie. Why would Dad help out some stranger? And the answer is really quite simple. He does what he does because he can.

"Now, a story within the larger story, if you'll let me ramble some more."

"I've got my hankie right here, Pack," she smiled. "I'm expecting there's a moral to your story."

Pack's eyes left hers for a long moment, as if locked into some remote memory, then returned. "Most of Dad's money was inherited from his father. I'm told that my Grampa Peter was a son-of-a-bitch by most accounts. A heavy drinker, manipulator, power-monger...some believed even a murderer. He gave my father up for adoption when Kevin was born and never saw him." Pack paused, "I take that back. Peter visited his son once—on Kevin's second birthday down in Duluth. Just once! Anyhow, when Peter Moran died. Under suspicious circumstances I might add, he left his fortune to Kevin."

Maddie's eyes widened but she held back her question—"A murderer?"

"Dad has always struggled with his legacy. Being an eighteen year old with that kind of wealth was a load to carry. Over the years he's given lots of it away. Yet, he would be the first to tell you that all that money hasn't bought him a friend in the world. In truth, more often than not, his money has been a curse. The *Moran curse*. Wealth has isolated him, and probably brought more misery to his life than happiness."

Maddie nodded at the insight.

"We talk a lot, Maddie—Dad and me. And you're right; we're both a lot alike in ways. After I had been back from Korea for a couple of years, I confided to my Dad that my life was empty—that sometimes I felt like a loner, like a leper people wanted to keep their distance from. I was really down at the time and feeling that I didn't have a true friend in the world."

Pack looked away from Maddie's eyes for a long moment. "And I didn't. Sometimes I still feel like I don't."

"You do too, Pack. Gosh, there's Rick, Peloquin and all the other cop guys you work with, softball buddies..."

"Nobody I'm close to, Maddie."

Maddie frowned without reply. Neither had mentioned Jerry.

"Anyhow, as I remember, Dad got kinda reflective when I told him. 'I understand your feelings, Son' he told me. 'We've got to make friends with ourselves, Pack. You must, just as I've had to'. You see, Maddie, Dad understood me exactly because at heart he's a loner, too. Always has been, I guess. He's got Gary Zench, Grampa Tony—and that's about it since Claude died."

Maddie shook her head in disbelief.

"And we're both brooders, too. Or, maybe overly self-absorbed is a better way to put it."

Pack squeezed Maddie's hand.

"Ouch! I'm feeling some of your tension my dear man." She

lifted his hand and gave it a soft kiss. "You're being too hard on yourself. And your Dad."

His smile was weak, he sighed. "Maybe you're right. We're decent enough guys, I guess."

"I'd say so. And I hope you know that you've got a friend. A damn good friend at that." Maddie felt closer to him at that moment than ever before. "And Kevin's got your Mom. I mean she and your father are like some ideal couple. Anyone can see that they're so much in love."

"Oh, they are that, for sure. Very much in love. And the very closest friends in the world. They understand each better than any two people I've ever known."

Maddie nodded without reply.

Pack laughed at a thought. "So, if Dad's got some flaws, what about my allegedly perfect Mom? Beautiful and talented Angela Marie Zoretek Moran. The all-together woman of Hibbing society."

Pack turned from his gaze on the gravel road ahead and cast sad eyes on Maddie. "Mom takes tranquilizers every day and spends a week at the Mayo Clinic every summer. She lives with the constant fear that something might trigger an episode; that's what she chooses to call her blackouts. She had a head injury when she was a teenager. Would you believe she had stolen her Dad's car and crashed it while running away from home?"

Maddie's jaw dropped. "You're not kidding, are you?"

"Not at all." A subtle brooding marked Pack's next words. "We got so much to learn about each other—our families...things shoved into our closets. Things we've kept hidden from others. Things that have shaped who we really are. Secret things."

Maddie began to sob again. "I know. We both do."

Pack bent over and kissed her. "Let's promise to open our closets, Maddie."

Maddie pulled him close. "I promise."

34/ EVERYBODY ARRIVES

"Where are they?" Angie was pacing the kitchen. Pack was never late and he'd said he be arriving a half-hour ago. Standing on her tiptoes at the kitchen window she saw Patrick's Ford coming up the driveway. As anxious as she was for her first glimpse of Maddie, she stepped away from the window and tried to busy herself at the stove.

When talking with Patrick earlier that morning, her son told her that Maddie was "kinda nervous about everything"—especially meeting his mother. "She has this crazy notion that you and Dad are like people out of some romantic story—like Lancelot and Guinevere, she said." Angie had laughed over Maddie's perception but well understood the apprehension of meeting the parents of your significant other for the first time.

At the side door, Pack encouraged Maddie, "Just relax, hon, they're all swell people. And you look gorgeous!" He gave another appraising look at her outfit—khaki slacks, and a green turtleneck under a beige cardigan sweater. "And your mascara's fine. Nobody will ever guess that you were crying, hon."

"Did you just call me 'hon'? Twice?" Maddie smiled, lifted on her toes and gave Pack a quick kiss on the cheek. "And, gorgeous, too?" Pack's words would make everything else that happened that day pale in comparison. "Well, let's meet the family."

From the first moment, Maddie was enthralled. Angela was delightful and gracious and warm. Giving her a hug was as natural as embracing an old friend. "I brought this, Mrs. Moran." Maddie had been up early baking her mother's recipe for peach cobbler. "I didn't want to come empty-handed."

"I simply love peach cobbler—what a wonderful contribution. And, Maddie...please, I'm Angie to all my friends. And Patrick's father is Kevin."

Maddie laughed, "Okay, Angie. And I've been told that when you're around, my...er, boyfriend...is called Patrick. I like that."

After introductions and compliments on Maddie's striking outfit, Angie offered coffee.

"Everything's pretty much finished in the kitchen, Maddie," Becca said. "Lets all go outside and join the others. Maribec wants you to meet her beloved grampa, Tony. And all of us can relax a bit before our other guests arrive."

Nearly an hour later, Rick Bourgoyne and Maury Loiselle arrived. Maddie's mother and Rick knew everybody there and mixed easily. Rick got immediate attention with his loud pronouncement, "My bachelor days are numbered!" Putting his arm over Maury's shoulder and kissing her fully on the lips, he continued, "This lovely woman is willing to have me for her husband. God help her."

Everybody laughed, congratulated, and offered their various toasts to the couple. "How romantic you are, Rick," Maury teased with an embarrassed smile. "I've agreed to marry a man of such profound expression!"

"Marry the boss and get a raise," Rick chided.

The news got the afternoon off to a marvelous beginning. Surrendering his brief center of attention, Rick slid a chair between his best friend, Marco, and Kevin Moran. Marco had brought a cooler of Hamms Beer and the men heartily toasted the groom-to-be. Tony offered his glass of milk to the clink of bottles.

Already, the separated groupings of men and women were beginning to define the get-together. Tony smiled to himself over the inevitable segregation. Maribec and her mom, Becca between the two of them, and Maury Loiselle with her chair turned in toward the other three women. Above the deeper male voices around him he could overhear Angie's compliments of Maury's sparkling diamond engagement ring, Maddie's casually modern hairdo, and Becca's new soft yellow sweater.

The men rehashed the Dodgers 13-8 victory over the rival Yankees in game two of the World Series (which held no interest for Marco), the football season (Hibbing's Bluejackets, Minnesota's Gophers, and the Green Bay Packers), golf and hunting. The typical male fare. What was conspicuously avoided, however, was any talk about the Zench matter. Everybody knew that Gary, Nora, and Naomi were soon to arrive.

Kevin broke the ice. "I don't have to tell any of you that the Zenches are going through absolute hell. As hard as this might be, I think we all should try not to go overboard in treating them with kid gloves. If they want to talk about Jerry, they will." Heads nodded at Kevin's suggestion,

Upstairs, Stevie and Bobby were jamming some melodic calypso—Harry Belafonte's Jamaica Farewell. Bobby was strumming his Silvertone and Stevie's fingers were sliding skillfully over the ivories of his spinet. "I like the rhythm, Stevie. Follow me now...I'm going to lead you on to something else—just follow, okay?" Bobby switched chords and began to wail, straining his voice to a high pitch; "Baby...my sweet baby—" as he picked up on the Mickey and Sylvia hit song.

Finishing several popular melodies, Steven pushed away from the piano. "What are we going to do this afternoon? What songs, I mean?"

"On the drive out, your uncle suggested we do some mellow stuff," Bobby said. Knowing that his friend played the saxophone, he suggested, "Maybe some Fats, some Ricky Nelson...a couple of Elvis songs—how about Heartbreak Hotel?"

Steven would have no trouble with any of his friend's suggestions. "D'ya wanna see the house, or go outside for a while?" he offered a diversion from remaining cooped up in his bedroom.

Bobby leaned his guitar against a nearby dresser, looking around as if for the first time. "They call your house 'the mansion' you know. The other kids at school, I mean. They even say it's spooked. They say that someone was killed inside a long time ago. Do you know anything about that?"

Steven did, but was reluctant to talk about it. "Kids say lots of things. Lots of it is just foolishness. Wanna have a little tour?"

Showing his friend around the house, Stevie got the impression that Bobby was awed by the elegance. "My dad had it moved out here from old Hibbing years ago. Belonged to his father."

"I'm gonna have a place like this someday," Bobby boasted. "But never in Hibbing. Maybe California."

In the kitchen, Stevie got them each a bottle of Coke. "Want to meet my parents and their friends outside?"

Bobby, uncomfortable in social situations with grown-ups shook his head. "Nah, we can do that later. Maybe when we do our music. Let's see what we can get on the radio."

Steven puzzled. "Only take a minute to say hello to the adults."

For a long moment Bobby said nothing, his eyes cast beyond his friend. "Any of them Jewish, Stevie?"

Steven sensed something he hadn't before. Maybe the key to Bobby's negative attitude about all things Hibbing was rooted in his perception of being Jewish. Maybe that was why he dreamed of getting as far away from this place as he could—whenever he could. Stevie had never made any distinctions between people, but perhaps most people did. Bobby's question still hung between them. "I don't think so," was all he could say.

Taking Stevie's elbow, Bobby pulled the taller boy away from the doorway out to the porch where the adults were congregated. "I don't like feeling awkward, Stevie. Let's just leave it at that. Okay? Anyhow, there's gotta be some 'top forty' on WEBC."

"Sure...but, I promised my dad we would include Naomi in what us kids were doing this afternoon." He wanted to remind his friend that Naomi was an even more conspicuous minority, but didn't. "I think she's bringing along a girlfriend of hers—do you know Echo...Echo Helstrom?"

Bobby nodded that he knew the girl. "Sure, why not?" He knew Echo better than he'd admit to his friend. Echo smoked and he had not dared to bring any cigarettes along with him.

The Zenches arrived after one o'clock. Gary wore his stress like part of his outfit. Nora was expectantly relaxed. Today was her first social outing in weeks and she desperately needed to be around people.

Naomi and her blond-haired friend found the boys listening to popular songs on the dual-speaker Zenith radio and joined them in the living room. After a few minutes, Bobby and Echo went outside "for a few minutes" leaving Stevie and Naomi to converse awkwardly about their favorite teachers, music, and various high school social cliques. Stevie liked the self-conscious teenager's perspectives on the aloofness of athletes and cheerleaders. "Sometimes it seems like the school belongs to them. And the 'meat line' on second floor—how embarrassing when I have to walk by those guys on the way to my locker."

Steven laughed, "I know what you mean." The cluster of boys, mostly seniors, were notorious oglers.

"Some girls love it and walk past the boys for half an hour before first hour classes."

During a lull, Naomi softly voiced the lyrics of Pat Boone's number one song Ain't That a Shame. Steven liked her voice, her perspectives on school, and was flattered when Naomi said that his uncle—Mr. Z—was one of the best teachers at Hibbing high. She carried the melody of Boone's song perfectly.

"I didn't do too well in his music class but it sure wasn't his fault. He was encouraging...and I do love music, but not playing an instrument—you know what I mean. He's Mr. Band."

"You're in choir, though—aren't you?"

"I love to sing."

Steven complimented, "I can tell. And you've got a great voice."

Naomi blushed, "Pat Boone's my favorite. But I like Elvis, too. I've got lots of his records at home. My mom isn't too crazy about that."

"Say, Bobby and me—and my uncle, too—we're going to play some music later this afternoon. Would you sing along with us, Naomi? Echo can join us if she wants to."

Naomi smiled widely for the first time in their conversation. "Sure. Why not—if you guys don't mind. What songs are you going to do."

The two of them talked music until Bobby and Echo returned, their breath smelling strongly of Dentyne. The four of them all agreed upon two songs for their little program, Elvis' Heartbreak Hotel, and Singing The Blues by Guy Mitchell. But they argued over two others. Bobby would agree to let Naomi do the Patty Page, Que Sera Sera, if he could do Be-Bop-A-Lula by Gene Vincent. Echo would accompany the group with Steven's tambourine. Steven wrote down the song selections and excused himself. "I'm going to run out and tell Uncle Marco what we've decided on. He can play anything."

33/ 'BLEST ARE THOSE WHO WEEP...'

From a patch of shade on the wide deck, Tony had been observing the dynamics of everything around him for nearly an hour. His thoughts focused on each person individually, apart from the context of the entire group.

Watching Becca was like falling in love all over again.

In Angela, he saw the striking beauty of his first love, Mary Samora.

Mary Rebecca had her mother's loveliness and spunk, her father's fortitude. But, he worried about her. And why didn't she have a date?

Maddie was beautifully radiant and seemed especially drawn to Angela. Yet her eyes kept Pack in constant connection.

Maury was pleasant but aloof. Too often she wore the frown of one with doubts.

Nora was easily the most animated among the women and spoke with her hands and words in marvelous coordination.

Within his own group, Kevin engaged Tony's contemplation more often than any of the others. As he mused, a smile danced lightly across his sharp features—if ever he were to write a novel, a figure like Kevin would be his central character. As Tony searched for a word—elegance came first to mind. No maestro in heaven might have orchestrated a better symphony than Kevin and Angela. Although each was compelling in their own right, they were ever so much more when together. Strength draws from strength, he concluded.

Pack. He often wished that had been more involved in his grandson's twenty-six year assent to manhood. Tony remembered Pack's athletic prowess more than other life experiences. Why was that? He caught the quick smile Pack shot across the porch to Maddie. It was a happy smile—the familiar smile of a man in love. He had seen that same smile on Kevin's face years before when Pack's father was courting Angie. A smile that generations will never change.

Rick Bourgoyne was a wordsmith with thoughtful views on every topic that arose. As the man tugged absently at his untrimmed beard or adjusted his glasses on the bridge of his narrow nose, Tony wondered what Maury found attractive. Goodness was the best answer.

Marco was a deceivingly insightful man, but a man of few words. Tony regarded his son lovingly. An introvert flourishing in a profession more natural for extroverts. A musician who was a master in his realm.

Gary Zench wore the face of a deeply troubled man. When he spoke, which had been seldom that afternoon, his tone was subdued. Tony puzzled at the close friendship between Kevin and Gary, a companionship that went back to the days of their youth. Smiling again to himself, he recalled the first question Pack had asked him only an hour before. "Tell me about the time Dad and Mr. Zench hopped a train from Duluth to Hibbing when they were kids." It was true, of course, and Tony acknowledged that their secret had never been divulged. Childhood friendships can have a bond of steel, Tony realized. So it had been with Gary and Kevin. Whatever the depths of Gary's pain on this day, Kevin was feeling the hurt nearly as much. On more than one occasion, Tony saw Kevin's reassuring hand patting Gary on the back—an "I'm always here" gesture.

It was Rick, not Kevin, who brought up the question. "What's the latest on your son, Gary?" The question was open-ended and sensitive to whatever Gary might deem appropriate.

Rather than fix his eyes on Rick, Gary looked first toward Kevin for a long moment, as if to find some acknowledgement—however subtle—to explain what had been happening. A meeting of eyes was a meeting of minds between them. Gary found a necessary confidence, "Despite what the police and local paper have said, Jerry is not in Minneapolis. I would bet my own life on that." Gary bit off the last sentence.

"I didn't think so," said Rick. "I know Jerry well enough to be certain he wouldn't go anywhere without letting you know."

Eyes downcast, Gary nodded without reply.

Everybody in the circle of men had thoughts of consolation to share, but somehow, no words were spoken for a long minute. A silence of respect.

In the strain of the moment, Rick realized that the few words he'd already spoken were sufficient. Any elaboration would be up to Gary or Kevin.

Kevin was not the elder in this group. He looked levelly at Tony, "What do you think, Dad?" He had already told both Tony and Rick about the evidence discovered at the Rosnau hunting shack the day before. Tony had been candid in telling Kevin that he believed Jerry Zench had been murdered. That belief weighed heavily on Kevin's thoughts.

"I agree with both of you," Tony's eyes moved from Gary to Rick. "Jerry didn't run away. I think by now we all know the prospects of finding him alive are bleak at best."

Forcing back his tears, Gary nodded.

Kevin spoke, "Pack and I are going down to Minneapolis tomorrow. We have an appointment with a private investigator that an old friend of mine has the highest respect for. And we have something to be examined by the State Crime Bureau. Gary has—"

Leaning forward in his chair, Gary finished what Kevin has started to say. "This morning Nora and I went to the clinic for blood type testing." He met Tony's eyes. "Becca has agreed to write down all the possible matches of Jerry's type from that information."

That revelation brought a long moment for all to contemplate.

Of the men, only Marco was in the dark about the rag which had been discovered. "Do you really think that this detective going can find Jerry down there, Kevin?"

Gary answered, "Kevin's heart is always in the right place, Marco. But, I think we both agree that searching the Negro neighborhoods down there would be a waste of valuable time. The Minneapolis police can do that if they want to."

Kevin nodded.

Pack wanted to talk about what the Crime Bureau might be able to do—but, chose against it. He and his father would have plenty of time to discuss forensic potentials on their trip to the Cities tomorrow.

Rick, who had opened the matter, would try to close it. "Something's going to break, Mr. Zench."

"That's our prayer, Rick. Something?" Gary shrugged.

Rick stood, "Maybe we should find our women...give them the pleasure of our company."

"I've got to get going on our steaks," Kevin said. "It's almost three."

Gary and Tony lingered on the porch as the others moved toward the kitchen. "I don't know you well, Mr. Zoretek," Gary said, "but I have great respect for you." He swallowed the lump in his throat and met the eyes of the taller man. "It was courageous of you to say what you did, sir."

The dull pain in Tony's chest had returned minutes ago, while Kevin was explaining his Twin Cities itinerary. His eyes held compassion, his voice sincerity as he said, "If prayers could find your son, he would be with us today. Gary, I was only being honest. Our conversation needed that."

Gary nodded, waiting long seconds before responding. "I had a very strange experience yesterday. For the first time in weeks, the feeling that I had lost my son gave me a sense of peace. The peace of resignation, I suppose. It's one thing to believe something in your head, and another to feel it in your heart."

Tony was struck by the sadness of the moment. He could see the welling of tears in the dark, hopeless eyes which had strayed beyond him, to something far distant. He fought back tears of his own and reached across the space between them for the large black hands of the tormented man. Gripping Gary's hands, he chokingly offered the only words of comfort his soul could provide, "Blest are those who weep...for they shall be consoled."

Gary knew the Beatitude well. "Sir, would you be kind enough to pray with me for a moment?"

~

On that sunny Saturday afternoon, twenty miles south of the Moran's gathering on Maple Hill, Leonard Rosnau felt the cold chill of fear. Approaching his hunting shack he saw fresh tire impressions in the sandy soil, then footprints leading to his cabin. A piece of two-by-four lumber lay below the side window. "Sonofabitch!"

Inside the structure, everything looked the same as he remembered from weeks ago. Whoever had been inside were not burglars. His mind raced. Had Carl been there? The boys—Tobin and Dahlberg? Who? Why? What were they looking for? What did they find?

Then it struck him like a stomach punch. Pack Moran!

34/ A SUNDAY BLIZZARD

The transition from bright and mild to dull and chilly was a sudden one. A Canadian front swept banks of ominous gray clouds across northern Minnesota darkening the early Sunday afternoon skies. Large, moist flakes of snow began to set a white blanked over the ground. In less than an hour, the texture of the snow began changing to lighter flakes that swirled in the rapidly cooling air. A storm was brewing.

Sitting on an overstuffed beige sofa near the living room window, Angie gazed upon the western slope of the Moran's Maple Hill property. The winds were shifting from the southwest to the north, bending the trees and stripping the last leaves from their naked branches. As minutes passed, the snowfall became thicker, obscuring her view of the lower reaches of the tawny meadowlands beyond the window.

Her thoughts were conflicted. Angie loved the paralysis of a blizzard more than any phenomenon in nature.

The wind's eerie howl rattling window panes and the wildly drifting snow inspired her creativity like nothing else in nature's handiwork. Her finest artworks were expressed in vividly imaged winter landscapes. Contrasting shades of white were an essence she had mastered on several celebrated canvas oil paintings.

But Kevin was not home this afternoon and the huge house held an empty feeling. She worried. Kevin and Patrick had left for Minneapolis more than two hours before. Both were sensible men, she reasoned, and if the weather became too hazardous, they would be careful not to take any foolish risks. Or, would they? Both were determined to resolve Jerry's disappearance and their meeting with a professional investigator was a critical link toward that end.

Angie tried to dispel her troubling thoughts and concentrate on the large sketch pad resting in her lap. It had been weeks since she had painted anything that spoke in clear voice to her artistic imagination. She willed an inspiration that might capture the bluster of the magical transformations occurring beyond her window.

Off to her right was a low picket fence she had been meaning to paint before the onset of winter. Her thoughts focused. As the howling wind intensified, the rapid accumulation of snow brushed itself into low curving drifts. Without looking at the pad, her instincts guided the charcoal pencil over the paper in precision strokes. From her visual sensations, through her mind's eye, down her arms, and into her delicate fingers—perceptions became feelings, and feelings became bold lines of expression. Lost in a warp of time she became one with the fury of nature's stormy bluster.

As the room darkened, her concentration lapsed. Looking down at her creation, Angie appraised the imagery on the page pinned to her thigh by the palm of her left hand. The abstract expression brought a smile of satisfaction. Maybe later she would go upstairs to her studio and begin transforming this sketch into a landscape portrait.

Thoughts of Kevin and Patrick, however, creased lines of worry on her forehead. Putting the tablet aside, she stood and walked to the window. A chilly draft deepened her apprehension of the moment. The temperature had plummeted dramatically in the lost space of time. An ache, at first only subtle, had moved from her lower back into her shoulders. The symptoms frightened her. "Don't stress yourself, Angela," she commanded. "They will be fine. Relax." Maybe a hot bath? Something soothing. Angela's greatest fear was a headache. It had been years, but—a headache could bring a blackout. She thought of calling Steven who was upstairs listening to his music. Turning away from the window, however, she regarded the sofa. A nap—yes, that was what she needed now.

As she slept, the afternoon faded into early evening and the storm outside raged in unabated fury. When she stirred awake, it was after five. The nap had left her feeling lethargic rather than rested. Although it was dinnertime, her appetite seemed dulled from her deep, fitful sleep. She heard the clank of a milk bottle—Steven must be rustling through the refrigerator in the kitchen. Bless his heart, he had allowed his mother to sleep. As she got up from the sofa to warm some leftovers from yesterday's cookout for her son...the headache split across her temples with blinding swiftness.

~

Pack fought to keep the car on the highway through nearly whiteout conditions. Fortunately there was a vague glimmer of taillights from a semi to follow between Cloquet and Moose Lake. But the truck pulled off the highway there. The storm had raged for nearly three hours and evidenced no signs of letting up. "We're going to have to sit this one out, Dad. It's blind driving now, guesswork more than anything. We can't risk going beyond Hinckley."

"No argument from me. I'll try to call Prentice in Minneapolis and let him know we can't make it there tonight. Then I'll let your mom know we're going to be stranded here for a while."

Pack nodded absently, eyes focused on the dark border of trees to his right. Visibility, limited to no more than a few feet in front of the car, seemed improved with the headlamps off. Yet the mesmerizing snow was making him drowsy. "Another ten or fifteen miles and we'll be in Hinckley. We could both use some coffee."

"I can hardly keep my eyes open. You must be a nervous wreck by now," Kevin said.

Within half an hour, the red neon of Tobies Restaurant shown dimly through the sheet of snow. Pack pulled off to the side of the highway well beyond the restaurant. The string of marooned cars and trucks stretched for blocks in both directions.

Tobies was packed with stranded travelers, many waiting their turn at the long, horse-shoed counter. Under the circumstances, however, everybody appeared in boisterous spirits. The unexpected Sunday blizzard rendered all of them equally discomforted. Sympathetic to their plight, the Tobies owner offered everybody whatever floor space they could find to lay out blankets and sleep for the night. "Nobody's going anywhere tonight, and we've got enough food and coffee for a few days."

A grizzled-looking trucker laughed, "A few days? Might be more like a week. I ain't never seen worse conditions around Pine City in twenty years. Highway 61 is buried all the way down to the Cities."

Pack bought coffee and found Kevin waiting his turn behind a line of people at the wall phone. "We're number eight for a place at the counter," he said.

"And about the same for a place at the phone."

Steven answered. "Mom's had one of those headaches, Dad!" The boy had found his mother passed out on the living room floor. "I called Becca right away. She's going to try to get here if she can—but, it's really been storming up here, Dad."

"What? Tell me, Steven...is she okay?" Kevin tried to keep panic out of his voice. Another blackout was his greatest fear. Years before Angie had lapsed into an amnesia condition that lasted for months.

"She's awake right now. I broke one of those ammonia things like she told me to do if this ever happened."

"Good thinking, son. Can she talk to me right now?"

Angie took the phone. "Are you okay, Kevin? I've been worried sick." The unsteady edge to her voice betrayed her unsettled condition of the moment.

"We're fine. It's you I'm worried about, sweetheart. What happened?"

She explained briefly. "I'm going to be just fine—I can remember everything. I'm going to call Becca this minute and tell her not to even attempt to drive in this storm. It's just too dangerous."

"I'd better not tie up the phone then. Just take it easy, sweetheart. I'll call again later. We're going to be stuck here for quite a while, I'm afraid." Kevin briefly described their circumstance. "Let me talk to Steven for just a moment, dear. I love you." Kevin instructed his son to keep a close eye on his mother and gave him the Tobies phone number in case of any emergency. "Write it down on the pad by the phone."

The storm's fury continued unabated throughout the night leaving central Minnesota under an eighteen-inch blanket of drifted snow. Monday travel would be impossible. Even the highway department's snow removal equipment had been socked in. Like all the other stranded motorists, Kevin and Pack contemplated changes in their plans. Their time in Minneapolis would be abbreviated.

35/ THE STAIRWAY TO HEAVEN

Tony Zoretek hadn't slept well again that night. Nausea, more than the howling winds, kept him awake. Slipping out of bed careful not to rouse Becca, he found his long underwear, a pair of corduroy trousers, and a wool sweater. Quietly he went downstairs to appraise the aftermath of the season's first major snowstorm.

A visage of the world outside, dressed in her pristine coat of white tranquility, struck Tony's tired eyes. From the living room window he pondered the beauty. An exhortation of two voices crossed Tony's placid thoughts of the moment. One impelled him to venture out into the fresh air and shovel the front walkway; the other cautioned against risking the exertion.

For countless days, Tony's inner voices had been conflicted: Becca's urgings to see a doctor and his resistance to interfere with some arcane force he could neither define nor talk about. He had struggled with the essence of honesty—to share his thoughts or to keep them private. All he might say was that there was a summons of some kind, a powerful desire to refocus his priorities, his purpose. For long hours he had contemplated the most sublime meanings of life, both ethereal and eternal. His clearest understanding was that this life now held little more than a temporal fascination for him.

Tony found his parka on a hanger in the far corner of the foyer closet and his lined choppers on the shelf above.

Stepping outside, he smiled as the fresh morning breeze stung his face. Everything was so incredibly white that it blinded his eyes for a moment. Sucking in the chill he felt the pang bolt through his chest, gripping like a vice—then, suddenly relaxing its clutch before seizing again. He could feel himself falling backwards, ever so peacefully, into the soft fluff of snow beside the front steps where he had been standing. Looking upward, a marvelous tunnel of light rose into the marvelous blue of an endless sky. The warmth was overwhelming—the surreal glow incomprehensibly alluring.

He saw her first. Her arms open wide, hands reaching out to him, her radiant blue eyes smiling...Yes, there was no doubt, it had been her voice he had heard only moments before. Somehow, he'd known that before stepping outside—known that Mary was waiting for him. Rising like a splendid staircase into a majestic corridor he could see his spent body lying in the snow as he lingered in the blinding light.

And Becca's face was in the upstairs window of the vanishing house...tears in her eyes, horror masking her lovely face! Tony wished he could tell her of the marvelous peace. Tell her that he loved her one more time. Tell her that he would be there for her when...And, he wanted to say goodbye to his children, too. But there was no time for that anymore. He had been called on this pristine morning. Many of his loved ones were waiting for him now; beckoning him up the glowing staircase.

Tony felt the youthful lightness of his steps as he hurried to embrace her. The years since he last held her were but moments. And there were all the others...his brother Rudy, his Slovenian parents, Father Foley, Steven, Senia, and Claude—all his friends were waiting in line behind her.

Looking down to where he had been only moments before, his former life slowly trailed off like a pleasant dream.. All the things he so deeply loved and cherished seemed strangely insignificant from this celestial perspective. The power at the top of the stairway so compelled him that any desire to go back was lost in the new hope for everlasting happiness.

He took her hand and let her lead him home.

~

Angie's call to Hinckley caught Kevin as he and Pack were heading out of Tobies to begin shoveling the Cadillac from a drifted ridge of snow.

"Is there a Mr. Moran here?" bellowed a voice from behind the counter of the busy restaurant. "A call for Kevin Moran!"

Something was wrong! Kevin knew it before he clutched the phone. His first thought was of Angie. Another headache? Or, Becca. Had she gotten into trouble driving out to Maple Hill? God, what would he be able to do? All the roads north and south were closed to traffic.

Pack could read the grief on his father's face as Kevin listened to the person on the other end of the line. "No!...My, God, No!" He saw tears welling in his father's eyes. "I'm so sorry, Angie." Kevin's voice strained. "We'll get back as soon as we can."

Pack moved closer to his father and heard the wail of his mother's far away voice.

It was late Monday night before Kevin was able to get onto highway 61 north toward Duluth. Earlier that day, Kevin and Pack had argued. His son was insistent on taking a Greyhound to Minneapolis—Kevin wanted him to return home. "Dad, for God's sake, let me take care of the business we started out to get done. We promised the Zenches."

Kevin believed that his son had a greater responsibility to his family. "Your mother will need you there."

Disagreements between two men who respected each other without reservation, were so rare that each struggled with what was the right thing to do. Ultimately, the father yielded to the son. Pack would keep the appointment with Prentice Garvey and Damon Porter. After delivering the evidence and discussing the case, he would catch the first bus back to Hibbing the following day.

"You'll be in my prayers, son. Give my best to Prentice..." he smiled an afterthought. "And have no doubts that you're doing the right thing, Pack."

Embracing his father, he said..."Give both Mom and Becca a hug for me...and, tell them how much I loved..."

36/ EDITORIAL COMMENTS

It was nearly three in the morning when Kevin arrived in Hibbing. Having phoned Angela from Duluth around midnight, he went directly to the Zoretek house.

"Thank God you're home safely," Angela clung to her husband in the doorway, sobbed into his wool coat. For a long moment nothing was said. Massaging his wife's shoulders, Kevin could feel Angela's tension, wished he could take it upon himself. Kissing her silky hair and inhaling it's freshly-washed scent, he whispered 'I love you' and 'I'm sorry' over and over.

Angela released her grip, took Kevin's hands in hers, met his eyes, "Becca's upstairs...she's not taking this very well, I'm afraid. Maybe you could—"

"I'll do my best, sweetheart. I'm pretty broken up myself." Fighting his own emotion, Kevin pulled her close—hoping she would not see his tears. "How are you, my love? I've worried so."

"Tired. Very tired. But..." she choked, "I'm making it, Kevin. Now that you're here I'll find the strength I've needed. All of us will."

Kevin took a moment to ask about Maribec and Steven. "Patrick sends his..." He explained how hard it was for Pack to stay back. "Well, I'd better go up and visit with Becca. You take a nap—we can talk more later." He kissed her fully on the lips, "Please. You've got to rest. If anything happened to you, Angie..." he let the painful thought drop.

~

Pack stepped off the Greyhound and found both Prentice Garvey and detective Porter awaiting his arrival. Both men had talked with Kevin and learned of the family emergency that had changed their plans. Although it was already nearly nine o'clock, both men wanted to talk as much as possible about the case before Pack caught the early morning bus back to Hibbing.

Pack was impressed with Garvey and Porter—and they with him. After condolences and small talk about the storm, the three men walked down the block to a café away from the busy terminal. The University professor looked exactly as Pack had pictured him from his father's description. Garvey was a slight, balding, and neatly dressed Negro man with an incredibly warm smile. Pack could almost imagine a kindred spirit between Prentice and Gary Zench—a link that transcended race.

"I can certainly see your father in you," Garvey said. "He was an outstanding student and an even finer young man. And, despite all the miles and years between the two of us, we still manage to keep in touch with each other."

Pack nodded, returning the man's congenial smile.

Inside the café they found a corner booth and ordered coffee. Porter spoke for the first time since leaving the terminal. "I've made several phone inquiries in the northeast neighborhoods of Minneapolis over the past few days. Nobody's heard of your friend, Jerry. I'm sorry but not surprised." Porter, probably in his late forties, was taller than Pack, wide-shouldered, and thick around the middle. His eyes were deep-set under thick brows, his complexion ruddy. He frowned, "But we've got the word out on the street." Turning from Pack to Prentice, Porter said, "I'll be frank. I believe that my time will be better spent up in Pack's neck of the woods. From what Kevin has already told me, there are some people and places to check out in the Hibbing area."

"I'm glad to hear that, Mr. Porter," Pack's sighed his relief. "I had hoped you'd want to focus on things up there. We need some help."

"Your dad, in typical lawyer fashion, has filled us both in on just about everything we wanted to know, Pack. But you can give us more details, I'm sure. I don't have to tell you that your father has great confidence in you."

Porter flipped out his notepad, flipped some pages, set it on the table. "I've got some questions about the various hate notes, the banquet episode, and, most importantly, about this cop Rosnau and what you fellas found at the hunting shack. You've got the evidence with you?"

Pack reached into his jacket pocket and took out the rag which was in a cellophane wrapping. "Dad said that you've already made arrangements to have the Crime Bureau's lab run some tests." He handed Porter a card with blood type information. "These are from the tests that Mr. and Mrs. Zench had done last Saturday."

In a sober voice, Porter said, "I don't want to hold out any false optimism. Blood-typing will only give us some broad parameters and I have serious doubt that we'll be able to lift any prints from the cloth."

The three men talked for nearly an hour. Porter suggested that he might be up in Hibbing by early next week. "Your family has more important things to deal with right now."

Pack nodded without reply.

"I'll be working with the crime lab people, running some profiles, and figuring out how to approach things. This snow cover's not going to make our task up there any easier. And Mr. Garvey will keep in touch with our contacts in the Negro community down here."

While listening to the detective, and answering his myriad of questions, Pack became increasingly impressed with the detective who's large hands made the coffee cup appear to be no larger than a shot glass. Porter was intelligent, his physical presence intimidating.

"As I said, Pack, I doubt if we're going to find much in the way of viable evidence. We're going to have to break somebody down—

that's all there is to it." He smiled confidently, "And I'm pretty damn good at that."

The men parted company about midnight. Pack declined an invitation to stay overnight at Professor Garvey's house. "I've got an early bus and Dad's already called in reservations at the Palace."

Pack made his way to a hotel on Hennepin Avenue only blocks from the bus station. The Minneapolis main drag of theaters, cafes and bars was a dynamic lit in colorful neon and alive with late-nighters of every description. Passing a striptease club, Pack declined a "great time upstairs" proposition from a busty redhead, contributed some change "for a cup of coffee" to a soliciting wino, and resisted the temptation to have a stiff drink before calling it a day. The big city was not the least bit appealing to him.

A Minneapolis squad car cruised slowly down the street and the cop at the passenger window eyed Pack suspiciously—probably a routine practice with any new face on the city street. Head down and collar up against the tunneling wind, he ignored the curious stare and continued walking to the blinking Palace neon at the end of the block.

~

There were days when Neal Beamons felt washed-up as a journalist. This cloud-shrouded Wednesday was one of them.

The *Hibbing Daily Tribune* reporter had bounced around newsrooms for years—a career that always took him one notch down from where he had been before. From St. Paul to St. Cloud and from Winona to Hibbing. That Beamons was a gifted writer none of his former employers would dispute, but his alcoholism tripped him up at every turn in the road. Most days he could make it with a vodka-coffee in the morning, a vodka-coke with his sandwich at lunch, and a stolen pull on the bottle hidden in his bottom desk drawer sometime during the late afternoon. He hated the office and spent much of his workday drinking black coffee, watching the tedious sweep of the clock, and trying to look preoccupied. The local stories he was routinely assigned each day came easily, his weekly 'Around Town' column could be composed and edited in a matter of a couple of hours on Tuesday mornings—but, every Wednesday he was responsible for the Tribune's editorial. Neal Beamons sat in his corner cubicle staring at the blank white sheet in his Underwood typewriter.

On his desk was a notepad opened to the scrawled lines he had jotted down while talking with Lieutenant Rosnau days before. The Zench disappearance story was still highly newsworthy, and today Beamons had something that might boil the kettle a bit. The journalist fingered the keys and watched as his first few words began to line themselves in a black row across the page...

> *Shame on our local school officials. As our beleaguered police department has struggled to uncover leads in the Jerry Zench disappearance case for the past month, it seems that our school superintendent has been sitting on potentially vital information. The Tribune has learned through an unnamed, but impeccable source, close to the investigation that one of our schoolteachers might have been among the last people to have had contact with the missing young man.*

Beamons looked over the first paragraph. Erasing on the paten, he penciled in a few word changes—dropping potentially, and changing impeccable to 'a highly placed' source. This editorial would put him out on the proverbial limb. Hibbingites cherished the institution of education nearly as much as they did family and church. Any allegations that might cast aspersions on the integrity of her schools were dangerous business. Both Chief Lawrence and Rosnau, he was certain, would have to deny that they were the 'unnamed source' of his editorial reference. But, school officials would be hard-pressed to disclaim his contention that they had not acted in an appropriate manner. When his editorial was published, Beamons was certain that he'd be contacted by Mitchell and Slattery at the school. Maybe, just maybe, he had a dynamite follow-up story in the making. Maybe he could get some names. Every journalist lived for that one story—that prize-winning kind of story.

Carefully crafting the remainder of his article, Beamons suggested that everybody in the community had a civic responsibility to cooperate with the police. His rough draft concluded with...

> *We cannot handcuff those commendable officers who serve and protect us by withholding information—any information—that might open a window and bring some fresh air into an otherwise stale police investigation. All of us deserve to know the identity of this teacher and what, if anything, might have been that faculty member's connection with the missing man.*

37/ "TELL MADDIE I LOVE HER."

Pack would have nearly ten hours to think about things on the two-hundred mile Greyhound trip north from Minneapolis to Hibbing. Lots of time to think, and lots of things to think about. Grampa Tony was dead. He thought about that harsh reality more than anything else for the first few hours. Mingled with his memories were thoughts of how his family—especially Mom—was coping with the loss of their beloved patriarch. Such a good man, and strong, devoted, wise...so like his own father in every way.

His father once told him that life was like a river making it's way to the sea. Pack pondered the insight for long minutes. Perhaps Tony's life was more like a boat on that river, carrying all of his loved ones to places along the way—allowing each to get off where they needed to land and develop roots of their own. Becca had been his last passenger, so now his empty boat could sail on to its promised harbor. His analogy gave him a measure of solace. Yet, the vessel that had been Tony Zoretek would be painfully missed by all.

Pack thought about death in ways he never had before—even more than he had during his two years in Korea, when his own life was often at risk. Up until now, his Uncle Rudy had been the closest person in his life to have died. He remembered how much he had cried at that time and wondered why there were no tears now. Perhaps feelings were linked to how one died, or maybe it was more about the number of years a person had been given before life was taken away. Rudy was too young, too full of promise—Tony's years, on the other hand, had been full and richly blessed.

His introspection with death led inevitably to his friend, Jerry. Pack no longer had any doubts. Jerry was dead. He could perceive that reality at two levels—in his head, and in his gut. And, it was the gut level stuff that Pack trusted most.

Pack gazed out the window at the white countryside. His thoughts took him to Damon Porter. "I'll be working more closely with you than anybody else," the detective had told him the night before. "We've gotta pin down motive, Pack." Porter had said. "Then we find the murderer. One way or another, we're going to get to the bottom of it." Porter had said murderer—not kidnapper!

A fellow traveler intruded on his thoughts, wanting to talk about the economy of traveling by bus—rather than driving a personal vehicle. He was a salesman whose driver's license had been suspended for a series of speeding tickets. "Heard somewhere that this whole Greyhound operation started up in Hibbing years ago. Any truth to that?"

Pack was familiar with the history and shared the story of a man called 'Bus Andy' and the early days of what eventually became the Greyhound business. "Probably that and the Hull-Rust Mine are Hibbing's most notable claims to fame. And, our high school." Pack engaged the stranger for fifteen minutes, then offered him his copy of the morning paper. The salesman promptly screwed up the crossword puzzle Pack had been saving for later in the trip.

A pair of does were chewing at tufts of alfalfa in a wide clearing between stands of poplar and birch. He wondered if they would make it through the coming dear hunting season and hoped they would. The passing countryside became as blurred as his focus. On the window's film of vapor, Pack traced the name Maddie across the glass. He smiled to himself. Regardless of where his thoughts wandered, they always came back to Maddie. He was hopelessly in love and happy to embrace that reality.

At the coffee stop in Pine City, Pack called home. Nobody answered. Mom and Dad must be at Becca's. Steven would be in school. He considered trying Becca's number but decided against it. He rather give his condolences in person later that night.

More than anybody he had wanted to talk with Maddie, but she would be teaching her first graders and Pack didn't want to interrupt her class. He remembered how much he adored his own first grade teacher, Miss Devaney. Smiling to himself, he recalled that his former teacher was a striking blond—just like Maddie. How the boys in Miss Loiselle's class must enjoy coming to school every day.

At the Duluth terminal there was a half-hour layover before the bus continued on to the string of Iron Range Cities—from Eveleth and Gilbert to Virginia; then stops in Mt. Iron, Buhl, and Chisholm before finally stopping in Hibbing. It was nearly four o'clock now and Maddie should be home from school.

Maury Loiselle answered the phone. "She's not home yet, Pack. Must be something going on at school because she's usually home by four."

"I've got to hurry, Maury, there's a line forming behind me. Will you ask Maddie to pick me up at the depot...around seven, I think?" He paused a moment before surrendering the phone. "And tell her..." Pack considered two options to complete the thought—'miss her' or 'love her'? "And tell Maddie I love her!"

~

After school, Maddie stopped by the Cobb Cook grocery store, a block down from her school, to pick up a few items for supper. It was her turn to prepare dinner and Rick would probably be joining them. Rick liked pork chops. After the meat counter, she picked out some baking potatoes, and a head of lettuce from produce, and found a large bottle of applesauce on a nearby shelf. After paying at the register, Maddie had an afterthought and grabbed a copy of the Hibbing Daily Tribune from the rack. She slid a dime toward the clerk and tucked the newspaper under her arm.

While her car heater warmed up, Maddie scanned past the front-page election campaign stories (Ike was in Pittsburgh blasting the Democrats' position on ending the draft while Adlai called for a halt to H-bomb testing while stumping in Seattle), and the Yankee's World Series triumph, to the editorial page. Maddie enjoyed figuring out the clever Jimmy Hatlo political cartoon 'They'll Do It Every Time'. Today, the Royal Order of Loons was meeting to discuss nominating a guy named Vermin Sneaker to some committee. She laughed to herself over the men's dialogue, but didn't quite get the gist of the issue they were discussing.

Before closing the paper and shifting her car into reverse, Maddie's eye caught the Beamons article along the left side of the Editorial page. *'Local teacher connected to Zench disappearance.'*

Maddie's jaw dropped..."Oh my God!" Tears welled in her eyes as she read down the column in stunned disbelief. Where did this information come from? Why—after all this time? What would she do? Her mind raced...how long before her name made the paper? Beamons allegations would surely give rise to a flurry of questions. Before too long, Maddie was certain, her reputation would be ruined!

Spinning her tires on the icy snow pack, Maddie backed out from the building, shifted, gunned the engine, and turned a sharp left onto First Avenue. She didn't see the pickup truck traveling north. The jarring impact flung her forward, crushing her chest against the steering wheel. "Oh, my God!" Maddie felt her Nash slide into the snow bank. Rubbing at her reddened eyes with the sleeve of her coat, she tried to collect her thoughts. "My God..." Maddie glanced into the rear view mirror, saw the man getting out of his truck. Then, slouching behind the wheel, she began to sob uncontrollably.

"What an' hell ya doin', lady. Are ya blind or somthin?"

The question at her foggy window shook her back to reality. Cranking the window she choked an apology. "I'm so sorry...I just didn't..."

"I'll say ya didn't. Ya pulled right out in fronta me." The heavyset man with wool cap pulled down over his ears, gestured for the traffic behind them to pass. "I couldn't stop."'

"It was my fault, sir. I know that."

Seeing her stream of tears, the man softened his tone, "Are ya hurt, Miss?"

"No, I'm fine, I think." Maddie opened her car door, stepped outside to look at the damages. "How about you?"

"Nothin' more than my everday aches and pains." He smiled at the distraught woman. "Let's take a look." Standing off to the curb side of the avenue, the two of them appraised the situation. "I guess it's ain't too bad. Yer car's banged up a little...my truck looks okay ta me."

Maddie reached into her handbag for her billfold and drivers license. "I'm Maddie, Madeline, Loiselle, sir." She handed the man her plastic card. "My insurance is with Mr. Matetich. Should we call the police?"

"Erickson. Herbert, or just Bert." He glanced at the license, offering his hand. "Sorry I snapped at ya like I did, Miss. Ya jus scared the hell outta me when ya pulled out like ya did."

The two of them heard the siren before they saw the flashing lights.

A Hibbing police squad car pulled in behind the two vehicles and a tall officer approached. Lieutenant Rosnau had been on his way to the station to close out his day shift when he noticed the slowed traffic flow. Just ahead he spotted the accident scene across from the corner grocery story. "What have we got here?" Rosnau mumbled to himself. From the looks of things, however, what had happened seemed obvious.

As he approached, the police officer recognized Bert Erickson standing by his Dodge pickup truck. "Looks like you hit the Nash, Bert. Were you driving a little too fast for the conditions?"

"No, officer, it was my fault. Entirely, my fault. I pulled out in front of Mr. Erickson," the blond woman said apologetically. "He wasn't doing anything wrong at all."

Rosnau could see that neither vehicle had sustained much damage but presented a problem blocking traffic. "Nobody's hurt?"

Maddie and Herbert Erickson both assured the lieutenant that they were fine.

"Bert, give me a hand here. We'll push this Nash out of the bank—then I'd like both of you to drive over there for a few minutes," Rosnau gestured toward the service road bordering the Greenhaven neighborhood to his right. "I'll just get some information for an accident report and we can all be on our way. It's cold out here."

On the side street out of the traffic flow, Rosnau put his foot on the pickup's bumper while resting his clipboard on his knee. He quickly scribbled plate numbers and other descriptive information on the yellow form and walked around the two idling vehicles. "Not much damage that I can see, but we gotta do the paperwork, you know. What's your name, Miss? I'll need to see your license. Yours, too, Bert."

Rosnau's eyes widened. "Madeline Loiselle." Appraising the attractive woman, he made an immediate connection. Pack Moran's girlfriend. Rosnau chose not to comment on his recognition of the name and continued jotting down the required information. "You'll want to get a copy of this report at the station tomorrow. For your insurance, Miss Loiselle." Then taking his stare from the blond woman, he offered a faint smile toward Herbert, "You, too, Bert. But from what I can see you've only got a little bumper dent."

Circling the two vehicles one last time, Rosnau tucked the clipboard under his arm while rubbing his hands together. "Let's call it a day. I've got all I need here...and I think we're all freezing our as—our behind off out here."

"Thanks officer, you've been most helpful." Maddie forced a smile. "I don't think I got your name."

"Rosnau, Miss. Lieutenant Leonard Rosnau."

38/ A LIFE IN CRISIS

Rick and Maury were having coffee at the kitchen table; an open copy of the *Tribune* with Beamons' editorial between them.

"What are we going to tell her about this, Rick?"

Rick shook his head, "I don't know. Maybe she's already—"

The both heard the car door outside. "We'll know in a minute," Rick said.

Maddie virtually burst into the kitchen, slamming the door on a cold draft following her across the linoleum floor. "Here's supper, but you'll have to fix it yourselves." She dumped the grocery bag on the counter, "Have you seen our rag-ass Hibbing paper yet? Let me tell you both, I'm getting out of this place—for good!"

Maury stood, nodded, stepped toward her daughter, "We were just talking about it, Maddie. The innuendos are slanderous!"

"The guy's a fucking jerk, Maddie. I called Hitchcock at the *Trib* before coming over. He's a damned Pilate. Your mom's going to call Jack Fena tonight." Rick put an arm around Maddie's shoulder. "We put this crap to bed once before and we'll damn well do it again." He tried to smile, "Don't let this bullshit get you down."

Maddie pushed herself away from Rick's consolation. "It's my reputation he's messing with, not yours. 'Get me down'?—his sleaze is devastating! Right out there for every parent in Hibbing to see.

You don't think there will be a hundred phone calls wanting to know who the teacher is?"

Tearful, Maury didn't know how to respond to her daughter's distress. Maddie was right about the community reaction.

"I'm not going through this again. That's final! I'm getting out of this town."

"Let's call Fena right now, Maddie. And Rudy Perpich," Maury said.

"You can call whoever you want to. I'm packing my suitcase tonight."

"Maddie, be reasonable. This cheap shot won't go any further—I can promise you that. The Trib doesn't want any lawsuits," Rick assured.

"I'm sorry. Sorry I snapped at you, Rick. But it's too late. I've already made up my mind. I'm quitting my job and getting away from here as soon as I can."

Looking to Maury for support, Rick shrugged his shoulders.

"Oh, just to put some frosting on my shitty cake, I piled up my car on the way home from school. Pulled right out in front of a guy."

"You what?"

"Just a fender-bender—nobody was hurt." Maddie would not tell her mother about the soreness behind her neck. "After seeing that article I was an emotional wreck, just pulled out on First Avenue without even looking. Stupid—stupid me!"

Maddie began to sob. Maury took her daughter into her arms. "There, there...please try to calm down, sweetheart. Let me fix you a drink, we can figure this thing out."

"Sorry, Mom. I've done enough figuring out in the past half-hour. Pack's coming back tonight..." The thought of Pack put her emotions in turmoil again. If only he were here right now.

Maddie had not taken off her coat. "Sorry about dinner. See you both later. I'm going over to Maribec's for a while. Cry in my beer." She turned toward the door.

"Oh...Pack called just a few minutes ago. He's getting back about seven and wants you to meet him at the bus depot. And he..."

Maddie stopped, turned toward her mother, "Mom, I don't think our relationship is going to survive this mess. I don't know if I can dump all this on him—especially now, with his grampa's death...and being on the road all day."

"I think you can. He's the best thing in your life right now and you know it. You can't just shut him out, Maddie."

"Seven? Okay." Maddie glanced at the kitchen wall clock. It was after five. Regarding Maury and Rick standing there watching, she felt remorse over her juvenile tantrum. Stepping toward Maury, she buried her face on her mother's shoulder. "I'm sorry, Mom." Raising her left arm, "You too, Rick. I love you both."

As the three of them embraced, Maury said, "Pack said something else when he called, honey. He wanted me to tell you that he loved you."

~

Sitting on the living room floor, Maribec regarded her photo album and an assortment of pictures. After returning from Becca's crowded house a short time before, her emotions were drained. "Why couldn't they have buried you yesterday and gotten this whole thing over with," she said to the empty room as she held a favorite photo of her beloved grampa at arms length. She had never experienced a loss like this—someone so dear to her heart. And the prolonged arrangements process was becoming almost intolerable. How would Becca keep her sanity? And, her parents? Angela hadn't slept for two days. The wake at Dougherty's would be tomorrow night, the funeral the following morning.

She nibbled on some Ritz crackers along with slices of Colby cheese as she cropped some weekend pictures developed the night before. The one that riveted her attention at the moment was of Grampa Tony musing in the porch lawn chair at Maple Hill. She tried to read his thoughts. Grampa's face held a trace of smile.

Obviously, something had amused him at the moment. "I'll always love you, Grampa...your warmth, your gentleness, your wisdom. I wish I'd told you how very much you meant to me...before...but—I think you knew. Didn't you? I didn't have to put words to my feelings, did I? You could always sense how much..." Maribec choked on her emotion. "How much I loved you." Kissing the photograph, she held it to her breast and cried. She vaguely remembered Becca telling her that Tony had a smile on his face when she first saw him lying in the fresh snow that morning. "He was totally at peace with his world," she had said. Maribec could understand that peace. Grampa had walked the road of life with such dignity and grace. He was prepared for a new life, free from the grief of mortals.

The knock on her door startled her from the reverie of the moment. Rubbing away her tears with a tissue, she tried to get up from the floor. Her legs had fallen asleep and the numb tingle would not allow her to lift herself from the floor. "Come in," she shouted. "I'm in the living room."

Maddie could see that she was not the only hurting person in the world when she entered the room strewn with photos, clippings, discarded tissue, and cracker crumbs. A bottle of wine rested in the midst of Maribec's clutter. Before she could say a word, Maribec said, "Grab a glass in the kitchen cupboard. I'm having wine with my tears."

Maddie's eyes, like those of her friend, were red. Seeing the photo of Maribec's grandfather resting on her lap, Maddie broke into another crying jag. "I'm so sorry for you. I always get so damn self-centered with my problems that I forget..."

"Just grab a glass, Maddie. No apologies necessary. You know what's on my mind—what's going on with you?"

The two women talked until nearly seven o'clock and Maddie was no better off than when she first arrived. "Part of me can't wait to see Pack. God, Maribec, I've missed him. But..." she paused in her thought. "another part just dreads putting all my crap on the table. He's had a hell of a couple days as it is—-and, he hasn't even had a chance to visit with family yet. That's going to be hard enough for him. What should I do, Maribec? My head's spinning. I love him and I need to share what's happened."

"Talk to him, Maddie. When you love someone it's not like dumping—you're having a crisis right now. If you don't know it already, you are the most important person in Pack's life. Get that through your thick skull, girl! If I know my brother, he's already at peace with Grampa's passing. He's better at getting his thoughts straight than anyone else in our family. Always been that way, I guess. Pack's a pretty deep guy."

Maddie pictured Pack traveling the long trip from the Cities cooped up on a bus with so much time to think things out. Maribec was probably right. He was an introspective man—a deep thinker. "But maybe I shouldn't say anything about my decision to get out of Hibbing until after the funeral. What do you think?"

"Put it all out there for him. He can handle whatever you've got to give him. Somehow, I wouldn't be at all surprised if he decides to go with you," Maribec offered with a smile. "He's impulsive, just like you."

39/ *"ALWAYS LISTEN TO YOUR HEART..."*

After making his afternoon rounds about Hibbing, moving in a pre-determined pattern from one business to another, Dewey Bartz often stopped by the police station to meet up with his friend, Johnny Beck. Beck was a slow-minded custodian at city hall, and usually finished with his routine chores by four o'clock. Often the two men would walk over to the Sportsmen's Café for a bowl of soup and crackers after 'Beck' punched his time card. Their meal was always 'special priced' at twenty-five cents, and if Louise was waitressing, the two men usually got a sandwich on the side.

Whenever Dewey lingered on the second floor of police headquarters, few employees gave him any more notice than a casual "Hi Sweep." (At the department, everyone called him Sweep.) His presence wasn't much different than any other fixture in the office environment.

Dewey waited in the hallway where he would meet Beck. Realizing that he was a few minutes early, Dewey leaned against the wall near a water cooler just feet away from a half-open doorway. He hummed a simple tune to himself. Inside the office he could recognize the voice of the Lieutenant talking on the telephone. Rosnau was talking in hushed tones.

Dewey heard: "Should'a dumped him in the lake like we planned."

"Hi, Sweep." Officer Leland Krause said in passing. "Beck'll be along in a few minutes. He's finishing up downstairs right now." Krause didn't even slow down as he hurried toward the front desk.

"Ya, ya..." Dewey responded with a vacant smile on his wide face.

Although Dewey wasn't eavesdropping on the conversation, he couldn't help but hear Rosnau mumble, "Snow's already melting. Someone's gonna find the fuckin'—" Dewey wasn't sure that he'd heard the last word. Sounded like body? Police work was exciting to him.

In the remaining five minutes, Dewey was certain he heard the word body mentioned twice more. But what seemed especially puzzling to the smiling imbecile was a mention of the name Moran. Must have something to do with Tony Zoretek. Dewey had cried when he learned of Mr. Zoretek's death. Tony was like Kevin Moran—a generous and friendly man. Everybody in town was feeling badly for the Morans.

"I'm 'bout as hungry as a horse, Deweee." The familiar voice of Johnny Beck echoed down the hallway. "I'm gonna ask'em for chili tonight—yes, I am. A big bowa chile'll do me just dandy. You betcha!"

~

The sight of Maddie's Nash parked near the depot brought a smile to Pack's face. The bashed in rear fender of her car raised a frown. Although curious about what had happened, he'd let her tell him about it and resist any temptation to be facetious about women drivers.

She ran out to meet him when the bus pulled in. Holding her in his arms thawed the tensions of the long ride like melting ice. Maddie felt better than anything his imagination could conjure. "I love you!" were the first words he said, whispering them softly into the blond hair over her ear. "You've been on my mind more than anything these past few days."

Maddie couldn't help but sob. She too felt better at this moment than he had since saying goodbye to him on Sunday. "I love you, too, Pack. More than you can possibly know."

"I think I need an hour of...just looking into your eyes, Maddie. Even before going over to Becca's with my belated condolences." Stroking tears from her cheeks with his gloved fingers, Pack gave her a soft kiss on the lips. "Don't cry, sweetheart." He misread her tears, "Tony's already in heaven."

"I know he is, Pack. But I'm so sorry for those he left behind—he was a beloved man."

"He was that." Pack took her hands and led her inside the quiet terminal building. "I'll be talking about Grampa all night, Maddie. Right now I want to catch up on you. On us!"

Over coffee at a table in the bus station, Maddie told him everything—from the Beamons article to her accident that afternoon. "I'm quitting my job. I've just got to get out of here for a while. My God, there's Jerry and now the Beamons allegations—this place is driving me insane, Pack!"

Holding her hands in his own, Pack listened patiently, hurting deep inside over Maddie's pain. "I wish there was something I could do—" He wanted to comfort her, even support her compulsion to leave Hibbing. Rather than try to dissuade her, or suggest that she give the matter more thought, he asked a question instead. "Where would you go, sweetheart?"

Maddie smiled for the first time. "I think you could probably guess, Pack."

"You're going to find your father." His words were a statement—not a question.

"I've always wanted to."

"I know." The two of them had shared dreams about traveling to California some day. Pack tried hard to return the smile she had given him while considering his next few words carefully. Behind what he would say were all of the perceived consequences of being impulsive himself. The investigation would surely be heating up in the coming weeks, and he was expected to play a major role. But, he was in love. His head reasoned he could do whatever he wanted with his life—his heart negated most options. "I want to go with you, Maddie. I need to go with you."

~

Maddie kissed him goodnight at her back door and promised to see him after school the next day. She would resign her position effective the following Monday and did not expect any protest from Mr. Dietrich. She and Pack would attend the wake together tomorrow night. Tonight she would have a long talk with her mother.

~

Pack remained dry-eyed throughout the painful condolences at Gramma Zoretek's house. Becca looked drained but her spirits were elevated when her grandson hugged her. "Now we're all together,

Patrick. I know it was hard for you to go to Minneapolis with everything going on here. But you did the right thing and we're all proud of you."

Pack found his mother feeling even more out of sorts than Becca. Mother and son clung together for long moments. "He was always your rock, Mom—I know that. But he's in a much better place now."

Angie wept on her son's chest. "I'll be fine, Patrick. I've still got my three wonderful men to take care of me. I'll be fine..."

After visiting briefly with Maribec (who had returned to Becca's after a needed break from the disconsolate scene earlier in the evening) and greeting several family friends, Pack managed to get his father off to the side. "Can we talk for a few minutes, Dad? Maybe go for a walk down the street?"

Kevin embraced his son. "I could use some fresh air, Pack. I've been waiting for your report on the meeting and getting your first impressions of Detective Porter."

The night air was brisk and the sky star-filled. For a few minutes they walked side by side in silent contemplation down the Brooklyn neighborhood street. Each waited for the other to pick up the thread of conversation left in the house behind. Kevin broke the ice. "Prentice called this morning. You made a good impression. Both the professor and Porter had compliments." Kevin put his arm around his son's shoulder. "Thanks for doing what you did. You know how badly I wanted to take you home on Monday, but—"

Pack kicked at a frozen chunk of snow on the street. "I suppose Mr. Garvey gave you a thorough report on what we talked about. Any questions? I was impressed with Porter. He's going to be a huge help. Plans on coming up one day next week."

"That's what Prentice told me."

Pack told his dad about Porter's theory on motive. "I'd hate to have that guy interrogating me."

Rounding the corner and approaching the Zoretek house, Pack took his father's elbow. "There's something else, Dad."

"I had a feeling there was, son. What's on your mind?"

"Have you read tonight's paper?"

"Haven't had the time. With all the calls, people stopping by with hot-dishes and brownies...you know. We've been so blessed with wonderful friends. So, what did I miss?"

Pack explained. "So, Maddie's determined to resign her position at school...and get out of here, Dad. She's serious."

Kevin met his son's eyes, "And?"

"I want to go with her. I need to, Dad. I know this is the worst possible time to be leaving Hibbing—and Porter's expecting me to help out...but—"

Kevin pulled his son closer, "Always listen to your heart, son. Always! That's something your grampa told me before you were born. Your mother and I left Hibbing for a while ourselves—under similar circumstances."

Pack knew the story well. He was born in St. Paul during that time.

"If Maddie is the one, and both Mom and I are sure that she is, you need to go with her. That's all there is to it. She needs you more than we do right now—and you need her."

Pack felt the swell of emotion moving from a place deep inside up into his throat. Losing himself in the well of his father's eyes, he did something he hadn't done since early childhood—he gave him a kiss. "I love you, Dad...thanks," he choked the words.

~

The somber funeral mass filled the huge Blessed Sacrament Church to overflowing. Becca had been given special permission to have her husband buried in the old Hibbing cemetery north of Bennett Park. The gravesite she had chosen was next to that of Mary Samora Zoretek.

40/ TRAVEL PLANS

At the church reception following the funeral, Pack chatted briefly with Chief Donald Lawrence. "It was heartwarming to see so many fellow officers at the cemetery," Pack said. "Thanks for giving them the time off, Chief."

Lawrence was a member of the parish and rarely missed a funeral.

"A real tribute to your Grandfather, Pack. I can't remember the last time Blessed Sacrament was so filled."

Condolences were brief and Pack had a reason for seeking out Lawrence that afternoon. "Chief, will you be in your office later? I have something...something personal, I need to talk to you about."

Lawrence nodded, "About five?"

Pack had reviewed the personnel polices the night before. He needed written approval from the supervising officer and authorization from the Police Commissioner Board in order to get an indefinite leave of absence from the department.

"This really surprises me." The Chief put his arm around his sergeant's shoulder, "These past few weeks have been tough on you, Pack—I know that. Your friend's disappearance, and Mr. Zoretek—" He met Pack's level gaze, "And maybe I've been kinda tough on you as well."

Pack nodded without reply at the unexpected warmth. Lawrence, he sensed, had more to say.

"Let me tell you, and I mean this sincerely, Pack—you're one of the best damn cops I've got. Just between the two of us, if I were to step down tomorrow, I'd have no reservations about recommending you for my job." Lawrence was uncharacteristically emotional. "I've been around here for a while, picked up what I call 'cop instincts—you know. And sometimes I think—" Lawrence looked away as if he didn't want to say any more. But, he did "...I think I smell a rat on board my ship."

Pack gave the Chief a puzzled expression, but Lawrence let his train of thought go uncompleted. "I'll write up an authorization letter, Pack. I don't think the Commission will have any problems with your request. But, I'm sorry to lose you right now."

"Thank you, sir."

Pack left the police department in disbelief. Had he seriously misjudged the Chief? Or, was his boss just happy to have him out of the picture for a while? Something told him—maybe his 'gut feeling' that Lawrence meant what he said. Time would tell.

~

On that same afternoon, Robert Dietrich was completing the tedious daily attendance forms that cluttered his desktop. His concentration on details had been strained all day. The school principal wrestled with the paranoia that his job was in serious jeopardy. The Beamons editorial in yesterday's Tribune had hit him like a stomach punch. If only he'd thrown that racist letter in the trash where it belonged, none of this would be happening. Now, it was like ripping the scab off a wound he thought had been healed.

Yet, what piqued his consternation most was the routine of his day.

Nobody had called—not Mitchell, not Slattery—and not that do-gooder, Rudy Perpich. Robert could not help thinking that there was a conspiracy taking shape, behind closed doors in the Superintendent's office. He looked at the wall clock and counted the minutes remaining in his workday. Thirty-five. Lately, the bottle of bourbon at home had become his only escape from the stress that goddamned letter had caused him! Thirty-five minutes.

He heard the rap on his door and, without looking up from his paperwork, called out—"door's open."

"Mr. Dietrich, I'd like to speak with you for a few minutes." Maddie slipped her letter of resignation onto the principal's desk. "I am resigning, sir—effective after classes tomorrow."

Dietrich's flaccid lower lip dropped. "You're what?"

"Resigning, sir. You heard me correctly." Maddie spoke without emotion, measuring the reaction of the man she despised. "Quitting!"

Dietrich checked his first reaction. An employee could not arbitrarily break a contract without appropriate school district and board action. This, however, was a unique situation and he knew it. The principal did not want to deal with Miss Loiselle's lawyer, or Rudy Perpich and more than necessary. He would be happy to have this thorn out of his side—and he could find a long-term substitute easily enough—probably that very afternoon. "I'm sorry..." How would he finish his lie without making any reference to the issue that both were keenly aware of? His smile was a failure, "I'm sorry to see you go, Madeline. You have been an excellent teacher."

Maddie bit off her next few words. "Is there anything else you need from me besides this letter?"

"No. I'll take care of everything from here."

"You're right you know, Robert—I have been an excellent teacher," she said coolly, reciprocating the first name reference. There was nothing else left to say between them—no apologies, no good wishes, no thank-yous. Maddie turned and left the office.

~

While Pack spent early Friday evening with his parents at Maple Hill, Maddie visited with her mother over a highball in the living room. The two women talked about the funeral, Maddie's resignation, and the trip to California. Old photographs were strewn across the coffee table. All of them from fifteen or more years ago.

"I haven't talked with your father in years, Maddie. Let me see, the last time he called was the night of your high school graduation. I think he's remarried a couple of times and probably still has his problems with drinking and gambling." Her thoughts drifted back to her former husband, Sean McDougal. It was impossible to avoid comparing Sean and Rick Bourgoyne—opposites in every sense of the word. Tall, handsome, Gregory Peck-looking Sean—and short, homely Rick. She always laughed to herself when making the inevitable contrast between the two men. Sean had swept her away with his charm while Rick had slowly grown on her—one was like a sudden storm the other like an evolving season. Maury was holding a picture of herself and Sean holding their newly baptized daughter outside of the Good Shepherd Church in West Duluth more than twenty years ago. "We were young and wildly infatuated with love, Maddie. Our years together were probably the best and the worst that I've ever had."

"You've never had anything good to say about my father, Mom. I don't want to go out to California thinking I'll find someone despicable." Maddie gazed at the photo, "We've all made mistakes...but none of them unforgivable."

Maury met her daughter's eyes. "It's hard for me to say this, Maddie, but you'll love the man. I did—and, maybe in that same crazy way of years ago, I still do. Rick knows about my feelings. Bless his heart." Tears welled in Maury's eyes, "Sean is not a bad man. Like Peter Pan, I guess, he just never wanted to grow up and be responsible. Marriage and parenthood were just too much. But don't ever get the idea that he didn't love us both."

Maddie put down the photo, took her mother's hand, and smiled. "How could he not love us, Mom? We're pretty special people."

~

"I'm glad you left the department on good terms with Lawrence," Kevin told his son. "I don't care much for the man, but it's possible he's not our adversary in this investigation." Pack and his father had been talking about what might be happening when detective Porter came to Hibbing next week.

"I still feel badly about talking off in the middle of everything," Pack admitted. "But as you've assured me, Porter can manage things pretty well with you and Mr. Zench pitching in." He swallowed hard, "If I could believe that Jerry was still alive out there somewhere...I'd stay home.

Kevin nodded without reply.

Angie joined her two men at the kitchen table. "I couldn't help overhearing you from the living room, Patrick. Please—don't feel guilty about your decision to go with Maddie. It's the right thing to do."

Angie smiled as a memory passed behind her eyes. "Your dad and I took off together years ago—left everything in Hibbing behind. Our love for each other was the most important thing in our lives—and, still is." She beamed at her son, then at Kevin. "When we came back home we were happier and more complete than we'd ever been."

Pack could not help but smile at the familiar reference. His mom, however, always told the story better than Kevin—more detail, more feeling, and more 'mush'! "I know the story pretty well by now, Mom." He couldn't resist the opportunity, "Why was it...the reason you and Dad went to St. Paul back then?"

Angie blushed. She had been three months pregnant and three weeks married at the time. "I told your father that we would take care of your house while you're away," she diverted.

The three of them talked for nearly an hour about Maddie, the California trip, hopes and dreams and responsibilities. Pack promised to keep in close touch with them while away and Kevin promised to let him know immediately if there was any break in the case.

41/ A BAND OF FOIL

Pack and Maddie headed west from Hibbing on Highway 2 early Monday morning. All good-byes had been expressed and emotions spent the day before. In the back seat of Pack's Ford were suitcases of lightweight clothing, the trunk was packed with camping gear. For both of them, the cross-country trip was more adventure than escape. They would take their time driving to Sacramento and soak up the varied scenery of the Western states.

Their first night, in Minot, presented them with an awkward situation. Although sleeping arrangements had been in the back of their thoughts for days, neither had said anything about what they might do when that inevitable time arrived. After pitching their tent and making burgers on the campsite grill they watched the sun drop into the western horizon. The night air held the chill of late autumn and a brisk wind swept the Dakota prairie land, flapping the canvas tent like a flag.

Sitting on an old wooden picnic table, Maddie broke the silent wonder of the sunset. "Pack, we've talked all day about the scenery, my dad, California...and, all the while both of us have been afraid to broach the 'big question'...and you darn well know what I'm talking about."

Pack laughed easily at the reality, put his arms around her shoulders. "It's been like having an elephant in the front seat for twelve hours and trying to pretend it isn't there. Yes, sweetheart, it's almost time to call it a day and the elephant is waiting for us in the tent."

"What are you thinking, Pack?"

"I'm thinking that maybe...maybe, what I'd like to do and what's probably the right thing to do, are two different things." Pack paused significantly, looking from the amber glow of dusk into the deep brown of Maddie's eyes. "I've thought about sleeping with you all day—long before today. A thousand and one times since I first saw you. But..." he stammered, " but, I don't want to do anything that you're not ready for. I mean, it's going to happen at some point; at least I hope so...still, it's got to be special for both of us. I mean, when we do..."

Maddie knew that Pack was struggling with both his words and his feelings. She had the same conflicting thoughts, and expressing them would be equally difficult for her. She wanted to do it as much as he did and had thought about it for just as long. But! Maddie kissed him lightly on his stubbled cheek. "Can you wait? I want to be...absolutely sure that it's perfect. Do you understand?"

"Sure. I want that, too. We'll both know the right time to..." he searched for the right way to put it, "...to make love."

Maddie laughed softly, "Thanks for giving it a proper association."

Pack was overtired from the day's driving and unaccustomed to sleeping within the tight confines of a cocoon-like bag which often slipped off the too-narrow air mattress. An habitual sprawler in his double bed at home, the bag made comfort virtually impossible. For more than an hour he tossed and turned trying not to wake Maddie from her sleep.

But Maddie wasn't sleeping either. It wasn't the chilly space or any discomfort so much as it was her conflicted thoughts. She loved the man trying to pretend he was asleep at her side—wanted him to hold her in his arms. She wanted to caress him, to feel his warm body against hers, experience the tenderness she imagined his passion would be. And, she knew how much Pack wanted her. His thoughts, she was positive, were the same as hers. But—that three-letter word was like an invisible wall between them. But, when was the right time for having s-e-x?

Pack heard the zipper of her sleeping bag open. Like him, she hadn't fallen asleep yet. "What's the matter, sweetheart?"

"I'm freeeezzzzzinggg, Pack!" her voice exaggerated the shivering.

Pack unzipped his bag, "I'll find you another blanket," he offered, beginning to crawl into the chilly space.

Then he felt her hand on his bare thigh.

"I don't need another blanket. That's not going to help me warm up." She sighed deeply, reaching for his hands. "I need you...I won't sleep knowing that I might have you tonight. Pack, I think...no, I'm certain, the right time for me is now."

Pack pulled her close to him, "I want you, Maddie...more than anything." He stroked her hair, found her mouth with the light touch of his finger, parted her lips, kissed deeply.

Maddie sighed expectantly. Opening the front of her flannel shirt she placed his hand over her warm breast. Heat rushed through her body as Pack's thumb moved slowly and sensually over her nipple, then down. Her stomach tingled at his touch, then she gasped as his hand slipped into her panties. She could feel his hard arousal against the bare flesh of her thigh and began her own exploration of his muscular body. Her fingers flitted across the coarse hair of his flat stomach...her mouth followed her hands down.

"I love you." Pack's passion came in heavy breaths as he uncovered her secrets and the anticipated ecstasy her body invited him to possess.

On their third night the lovers dined in a hotel north of Denver. After a frugal meal, they enjoyed a bottle of two-dollar wine at a patio table with a spectacular view of snowcapped mountains stretching their enormous glacial mass across the western horizon. For both Pack and Maddie, this trip had been like a honeymoon. Sitting beside her with his arm caressing her shoulders, Pack said "I love you" for the hundredth time that day. But, there was a noticeable tension in his words. Throughout the afternoon drive he had rehearsed his proposal so much that it should come out perfectly. His thoughts had processed a profound pledge of love and commitment, along with his dream of having children together. He could be an articulate man when he set his mind to it, and every word he had planned for this special moment had been perfectly composed.

But, as fate would have it, his proposal didn't come out the way it was supposed to. Getting off the table, Pack awkwardly dropped to one knee and groped for Maddie's hands—which she had tucked into her sweater. Once he held her delicate hands in his, his voiced choked with emotion. "I want you to be my wife, Maddie...will you marry me?"

His elaborate profession of love was spent in twelve words!

Maddie squeezed his hands and gave him a wide smile. A smile, as Pack would later describe, "that dwarfed the sun dropping into the mountains". The man on his knee was more than her young girl's fantasies might ever have imagined. He had become the everything of her life. "I will, Patrick Anthony Claude Moran...and I will pledge my love forever." With her profession came a stream of happy tears, "Forever!" she repeated.

Earlier, while Maddie had been taking a shower, Pack had fashioned a ring from the foil of a Wrigleys gum wrapper. "I'll get you something beautiful in Sacramento, sweetheart," he promised as he reached into his shirt pocket. Slipping the silver band on her finger, he repeated her profession "Forever, Maddie. You and me...always."

~

Turning west off south Highway 85 onto number 50, they wound through the narrow Rocky Mountain passes toward Grand Junction, then onto the elevated flatlands stretching across Utah and Nevada. Taking their time and enjoying the varied landscapes—the shared experience was an adventure neither believed possible. The issues both had left behind were almost forgotten and rarely discussed in the swim of diversions they encountered through every hour of each day. "Sometimes I have to pinch myself to see if what I'm feeling is real, Maddie."

Slipping her hand along the back of the driver's seat without Pack's notice, Maddie found the flesh on the side of his bottom and pinched.

"Ouch!" Pack laughed. "It is real, isn't it? This is really happening." He found her hand beside him and squeezed, "Thanks for the reality check."

Car trouble stalled them for a few hours in Fallon, Nevada where Pack's overheated Ford required a new radiator hose and fan belt. On Monday night, the one-week anniversary of their lovemaking, the couple was settled in a Carson City motel. They celebrated with the best steaks they had ever eaten and a bottle of Napa Valley wine. The next day they would conclude their eighteen-hundred mile journey to Sacramento.

Pack and Maddie made their promised phone calls home from Carson City later that night.

Maddie's voice brimmed with exuberance when she told Maury about her engagement. "It took me four days of begging to get this stubborn cop to commit—but, I've got him now! And, I'm not going to let him go." Maddie teased, poking Pack in the ribs as she sat beside him on the bed. Pack could hear Maury's excitement through the static of the long distance connection.

"Just north of Denver."

"Very romantic!"

"Yes...it's so...so shiny—I can't wait to show you."

"Honestly. No. Descriptions can't do it justice. You'll just have to wait and see it for yourself."

"Tomorrow, Mom. Late afternoon we think."

"We'll start with the phone directory."

"Why should I be nervous?"

"Pack's been absolutely wonderful."

"I know I'm lucky."

"He'll be calling them when we're done."

"Money? No problems."

"Two days ago in a place called Fallon—in Nevada."

"Absolutely beautiful."

Maddie's conversation was easy to follow even without hearing the rejoinders from Maury back in Hibbing. "Give my best to her and to Rick," Pack whispered over her shoulder.

"Sure, just for a minute though."

"I'll tell you all about it later, Rick."

"Yes. Right here next to me. I will...give Mom a kiss for me."

Kevin and Angie were also having a glass of vintage California wine, watching the snapping flames in the living room fireplace, and awaiting their son's promised call. Kevin tried to placate Angie's nervous prattle by assuring her that Patrick had brought enough money, his car was in excellent condition, they would have water in the car, and reminding her that "it's two hours earlier out there, Angie." He chose not to comment on his wife's overly Catholic concerns about the unmarried couple sleeping together.

The phone rang only once before Angie blurted the predictable mother's lament, "I've been so worried..." Within the first minute came an elated shriek, "Kevin...Patrick and Madeline are engaged! Can you believe...?" Angie and Patrick talked for nearly fifteen minutes; covering the same ground as Maddie had with her mother only minutes before. Angie and Maddie rehashed the love story for another ten minutes.

Kevin smiled to himself as he watched his wife on the phone. How could it be, that after all these years, his love for this woman took on new dimensions with every day. Kevin would never be able to explain. Just watching her was falling in love again.

Kevin patiently waited his turn. He wished there was something new to tell Pack about Jerry—but, this past week had not been much different than the past several.

Smiling and rejuvenated, Angie spoke another long minute with her son before passing the phone to Kevin. "Patrick sounds just wonderful."

There was little in the manner of small talk between the two men. "I met him for the first time yesterday," Kevin reported on his two-hour conversation with Porter. "Yes...I had a good impression. We did a lot of profiling the people on our list."

Several questions were answered. Kevin said, "After deer hunting season he's going to go out there and look around. Oh, there is something else I wasn't aware of. It seems that Porter knows Don Lawrence. They're not old friends or anything, but their paths have crossed in the past. Porter seems to think that Lawrence is a credible cop. I think the two of them are having dinner together tonight.."

Toward the end of their conversation Kevin acknowledged his concern about Gary Zench. "Not too well, I'm afraid. He's been despondent...talks about selling his house and moving. Your mom talks to Nora every day—she's been propping him up and keeping him going."

In ten minutes, father and son had caught up. "Congratulations, son. Now let me talk to my daughter-to-be. I've got some news that she'll get a kick out of." Kevin gave his love to Maddie, then added, "Don't break out in tears, but Bob Dietrich has taken an early retirement. I think that Rudy Perpich twisted his arm a little at the board meeting last Wednesday." Steven pouted his disappointment. He hadn't been given a chance to talk to his big brother. All he got was second hand information and an apology from his mom. As a compensation, however, Angie gave him permission to call his friend, "Only five minutes, Steven. I have to call Maribec."

Bobby's father answered the phone and asked who was calling. Abe Zimmerman knew the Morans and warmed to young Steven. "I'll try to get him away from his phonograph. Steven—say hello to your father for me."

Stevie rushed his news. First, he wanted Bobby to know about a Shreveport blues station he found on his radio, and the disc jockey called Brother Gatemouth. "He plays Muddy Waters and John Lee Hooker all the time." Then he whispered so his mother couldn't hear, "The show's called No Name Jive—but, he's on at two in the morning!"

With his few remaining minutes, Steven bragged about his big brother's trip to California. He enjoyed any opportunity to impress his friend. Bobby Zimmerman always had something to boast about. "Yeah, Pack and his girlfriend will be there tomorrow. Can you believe, he drove half way across the country in just over a week."

"I'm going to do that after I graduate," Bobby said in a voice full of himself. "California or New York. Whichever is further from Hibbing," he laughed. "Maybe both places. Who knows?"

"My brother can tell you all about California when he gets back," Steven recovered from Bobby's boast. "I'll bet you don't know anybody else who's really been out there."

Young Zimmerman's personality was a contradiction. Although quiet, almost shy, in school—with his few close friends he could be effusive and conceited. Realizing that he might have hurt his friend's fragile feelings, Bobby's empathy conjured words from a seldom opened, yet deeply sensitive, realm. "Hey, later you'll have to tell me more about his trip, Stevie. Pack's a really neat guy. Maybe he'll find some cool music spots out there to tell us about."

Steven smiled.

42/ SACRAMENTO

From West Highway 50, the skyline of Sacramento slowly came into view. Maddie had a California map spread on her lap. As the traffic got heavier, Pack said, "Keep an eye out for Fulsome Boulevard, hon. It shouldn't be too far from here."

Maddie was watching the intersections. "I think it should be coming up just ahead—yes, you should turn right at the next light. That will take us in to Capitol Square." Both marveled at the incredible greenery of the city landscape.

"Makes you wonder why anybody lives in northern Minnesota, doesn't it?" Pack offered an enigmatic smile.

"But, home is where the heart is—isn't it?" Maddie wondered how long they would be in this new and different place. "I think, if we try hard, we'll get used to palm trees and sunshine."

They drove along the lush avenue past the State University campus as they approached the heart of the city. Pack had made reservations at the Capitol Hotel while fueling in Placerville, east of Sacramento.

Maddie became absorbed in her own thoughts as they moved slowly through the congestion. Sensitive to her growing apprehensions, Pack respected her need for a private contemplation of what was ahead. They had talked for hours along the way about what they would do once they arrived. Now—they were here!

Maddie stared at her yellowed photographs of Sean McDougal. "How much different does a man look in fifteen years?" she had asked. Her excitement and anxiety were mixed in near equal measure. Fifteen years!

Pack thought about his own father, remembering stories that Kevin had shared with him. Kevin had seen his father only once—when he turned two years old—and had virtually no memories at all. In his library, however, Kevin displayed an old teddy bear that his father had given him on that occasion. Like Maddie, Kevin had a few old photographs. Pack considered that Kevin's father was a void that would never be filled. At least, Maddie had a chance!

"I can see it up ahead," Maddie said excitedly as the hotel's marquee came into view. Pack found a place to park near the corner of Tenth and J Street, only a few blocks from Capitol Square in downtown Sacramento. Outside, the seventy-degree heat put a bounce in Pack's step. "Seventeen-hundred and ninety-one miles, hon..." He hoped to uplift his wearied and anxious companion, "And, as great as our trip has been, I think the best is yet to come, Maddie. I'm sure of it."

Maddie smiled at the well-intended thought. "Help me keep my chin up, Pack. This is going to be the hardest thing I've ever done."

After checking in at the Capitol Hotel, they found a phone book. Thumbing down the column of small print, Maddie's finger stopped at the only Sean McDougal listed in Sacramento. "Now what?" she asked.

It was late afternoon. Was Sean still at work? Did he work? Who might answer the phone? Was he married? What would he say? But all the questions racing through her mind had been replayed countless times. She noted the address on 42nd Street. "We should go and see where he lives before we call, Pack." Maddie had gotten into the habit of referring to everything they did in terms of 'we'—it gave him a good feeling.

Shortly before five, Pack found a shady place to park just in from the corner, three houses down from 2618 42nd Street. He and Maddie ate White Castle burgers, sipped Cokes, and whiled away their time talking about the weather and palm trees—conspicuously avoiding any more dialogue about their impending reunion with Sean McDougal.

After a few minutes, a slender woman with dishwater blond hair and dark-framed eyeglasses came out the front door. She wore a simple denim shift, red paisley bandana, and floppy sandals. Near the front steps she picked up a garden hose, turned on the spigot, and began to water the flowerbeds lining the front of the stucco house.

"I feel like a spy, Pack," Maddie squirmed in the seat. "Here we are watching this woman and she has no idea. Somehow, I can't help feeling as if we're violating her."

Pack put his hand on the bare thigh below Maddie's cotton Madras shorts and smiled his amusement at her obvious stress. "Just look at it like detective work, hon. Trying to find some pieces for our puzzle."

"Yeah...easy for you, Mr. Cop! I'm too sensitive, I guess. I sure wouldn't want anybody watching me when I didn't know about it."

For long minutes nothing was said. Maddie analyzed the woman—her looks, clothes, and mannerisms. If this was actually her father's wife...? "Do you think she's attractive?"

"Yes, I guess so—in a wholesome kinda way. Not striking, for sure, but without the glasses and wearing a fancy outfit...then, maybe. Hard to tell from this distance. Why? What are you thinking?"

"Nothing, really. Well, that's not true. I just thought that my dad would have some voluptuous woman, I guess. From everything Mom's told me, Sean always had an eye for beautiful women. And, she's not what I'd call great-looking at all. Don't I sound awful, Pack?"

"Well, I've heard that women can be awfully catty when it comes to—"

Before he could finish his tease, a shiny new '56 Crown Victoria pulled to a stop in front of the house. A tall, handsome man stepped out of the car and walked slowly up the sidewalk. Apparently, the woman had not heard the slam of the car's door and continued with her watering. The man was well-dressed in a navy blazer, blue dress shirt, and beige trousers. Creeping slowly, he stepped behind the woman, threw his arms around her shoulder, and kissed her on the neck.

Startled, the woman dropped the hose, spraying herself and the man as she did so. The sudden spray caught the man directly in the crotch of his pants. He jumped, threw out his arms, and laughed like a boy in a squirt-gun fight. Seeing what had just happened, she laughed as hard as he did at something he must have said. Then she embraced him. They kissed unashamedly.

Maddie couldn't contain her laughter as the scene unfolded. This was a happy couple—of that reality all doubts were dispelled. The thought brought mixed emotions. Had this man and her mother had similarly happy moments together? From the memorized picture images, she had no doubt that this man was Sean McDougal. "That's my dad, Pack!" Her voice betrayed her excitement. "And I'd bet anything that is Mrs. McDougal." She watched the couple walk to the front door holding hands and laughing like teenagers.

~

Despite the fact that Miller Fontaine was his closest friend, Sean McDougal did not enjoy his sales job at Fontaine's Ford Plaza. Pitching new and used cars for hours every day was stressful. And success required fast talk, manipulation, and—all too often— deception as well. His pay was commission-based and the fall season had been slow. Most days he couldn't wait to get home and enjoy Gayle's companionship. His fourth wife was the best thing that had happened to him in his fifteen years of California life.

Sean had sold her the odometer-altered lemon several years ago. When Gayle Young brought the car in for transmission repairs (her third trip to the dealership in a month) she located Sean at his desk off to the side of the showroom floor. "I trusted you, Mr. McDougal—and this car has given me nothing but grief. I had to leave it parked in the street this morning and walk to school."

Sean had known the DeSoto would give the unassuming schoolteacher problems when he sold her the car. He apologized with the standard "these things happen" line and some of the mechanical bullshit he'd picked up over the years.

Miss Young leveled her gaze on the salesman and repeated, "I trusted you, Mr. McDougal." Then she cried.

Sean was too sober at the time to cope with the woman's tears. For reasons he might never explain, he felt a sense of guilt. "I'm truly sorry"—this time his apology was sincere. "I'll take care of the bill."

Sean McDougal did something he'd never done before that day. He paid for the repairs out of his own pocket. Further, he gave away his commission in offering Gayle Young a '50 Chevrolet coupe as a trade-in for her DeSoto sitting in the lot.

It was nearly six o'clock when they signed the transaction paperwork. Although he needed a drink, Sean further surprised himself—he offered to buy the woman dinner at a restaurant across the street from the Fontaine's lot. "No thank you, Mr. McDougal!" Gayle said emphatically. "Despite your help this afternoon, I'm afraid I've seen quite enough of you for one day!"

And, Miss Young said 'no' to invitations to dinner on three subsequent occasions. Sean was frustrated. He had always had his way with women—but not with this woman! And, she wasn't particularly attractive at that!

A bouquet of roses several weeks later finally got him the date he'd tried so hard to get. To his invitation to "do anything you'd like" Gayle suggested bowling. Not only did the petite English teacher 'bowl him over' (words he often used to describe their date that night), Gayle Young had the audacity to suggest that he get treatment. "You have a drinking problem, Sean. If you ever want to see me again, you'd better do something about it. My father was an alcoholic, so I know all the symptoms and the lies that go with them."

That night, and that woman, changed the course of Sean McDougal's life. He sobered up, joined the Catholic parish in his neighborhood, and began putting his booze money into a savings account. For the first time in years he wasn't broke all the time. After six months in AA, he had his second date with Gayle Young.

~

On this Tuesday, Sean and Gayle had been married for over four years. Pulling up to the curb, Sean saw his wife watering her flowers. He closed the door of his car quietly. He was certain she hadn't seen him come down the street. He approached carefully from behind—then grabbed her tightly, and kissed that special place on her neck. The icy chill shocked him! "Oooops, I think you just froze the snake!"

Seeing his drenched trousers, Gayle shared in the hilarity of the moment. "Sometimes I wish I could," she said.

43/ A TEARFUL REUNION

Indecision. Pack and Maddie had returned to the hotel to consider what they would do next. Pack was of the opinion that a phone call would be the best next step; "We can't just show at their house unannounced. After fifteen years, I think any sudden confrontation might be too much for your father to handle, Maddie. Too much for both of you."

"And, giving him time also gives him an opportunity to fabricate excuses...don't you think? I mean, Sean's got a lot of explaining to do." Maddie looked at the ceiling for the longest time—as if some answer might drop onto her lap. She was torn between the two options—calling first to let Sean know she was in Sacramento; and simply knocking on his door. Seeing him in his front yard only an hour before had softened her—yet, she seemed to prefer meeting him face to face without warning. Maddie had a flair for the dramatic; Pack was a pragmatist. "Would you jump off the dock...or wade in, Pack?"

He smiled at her analogy. "Depends. To save somebody's life...or to enjoy a swim...?"

A befuddled look crossed Maddie's face as she checked her wristwatch. It was after seven and the street lamps below their fifth floor window were coming on. "I'm really torn."

"We don't have to decide tonight. We've just arrived and don't even know our way around here."

"But this hotel is going to cost us blood, Pack."

They talked about finding an apartment and looking for jobs to help with the expenses. Half an hour slipped by. "I remember Grampa telling my dad once that to make no decision was really making a decision. I thought that was kinda profound at the time."

"Procrastinate? Can you remember what your dad did with the advice?"

"He made a decision, of course."

Maddie laughed, stood, then walked slowly to the window. "To hell with it, Pack! I won't be able to do anything until this is resolved one way or another. I'm calling Sean! Right this minute!" Maddie turned to face him, her jaw set in resolve, her eyes riveting..."Say a prayer for me—for both of us."

She took the phone and dialed the number she had written on the cover of a matchbook. Hesitating for long moment at the last number, she let it spin. On the third ring the woman answered. Her voice had a pleasant tone. "Just a minute, please—I'll get him."

"Lo...this is Sean."

Maddie froze. On her notepad she had scribbled some different versions of her first words. Her eyes tried to focus on what she had written down: "Hello, this is Madeline Loiselle"..."This is your daughter, Maddie"..."This is a voice from your Minnesota past..." (she'd drawn a line through the third option).

Another "Hello" from Sean.

Confused, Maddie simply blurted, "Hello, Dad...this is Maddie. I'm here in Sacramento."

"My God!" A long pause followed the exclamation. "Maddie!"

She could hear her father call to the woman, "Gayle...it's my daughter on the phone! She's here."

"Dad?"

"My God," he repeated. "I can't believe...where are you now?"

Maddie explained that she and her fiancé were at the Capitol Hotel. "We just arrived this afternoon and found your number in the book."

"Your fiancé? That's wonderful news, Maddie." Sean McDougal was stricken with a loss for words. What could he say to let her know how happy he was. Maddie's voice, so much like Maureen's, brought back a flood of memories. "My God...when can I see you? Meet your fiancé? Maddie, I'm just overwhelmed."

Maddie's throat constricted. "That's up to you."

"You have my address, don't you? We're not far from the hotel...Tonight! I want to see you tonight—if that's okay? Waiting would make me a nervous wreck. I already am, Maddie. I've got to see you," he repeated. I want to meet your fiancé. And I want you to meet Gayle, too." Sean could not contain his excitement. "Or, we could come over to the hotel, Maddie. Whatever? I just want to see you."

Pack pulled in behind the Crown Victoria on 42nd Street.

Maddie was a bundle of nerves.

"I hope I told you how fantastic you look in that dress, sweetheart." He wanted to soften her stress with the compliment. She wore a simple but stylish green A-line shift. Green was her favorite color. "Your dad's going to get a knock-out punch when he sees you."

"Do you really think so?" She adjusted her pearl earring, moved the clasp of her necklace to the back of her slender neck. She wore her long blond hair brushed to the back. "I might look good, Pack...but it's only a mask for what's going on inside. I'm so nervous...I think I could actually vomit."

"You'll be fine. Just think about how Sean must feel waiting inside.

And, don't forget that both you and your dad do have some support...I'll help you out in any way I can, sweetheart."

Her thanks was the beam of a confidant smile.

Sean was wearing a path in the carpet, striding back and forth across the living room, looking out the window at every turn in his nervous pace. What was he going to say to Maddie? What did his daughter look like? Like Maury...or him...or both? What did she think of him—of what he had done? Was she angry? (That fear bothered him more than anything else). Was forgiveness possible?

Gayle watched her husband, unable to find the right words to comfort his uneasiness. She was nervous, too. Meeting Sean's daughter would be awkward for her, but Gayle had more self-confidence, and far less anxiety, than her tormented husband.

"They're here, Gayle!" Sean saw the Ford pull in behind his car. He said a silent prayer—the same prayer he had said countless times every day for the past five years: God grant me the serenity to accept the things I cannot change, the courage to change the things I can, and the wisdom to know the difference.

Standing in the open doorway, Sean watched the young couple walk arm in arm up the sidewalk. Upon his first sight of the lovely woman his mind swept back over the years—there could be no mistaking her features...this was his daughter!

Seeing the tall man framed by the foyer light him, Maddie lost her composure and began to cry. In that moment every repressed anger and fear was gone. Finally! Her father's arms were open.

Neither of them could summon words. Everything that needed to be said between them was spoken with a clinging embrace and a swell of tears.

Pack watched the reunion with a lump in his throat and tears of his own. Tears of happiness, tears of relief, tears of hope.

Gayle found Pack's eyes from behind the emotional embrace. Slipping around her husband and out onto the porch where Pack was standing, she smiled and said in a soft whisper, "Let's give them a bit of time—just the two of them." She took Pack's arm and led him down the sidewalk. "I'm Sean's wife, Gayle."

Pack was warmed by the small woman's considerate gesture. "Patrick...Patrick Moran, Mrs. McDougal. It's a pleasure..."

"The pleasure is mine—ours, Patrick. I can't tell you how fulfilled I'm feeling right now. This is like a dream I never dared to dream." She dabbed at her nose, "I can't help crying. Happy tears, Patrick."

"For all of us—the two of them most of all." Pack felt an immediate fondness for the woman at his arm. "Thanks for inviting us over to your home tonight...Gayle. I don't think Maddie could have waited another day."

"Nor could Sean," Gayle laughed her amusement. "After he hung up the phone, he called his boss and told him that he wouldn't be going to work tomorrow. 'I've just experienced a miracle' is what he said to Mr. Fontaine at the dealership. Then, he insisted that I run down the street for a bottle of champagne." Gayle hesitated..."Sean doesn't drink anymore, but—" She went on to explain that her husband was 'recovering'.

Having known some of Sean's history, Pack smiled, "You must be proud of him. It's a tough thing to do."

"Words can't express..."

From the porch, Sean called, "Pack...Gayle...let's all of us go inside and celebrate!"

Sitting next to her father on the sofa, Maddie studied Sean as he thanked his wife and Pack for giving them those precious few minutes. Lines of a hard life were etched in his features. His dark hair was streaked with gray, but his deep-set green eyes were like soft pools of serenity. In most respects, Sean looked older than this forty-two years.

After pouring three glasses of champagne, Sean opened a bottle of Seven-Up for himself. "Let me toast to one of the happiest days of my life—or to be perfectly honest, one of the happiest days that I can remember."

After the toast, Sean cleared his throat and candidly explained a life that had been "wasted on alcohol, womanizing, and gambling" and how Gayle had "saved his life". He also shared fond memories of Maury and Maddie, "Your mother put up with a lot of my irresponsibilities, Maddie. I know I hurt her a lot. Both of you for that matter."

Gayle understood her husband's painful past better than anybody and had worked with him through his 'Twelve Steps' of recovery. Sean had changed more than any words could describe since she first met him. "I'll pray that this wonderful reunion will finally get you over that 'Ninth Step', honey." She explained how much he had struggled with seeking forgiveness from those he had injured through his years of alcoholism.

Later in the conversation, Maddie mentioned her mother's recent engagement. Sean was delighted, "This Rick is a lucky guy. Maury is a great woman—I honestly mean that. She deserves the best, and

I'm happy for her—for both her and Rick." He took Maddie's hand and met her eyes, "I'm going to call her tomorrow and offer my congratulations."

"She'd be happy to hear from you, Dad." The word Dad rolled easily from her tongue on this miraculous evening.

~

The following day, Sean gave the young couple a tour of the bustling capitol city on the Sacramento River. The older commercial area around Front Street evidenced the urban decay of neglect as the city's new growth sprawled out to the suburbs. Sean explained that here was a lot of talk about restoration but nobody was doing much about it. He had applied to the mayor for an appointment to the Planning Commission. "I've never been very political so I probably won't be considered."

In his years of Sacramento life, however, Sean McDougal had made many acquaintances. The ones he cherished the most were his friends in the AA community. Miller Fontaine, his boss at the dealership, was his sponsor and best friend. Sean stopped by the car lot and proudly made introductions. "This lovely woman is my daughter...Madeline." His eyes teared when he said her name.

They all talked for half an hour over coffee and sweet rolls at a window table in the large showroom. Miller's brother owned the Town and Country Shopping Center. "If you'd like to find a job, Maddie, my brother can have you working at one of his shops tomorrow."

Another friend of both Sean and Miller was Archie Rudolph. Arch was a supervisor for the Pinkerton Agency. Miller suggested, "Sean, why don't you take Pack over to Archie's office and introduce him. With his background in police work, I'm sure Arch could find him a job as well."

By four-thirty that day, after making stops all over Sacramento, Maddie had a job in a woman's clothing shop (Estelle's Fashions) at the Town and Country Center, and Pack was scheduled to begin a training program with Pinkerton on the following Monday.

On Thursday, the couple planned to go apartment hunting. Gayle had warned them earlier that finding a place would be difficult under the circumstances of their relationship. "I'm afraid that lots of landlords won't rent to unmarried couples."

Upon hearing Gayle's caution, Pack had winked at Maddie. "What do you say, sweetheart. I'm ready and willing to tie some knots...and you've already got my fancy ring on your finger."

Maddie had shared the engagement story to everybody's amusement. "What do I say? Well, I'm pretty old-fashioned, you know. I want a wedding and a reception to go with it." She gave a coy smile, "But I'm not so old-fashioned that I couldn't pass myself off as Mrs. John Smith for a while. After all, this is 1956!"

Pack nodded. Sean winked. Gayle grinned.

Maddie said, "What do you think about that...John?"

44/ EAVESDROPPING

Early November mornings brightened later, changing the routine of Dewey Bartz's day. He would savor his first cup of coffee (half cream and half sugar) at the Sportsmen's Café before beginning his rounds about town. Just before seven, he'd cross Howard Street and begin sweeping the long stretch of sidewalk wrapping around the corner of the Androy Hotel. On his fortunate days, he'd see Mr. Moran. Kevin was his favorite person in Hibbing and the only one who took time to chat with him.

On this Thursday morning, Dewey sat on his usual stool at the end of the long counter stirring his four spoonfuls of sugar into the steaming cup. He knew all of the café regulars by heart—their booths of habit, favorite breakfast choices, and those who always ordered orange juice. He often thought that if he were the waiter, he could have every order filled before the regulars sat down. Sometimes Dewey wished he were a waiter.

Eavesdropping on conversations was almost better than listening to

Rick Burgoyne's radio program which he could hear from the kitchen. Almost better. Dewey really liked Rick's mix of music and news. Yet, he picked up more 'local news' in the café than he was ever likely to hear on the airwaves of KHNG radio.

On this particular morning, two familiar young men were sitting in the booth behind his back and to his left. Randy Tobin and Dave Dahlberg were softball players on Mr. Moran's team. Because the two men were not Sportsmen's regulars, Dewey was curious to find out whether they would order the breakfast special. And, perhaps, learn something about his favorite sport at the same time. Any softball talk would give him something to share with Mr. Moran later. Once, at a ballgame, Dewey heard Pack (his favorite player) tell Jerry Zench "great sacrifice bunt". After the game, he told Mr. Moran, "that sacrifice bunt was great" and Kevin was very impressed. Dewey had no idea what 'sacrifice' meant, but he knew a bunt from a full swing.

Dewey smiled to himself and tuned-out the background radio. His left ear was his best ear. His head bobbed as he hummed to himself, still concentrating on the voices behind him.

"Just coffee," Dahlberg said. Tobin ordered eggs over easy and hash browns—no toast.

"Should'a dumped it in the lake like Rosnau said." Dahlberg said. Then something from Tobin that Dewey couldn't pick up.

` "He's gonna be pissed if he finds out."

"When huntin's over. It's gonna stink like hell, ya know." Tobin said.

Dewey heard the click of a lighter. Players shouldn't smoke he thought. Then the word 'body' from Dahlberg. Was it "dump the body"?

Tobin had a deep voice and was sitting further from Dewey's left ear.

"Saw Moran's new detective yesterday. Big sonuvabitch," Tobin said. The mention of a detective got Dewey excited. Detectives were in television shows. "Talkin' to Lawrence."

After Tobin's order was served, Dewey heard Dahlberg say something about J. R.'s "knowing too much."

"Gonna hafta get rid of him, Dave," Tobin said through a mouthful.

Dewey frowned. J. R. was a pretty good first baseman—why would they want to get rid of him? He'd have to ask Mr. Moran about that.

"When huntin's over I'm getting' my ass outta here for a while," Dahlberg said. He mumbled "California" but the rest of what he said got lost in the clinking of plates behind the counter.

Dewey's favorite song wafted from the kitchen radio—"You ain't never caught a rabbit and you ain't no friend of mine..." he hummed along with Elvis.

Dewey was losing interest in the conversation. The two men weren't talking enough about softball. Dewey thought about a detective in town and Dahlberg's going to California. Then it struck him, Mr. Moran's son was on his way out to California—wherever that was. He'd have lots to talk with Mr. Moran about after all. Pack's friend was going out to visit him. What a nice idea. How far was it—California? Probably as far as Canada.

~

Thanksgiving was not the same in the Moran household without Pack—and Tony! The dining room table would have two very conspicuous gaps. Angie planned to take the turkey from the oven at about two. Her timing was based on a promised phone call from Pack and Maddie before noon—Pacific Time. Angie's eyes were rarely focused on anything beyond the kitchen clock. It was just after one.

Becca, with her freshly baked pumpkin pie, had arrived at noon. The recent widow was playing gin rummy with Kevin and Maribec at the table while Angie fussed over her cranberries and garden green beans. The potatoes would wait for another half hour on the back burner. Where were Rick and Maury, Angie wondered? They said that they were going to arrive before the phone call.

Kevin had invited the Zenches but Nora pleasantly declined, "I'm so very sorry, but Gary just isn't up for anything social these days. He just wants to stay home with Naomi and me."

Gary's depression had worsened. He had requested a cutback schedule of three days a week. Kevin supported the arrangement. There had been no new developments. Even Detective Porter's investigations had been as cold as the November days.

Shortly after two-week deer hunting season, Porter examined the Rosnau hunting shack south of town. He found the place had been scrubbed clean with freshly painted walls. Much too clean! He could only wonder about what evidence may have been purged, or what had motivated painting the wall in a pastel yellow. A man's hangout, with a trophy deer head and mounted fish, would not have this distinctly feminine touch.

Mostly, the investigation was a waiting and watching routine. Donald Lawrence had offered Porter every possible assistance and approved his surveillance of the five suspects—including his own police lieutenant. Rosnau had taken a week off during deer hunting season. Carl Wicklund had joined him at the shack for both weekends. Tobin, Dahlberg, and Roberts did not hunt.

The only valuable insights came from Kevin's conversations with Deward Bartz. In his own innocent manner, Dewey had gleaned more information than all of those who were purposefully looking for leads. Yet, the retarded man had no idea about the relevancy of what he divulged to his friend, Kevin Moran.

"It's nothing to feel guilty about, Deward." Kevin had consoled the diminutive man when told about overhearing Rosnau's conversation about "dumping a 'body' into a lake" several days before.

"Ya, ya...not a bad thing—if ya say so. But when yer name was said—ya know, I jus hadda tell ya."

Then, Deward's most recent revelations about the Sportsmen's Café conversations provided a link between Rosnau and two other suspects—Tobin and Dahlberg.

"Herd yer name agin, Mr. Moran. And a deetektif, too. Wadda 'bout that?" Kevin explained the detective was helping Mr. Zench find his son. That made Deward happy, "Gooood fer you. Ya gotta find yer shortstop somewheres don ya?"

Kevin also told Deward that, just between the two of them, he might have to let go of J.R. before next season, "I'd like to give Rick a chance to try first base." Deward thought that was a pretty good idea, too.

Pack's call home was perfectly timed. Maury and Rick had arrived about one-thirty. Everybody—including Steven—had a chance to talk. Kevin waited patiently and when his turn came, the others returned to the kitchen to allow him some privacy. "I wish there were more to tell you, Son." He explained the latest Deward Bartz information and how Porter had been watching Tobin and Dahlberg's activities. "Porter's spending the weekend with his family in Minneapolis. He told me that next week he's going to start leaning on some people."

"Tell him to lean on Roberts. He's the weakest link of the five, Dad. J.R. might not have been involved in whatever happened, but I'd bet he knows something about it."

"Dahlberg's comment about leaving town for California makes us feel that he's more than a little nervous about something. He's the guy Porter wants to visit with first."

Pack disagreed. "I know these guys, Dad, and for what it's worth I'd want to get Roberts in a room before Dahlberg."

Kevin would pass his son's ideas along to Porter on Monday.

~

Monday morning found Leonard Rosnau in a foul mood. The long holiday weekend had done little to ease the gnawing fear that the Zench matter might be unraveling. Too many people knew too much. That was his mistake. Yet, what troubled him the most were the little things. His depressing neighbor, Dietrich, was drinking and talking too much. The other night he had told Rosnau, "My wife agrees with you about most local folks thinking niggers should know their place"—Iris was a blabbermouth.

And Neal Beamons. Rosnau's reporter friend had called last week to let him know that he was leaving the Tribune to take a "less stressful job" in the wilderness resort town of Ely. Beamons' recent editorial had caused an uproar between the school district and community—the resulting 'stress' was too much for the closet alcoholic to cope with.

Rosnau's best friend, Carl Wicklund, hadn't stopped by the house since the end of deer season two weeks ago. The apparent estrangement of his co-conspirator was both unusual and disturbing. Carl had been against the lynching scheme from the onset. But Carl was a bulldog—under pressure his friend would never crack. Rosnau had to believe that.

It was the 'boys', however, that made Rosnau the most nervous. They had fucked up good. Randy Tobin didn't throw the body into the lake as he was told to do. Instead they dumped it in a ditch off of Highway 73, south of Hibbing. When Rosnau found out about it two weeks later, he chewed Tobin's ass and demanded that he recover the corpse and haul it out to Island Lake. Tobin became insolent. "Ain't gonna do that lest you come along, Lefty. You shoulda been with Dave and me that night. It was creepy having Zench's dead body in my trunk. We wasn't gonna throw it in no boat and go out on no lake. It was pouring rain—we kinda freaked out."

Smart-ass kids! When Rosnau told Tobin to do what he was told without any lip, the punk gave him the finger and a 'fuck you'!

The winter ice sheet could only be days away and the body had to be dumped in Island Lake or Janet Lake or Day Lake—there were lots of lakes to choose from. Maybe he and Wicklund would have to do the dirty work themselves? But, Rosnau wasn't sure of the exact spot to look. Only Tobin and Dahlberg could take him there. All Rosnau knew was that the ditch was near Townline Road, on the east side of the highway, in a patch of cattails. And, now there was snow cover.

Maybe he was worrying too much. If the lake froze over, they could auger a hole and dispose of the body during ice fishing season. Keep your cool, he reminded himself.

Yet, despite his resolve, Rosnau's pessimism was consuming. Tobin and Dahlberg were smart enough to know the consequences. They were tough kids—not the kind that were easily bullied. Both had been keeping to their daily routines. Both had been questioned by Lawrence and handled themselves well. Dahlberg had talked about getting out of town for a while...and, maybe that was not a bad idea. Maybe? That needed more thought. It was JR Roberts that worried him most. JR's hands weren't as dirty as those of his two companions. Rosnau had instructed Tobin and Dahlberg to keep tabs on JR's comings and goings. Maybe he was the one who should be leaving town.

Rosnau mused about other concerns. Pack Moran was gone for the time being. That was good. Pack worried him more than anybody. The big city detective hadn't done much of anything for the past two weeks—besides visit with Lawrence on three or four occasions. In fact, the two of them would be meeting again later this morning without him—that was just as well. The less he saw of the guy, the better. Rosnau had met Porter only once, and only briefly. Porter's size and demeanor were imposing—but that was all. The detective Moran had hired seemed out of place in Hibbing, and there wasn't much Lawrence could give him about the Zench case that wasn't already common knowledge. No, Porter had nothing tangible to go on...especially if he was relying on Lawrence to be of help. He laughed to himself, *Kevin Moran's just wasting his money to impress folks, to make his nigger buddy feel good.*

~

"I've got to start leaning on some people, Don." Porter told Lawrence over coffee in the Chief's office. "And, I don't want Rosnau involved in any of my interrogations. Is that okay with you?"

Lawrence nodded. "You don't trust him, do you?"

"I'm certain that your lieutenant knows a helluva lot more than either of us do. Call it instinct if you want, but that hunting shack business really sticks in my craw. Something happened out there."

"Where do you want to start, Damon?"

Porter and Kevin had talked earlier that morning. "Pack told his dad that JR Roberts was..."

"Oh, shit!" Lawrence interrupted. "Damon, do you know who JR's father is?"

"I've done my homework. Used to be a big shot mining company official, family's got some bucks, belongs to the Algonquin Club— so what?"

"We've already had a run-in with Ian Roberts."

"I need to start a little fire around here, Don. Get people talking. The more talking going on, the more shit we've got to kick around. And, most of what's out there might well be shit. But, talk makes people nervous and I need a lot of nervous people."

"You're not talking about a little fire."

Porter smiled. "You know, Don, once you start a fire on a ship the rats start running like crazy. I want to see that happen." He paused significantly before making his next observation. "And one of those rats might very well be holed up in an office just down the hall."

Lawrence gave Porter a pained look. For the fiftieth time in the past two weeks he thought about retirement. He had been eligible for a pension since last June. "What the hell. We might burn our fingers, but I'll have Roberts here in my office at two this afternoon."

45/ DETECTIVE IN TOWN

Randy Tobin followed JR Roberts' car from a safe distance, and watched his friend park in front of the City Hall building. He was doing casual surveillance that afternoon. Dahlberg was working. Tobin was curious. Why had JR left his Lerch Brothers lab early that afternoon? Who was he going to see in the City Hall Building? He watched Roberts walk stiffly toward the east entry door—the door most people used to go to police headquarters on the second floor. Roberts appeared to be talking to himself and seemed unusually agitated about something. What? Maybe Rosnau wanted to talk to him? Tobin would check with the cop later.

"I'm not going to beat around any bushes with you, Roberts." Damon Porter's smile was a crooked line across his ruddy face. Loosening his tie and rolling up the sleeves on his shirt he paced. Lawrence sat off to the side and had agreed to let Porter do the interrogation. The imposing detective stopped, turned, and faced the young man seated in deliberate discomfort on a wobbly wooden chair in the center of the room.

JR Roberts had expected to meet with Lawrence—not the detective. He looked away from Porter and met the Chief's eyes. "What's goin' on here? You didn't tell me about this galoot when you called."

From his chair off to the side, Lawrence said. "This galoot, as you called him, is Inspector Porter from Minneapolis. He's helping us out in the Zench investigation, JR."

JR said nothing. It was logical that the Cities police would be following up on the letter.

Porter lit up a cigarette and continued. "Mr. Roberts, we've got five names on our list...and you are one of them. Five people we need to talk to." Porter emphasized the number by displaying his large open hand. "Okay? Now, you can tell me any number of things, Mr. Roberts. You can tell me that I have bad information, you can tell me that I'm only blowing smoke, you can tell me I'm crazy..." He blew a cloud of smoke toward JR's face, "Or, you can tell me the truth. I have five suspects." He repeated the word 'suspects' in an intimidating tone. "Now, what's it going to be?"

JR Roberts masked his tension with an insolent smile. "You're crazy. Both of you are crazy. I don't know what kind of list you're talking about. And, I can count without your God-damned hand in my face."

Porter smiled, measuring the youth with experienced eyes. "We're going to find Jerry Zench—and, sooner than later—I can assure you of that. And when we do, some people are going to end up in Stillwater for a long time. You heard of Stillwater, JR?"

JR scowled without comment.

"Now, one of those abductors, or murderers—if that's the case— is going to surprise the local folks...isn't that right? One of the five is somebody nobody in their right mind would ever expect..."

Porter noted a dilation in JR's eyes, a slight twitch in the young man's jaw. "Someone's going to talk to me, JR. Someone's going to want to save their ass and come clean. That always happens. Always!"

Lawrence spoke from the side of the room. "Porter's right, JR. It's going to go easier for anyone who gives us the information we need. There are rewards for cooperation—I can give you my word on that."

But JR gave Lawrence a twisted smile of contempt. The 'good cop', 'bad cop' technique was elementary school stuff. "I don't know what you guys are talking about. Five names on your 'suspect list'? That's a fucking joke if you ask me. You otta have a hundred names. Zench was a flake—you know that Lawrence. A loner. I went to high school with him, played on the same teams. Nobody really liked the guy." JR realized he'd better be careful. "He probably skipped town for the Cities...just like the newspaper's said. Make some friends with people like himself."

Porter detected a slight squirm in the wooden chair. He would go for the jugular. "The letter from Minneapolis was bogus, Roberts. We know that. And, I think you do too."

JR bit his tongue. Don't let this guy get to you, he cautioned himself. Let him do the talking. But. He could feel a damp perspiration under his arms. How much did Porter really know? How much was clever technique? In his mind he ran the five familiar names. Who had this big city cop talked to already? He wanted to ask, but playing dumb was the smartest thing to do. One way or another, JR was not going to be intimidated or fall for any ruse.

Porter, sensing that he had struck a nerve, would play his trump card. "Let me tell you something else, JR. You are the one that all the others are worried about. I've got that on good authority—you can choose to believe me or not." Porter stepped closer to the young man, leaned over so that his face was only inches from that of Roberts. "Watch your step, JR. We think you're in danger. And, if you think that I'm only trying to scare you—well, that's your business."

JR was scared. Before he got up, however, he'd take his own initiative. "If anybody's in trouble its Pack Moran. Tell me why all of a sudden he and his bitch took off for California? Either he's scared...or, he's got something to hide. Five suspects? Hell, I can only count one. Pack's girlfriend was screwing Jerry Zench. You guys already know that, don't you?" Feeling a surge of confidence, JR met Porter's eyes, "Even Rosnau thinks that Pack could'a done it...Pack's the one with the best motive, wouldn't you say?"

Porter jumped on JR's slip of the tongue. "Done what? You just said 'done it'—what is that supposed to mean?"

"Nothin'!"

Porter's experience told him to shift from one point to another quickly. "You know Rosnau, then?"

"Not really. Just know who he is—that's all."

But the edge in JR's voice was unmistakable. Porter glared without comment.

"Rosnau talks to lots of people I know—word gets around. Hibbing's that way, Mr. Porter. Do you think Pack Moran just up and decided to take a November vacation? After having three weeks off?"

Lawrence intervened. "I can assure you that Pack Moran is not on our list, JR. He's on leave of absence. And, Miss Loiselle's affairs have nothing to do with Mr. Porter's investigation."

JR stood up from this chair, glared at Lawrence. "I've had enough of this. Christ, I came here of my own..." he searched for the word "...avolutin—and, you guys know damn well I ain't done nothin wrong. This is the second time you've harassed me, and the last." He brushed past Porter on his way to the door. "The next time we talk it's going to be with a lawyer present. Just wait until my dad hears about this bullshit. He's going to be after your ass, Chief. My dad and Les Bowman are damn good friends, you know." At the door he sent both men an arrogant smile. His reference to the chairman of the police commission would give Lawrence pause for thought. "Think about that!"

Porter got in the last comment. "The one who should do some thinking is heading out the door. Remember what I told you a few minutes ago." His tone became conciliatory. "That's not bullshit, JR. I want you to watch your step."

When Roberts was gone, Porter regarded the police chief. Lawrence was visibly shaken by the angry youth's threat. "Do you think I went too far, Don?"

Lawrence wore a pained expression. "Hibbing is a small town, Damon. Crazy, behind the scene politics going on all the time. As you know, my position is appointed...and Ian Roberts throws a lot of weight around here. He and Bowman can make my life miserable."

Porter understood the man's grief and struggled to offer a measure of consolation. "We're only doing our job, old friend—a damn tough job at that." One his words were spoken, Porter realized that he had called the tormented lawman, 'friend'. The word felt good on his tongue and the weak smile he received assured him that the thought was reciprocated.

~

Tobin watched JR Roberts drive past the Androy and turn left toward Frank Hibbing Park south of Howard Street. Apparently, JR was not returning to work this afternoon. JR parked his car in the driveway of his father's stately house on affluent Wisconsin Street. Tobin glided to a stop, watched JR slam the car door, and stomp toward the front door. His friend was really pissed about something.

Tobin looped back toward Howard Street and pulled into a Standard station on the corner. From the public phone inside the entry, he dialed Rosnau's number at the police station. "So, what was Roberts doing over there, Lefty?" His tone was unnaturally high-pitched. "He looked damn angry when he left. I followed him over to his dad's place."

Rosnau's stress could not be disguised. "Don't know. He was in Lawrence's office talking to that dick Moran hired."

"You must have some idea about what's going on there for crissakes! This shit is making me nervous."

"Both of us. I'm not in the middle of things like before. I'll ask Lawrence when Porter's gone. But—"

"And, if the Chief don't tell you nothin', then what, Rosnau? You better get a grip on what's happenin' behind your back. Find out what Roberts told them, okay?. Like I tol ya, I'm gettin' damned nervous."

Rosnau knew he needed to check Tobin's panic with confidence. "Hey, don't sweat it. I'll find out what I can here. Meantime, you and Dahlberg see what you can get from Roberts. Lean on him if you have to, Randy."

Tobin was frustrated, "Yeah...we can do that. But you know as well as I do, whether JR spilled his guts or not, we're gonna have to get rid of him. He's the only one..."

Rosnau saw Lawrence heading down the narrow hallway toward his half-closed door and quickly hung up his phone.

Tobin cussed at Rosnau's cut-off. What was going on? The rock of their conspiracy was becoming more like jello. He'd get in touch with Dahlberg, then the two of them would have to figure out the best way to cover their asses. He yanked down the cradle and redialed. Dahlberg's phone rang without answer.

46/ BLESSINGS OF FRIENDSHIP

Within a few days, Pack and Maddie found a cozy one-bedroom apartment between their respective jobs on the eastern perimeter of growing Sacramento. Their lease (in the names of Mr. and Mrs. Patrick Smith) was established for renewal every three months so the couple could decide what they intended to do with their transient lives as they evolved from week to week. Both of them planned to return to Hibbing at some point in time—but, maybe not permanently.

Their first California month swept past like a whirlwind.

Pack had completed a two-week training program with the Sacramento Pinkerton Agency. The coursework was a snap. At times he knew he could have taught the classes far better than the agency's instructors. His supervisor, Rolly Jackman, was of the same impression. "Mr. Moran, your final test batteries were perfect. Congratulations." The squat, balding agent extended his hand. "For these past two weeks you've kept your teachers on their toes. Have you ever considered being a teacher yourself?"

Pack considered the question. Teaching would offer him an opportunity to use his police-work experience. "I would enjoy that very much, Mr. Jackman. To be candid with you, the basic training concepts could use some vitality."

Jackman laughed at the reality. "No argument on that. But, I was thinking of something else. Pat, we need to give our veterans some long-overdue refresher courses. Many of our people haven't had advanced training since completing this orientation program. And police work is changing so rapidly these days."

Pack and Jackman talked for nearly an hour about how the new technologies of modern police (and security work) were revolutionizing the field of investigation. The word 'forensics' came up often in their discussion.

"I'd like you to look this over," Jackman said. He handed Pack a catalog from Cal State-Sacramento. "There's a professor over there named Paul Cragun. He's top-notch. Introduce yourself to him and see what the two of you can work out. We'll pay all the tuition, and put you on salary while you're doing curriculum work. How does that sound to you, Pat?"

By the end of those same two weeks, Maddie Loiselle had been given the job of assistant manager at Claire's Apparel. Sales came naturally to the former schoolteacher and Claire Valine recognized her skills immediately.

Her promotion meant ten-hour days, but Maddie thrived in her new career. Working in the busy shopping center gave her an opportunity to meet many people—several of whom were transplanted mid-westerners—and get in touch with the essence of California's casual lifestyle. At times she was convinced that Hibbing existed in a different world.

Maddie's spirits were high. Her menstruation had resumed, her relationship with Pack gave her a noticeable glow, and her outlook on life had never been brighter. She loved the change and the sun and the newness of everything. Sixty-something, Claire Valine, talked often about selling her shop and retiring to Santa Monica where her married daughter lived. Maddie could imagine an interesting opportunity on the horizon.

At least twice a week, she and Pack spent an evening (or weekend day) with Sean and Gayle McDougal. The new bonds between Maddie and her father were powerful. Gayle was always fun to be around and, as a schoolteacher herself, had much in common with Maddie.

And Pack, spending most of his time at the Cal State campus with Professor Cragun, was making progress in organizing an updated curriculum for the Pinkerton veteran staff. Cragun was a consultant with the Sacramento police and introduced Patrick to some of the officers there. It didn't take long for Pack to join the 'Kops Krew'— a local softball team. Sean and Pack, along with Miles Fontaine, golfed on Wednesday afternoons.

In almost every respect, the young couple seemed to be flourishing under the California sun. Almost every regard. Although he kept his feelings to himself, Pack was less enamored with Sacramento than his partner. His work was challenging, the varied recreational opportunities satisfying, and the weather unbelievably pleasant—but, all of this was small compensation for a gnawing guilt. Pack found himself living more in the life behind him than in the present. He was still obsessed with his friend Jerry's disappearance...and, often regretted not being directly involved in what was happening back home. Without confiding to Maddie, each Monday morning he called Porter at the detective's Androy Hotel room for an update.

Pack missed his family much more than Maddie did hers. The weekly phone conversations seemed always to be too superficial and left his heart aching. For Maddie's sake, he kept his feelings to himself and tried to bask in the glow of her perpetual happiness.

From their small kitchenette, Pack and Maddie watched the Friday evening news on the small television screen in the living room while they ate take-out Chinese. "I think I've got this refresher course worked out, Maddie. Both Cragan and Rolly Jackman are enthusiastic—and I'm anxious to give the first two lessons a trial run on some of the old-timers next week. I hope I'm as good at teaching as I've been at organizing materials."

Maddie smiled her pleasure and teased, "You're great at everything you do...when you have a mind to do it!" Her allusion to the night before was obvious by her tone. The night before Pack had fallen asleep on the couch. "I was sooo horney again last night."

Laughing at her cajole, Pack apologized. "Well, I'm going to make it up to you tonight. How about a movie? *Giant's* playing at the drive-in." The new James Dean film with Rock Hudson and Elizabeth Taylor was getting rave reviews. "And a glass of wine when we get home?" Pack winked, "Whatever it takes to get you back in the mood I missed out on last night."

"That might just work, Mr. Smith." Maddie smiled, leaned over and gave Pack a kiss on the cheek. Returning her gaze to the television, she groaned, "Oh, Pack...look at the weather map." Another Canadian cold front was settled over Northern Minnesota. "Highs in the single digits. My God, how I miss being home," she laughed. "And what is it outside here right now—seventy?"

Pack forced a laugh without reply. A big part of who he was would much rather be lodged below the artic air of home.

~

From as far back as she could remember it usually took Maddie an hour or more to fall asleep. Tonight was no exception. Although pleasurably drained from their love making, she couldn't let go of thoughts playing along the edges of consciousness. Having read the Edna Ferber novel *Giant*, Maddie could not help making comparisons between the book and the sweeping movie adaptation. As thoroughly absorbing as the movie had been, the book was better. Yet, James Dean's portrayal of the obsessive Jett Rink had been exquisite.

Turning on her side, she regarded Pack sleeping soundly and taking up most of the bed. The warm feeling of love brought the trace of a smile to her lips. Her handsome man. Lightly tracing the line of his strong jaw with her finger, she made the inevitable comparison. Yes, Pack was every bit as good-looking as the movie icon. She touched the scar on his chin and remembered his telling her about the hockey incident when he was a sophomore in high school. The small cicatrix above his right eye, however, was something he never talked about. Or, was it that she had never asked? Sometimes it seemed that much of Pack's life was a mystery. Although he could talk about almost anything, and was always open to sharing his feelings, there were many closet doors that seemed closed—areas and places that were never discussed.

Rolling over onto her back, Maddie stared at the ceiling. Everybody had closets she reasoned. In time, they were opened and aired. But, what was it about this man that perplexed her? At times so gregarious and at others so aloof, remote—seemingly lost in some self- absorbed reverie. She remembered Pack telling her once that he spent too much time by himself...that he was a loner at heart. At the time, she had laughed at the admission. Yet, tonight it was keeping her awake.

Pack had his own little house off Lindquist Road south of town. He told her that he bought the place because of the four-acre lot backed by dense woods. He told her that it was his retreat from all the stresses of life. What those stresses were—he never elaborated. In the months that they had dated, Maddie had only been out to his house a couple of times. Once, on a Sunday afternoon, she had dropped in unexpectedly when Pack was deadheading some flowers in his garden. That was the only time in her memory that she actually wondered if Pack was happy to see her. She felt almost like an intruder. But, after his initial surprise at seeing her, he was as congenial as ever. They shared a wonderful day together.

Maddie fell asleep that night with a headache. Was Pack really happy here in California? Was he really—deeply and honestly—

happy with her? How did a woman open the closets of a man's life without risking trouble?

~

When winter's talons clutch the North Country, long, gray months follow in seemingly endless monotony. As Rick Bourgoyne promised on his 'Morning Show' this first week of December, subzero temperatures were on their way and would linger for several days. Preceding the cold front had been a measurable snowfall. "Winter is here, folks!" Raising his voice to emphasize his detest of the inevitable, Rick added with a laugh—"Let me remind you once again, we're all up in this frigid neck of the woods by choice. So, let our complaints be tempered by that reality. Now, on the up side of things, the city crews are putting in the hockey boards and all of the local skating rinks should have a good sheet of ice. And you ice-fishermen out there—and I'm not one of you—can get your houses on the lakes. Ahhh, the wonderment of Minnesota winter."

Despite his facetious reference, Rick was proud to be an Iron Ranger. To him, an avid cross-country skier, no place on earth offered a better quality of life. Like other natives of the area, he had learned to cope with the adversities Mother Nature imposed by taking advantage of recreational and sporting activities the climate presented. Range towns were nationally acknowledged hotbeds of hockey—especially the small mining city of Eveleth where the fabled Hippodrome ice arena had produced countless hockey legends. Year after year the Eveleth high school teams skated off with state championships. Yet, if hockey was the major spectator sport, curling was even more popular in terms of participation. Bonspiels across the Range brought weekends of boisterous revelry to curling clubs throughout the winter months. Add ice fishing, skiing, sliding and tobogganing to the mix—along with fur-trapping in the abundant forests—and the diversity more than compensated for any adversities imposed.

~

Kevin Moran and Gary Zench listened to Damon Porter's account of the JR Roberts interrogation that afternoon. "You only did what you had to do, Damon," Kevin said. "You started a little fire. God knows we needed that to happen. Finally, these guys are going to feel some heat."

"I warned JR," Porter shook his large head. "Behind his phony tough-guy attitude I could tell he was scared shitless. And, the cop Lawrence has watching these guys called in to say that JR was being tailed by Tobin. As we expected, JR went right to Daddy."

Kevin frowned. Ian Roberts was a formidable adversary. "I'll talk to Ian. Let him know that we've got his son's best interests in mind. The two of us are not friends by any stretch...but I think he'll listen to me."

"Thanks, Kevin. I'm sure Don Lawrence would appreciate that. Maybe you could give Lester Bowman a call as well." Porter sighed to himself and realized how much he needed to learn about small town politics.

Gary sat quietly, his long fingers stroking the line of his jaw. In the back of his thoughts he was counting the weeks since September twelfth when his son was last seen. Resignation was etched in the lines of his tired face—fifteen weeks! He regarded Kevin with doleful eyes. Throughout these difficult times no one had been more committed to resolving this tragedy than his lifelong friend. As he had done so many times of late, he was counting his blessings. His devoted wife, Nora, was at the top of his list, Kevin next...and so many friends. The surety that his son was dead had settled in his psyche long ago. From now on, Gary would learn to be content with memories. Wonderful memories. Self-pity was no more than a cold, dark, and endless cave. A cave from whose labyrinths he must escape before it swallowed him up.

Gary contemplated Kevin almost as if for the first time. His friend had just consoled Damon Porter and offered his help for the beleaguered police chief. Always seeking to mollify potential problems, always looking out for someone else, always willing to involve himself...Kevin the peacemaker! Gary recalled the Beatitudes from Scripture. "Thanks, Kevin. Thanks for everything," Gary blurted, filling a pause in the conversation.

Kevin gave his friend a befuddled smile, "For what, Gary?" He was confused by the well-intended comment dropping from out of the blue.

Gary smiled, "For being my best friend in the world, Kevin. That's all." He smiled for the first time. "My friend! What a blessing you are."

~

Angela Moran called Nora Zench from her downtown art studio that afternoon. She had not talked with Nora since last Friday and had a quiet moment to share with her friend. Angie had just put the finishing touches of gray highlights on the winter scene she had sketched during the blizzard more than a month ago. The canvas oil painting was one of the best she had ever done and would bring several hundred dollars at an art show in the Cities or Chicago. The wispy drifts along the picket fence were vividly captured in her typically broad strokes of white. The portrait's overall effect was chillingly winter. Standing away from the easel with a brush in her hand she eyed the finished product—"Perfection!" she complimented under her breath.

As satisfied as Angela was with her new work, she would not sell this winter landscape. "Hello, Nora..."

Nora Zench was speechless. "You've been working on that painting for weeks, Angie. How can you do this? I'm at a loss for words. I just can't—"

"A painting is only as special as the people who behold it. I would be honored if you accepted the painting in the spirit in which it's offered, Nora. Your son has been my inspiration from the start and there's no one else I could give this to." Angie paused in her thoughts. "...You are my friend—and a friend is the treasure of life."

Nora's eyes teared, her voice choked with emotion. "You have made this day beautiful, Angie—my dear friend, Angie." There were no more profound words than these to offer—'my dear friend'.

When she hung up the phone and wiped at her tears, Nora thought of something her mother had told her long before. "It takes a solitary person to truly appreciate the meaning of friendship." Her mother's wisdom always helped Nora keep a grip on the genuine pearls of life.

47/ WATCHING THE LITTLE FIRE

Randy Tobin drove to Dahlberg's apartment and found the shades drawn and garage empty. "Shit! Where in hell is he?" Tobin knew Dave had the day off. Nobody at the pool hall had seen Dahlberg since Saturday night. The same at Sully's Pool Hall and the Homer Bar. It was nearly six and Tobin was frustrated. He returned to the Standard station's pay phone and dialed. Rosnau had told them never to call him at home—he'd be pissed. But Tobin was feeling too vulnerable to give a damn. Things were getting strange.

Rosnau barked, "I'm eating supper, damn it. You otta know better than—"

"Fuck you, Rosnau. I wanna know what's goin' on. I think Dahlberg's skipped town. Have you talked to him? And, what did you find out about JR?"

Rosnau whispered across the table to his live-in, Nel Trask. "Norgren down at the station—some domestic crap."

When police matters came up, Nel gave Leonard privacy.

"Meet me in an hour." He considered where he and Tobin might be inconspicuous. The Homer and Sportsmen's wouldn't work. "Randy, find a place in the Memorial Building parking lot. There's curling tonight—should be lots of cars. Keep your eyes open. I'll find you. Hope you've got a good heater in that heap of yours—it's damn cold outside."

It was six-fifty and the evening well into winter's early dark. Snowfall softened the edges of a chilling northern breeze. Rosnau was not a spontaneous man. Mistakes were the result of acting without forethought. But clear decisions had to be made—soon! One thing seemed certain, JR had to be dealt with. After meeting Tobin, Rosnau would swing by the Androy and visit with Carl Wicklund. He circled the parking lot a second time scanning for idling cars.

Dave Dahlberg was in Grand Forks on that frigid Monday night. Without telling anybody, he had left Hibbing the previous afternoon to hang out with his University of North Dakota student cousin. He had spotted Porter following him home from the Homer on Saturday night, then again on Sunday morning when he went out for coffee. Porter freaked him. Why was the big city detective so damn interested in his whereabouts? What did he know? Were Tobin and Roberts being watched, too? And, Rosnau? He didn't trust the cop. Worse, he didn't know if he trusted Tobin and Roberts. It crossed his mind that he might be the fall guy if shit started coming down.

Dahlberg had a long weekend from his Agnew Mine job and didn't have to punch in again until the next afternoon. Maybe he should head west. Get away from everything for a while. He needed time to think. One thing was certain in his thoughts, he was not going near the Zench body again. For all he cared, the corpse could rot where they left it.

But, if he took off somewhere...then he'd be playing into their hands. Dahlberg felt stuck.

Rosnau parked his rusty GMC pickup several cars away from where Tobin was waiting in his idling '52 Mercury. Slipping inside the smoke-filled car, Rosnau coughed and cussed. "Roll down your window for God's sake." He pulled up the collar of his leather bomber jacket and put his back to the passenger window. "Lets make this quick, Randy."

"Fine with me. Where the hell's Dahlberg gone? I've looked everywhere."

"No idea—he's your buddy, not mine." Rosnau blew warm breath over his ungloved hands. "That chicken-shit bastard might've taken off on us. You shouldn't be surprised, Tobin—he told you he was thinking of running two weeks ago."

"That's what I'm thinkin'. Maybe JR spooked him or somethin'. I ain't heard from him since Saturday and he's got the weekend off."

"Maybe it's just as well if Dahlberg's skipped out for a while. Might throw a wrench into what Porter's up to. If he thinks Dahlberg knows something, maybe he'll head out of town looking for him."

Tobin said nothing for a long minute. Rosnau's theory seemed stupid. Porter wasn't going anywhere. "So, what's the scoop on JR anyhow?"

"Don't know. If he told Porter anything Lawrence would have said something to me. I'm still in charge." Rosnau hoped Tobin took his line. "Regardless, I think JR's a problem we've got to take care of. Now. Dahlberg's something we can deal with later."

"What's Wicklund been up to lately? I never see the guy. Lately, you're the only one I've talked to. That makes me nervous."

"Fuck the nervous! I've got a good handle on things. Gonna check in with Wicklund later tonight." Rosnau's tone became take-charge. "Let's get back to JR."

Tobin leveled his gaze on Rosnau. "If you think I'm gonna get rid of Roberts...well, think again. I ain't doin' nothin' by myself."

Rosnau paused as a car with its lights on pulled into the vacant spot behind Tobin's Mercury. His first thought was Porter. What if the detective found the two of them together? Hunching his shoulders, he watched through the side view mirror. False alarm! Rosnau breathed easier as the man hustled across the snowy lot from his car to the side door of the arena. "I just want you to talk to Roberts. That's all for right now. Find out what his meeting at the police station was about. Get a read on where he's at. Can you do that? It's not too late, maybe you can pick up a coupl'a six packs, swing by his apartment."

Tobin nodded at the reasonable suggestion. "I'll see what I can do. But, what if he's already spilled his guts to Porter? What then?"

"Don't worry about that. If he had, we wouldn't be having this conversation." Opening the door to the frigid draft, Rosnau started for his truck. "Give me a call at the station tomorrow. We'll get this figured out. Don't worry, Randy."

"Don't worry?" Tobin muttered loud enough for Rosnau to hear. "I think you're as scared shitless as I am."

From his nondescript gray Chevrolet parked at the corner of Twenty-third and Sixth Avenue East, Porter watched Rosnau's pickup leave the lot. His gut instinct told him to follow Tobin rather than Rosnau.

~

JR Roberts, already three deep into his own six-pack, was watching television when Tobin knocked on his door. "Door's open," he called without turning away from the screen.

Tobin stopped in front of the set, turned down the volume and found a chair across from his friend. "So, whatta ya been up to, JR? Ain't seen much of ya lately."

"Nothing much—same old, work and sleep. You know."

"Ain't seen Dahlberg, neither. Thought you two guys might be hanging and forgettin' your old buddy. Ya seen Dave?"

JR forced a laugh, finished his beer. "Not for a while. I was thinking the same about you two."

Tobin opened a can of Schmidt, pushed the bag of beer toward JR. "Have another."

"I think Dave's on his long weekend from the mine. Must be shaking up with that babe in Virginia—Jeannie something or other. Say's she's hot and easy."

"Yeah. Maybe so." Tobin swallowed half his can in one gulp. He knew that Jean Pauletti had given Dahlberg the brush two weeks ago.

"Stopped by Lerch this afternoon to see if ya wanted to bowl tonight, or take in a movie. Giant's at the Lybba. But that big-titted secretary tol me you left early." Tobin tossed his bait.

"On a Monday night?" JR looked puzzled.

"Why not?" Tobin tried to fix on JR's eyes. "Where were ya?"

"Had some stuff to take care of. The bank called. My checking account's all screwed up. Got that taken care of...and then came back here and crashed on the couch."

Tobin let the lie drop without comment. JR was beginning to feel the beer. "Hey, drink up. I've got two six-packs here."

They polished off two more beers, watched Red Skelton, talked about cars and girls they planned to lay. JR's eyes were getting heavy. "High school team drubbed Grand Rapids Saturday. Ya go to the game?"

JR yawned. "You know I don't give a damn about basketball." He slurred the word. Another yawn—deeper. "Say...Randy...I'm wiped.

Why don' ya put the beer in the fridge. Save some for tomorrow."

"Rosnau tol me ya were at the police station this afternoon."

JR's head lifted. "Yeah...just stopped by on my way to the bank." He thought quickly. "Parking ticket."

Tobin had had enough bullshit. "I didn't know this Porter asshole was takin' care of Hibbing parking tickets. I thought Moran brought him here to find out 'bout Zench." Tobin leaned forward—if he needed to, he'd get tough with Roberts. "What did Porter want to know, JR? And don't give me anymore fuckin' lies, goddamn it!"

Roberts remembered the detective's warning about his being in trouble—even "in danger". And, he remembered his father's advice—"Stay away from those two hooligans and don't say a word to anyone about anything."

Tobin stood, moved to the couch only an arm's length from JR. "You don't tell me what's goin' on and I'm gonna bust up yer fuckin' face."

Suddenly sober and scared, Roberts was caught somewhere in the middle of an ugly situation—Porter on one side, Rosnau on the other. A no-win situation. His gut instinct was to fear Rosnau more than Porter.

"Rosnau send you here, Randy?"

"What's the difference? Talk to me, Roberts. No bull-shit talk."

"I told Porter I didn't know anything—and that's the fucking truth!"

Tobin grabbed JR's shirt, "Nothin' about what?"

"Jerry Zench for crissakes." JR saw the rage in Tobin's eyes. "He's just fishing for something—anything. We're on some kind of list because of that softball crap. You know that already. He kept mentioning this list. I don't think he knows shit, Randy. Honest to God, I swear..."

Tobin read fear in JR's face and 'Honest to God' always raised a flag. "I don't know what Porter knows, but I know that you know too much, JR. What you know can get the rest of us guys in big trouble."

JR remembered Porter's warning. Fear was a knot in his stomach. He gripped Tobin's fist which had tightened its grip on his shirt, tried to push the larger man away. "Leave me alone, will ya?"

Tobin twisted the shirt, rubbed his knuckles under JR's jaw. "Am I on this list of Porter's? Dahlberg?"

"He didn't mention any names. All he said was..." JR wanted to vomit. "All he said was that he had five names. Said that I'm one of them."

Tobin could do the calculations. Porter knew more than he thought. "So you didn't tell him anything?"

"Nothing. Shit, Randy...I don't know anything—really." In a quivering voice he appealed, "...Just keep me out of this—I don't want to know anything about what you guys did."

"What did we do, JR?"

"I told you, I don't know." He swallowed hard, "Look, all I ever did was mail that fuckin' letter from Minneapolis. That's all Rosnau ever asked me to do. So, whatever else happened—"

"What do you think happened?"

JR's eyes were wide with fear, "I told you, I don't want to know what happened." Then, trying to repress a sob, he looked directly at Tobin for the first time in twenty minutes. "Jerry is dead—isn't he?"

"What makes you think I know?"

JR wished he hadn't asked, felt himself stuck in a corner. He would try to show some bravado. Pushing with both hands at Tobin's arms he said, "I'm not deaf and dumb, Randy. Christ, it's not too hard to put two and two together. Dahlberg told me a while ago that 'one part of the nigger problem in Hibbing was taken care of'— that's exactly what he said. So, what am I supposed to think?"

"Dahlberg said that?" Under his breath, Tobin cussed—"That son-of-a-bitch!" He relaxed his grip, looked away.

"Don't you guys worry, Randy. I'm not saying anything to anybody. My dad's getting me a lawyer, too. Just in case, you know...in case they want to talk to me again. My dad says they can't make me say anything—and a lawyer's gonna make sure of that."

"A lawyer, huh? Your dad thinks ya need a lawyer." Now Tobin was nervous—more scared than he had ever been in his life. Porter had a list and his name was probably on it: neither JR nor Dahlberg could be trusted, and Rosnau was floundering. What was he going to do—kill the people who could put him in Stillwater Prison for the rest of his life? Things were crumbling around him.

"Okay, JR, just keep your fuckin' mouth shut—like ya been doin'." Tobin's let go of the shirt. "Like you, I don't know what might'a happened. Maybe Dahlberg does...maybe even Rosnau. But, you and me...we ain't gonna get our asses hung out to dry. Right?"

JR smiled at the apparent reprieve and his friend's false optimism. "Right, Randy. We've gotta hang together, don't we?"

With his fingers numbed with cold, Porter made a second entry in his notebook: Tobin arrived at Robert's apartment approx. 7:30. Left approx. 9:15. The detective could only imagine the conversation in the upstairs rooms of JR's apartment, but it must have had something to do with the earlier meeting between Rosnau and Tobin. A wry smile crossed his stubbled face. His little fire on Rosnau's ship was beginning to make the rats run.

48/ *A BONE IN THE SNOW*

The morning was mild, Angela Moran restless. After listening to the first hour of Rick's Morning Show and baking a batch of chocolate chip cookies, she contemplated spending an hour or two in her upstairs studio. There was something she planned on doing when the weather moderated, but she couldn't remember. On the phone table she found her calendar with scribbled notes—grocery lists, menus, and assorted reminders. "Ahaa," she smiled at something Kevin had penciled on the margin. Their neighbor, Nels Nordvold had called last week to inform Kevin that a section of fencing along the southwest corner of their property was in disrepair. Angie had promised Kevin that she would take a look at the problem when she took her next ride. This morning was a perfect time.

Angie pulled on her western boots, took out her wool plaid jacket, found warm mittens and wrapped an old scarf around her ears. Outside, she walked the treeline trail down snow-blanketed Maple Hill toward the barn. As she approached, she heard the nervous whining of the horses. Her eyes darted from the corral to the line of wood-railed fence off to her left. She froze! The fresh tracks were unmistakable—wolves! A pack of maybe four or five had circled the corral; probably within the past several hours. Looking beyond where she stood, her gaze followed the spores leading south and west toward the pond and the highway nearly a quarter of a mile away. Wolves.

Inside the barn, Angie raced to the telephone mounted by the tack room door. She dialed Kevin at the hotel. "Kevin—we've had wolves around the barn—the tracks are fresh—seem to be headed from here toward the pond—the horses are skittish." In her excitement, Angie's words and thoughts ran together like a racing train.

Kevin was not surprised. He had been told about wolves in the area by a dairy farmer on Leighton road just the day before. He smiled to himself, "Don't worry, sweetheart. I'll give the DNR game warden a quick call and come out to take a look myself. Just sit tight for a few minutes, okay?"

Nearly an hour later, Kevin found Angie waiting nervously inside the barn. She had two geldings saddled and ready for an exploratory ride. Kevin embraced his wife, "looks like you're anxious to get out and find those critters."

"I don't like wolves, Kevin. How can you be so calm? Wolves are killers."

Kevin laughed, "They're a lot more frightened of us than we are of them. I'll take the 'four-ten' along, but they're probably long gone by now."

The spores were easily followed in the fresh snow. As the predator's scent became stronger the horses snorted and pulled. The pack had traveled the full length of the Moran property, beyond the frozen stream, toward the pond which was buffered from the highway by a thick row of Norway pines. Kevin reined his agitated horse—up ahead was a disturbing sight. The pack had stopped near a ditch about fifty feet from the well-traveled roadway. "Looks like they found something over there," he gestured as Angie pulled her horse beside him.

Approaching slowly, Kevin could read the signs. A pained look crossed his face. "Wait here, Angie." He dismounted and walked to the track-compacted area among the cattails at the ponds edge. Kneeling at the edge of the ice he could smell rotted flesh. Brushing his hand into the snow where traces of blood had crusted, Kevin touched the bone. He choked at the swell that moved from his stomach into his chest and throat. A human bone! The size and shape suggested it was a femur. The bloodied fabric of bluejeans and burlap were frozen into the ice. He gasped at the horrific sight.

"What is it, Kevin?" Angie's voice betrayed her own fears.

Kevin set the bone back into the snow, looked up at his wife. "I think we've found Jerry." His eyes moistened, "How could anybody...?" The answer was beyond anything Kevin could fathom. As he hung his head and tried to say a prayer, Angie's hand touched his shoulder. Fighting against his tears he mumbled "eternal rest..." Then he broke down, unable to finish the supplication.

Kevin remained with the body, careful not to disturb the scene any more than he already had, while Angie raced back to the barn to make a phone call to Lawrence. He had no doubts that these remains were those of Jerry Zench—no doubts whatsoever. Flakes of snow drifted in the air as he contemplated how he might convey this tragic news to Gary and Nora. While waiting for Lawrence and Porter, he prayed and cried and wondered. Why? This dimension of human hatred could not be measured in his mind.

Kevin's watch read two when he called Gary at the hotel. "Gary, we need to talk. I'll meet you and Nora at your house in an hour."

Gary knew. He had seen Kevin leave the office nearly four hours ago. It was unusual for his friend to be gone that long without letting someone know where he was going. Very unusual. Something was going on. "I'll have Nora put on a pot of coffee, Kevin."

"Lots of coffee, Gary," was all Kevin said.

When she joined her husband on the couch, Nora's eyes were red from spent tears. "Kevin's bringing the news we've been expecting, isn't he?"

Nodding, Gary squeezed her hand. "Be strong for me, Nora. I'm going to need that. We can cry together later."

"Angie, I need you to come with me. I can't do this alone." Kevin said. "Sometimes I think you're a lot stronger than I am. I'm going to need that strength this afternoon."

Understanding his need, Angie embraced her husband. "We will hold our tears until afterwards, sweetheart."

That night, Kevin and Porter met with Gary in Kevin's Androy office, while Nora and Naomi, Reverend Lindquist, and Angela visited in the Zench living room discussing arrangements.

Porter reported that the body had been identified. "What remains of the clothing matches what Jerry was wearing the night he disappeared—including what appears to be an Androy softball jersey." He swallowed hard, "And we found a 1952 class ring." Sensitive to Gary's fragile emotional state, the detective would not elaborate and further on the condition of the young man's castrated remains. Nor would he acknowledge that the discovery of the body was the break his investigation needed.

Kevin sat beside his friend with a comforting hand on Gary's knee. He had poured each of them a stiff Bushmills Irish whiskey.

Gary spoke in soft tone, "As hard as all this is right now, things are probably going to get worse in the next couple of days."

Porter nodded. "The story's going to be in tomorrow's paper. Lawrence will make certain that details are kept to a minimum."

Gary turned from Porter to Kevin. "Now we're going to find out what happened. We needed the body, didn't we?"

The question floated in the air without comment. Gary was a pragmatist. That afternoon he had confided to Kevin that, for the first time in weeks, he might be able to sleep now.

~

Pack was working on some curriculum ideas at the kitchen table, and Maddie making a sandwich when the call came. "Just a minute, Mr. Moran..." There was no small talk between her and Pack's father. "Maddie, dear, I need to talk with my son." She knew something had happened back in Hibbing. Kevin never called at mid-day.

Maddie watched Pack's expression. For the longest minute, Pack only listened, nodding at words she could only imagine. Then, for the first time, she watched her man cry.

Her intuition told her that this call was going to change their relationship. This call was going to take Pack away from her. Despite the deep love that had grown between them, the fate of Pack's friend was something—a silent wall—that lingered always in the recesses of his private thoughts. Maddie would pray that this call would enable Pack to put his private torments to rest once and for all. When that happened, and only when that happened, he might then become hers—without reservation.

49/ SEAGRAMS AND CHLORAL HYDRATE

If Pack could almost feel his heart pound, Maddie could feel her heart drop into her stomach.

"I will, Dad. First flight I can get," Pack said.

Hanging up the phone, Pack wiped at his tears with the sleeve of his sweatshirt, stared off into the space beyond the kitchen window. He needed a minute to fully comprehend his father's emotion-strained words. Lawrence had just made a positive identification, Porter had told Kevin to "let Pack know—right away!" and his parents were going to visit with Gary and Nora that afternoon.

The irony of circumstance struck like stomach punch. His parents, of all people, had found the body. All this time, Jerry's corpse had been half submerged at the edge of the pond on his family's property. Despite his absence of weeks, Porter wanted him to be informed immediately. He sucked in the last swell of emotion, stood from the table, and turned to Maddie—"You know, don't you, sweetheart?"

Maddie collapsed into his arms, "Yes...I guess I've always known. And, how I've dreaded this day—this inevitable call."

Stroking her soft hair, Pack said, "Dad asked if I would come home." He tried to clear the lump in his throat. "I said I would."

Maddie sobbed at the painful reality of what was unfolding. "You have to go back, Pack. It can't be any other way—I know that. They all need you there...and I need for you to be there." She wanted to explain further, be more deeply honest, but curbed the temptation. Despite how wonderful things had been, Pack had not been wholly committed to their relationship. He couldn't be with so much unfinished business back in Minnesota. Now, perhaps, he might find some measure of closure. "Take this with you, Patrick. It's been our 'good luck'...and our promise to each other." She removed the foil band from her ring finger. "When I next see you—I'll want it back." With the gesture, she lost her composure and wept inconsolably.

~

Rosnau had not been informed of the discovery. Lawrence got Angela Moran's call and immediately contacted Damon Porter. After returning to headquarters, Lawrence stopped by Rosnau's office. "We've got the body," he blurted. "On Kevin Moran's property. Badly decomposed, and..." he spared other details. "And...in pretty sad condition. But we made an identification."

"Are you sure, Chief?" Rosnau shook his head in mock disbelief, wondered who "we" was. Probably Porter. "I can't believe it!"

"Now, we've got our work cut out for us."

At a loss for words, Rosnau offered a feeble—"I guess I had the wrong theory. Like most of us, I was certain that Zench skipped town."

Porter who had been listening in the hallway, entered the office. "I find that hard to believe, Rosnau," he scowled. "Every other cop on the force knew this was coming."

Rosnau bit his tongue on a "fuck you". This smart-ass detective would not get the best of him. "I don't know who you've been talking to, Porter, but this kind of thing doesn't happen in Hibbing. The last homicide here was five years ago. If you don't already know, the folks up here are pretty decent, tolerant, God-fearing...not like the crud down in the Cities where you're from." As soon as he finished, Rosnau realized that Porter had, indeed, provoked him.

"Did you say 'homicide', Don?" Porter asked. He let Rosnau's slip pass, paused for effect. "Yes, there are a lot of decent folks up here. And, it would seem there's a murderer in their midst. Now we've got to find him—or them—don't we, Rosnau?"

Seeking to gain some composure, Rosnau nodded. "And we will, Mr. Porter. And we will!"

Lawrence, observing the exchange, stepped to Porter's elbow. Over recent weeks he was beginning to share many of the detective's suspicions. Porter was certain that Rosnau knew something critical to the case. "Yes we will, indeed," the aging police official affirmed. "The pieces of the puzzle will finally start coming together. As sad as it is, finding the boy's body is what had to happen. Don't you agree, Lieutenant?"

Rosnau smiled weakly. "I do, Chief. What can I do to help?"

Lawrence regarded his assistant of many years with narrowed eyes. "We'll keep you posted, Leonard (it had been a long time since he had used the familiar nickname 'Lefty'). "Is there anything in your files that may be helpful to Mr. Porter? I'd like the two of you to work together as much as possible."

"Happy to pull the files, Chief." Then he met Porter's cold stare. "If you'd like, we can roll up our sleeves, right now, Damon."

"In the morning will be fine."

When the two men had left his office, Rosnau dabbed at the ridge of perspiration at his receding hairline. Under his wool police jacket, his armpits were damp and odorous. "Keep your cool..." he mumbled under his breath. Yet, nibbling at his fingernails, he could not dismiss a gnawing feeling of stress. Lawrence was playing games with him now. Work with Porter! But maybe that wasn't so bad after all? Many of his colleagues viewed Porter as an outsider—an intruder. And Rosnau had built a fair share of credibility in this town. "Focus on the positives, Len", he reminded himself. From now on he would be out of the dark, and apparently coupled with Porter every step of the way. That was a plus. And, maybe it was even possible that he could somehow win the confidence of the surly detective.

What to do? Taking off his jacket, Rosnau paced and pondered. It had been a big mistake to involve the kids—especially Roberts. If just he and Carl Wicklund had done it themselves, Rosnau would feel far less vulnerable. Tobin was a loose cannon, Dahlberg was...where had the chicken-shit gone anyhow? Think! Rosnau went to the window, peered absently into the abysmal December gray. The germ of an idea began to root in his thoughts. He and Wicklund might be able to do a frame-job—cops did it all the time. Frame Tobin and Dahlberg. If that was possible, it would be the word of a respected police officer along with a former Hibbing High School football star (Carl had been almost legendary in his day) against a couple of punks—racist punks, at that. He liked the idea and the odds, but how to pull it off? He'd need some incriminating evidence that he could plant—in the trunk of Tobin's car, or in his apartment. Something that could be clearly linked to Jerry Zench—rope, burlap, an item of clothing. As a cop, he had access to the body at the hospital's pathology lab, all of the trace evidence which was now in Lawrence's possession, and the Zench apartment. Maybe? He'd run his ideas past Carl.

In the meantime, Rosnau needed Tobin's help to take care of Roberts. Damn it! Still, if Tobin offed JR...and he nabbed Tobin...maybe that would be perfect. Complicated, but—

Another idea wormed into his thoughts. Maybe, working with the three others, Roberts could be made into the fall guy. What if Roberts confessed to murdering Zench? Rosnau remembered something he had read in one of his police magazines months before. A case study from—where the hell was the article? New Jersey? What magazine? He began rustling through his bottom desk drawer where old issues had been stuffed. Halfway through the stack he found what he was looking for. On the cover of March's Police Gazette was a bold caption: Was it Really Suicide? Flipping through the pulp issue to page twenty-four, he scanned the story to refresh his memory. Chloral hydrate was the drug he needed. "Could work", he mumbled as he stuffed the magazine back in the drawer. Wicklund's sister-in-law worked at a drug store in Chisholm.

Rosnau's scheme formed rapidly in his thoughts. Time was critical now. He glanced at his watch—four o'clock. Lifting the black phone from its cradle, he dialed the Androy. asked for Wicklund in the bar. If Carl could get the chloral hydrate yet today, Tobin could take care of JR tonight. A twisted smile crossed his face...this could work!

Tobin understood exactly what he was instructed to do. Maybe Rosnau wasn't so stupid after all. The cops plan would get them all of the hook once and for all. The vial of chloral hydrate was in one of his jacket pockets and the envelope in the other. With a bottle of Seagrams under his arm, Tobin knocked on JR's apartment door.

JR's eyes widened when he saw Tobin. Like everybody in town, he had heard about the body.

"Looks like you've died and gone to hell, JR. What's the matter?" He could read fear on his friend's ashen face. "A few good belts of this might do ya some good." He pulled the bottle from a brown bag, then went to the kitchen for glasses.

"Nah, I'm not up to any booze tonight, Randy."

From the kitchen, Tobin laughed, "Ain't gonna make your buddy drink alone, are ya? Shit's goin' on—we otta talk about, JR. Ya know what I mean."

Roberts watched Randy return to the living room with two glasses. "I'm fucking scared, Randy. I talked to my dad, he says the body was mutilated. Told me that if Porter calls again, I'd better damn well let him know right away."

"Drink up, JR. You and me are gonna figger out what to do. Don't forget, you an me don' know nothin' about what those other guys did."

JR puzzled. "Figure out what? You can bet your ass, I don't know what anybody did. All I know is that Porter is gonna—"

"Porter's gonna do shit." Tobin watched JR swallow half his whiskey. He drained his glass and stood, "Finish up, have another. Got any chips or anythin' in yer kitchen?"

JR finished what remained in his glass, handed Randy his glass. "Help yourself. And add some water to mine, this was pretty stiff."

"Don't be a pussy. So, what's Porter gonna do, JR?"

JR remembered his father's insistence that he not talk to anybody about anything. "Maybe the guy just freaks me out or something. He's not like the local cops. You ever talked to him, Randy?"

"What for?" Tobin handed JR another drink. "You think I'm on that list he tol ya about?"

JR didn't want to rehash the last conversation between the two of them. Yet, he wondered what Randy wanted to 'figger out'. His friend seemed out of sorts—even nervous. He matched Tobin's next two swallows. "Seen Dahlberg? We've got bowling Thursday night."

"Nah. He'll show up. When he does, maybe the two of us otta lean on him a little. He's been actin' kinda strange, doncha think, JR? I wonder 'bout him sometimes. Fuck, here's to our buddy..." Tobin finished his second.

Over the next half hour, Tobin watched the effects of the chloral hydrate on JR's speech and demeanor. They talked bowling and sports. During their fourth glass, Tobin's curiosity resurfaced.

"Whatcha think we otta do, JR? I can't help thinkin' 'bout that list. Think I shood ask yer ol' man ta get me a lawyer, too?"

JR responded slowly after taking another swallow. "Yeah...mebbe the same one...I ain't met 'em yet...mebbe..." He slouched forward, shook his head. "Yeah...mebbe..." He rubbed at his eyes, pushed himself back into the sofa. "Shhhhiiit... I... feel... I'm...like...shhhiiiit...Ran...dy..."

Sitting in his parked car, Porter was roused by what he thought was the sound of a car starting. Then, the man door of the garage behind the Roberts apartment closed. Why? Was Roberts going somewhere? He craned his neck, watched intently for activity—no car left the garage. Strange. Minutes later he saw the lights go out in the apartment window upstairs. Confused, Porter watched and waited. In a few minutes he saw Tobin leave through the building's side door and return to his parked car. Tobin's movements were suspiciously furtive. Following at a distance, he watched as Tobin drove several blocks to the Homer Bar on First Avenue. There, he parked his car and went inside.

Porter tried to put things together. It was only nine-thirty. Too early for Roberts to be going to bed. From his previous surveillance, he had learned the patterns of his suspects. Roberts was a night owl. Concerned, Porter decided to drive back to the Roberts apartment. Tobin would probably stay put in the Homer for a while.

Porter made a U-turn. If Roberts was asleep, he'd wake him up. With the discovery of the body that morning, maybe Roberts was getting nervous and have more to say than when they last talked. It was worth checking out.

Walking around to the side of the asbestos-sided building, Porter smelled exhaust fumes. Seeping from under the side door of the garage he could see the toxic vapors. The door was locked. Lowering his thick shoulder, he split the door from its frame. Choking, he found the light switch on the wall...

50/ A SUICIDE NOTE

At eleven o'clock the three men assembled in Lawrence's office. "I got him to the hospital in time—he's going to be okay when he comes to." Porter informed.

"Thank God you went back when you did, Damon," Kevin said.

"Another ten minutes and—who knows?" Lawrence added.

Using his handkerchief so as not to contaminate the evidence, Porter opened the envelope and carefully laid the letter on the desktop for the others to see. "What do you fella's think?"

The note was typewritten in capital letters:

> *I KILLED JERRY ZENCH BY MYSELF. I DON'T DESERVE TO LIVE. I APPOLOGISE TO THE ZENCH FAMILY AND TO YOU MOM AND DAD. I'M SORRY FOR WHAT I HAVE TO DO.*
>
> *JR*

Kevin shook his head, met Porter's eyes with a level gaze. "This is not JR's note. For one thing, he got enough college to spell correctly—'apologise' is misspelled—and, for another, I don't think he would sign his name for the last time with 'JR'. His parents always call him Ian.

Porter nodded at the insights. "You know him better than I do, Kevin. Do you think he could resort to something like this? He seemed to me like a tough-willed kid—almost defiant."

"Not the JR I know, Damon."

"Then we all agree on that," Lawrence said from behind his desk. "And the typeface looks awfully familiar."

Porter and Kevin agreed.

"When will we be able to talk to him?" Lawrence asked.

"Doc says sometime tomorrow."

"Don, first thing in the morning we'll need some search warrants. We've got to check JR's apartment and the Lerch labs—see if there's a typewriter there that was used for the note. And, try to find a match on the paper. Its cheap stationery." Porter stood to go. "I have my doubts we'll find anything that matches."

Lawrence opened his drawer, withdrew a master key. "Damon, you wanted to check the typewriter in Rosnau's office."

Porter smiled.

"What else needs to be done?" Lawrence asked.

Kevin stood, "As late as it is, I'm going to visit with Ian and Molly Roberts. They're across the street at the hospital right now. Do you think I should tell them about this note?"

Lawrence nodded. "I think so. God, that won't be pleasant, Kevin. But they should know everything we know."

Porter stopped at the door. "Kevin, when is Pack getting in?"

"Tomorrow afternoon." Kevin had a thought. "You know, Pack's been taking some forensics classes out there. Maybe he should look at the letter before we send it off to the crime labs in St. Paul."

"I like that idea." Porter rubbed at the stubble on his chiseled jaw. "Damn, it's going to be great to have another cop on board."

Lawrence cleared his throat, "Not just a cop—one helluva good cop, Damon!"

Kevin smiled at the compliment. "I agree, Don. He and JR go way back to elementary school. Maybe we should let Pack be involved in questioning JR. I'm sure there's still a bond between the two of them."

"Good thinking," Porter said. "JR's had enough of me and Don for right now. What about Tobin? When are we going to bring him in?"

"I've already put Anderson and Petroski on Tobin. If he so much as heads for the city limits, we're pulling him over. And, we've got an all-points out for Dahlberg. Both of them are on our agenda for tomorrow—after we've talked with Roberts." For the first time this evening, Lawrence felt 'in charge'. "I can't wait to visit with our lieutenant in the morning. When we bring in Tobin, I'd like him to be with me."

Before returning to his hotel room, Porter decided to stop by the Androy bar before the lounge closed for the night. Having known too many alcoholics over the years, he had an aversion toward drinking, and places that fostered the pathetic disease. Over the weeks since arriving in Hibbing, Porter had yet to meet the burly bartender, Carl Wicklund. From a distance he had observed the crew cut former football player on a few occasions, but only spare words had passed between them. Porter never sat at the bar, preferring a table off to the side.

"Scotch and coke on the rocks—without the scotch!" Porter said over his elbows on the long, oak bar.

Wicklund puzzled, nodded without a smile at the customer's wit.

Porter folded his large hands and watched the man pull a bottle from the cooler and unsnap the cap. Wicklund wore a white shirt, red bow tie, black apron, and a scowl on his broad face. Porter noted how tightly the extra large shirt strained across the man's bulging biceps. Wicklund would be a formidable adversary in the alley outside.

Only two other men were sitting at the bar and both were several stools away. Porter slipped a dollar bill across the polished oak as Wicklund poured the cola over ice in a tall glass. "Twenty cents," was all the barman had to say.

"Saw that basketball team of yours the other night. Damn good outfit." Porter tried to engage the man in some sports talk. "That Sabbatini kid, and Retica can really shoot."

"Good athletes," Wicklund mumbled.

"Name's Damon Porter," the detective introduced. "Played some ball myself. Down at Edison in the Cities. We had some pretty fair teams back then, but I don't think we could keep up with your Bluejackets."

"Heard of Edison," was all Wicklund had to say.

"You play basketball...? Sorry, I didn't catch your name."

"Football. Name's Wicklund. Carl."

Wicklund knew damn well that Porter knew who he was. Probably had a file on him. Let the asshole fish if he wanted to. But, he was curious. Why hadn't the cop talked to him before? Rosnau had kept him informed about what Porter was up to—mentioned some kind of list. Probably the body had something to do with the timing. Maybe, he'd do some fishing himself. "What brings you to Hibbing?" A question that both men knew the answer to.

Porter spoke in flat tone without hesitation. "The Zench case." He looked for a reaction.

"You a reporter or sumthin?"

"A detective."

"Oh. Working for Lawrence?"

"Your boss—Kevin Moran."

Wicklund was cool—no change in expression. "Thought you knew that," Porter said.

"Don't pay much attention."

"We had a major break today."

Wicklund couldn't play too dumb. "Heard sumthin about that. You guys found his body, right?" He forced a frown, "A tragedy—that's fer sure. Zench kid was a pretty good athlete himself. All sports."

"Did you know him well, Carl? Friends? Play on the same teams?"

Wicklund's eyes narrowed, "Hardly knew 'em at all. Negroes don't come in our bar very often." As soon as he said it he wished he hadn't. "His dad works for Moran here at the hotel. Nice enough guy, I guess."

"I've met him—a real gentleman. This has been pretty tough on him."

"Yeah. Hard on lots of folks." Wicklund has said enough. "Better check on the fellas down the bar, Mr. Potter."

"Porter, Carl. Damon Porter." He pushed his Coke aside. "You're going to know my name damn well in the next few days—you fucking bigot..." were the words he wanted to say but kept to himself. "See you around."

51/ "NO THOUSAND MILE..."

Still groggy from the effects of chloral hydrate and carbon monoxide poisoning, JR Roberts regarded his parents who had spent the night at his bedside. At some level, through the throbbing headache, he realized that Porter's warning was accurate—while at another level he was consumed with anger. He had regained consciousness hours before. His mother explained what had happened and how Mr. Porter had saved his life. She did not inform him of Mr. Moran's visit or the suicide note.

JR was scared. He told his father he had had too much to drink and fallen asleep in the garage without turning off the ignition. He knew the lie hadn't worked, but his parents didn't push the matter. Tobin had doped him and tried to kill him—but, he needed time to figure everything out. That he was lucky to be alive had become too obscured in a larger picture that he remained confused about. "Fuck...!" he mumbled incoherently. Then, "Sorry, Mom...I'm still having flashbacks or something."

Molly Roberts smiled her forgiveness without comment. Her confusion, however, was difficult to mask. Lines of spent tears streaked her tired face. She and Ian had argued about confronting their son about the note and it's connection to the death of Jerry Zench. Dr. Johnsrud had advised them to wait until he was more fully recovered. Reverend Haglund would be stopping by the hospital room soon. Molly contemplated the torment behind her son's blurted vulgarity, measured it against her own anguish. She met her husband's eyes before speaking, "We need to talk, son. Did Randy do something to you last night?"

Ian frowned, "Not now, honey, please. He's still sick."

Molly dismissed the caution, repeated her question.

JR looked away without reply.

"Your father and I don't believe you had an accident."

JR turned his back to her, "Leave me alone."

Ian Roberts shook his head. The unnerving questions he'd bottled up all these hours escaped his mouth. "Why, Son? How could you do this to your mother and me? We had no idea that things were so bad...so terribly bad in your life. Tell us why you did—"

JR gave his father a cold scowl. "Did what, for crissakes? Ma said you don't believe me. What do you want me to tell you, anyhow?"

"The truth," Ian pleaded. "Just the truth. We can deal with it—whatever."

JR puzzled. "Do you think I tried to kill myself?"

~

When the small prop plane taxied toward the terminal it was nearly six in the already dark evening. Pack could see his father and mother waving their welcome home from the building's large frost-edged window. As expected, Minnesota's winter was a full-blown contrast to the world already two thousand miles behind him. Pack breathed in the crisp air as he rushed from the plane. The cold wind stung at his face, but he smiled at the sensation. It was great to be back! Coming home was like Christmas—the gifts were loved ones waiting.

For the long hours—from Sacramento to Denver to Minneapolis—Pack had wondered if the events of yesterday would cast a pall over his reunion. He hoped not. But, this was a business trip, and despite his happiness to be home again, he was eager to plunge into the police work.

Rick and Maury had come to the airport along with his parents, Maribec and Steven and his brother's friend. Grandma Becca was there, too—along with Marco. The entire group would have dinner at the Androy, celebrate and catch up.

"You've lost weight, Patrick!" A mother's typical lament was the first thing he heard, and a mother's embrace his first good feeling.

"It's only the California suntan, Angie." Kevin beamed as he took his son's hand in his own. "You look great!"

Hugs and handshakes and questions along with greetings from Maddie crowned the warm reception. While waiting for his duffle bag, Pack told Steven and Bobby about a Harry Bellefonte concert that he and Maddie had seen two weeks before. Marco and Maribec were as intrigued as the two boys and probed with questions about every detail.

The Androy meal and homecoming were delightfully social. Nothing was spoken about the meeting which had been arranged for upstairs at nine o'clock. Pack would meet with his father, Porter and Lawrence for an update briefing before going to the hospital. As had been expected, JR Roberts had refused to talk with anybody about his previous night's brush with death. He was, however, visibly shaken. At his father's insistence, JR thanked Porter—but did so with impassive reluctance. When allowed to read the 'suicide note', JR finally broke down and cried.

~

Having visited with the hospital pathologist about the autopsy on their son in the late morning, Gary and Nora Zench met with John Dougherty at the funeral home about arrangements in the early afternoon. Wednesday, December 5—the day after—was proving to be the longest day of their lives. Kevin and Angela had been God-sent. Their friends brought breakfast rolls to their house and joined them over coffee for nearly two hours. But, both were making arrangements of their own for the return of their son that evening.

The thought of a returning son only deepened Gary's melancholy. How devoutly he had prayed that his boy would return in those early days, and reverently he prayed for Jerry's eternal rest in recent weeks. The workings of his God were not to be understood. All he could do now was find consolation in Kevin's good fortune. Pack, he knew, had his own cross to bear. When the young man called the night before to express his heartfelt condolences, Gary had another insight on friendship. "We only had one fight between us, Mr. Zench. We were just little kids, playing catch as I remember, at the time. Jerry said 'My dad's a better player than your dad'—well, I disagreed, of course. I said something like 'my dad's bigger and better than your dad any time.' Jerry pushed me, and I pushed him back. Next we were wrestling on the ground. When our scuffle was over—and he was on top of me—we both laughed at the silliness. 'Pack', he said, 'our dad's are both equal'. "

Sitting together in their living room in mid-afternoon, each absorbed in a private reverie, Gary and Nora held hands. Gary was lost in the pleasant memory of Pack's story from the previous evening, Nora absorbed in the solace of her prayers. Gary turned to his wife. "I'll pray with you if you like."

Nora smiled and nodded. "I was just thinking...remembering something my mother told me years ago—when Freddy was killed in the war. I didn't really know my brother very well. I think he was about twenty and I must have been about nine or ten." Nora always seemed to find pearls of insight when reflecting upon her wise and kindly mother's words. "I can't quite remember how my mom expressed it...but it went something like this: *'He doesn't give us our sons for no thousand mile, He think you need some sun and lends them for a while...'* "

Gary draped his arm over Nora's shoulder, pulled her close to his side. The thought was both profound and uplifting. He sobbed into her soft hair, "We must always thank him for the loan—and the sunshine!"

52/ A HOSPITAL VISIT

Decisions needed to be made. Among the weary men assembled in the Androy office, it was agreed that on Thursday morning Tobin would be arrested and the hunt for Dave Dahlberg accelerated.

"So, that's where we are right now, Pack," Kevin said. Along with Porter and Lawrence, he had explained the past forty-eight hours in detail. Pack had several questions—most of which centered on the alleged connections between Rosnau and Tobin. "A clever set up," he agreed. "JR had some role in this, but I'd bet not a major one. Once he talks, Tobin and Dahlberg will cave. Rosnau and Wicklund are the linchpins."

As impressed as Pack was with Porter, he was equally surprised with Don Lawrence. The police chief was not nearly as incompetent as he once believed. He was energized about working with this team of professionals.

"You must be more exhausted than any of us, Son." Kevin was ready to conclude the ninety-minute session. "Let's get you home for a good night's sleep."

"I'm running on adrenaline, Dad. It's a good feeling, believe me. I probably couldn't sleep tonight if I tried." Pack had his own agenda. "I'd like to go over to the hospital and check on JR."

Kevin looked disappointed, Pack read the feeling. He placed his hand on Kevin's shoulder, "We're going to have lots of time together over the next few days, Dad. You and mom and me. How about telling Mom that I'll be by for breakfast—early, about seven?"

Kevin smiled at the idea. "She'll be delighted." He turned to the other men, "We're on for eight, right? Don's office?"

"If all goes as planned, we'll have two people in custody before the end of the day. At least I hope so. Dahlberg has eluded us so far, but in a murder case we can count on a lot more help from other departments."

Pack thought of what Lawrence had just said. Yes, this was now a murder case!

Hibbing General Hospital was an imposing four-storied, brick structure which sprawled over an entire half of the city block between Third and Fourth Avenues East. On Second Floor West, Pack met the on-call physician. Doctor Luverne Johnsrud, a balding, sturdy man clad in a white jacket that looked too small for his sizable frame. The doctor was conversing with Nurse Rachel Elwell when Pack stepped up to the floor station desk. He looked up in surprise when the man introduced himself to the nurse and asked about JR Roberts. He recognized Kevin's son but hadn't seen him in months.

Pack explained that he was an old friend of the patient, a police officer, and had just returned to Hibbing from California. "I know this is out of the ordinary, but I'd really like to see JR tonight."

Johnsrud frowned. "I'm afraid I can't allow that right now. He's on sedatives. And he's been adamant about not seeing anybody— including his parents. Mr. Porter got him quite agitated earlier today. No, I'm sorry, Mr. Moran. If he were to awaken and find you...well, that might just be too traumatic."

Pack considered the physician's concern. A traumatic response was exactly what he hoped to accomplish. "Doctor, if I were to startle Mr. Roberts...would there be any adverse effects—I mean, might that set back his recovery in a significant way?"

"That's hard to say—but probably not." Johnsrud was more concerned with hospital policy and procedure. "Frankly, allowing you to visit would be more problematic for me than for my patient."

Pack went out on a limb, "What if we haven't had this conversation, Doctor? What if I had slipped by the desk without notice or authorization—while Nurse Elwell was at the filing cabinet and you...you were in the bathroom?"

Adjusting his spectacles on the bridge of his nose, Johnsrud smiled at the notion. If this young man were able to find out anything that might help resolve the Zench case—it would be worth the risk. "I'm sorry, Mr. Moran," he said loud enough for the nurse to hear. I just can't allow it. Now, if you will excuse me, I must relieve myself." He winked and glanced at Nurse Elwell.

Elwell turned toward the files, "I can't see anything, Doctor. If someone were to sneak past the desk and down the hall to Room 232—I'd never know."

Pack found the private room. JR was sleeping fitfully. Quietly, he pulled a chair to the bedside. With heavy eyelids, he waited and watched and pondered what to do. His thoughts were scattered at the moment. Being home, missing Maddie, and being back in the middle of what he had left behind—all became jumbled in his own fatigue. What would he say to JR when his old friend awoke. Should he be non-threatening? Could he be?

Pack glanced at the wall clock again. Counting minutes made them drag endlessly, only aggravating his fatigue. One o'clock passed. One-thirty. JR's snoring became deeply nasal, irritating. He wanted to nudge him...

Suddenly, JR's labored snoring stopped abruptly. In a mumbling voice, he seemed to be asking for water. Pack watched his arm slip out from under the blanket toward the pitcher on the portable bed stand. The tumbler was beyond his reach. In a clearer voice, "Nurse...Nurse Elwell...water."

Pack got up from his chair and walked around the bed toward the water pitcher. JR was still only half-awake. Without saying a word, he poured a glass of water and offered it toward the outreached hand. But, JR's arm went back under the covers and the snoring resumed.

Pack had waited long enough. Gently, he gripped the sleeping man's shoulder and shook him.

"Wha—?" JR's voice was groggy. "Nurse..."

Pack whispered, "You must be thirsty, JR. Here..." He handed the startled man the glass.

JR squinted in disbelief. "Pack?" He spilled half the water onto the bed sheets, tried to sit up.

"Hey, buddy—how you doing?"

"What the hell—?" JR, fully awake now, pushed his pillow behind his neck, shook his head.

"Just stopped by to say hello, JR. Heard you had a little accident."

"Wha time...? What you doin' here...?"

Pack sat on the end of the bed. "It's late—I mean, early. I kinda snuck up here when the nurse wasn't looking. How are you doing?"

"Why?" JR's face was a mask of fear—fear for his own safety. He wanted to scream for the nurse. Once again, Porter's warning brought an immediate paranoia. His thoughts were confused. Was Pack in cahoots with his cop friend, Rosnau. Was he going to accomplish what Tobin had failed to do? "Don't hurt me, Pack. Please. I'm not going to say anything. Tell Rosnau that. I'm not going to rat..." His voice became a weak sob. "Honest to God, Pack. You and Tobin don't have to be afraid of me telling anybody..."

Pack placed his hand on JR's leg. "I'm not here to hurt you, JR. I'm on your side for God's sake. You've got to believe that."

JR rubbed at his eyes. He had to believe someone. "Honest? You're not with Rosnau and Tobin? Tobin just tried to..."

"I know all about it. Just relax. You've got people on your side, JR. Me, and Porter, and Lawrence. Trust that."

JR leaned back into his pillow and looked at the ceiling for a long minute. He felt caught in the middle of this heinous Zench affair. He thoughts went back to his confrontation with Pack weeks ago. Maybe Pack knew something back then. As JR perceived his present circumstance, he considered two options. Protect Tobin and Dahlberg—and Rosnau, or tell Pack everything he knew. Talking to Pack put him on Porter's side—and, Porter had both warned him...and saved his life!

"You've got to trust me, JR," Pack repeated. "We're going to find out the truth about what happened to Jerry. You must realize that by now."

JR nodded, began to sniffle "...I didn't do it, Pack. I could never, never—"

Pack leaned forward so that his face was only inches away from that of the broken young man. "I'm willing to believe that. JR."

"I'm in big trouble—even if I didn't kill Jerry, aren't I?"

"Probably in some trouble—I won't bullshit you about that, JR. But, maybe it won't be so bad."

"God, I've really fucked up. Really! I know I'm going to do some time." His face was a mask of anguish and remorse. "I did something, Pack. I helped them...God, what a fuckin' mistake!"

"Let's start putting things right, JR. Tonight."

"I want to do that, Pack—'Put things right'." He cradled his face in one hand, leaned over his elbow, tried to smile. "Okay. I'll tell you everything I know...but, I can't be certain who did it—killed Jerry."

JR talked for nearly an hour. Going back to the banquet, and up to his conversation with Tobin two nights before. Pack asked questions and took notes, and asked JR to repeat certain relevant facts. JR's confession of his role in the overall murder scheme struck Pack as honest.

"So that's it. Like I said, that damn letter to Mr. Zench was all I was asked to do. I couldn't say no to a police officer who was investigating a disappearance." He paused for several moments, "...But I'd be lying if I told you I wasn't suspicious of Rosnau. And I could have refused to mail his letter. What I did was wrong to do—and I knew it, Pack."

"I believe that, JR."

~

Pack found the squad car Lawrence had reserved for him, drove through town with his window half open, smoked his last Pall Mall. It was after three in the morning and, although his body demanded rest, he didn't have the time to waste. His thoughts were swimming through the fog of sleep deprivation. At his house, a quick shower and shave failed to revive him. He brewed a pot of coffee and reviewed his notebook. On a blank page he did some event diagramming—linking named boxes (Tobin, Dahlberg, Roberts, Rosnau, and Wicklund) with incidents going back to the night of the banquet. From what JR had told him, Rosnau seemed to be the key—but, conjecture wasn't evidence. Still lots of work to do.

When he opened the door at his parent's Maple Hill house it was six. The aroma of fresh cinnamon rolls assailed his nostrils, brought a smile. Angie was taking the tray from the oven when her son stepped beside her and gave her a kiss on the cheek.

"I'd be less than honest if I said you look wonderful this morning, Patrick. Have you had any sleep?"

"Still shaking off the time zones change is all, Mom," he offered a half-truth. "Breakfast with my family should bring me back to the land of the living."

"Coffee's just finished perking," Kevin said from the table.

Bathrobed Steven entered the kitchen with a predictable plea, "Can I stay home from school today, Mom—spend some time with my brother?"

~

When Pack and Kevin entered police headquarters at five before eight, a line of officers were on hand to greet their colleague. Pack had always been among the most popular men on the force and his return to duty brought a variety of welcome-backs and well-wishes. "Damn good to have you back" was the consensus expression.

Inside Lawrence's office, Porter and the Chief were waiting. "It'll be just the four of us this morning, gentlemen," Lawrence said matter-of-factly. "Lieutenant Rosnau called in sick about twenty minutes ago."

A thermos of coffee and styrofoam cups rested on the table where the men sat.

Porter opened, "Anything happen at the hospital last night, Pack?"

Pack cleared his throat, "JR talked!" He went on to explain their conversation in meticulous detail. "Rosnau told JR to mail that bogus letter from Minneapolis. So, we've got that link...but, he couldn't say who wrote the letter."

Porter loosened his tie, "Rosnau could say that he had no idea about the contents—or, claim he was told to pass it along by someone else—Tobin, Wicklund...?" He scratched the thick hair above his ear, "It's something, but not enough."

Lawrence looked troubled. "We should talk to him, but I still find it hard to believe that Rosnau is behind the murder."

"He'll never admit to any involvement, Don—we both know that. He's too experienced and too clever. He knows how to cover his tracks. We've got to have more, a lot more. Proof beyond any doubt."

"I think we need to arrest Tobin, and the others, before we go after Rosnau. We don't have enough good information yet," Pack said. "We don't have any weapon, or even motive, and we haven't located the typewriter...too many loose ends. I'm positive that JR has told me everything he knows—but that only points us in the right direction."

"If we get into a 'his word against theirs scenario' we're not going very far. It's essential that we develop an air-tight case—even if it's built on circumstantial evidence," Kevin said.

Porter leaned over his elbows, "We need a confession. We've got to break down one of those guys. I'd like to start with Mr. Tobin."

"What about Wicklund? He's closer to Rosnau than any of the others—old hunting and fishing buddies," Lawrence said.

Porter seemed impatient. "Okay, lets go around the table. Each of you suggest who we start with—Tobin or Wicklund...or Rosnau. We can't include Dahlberg yet." He looked first toward Chief Lawrence, "Don, you can open."

"We've already got Tobin on suspicion of attempted homicide. We've got to bring him in now. But, I still think Wicklund is more likely to give us something."

"Tobin," Pack said. "But, I think the Chief has a point about Wicklund. If we put some heat around him—even the standard 'where where you on such and such a date' stuff. I think interrogating Wicklund is bound to stress his friend, Rosnau."

"We're all agreed, Damon. Tobin." Kevin said.

Porter nodded, turned to Lawrence. "Don, it's your call."

Lawrence sat up in his chair as if this really was his meeting. He spoke in a clear almost authoritative voice, "We'll bring in Tobin today. Wicklund after we've questioned Tobin."

~

Randy Tobin was awakened by Dahlberg's former girlfriend, Jeannie Pauletti, shortly before ten that same Thursday morning. "Someone's at the door," she whispered to the man stirring in her bed.

"Son-of-a-bitch!" was all Tobin could say.

The Hibbing and Virginia police were in surveillance mode since the day before. Tobin's Mercury had been parked on Chestnut Street in front of the Magic Bar overnight. Officers Moran from Hibbing and Lucarelli from Virginia entered the second floor apartment door.

"Get your clothes on, Randy. We're going back to Hibbing to talk about some things," Pack said as he dropped the warrant on the bed.

~

Approaching Havre, Montana, a quiet little town on US Highway 2, state patrolman John Frederick listened to the 'all-points bulletin' on his radio as he pulled into a small roadside diner. "I'll be damned!" he muttered to himself. Sitting in the lot was a car with Minnesota license plates matching the numbers he had just heard. A man named Dahlberg was wanted in connection with a murder investigation.

Inside, strung along the narrow counter, were five familiar local ranchers enjoying their bacon and eggs. Off to the end of the counter sat an unshaved stranger in a lightweight jacket.

"Who's Plymouth is that outside?" The Montana officer tossed out his redundant question. "The one with Minnesota plates?"

Dahlberg looked up from his pancakes. "Shit!" he mumbled under his breath.

The cop asked again, "Which of you guys is from Minnesota?"

Dahlberg stood from the counter. "It's my car, officer."

Frederick took the cuffs from his belt, "Your name Dahlberg?"

Dahlberg nodded without reply.

53/ THE PRIMARY SUSPECT

Agitated, Rosnau paced across the carpet in his basement office. This morning was the first time in two years he needed to call in sick. He was very sick—a psychological wreck! Porter was under his skin. The whereabouts of his smug nemesis had become an obsession. Since the discovery, every hour away from the office became consumed with surveillance work of his own.

The night before, from his pickup truck parked on Howard Street, Rosnau watched the lighted office of Kevin Moran. Porter was waiting for something—probably another meeting. It seemed like they—Porter, Lawrence, and Moran—were meeting all the time. It was nearly nine and bitterly cold outside. Scrapping the frost from his window and lighting a Camel, he watched the large frame of Porter through parted drapes. As expected, Lawrence's unmarked squad car pulled up to the Androy curb.

Shortly after nine, he saw Moran's Cadillac slip into the reserved parking place near the front entrance. Stepping out of the passenger door under the overhead lights was a man he hadn't seen in several weeks. Pack Moran was back in town.

Rosnau kicked at the small trash basket near his desk and cussed. All morning he had struggled with a plan. Tobin had fucked up his perfect Roberts frame...now he was desperate. Desperation was dangerous. What did Porter know? Fortunately, even if Roberts talked, he couldn't point any fingers. But, Tobin was another matter. How tough was the kid? How smart? Tobin ought to know he was looking at life in Stillwater.

But, Tobin was a string he couldn't pull right now—how to save his own ass was Rosnau's consuming concern.

Rosnau felt like his brain was burned from spinning his wheels in the dark for hours. What was going on downtown at headquarters, at the hospital, in Moran's office? By two o'clock his curiosity was driving him to the edge. Nobody had called him at home...maybe he'd check in.

"Lefty here..." He recognized officer Peloquin's voice. "What's going on down there today, Mike?" He left his inquiry open-ended. "I'm still under the weather, but I could stop by if there's anything important."

Peloquin knew that Tobin was being questioned and had just received word of Dahlberg's arrest. "Been damn busy here, Lefty. Maybe you otta come down. "Pack, and some Virginia cop arrested Randy Tobin this morning—found him shacking up with some broad over in Virginia."

Rosnau winced but didn't interrupt.

"Probably has something to do with what JR Roberts told Pack last night. Oh, I'm sure you heard that Pack's back. Great to see him again, and he looks super—suntan, you know, that California look—wearing his hair in a neat 'DA' kinda style."

The Roberts revelation was like a stab in the stomach. "Yeah, I'm sure he looks fine," Rosnau mumbled. "What's this about Roberts?"

"Pack spent the night with him at the hospital...snuck right in, I heard. Anyhow, seems like it was no accident and the suicide note was bogus."

Rosnau swallowed hard, "Anything else, Mike? Looks like this damn flu picked a helluva day to lay me low."

"Oh, yeah. Did I tell you about Dahlberg, Lefty. You know, Tobin's buddy? Anyhow, he got picked up, too. Somewhere out in

Montana this morning. Want me to look up the place—I've got it somewhere on my desk?"

"Not necessary. So, we've got both Tobin and Dahlberg?"

"Yep. Should have Dahlberg back here sometime on Saturday."

Rosnau had heard enough to bring bile from his stomach into his mouth. He had some heavy thinking to do and damn little time. "Any calls for me today, Mike?"

"Yeah. Your buddy Carl called, didn't want to leave a message. And, let me see...Jeeze, Lefty, I'm sorry as hell. Porter left a note on my desk to give you a call and update you on this Zench stuff. Want me to get him out of the meeting so you can talk to him?"

"Nah, he's probably pretty wrapped up. I'll get in touch with him later."

"You coming in tomorrow, Lieutenant?"

"Not unless I feel a helluva lot better, Mike. Tell the chief I called when you get a chance."

When Rosnau cradled the phone he noticed how badly his hand was shaking. And a throb was pounding in the back of his head. It was down to him and Wicklund now. He picked up the phone—Carl would be leaving for work in a few minutes.

Carl Wicklund didn't like the idea. "Call in sick? Shit, I was just heading out the door."

The edge in his voice was obvious. "Carl we've got to talk. I mean, got to talk! This whole fuckin' thing's comin' apart at the seams. If we don't figure something out...we're in deep shit, my friend." Rosnau gave a thumbnail sketch of what he'd just learned. "See what I mean?"

When Carl felt stress, his mind didn't process information well. What Rosnau had told him was deeply troubling, but he could not find any words to explain his fears. All he could think of was getting to the Androy on time. "Won't it look kinda suspicious? I mean both of us missing work on the same day?"

"Tell you what, Carl. Go to work. Then, after an hour or so, get sick. Make yourself vomit or something." His mind was racing now.

"Then go home, okay? Cut across your back yard to your brother-in-law's house down the block. Borrow his pickup truck—tell him your car's got a dead battery, some bullshit. Anything. But don't take your car. We'll meet out at the shack about seven. Got that, Carl? Make damn sure nobody is following you."

"Don't worry, Lefty. I'm not so fuckin' dumb, ya know. I can slip anybody hooze trying to follow me."

"Yeah, I know, Carl. Seven, then. Be damn careful."

~

Pack and Damon Porter were considering a plan of their own while meeting with Lawrence. The three men had interrogated Tobin for ninety minutes and come up with nothing. Tobin acknowledged that he knew who Rosnau was when confronted with some undeniable facts. "Sure we talk once and a while. So, what's the big fuckin' deal. We both curl, bowl, have a beer now and then—like everybody else in town."

Tobin was obstinate at times, defiant at others, and surprisingly clever throughout the questioning. He had an alibi for every critical date on Porter's list. And, his own version of what had happened on the previous Tuesday night. "We were goin' to go over to the Homer and tip a few more. JR was too drunk to drive and when I tried to take his keys away he got pissed as hell...tol me to get my ass outta his car. So, I left him there in the garage. He musta passed out. That's all I know. If he tol ya anything different—he's a fuckin' liar."

Dragging with fatigue, Pack skipped having lunch with his father and returned to the hospital to visit with JR. Tobin's version of the near-fatal night confused him.

"I told you, Pack, I passed out in my apartment. I can't remember much of anything after that." JR's eyes betrayed a fear that Pack hadn't seen the night before.

"That's not quite how I remember you explaining things, JR. Should I go back over my notes?"

"No. Maybe what Tobin told you was really what happened...I don't know for sure anymore."

"JR's waffling," Pack told the Chief. "He told me that he's not going to say anything more without his father's lawyer present. Said he was still groggy when we talked and can't remember the details."

Lawrence tried to shrug off his stress. The mention of lawyers always made him nervous. Especially Ian Roberts' lawyers. If his team didn't get a conviction—he might as well kiss his job goodbye. "So, what are we going to do from here? Tobin's saying the same thing—he wants a lawyer before he says another word. And, I'd expect Dahlberg will do the same."

Porter had been listening to the conversation from the open doorway without comment. An uncomfortable silence hung in the room.

"I think we all know who we've got to get next," Pack finally said.

Lawrence leaned back in his chair. As much as he dreaded the reality, his lieutenant had to be questioned. He knew that the reputation of his department would be gravely undermined, and his leadership brought into question, if the man officially in charge of the investigation was the primary murder suspect. This would be a nasty front-page story—not only in Hibbing, but throughout the state. The potential consequences were bad and worse...

Pack read the lines of worry on the face of his superior. Lawrence was in a tenuous political position. In fifteen minutes the Chief had a meeting with Police Commissioner, Lester Bowman. "What do you think, Don?" He had never used the boss's first name before, but considered it might be appropriate now. "Should we call in Rosnau tonight?"

Lawrence shrugged in apparent indecision. "Rosnau phoned the department just before you returned from the hospital, Pack. Asked Peloquin at the desk for an update on things here. So, he knows about Tobin and Dahlberg."

"That's got to shake him up. Did he say anything?"

"Said he talk to me later. Said his flu bug's bad and he won't be in tomorrow."

Pack nodded without surprise. Turned his gaze on Porter who had been unusually quiet while the two officers talked. "Damon?"

"Peloquin told me that Wicklund called for Rosnau this afternoon—that right, Don?"

Lawrence nodded, "Didn't leave a message, though." Looking at the wall clock, Lawrence stood up from his desk. "I've got another damn meeting at four, fellas. It's not going to be pleasant, I'm afraid. Bowman's going to want to know everything."

Porter offered the beleaguered officer and expression of empathy. "Maybe we can wait a bit longer before rocking Rosnau's boat, Don. Now that he knows about Tobin..." Porter closed his notebook and let his thought fade into the gloom of the gray December afternoon.

54/ WATCHING AND WONDERING

As City Hall's luminous tower clock swept inexorably toward five o'clock on this bitterly cold December Thursday afternoon:

Pack Moran watched the Rosnau house through a frosted windshield. His borrowed truck was parked inconspicuously behind two cars nearly a block away. He wondered what was going through Rosnau's thoughts as the noose tightened.

Damon Porter watched Carl Wicklund tend to customers as he paced behind the long Androy bar. He wondered if he could handle the burly ex-football legend if the two of them ever tangled in the street.

Donald Lawrence watched as Lester Bowman slammed the door behind him. He wondered if the Commissioner would press the matter of an early retirement to members of the board.

Randy Tobin watched a mouse nibble on some breadcrumbs from his lunchtime sandwich while sitting on his metal bunk. He wondered how many years of his life would be spent behind bars like these which now separated him from the world outside.

JR Roberts watched the news on the television screen in his private room. The Hibbing arrests in the Zench murder were the top local story. He wondered what good all of the lawyers in the world might do for him.

Kevin Moran watched Gary Zench review the payroll ledger spread across his office desktop. He wondered how this dear friend could focus his thoughts on anything but the pending funeral of his son.

Nora Zench watched Naomi pretending to be absorbed in her algebra homework while listening to the radio at the corner of her bedroom desk. She wondered if her daughter would be better off in a city school where she could make friends with other minority kids.

Maddie Loiselle watched the busy Sacramento traffic through her rear view mirror while driving home from the busy shopping center to her empty apartment. She wondered if Pack missed her half as much as she missed him on this sunny California afternoon.

Rick Bourgoyne watched Maury absently stir her cup of coffee across the kitchen table. He wondered what possessed this attractive and successful woman to love a homely and unambitious man like himself.

Dewey Bartz watched his friend Johnny Beck slide the mopping pail into the hallway closet on the first floor of the city hall building. He wondered if the two of them would have soup or chili for supper at the Sportsmen's.

~

Pack had borrowed the old pickup truck from his Grampa Tony's garage. The rusty Chevy, used for so many years by his grandfather to haul lumber to his garage workshop, held fond memories of that kindly man. The truck would be unrecognizable if, or when, he followed Rosnau. Every fiber in his body wanted sleep and it took total concentration to keep his eyes from closing. While he waited in the chill of the parked truck, he fondled the foil ring in his jacket pocket. There wasn't a minute without some thought of Maddie. It wouldn't be too much longer now. His every instinct told him that the vice was tightening on the killers.

Both his father and Rick were preparing to add some additional fuel to the fire this afternoon. Kevin was going to talk to Carl Wicklund about buying the hunting shack that the bartender owned along with Rosnau south of town. In that conversation, Kevin was going to comment that Porter had looked at the shack and really liked the improvements made inside. The ploy would let Wicklund know that Porter had been to the property and imply that he and Rosnau were being watched by the detective.

And Rick was going to put Rosnau on the spot.

Rosnau was too preoccupied with his torments to pay any heed to the pickup truck down the block. In a bag he had the shattered Adler typewriter and a ream of paper which he would dump in an alley garbage can before leaving town. He peered through the lightly falling snow for several minutes—looking for a squad car or any unusual activity. Nothing he saw raised any suspicions. Rick Bourgoyne had called less than an hour before and asked the lieutenant to appear on his 'Morning Show' the next day. "Everybody in Hibbing wants to know what's going on with the Zench investigation, and Mr. Lawrence told me that you're in charge of things at the department." Rosnau explained that he wouldn't be a very good interview. "I've been sick in bed all day, Rick." But reluctantly, he agreed to join the obnoxious radio personality for Monday's program. What else could he do? If he declined, that son-of-a-bitch would probably say so on the program and that wouldn't sound very good to those few thousand people who listened to Bourgoyne's shitty dialogue every day.

After leaving his house, and doing a round about the neighborhood to see if he was being tailed, Rosnau stopped by a liquor store for a bottle of brandy and package of cigarettes before heading south to the shack. Wicklund would be joining him there in another hour or so. By the end of the evening the two men would have their stories straight. Maybe the radio show was a blessing in disguise? Maybe he could spring their concocted story for all to hear on Monday. As the chief investigator, whatever he had to say would certainly ring credible. "Tobin and Dahlberg are in police custody right now," he might say. "We've got some solid reasons to believe that these two men are responsible for the Zench murder." He would be very careful. Over the weekend he would get his hands on a piece of burlap with the victim's blood, the castration knife, and a strand of rope to plant in the trunk of Tobin's Mercury.

Rosnau's plan was slowly evolving in his thoughts. He smiled to himself. Tomorrow, if Wicklund liked his plan, he'd find time to privately question JR Roberts. If he was persuasive enough, and JR scared enough, JR might back up his story. Rosnau would assure the youth that he was the one and only hope for JR to get out of this mess without doing any time. He was confident that he could intimidate the punk enough to believe that the three of them could pin Tobin and Dahlberg. "It's either my story or going to Stillwater, Roberts!" he would say.

Porter observed the stress on Wicklund's face as the bartender talked with his boss, Kevin Moran, over the polished oak bar nearly thirty feet away from the table where he sat sipping his Coke. After a few minutes, Kevin gestured a 'come over and join us' toward Porter's table.

Kevin's projected mood was almost jovial. 'Carl, I think you've met Damon, haven't you? He's been a guest at the Androy for weeks." He put his hand on the large shoulder of the barman to assure his attention. "Mr. Porter and I were talking about the Zench murder earlier today." For dramatics, Kevin had given the word murder an emphasis. "Not just a disappearance case anymore—it's clearly homicide in the first." This scenario had been rehearsed upstairs only minutes before. "Damon's been talking with JR Roberts at the hospital all afternoon," Kevin fabricated.

At the mention of Roberts' name, Porter noticed dilation in Wicklund's close-set blue eyes.

Kevin leaned over the bar in a manner that suggested confidentiality and spoke in hushed tones, "I was about to tell Carl that you were keeping close tabs on his buddy, Rosnau."

"We got someone watching right now—as we speak, Kevin."

Wicklund became noticeable agitated and tiny beads of sweat were evident along his crew cut hairline. Porter and Moran were making him damn nervous. Nervous enough to get sick—just as Rosnau had instructed. But, they were watching Rosnau right now. Shit!

"Did you say something, Carl?" Kevin asked.

Avoiding Kevin's eyes, Carl shook his head. "Thought we was talkin' about you wantin' to buy the shack, Mr. Moran?"

Porter jumped in. "Oh yes, your hunting shack with the pretty pastel walls. I've been out there a few times, Carl. Your wife pick out the paint?"

Wicklund forced a weak smile, "Ain't been out there since deer season. Don't know nothin' about paint. I think you guys got me a little bit confused. I think you better talk to Rosnau about the property."

"Oh, we will, Carl. Yes we will. But, we're talking to you right now. Anything you want to tell about the shack, or your friend...?" Porter paused significantly for effect, "...or...what might have happened to Jerry Zench?"

Kevin's hand was still resting on Wicklund's shoulder in a manner suggesting a friendly empathy. "You do look confused, Carl."

"And a little nervous. Do you sweat like this often," Porter chided.

"It's just a little warm in here tonight, Damon. That's all." Kevin glanced at his wristwatch—in a moment another player would be joining the conversation.

"Yes sir...Mr. Moran, damn warm if I say so myself. If'n you'll excuse me for a few minutes, I'll turn down the—"

"Well, isn't that Don Lawrence over there?" Porter feigned a look of surprise. "I'll call him over, let's buy Donald a drink. I'll bet he's off-duty right now."

If broken spirits could make any noise at all, Carl Wicklund would have been a thunderous din. His jaw sunk into his chest, his heart into his bowels. He knew what was going on—should have seen it from the start. Lawrence approached the bar with an envelope in his hand.

"What's that you've got there, Chief?" Porter asked.

Wicklund almost wanted to laugh at the clever setup and the predicament he was in. "I'll bet Chief Lawrence has some mail for me,"

Through town. Pack followed the pickup at a safe distance. When Rosnau passed the cemetery and turned south on Highway 73, he knew where his tailing would take him. Dropping well behind, he allowed two vehicles to slip between himself and Rosnau for the next several miles. Within half an hour, Rosnau turned left off the paved roadway and onto a county side road. Before turning, Pack cut his headlamps and slowed to a crawl. He knew the road well enough to find his way between the snow banks in the dark despite the flakes floating from the night sky.

Pack wondered if Lawrence had served the papers on Wicklund by now. In their late afternoon conference, the team had decided to make the two arrests tonight rather than wait for Tobin or Dahlberg to talk. He had a police radio on the seat beside him. The set, however, had been deliberately turned off. According to their plan, if Wicklund or anybody else confessed during Pack's surveillance, Lawrence would communicate with him using a code message containing the two words 'heart attack'. At that time, the undated Rosnau arrest warrant which the Chief had signed, would be executed. But, Pack was stretching his defined parameters by turning off the radio. Now he was out of range and Lawrence had no idea where he might be. Had he made a mistake in not reporting where he was going before leaving town? He feared that Rosnau might have a portable set along with him and would intercept any transmissions.

Pack wanted to do this himself. It was an ego thing and he knew it. However selfish and insubordinate, he had a compelling justification. Jerry Zench was his friend. And, it had to be just him and Rosnau! Hopefully, the others would understand. Hopefully, he would succeed.

Pack parked his borrowed truck across the entry road and noted the fresh tire tracks running across the unfastened strand of steel cable lying in the snow. He was warmly dressed and would approach the hunting shack by foot. Inside his hooded parka pocket was the warrant, in one rabbit-lined glove was his Smith and Wesson, in the other a flashlight.

The night sounds were an eerie reminder of the isolation of this remote place. The brisk north wind whisking through the naked trees brought a cracking sound to his ears, a distant owl hooted a nocturnal vigilance over his territory, and ice-crested snow crunched under his Sorrel boots. Pack's breath came in short, frosted wisps that hung like miniature clouds in the frigid winter air.

Pulling the hood over his head, Pack remembered the distance he must cover. Slow minutes passed. As he walked, carefully trying to keep his feet in the tire tracks, he focused his thoughts on exactly what he would do. Pack was certain that Rosnau would be armed. But, the cop would not be expecting anyone. Or, would he? Was it possible that Rosnau knew he would be followed out of town? Would Pack be walking into a trap? If so, this terrain was more familiar to Rosnau than to anybody else. Advantage Rosnau. He must expect that Rosnau knew—would be waiting for his pursuer. Pack's attention sharply focused—"Take your time...stay close to the cover of trees," he warned himself as he moved out of the tire tracks, closer to the roadside ditch. His eyes swept the shadows of mixed pine and aspen on both sides—the setting was perfect for a sniper to get a fatal bead on any intruder. Watching for any telltale footprints on either side of the narrow lane, his alert was heightened, his pace deliberately slowed.

Pack startled! His heart skipped a beat as he whipped his revolver in line with his right eye, dropped quickly to one knee and almost fired a quick defensive shot.

The snowshoe rabbit, only a few yards to his right, was equally frightened and leaped into the protective brush.

Pack caught his breath. His heart was somewhere in his throat. "That was close," he whispered to himself. Thank God he hadn't fired!

Twenty minutes later he smelled, then saw a waft of smoke spiraling into the frozen air. The dark outline of Rosnau's cabin and the pickup, parked outside the front door, were within fifty yards of where he stood. A dim glow shown from the shack's only window. Pack remembered the logistics from his site investigation the previous autumn. Stopping for a moment, he decided to follow the line of trees along the northern edge of the clearing surrounding the wooden structure. Without getting too close, he would locate himself in a position that allowed him to see inside the window. Crouching, he moved cautiously, never more than a few feet from the trees.

The window shade was drawn. In minutes he saw the silhouette pass. Although he had pictured this exact situation for the past hour, Pack was still uncertain of his next move. For the first time, he realized that his failure to arrange for backup support might have been a critical mistake. What did it really matter who apprehended this murderer? He considered a retreat. Rosnau wasn't likely to be going anywhere for a while. He could retrieve the radio, and drive—if necessary—as far as he needed to call in. No. He was already here. And, Rosnau might intercept any messages.

But, if Rosnau was already tuned in...?

Pack considered his two options for the hundredth time. He could go to the front door, holler for Rosnau to surrender, and hope the fugitive would allow himself to be arrested. He had the warrant and this approach was standard police procedure. But, Rosnau was like a rat in the corner right now—and, probably armed. The likelihood of his allowing Pack to take him was somewhere between zero and nil.

Or, on the assumption the suspect was armed and dangerous, Pack could justify a more aggressive approach. If he could get near enough to the window, he might be able to punch out the glass, tear away the shades, and freeze Rosnau with his aimed pistol. The inside space was small and exposing. He imagined—a bed, a sofa, table and chairs—not much in the way of cover. He'd order Rosnau to drop the firearm, if he had one, raise his arms, step backward to the door, and open it. In seconds, Pack could move from the window to the door. Three or four seconds. Critical seconds!

The window plan was risky. However, both options seemed equally perilous, even for a trained officer. He wished he had brought a rifle. From where he was hiding thirty feet away, a good shot through the window would certainly disable Rosnau.

Pack made his decision. He would go for the window. Rosnau had to be taken at gunpoint. From his exposed vantage position, Pack strained his eyes upon the frame of light on the north side of the cabin. Once again he saw Rosnau's silhouette pass across the inside space. Pack reconsidered his plan one last time. He was in the cold outside, Rosnau was warming inside. The longer he delayed—the greater his adversary's advantage. Cautiously, he started toward the window. One step, pause, then another...his focus on the window intent. A third step...

Crack! A dead tree branch snapped under his foot.

Pack froze in his tracks!

Rosnau paced across the cold room, rubbing his hands together, stopping occasionally near the front door of his Franklin Stove to absorb the slowly developing warmth. It would take some time before the shack would offer much comfort, and Rosnau was an impatient man. He stuffed two more birch logs into the stove. His police radio, next to his pistol on the table, squawked static. He shut it off, listened to the raging fire fill the air with its snapping sounds and rich aroma. The Coleman lamp on the table added a warm glow to the space.

It was after seven. Wicklund would be here soon. From time to time he put an ear to the door—listening for the sound of his friend's car. Rosnau's thoughts were in turmoil. Tobin, Dahlberg, Roberts—his vulnerable accessories. How stupid it had been to involve them. At times like this he wondered if he wouldn't have been much better off to have run—days ago, when he first began to feel the heat of Porter's probing. Now...now, it was too late! Now, there were few options remaining. He and Carl had to pull off a 'frame job'.

Unable to sit down and relax, Rosnau paced across the small space. Stopping by the fire to warm his hands, then past the draft from the window.

Crack!

He startled. The crack was not from the fire—it was outside. Carl?

Rosnau grabbed his pistol, raced to the front door, threw it open...there was no car!

As Pack's step came down on the dead branch, he dropped to his stomach instinctively. A second later, the door swung open. Rosnau was waving his revolver in his direction. Pack was too exposed. Quickly he got to his feet and zigzagged toward the trees. A shot whistled past his head—then a second. He felt the sting on the side of his neck, felt the warm blood ooze under the collar of his flannel shirt. Sighting a stump only two steps to his right, he dove face first into the snow.

Rosnau saw the shadowy form of an intruder less than twenty yards from the doorway. Instinctively he fired two quick rounds. Despite the darkness, Rosnau was an expert marksman and from this range even a random shot might be disabling—maybe even fatal. He saw the figure go down. His mind raced. The cabin was a death trap. He dashed out of doorway to the protection of his pickup. From here he could see the clearing and be safely protected from any return fire.

Through the open door, Rosnau saw the Coleman lamp glowing on the table inside. Background light was to his disadvantage. Taking quick aim, he fired a shot and sent the lamp spinning to the floor.

"Who's out there?" he called from behind the front fender of the truck.

The two-foot Norway pine stump offered only scant cover while Rosnau was situated behind a ton of steel. Even in the dark Pack could see the stain of his blood in the snow by his face. Only a graze.

Hearing Rosnau's question, Pack responded in a voice straining to convey all the confidence he could muster under dire circumstances—"Police officer. Here to take you in, Rosnau."

Rosnau recognized the voice. He had considered his fate coming down to this confrontation—Pack Moran and himself. A crooked smile creased his face. "Identify yourself, officer!"

Pack did not respond. He knew that Rosnau knew. Situations like this were more psychological than physical. He considered what to do next. He was pinned down. Any movement might be fatal. Maybe he could play the waiting game. Rosnau, Pack was certain, was not wearing outdoor winter clothing. Without a jacket or gloves, it wouldn't be long before the frigid temperature took its toll. The cold was his only advantage. Rosnau was no less than twelve feet from the cabin doorway. Pack's line of vision had the space covered. Under his breath he uttered a quick and unusual prayer..."God, please make this night as cold as it can possibly be."

Both men waited, contemplated what might give the slightest advantage.

Clearly, Rosnau's truck afforded him superior cover—equally critical, Pack's clothing gave him an edge in any protracted stalemate. It was a war between the innate patience of Pack Moran, and the natural hunter instinct of Rosnau.

Only the rustle of wind in trees broke the spell of winter's dark stillness.

Rosnau broke the silent chasm. "I know it's you, Moran."

Pack smiled inwardly. Rosnau had just lost the steely battle of patience. "Me and several others. In a few minutes you'll be surrounded by cops." Pack tried the timeworn ploy of cheap novels and Hollywood B movies.

Rosnau chuckled to himself.

Absolute stillness pounded in the ears of both men. It was a counting game now. Counting the minutes that might become hours—counting the rounds of ammunition spent. Pack was certain that Rosnau had the same standard issue Smith and Wesson he was carrying. Eight rounds in the clip—Rosnau had used two, Pack none.

Pack was beginning to feel a tinge of numbness in his hands and feet. How might he draw another round, or two? Another stump was only an arm's length away. One roll in the snow was all it would take. But, Rosnau was a crack shot and probably had a good bead on him already.

Rosnau knew how his adversary thought. Go ahead and use a round, Moran. I know you're counting.

Pack was not going to get shot or freeze to death with a full clip remaining in his pistol. He was loosing blood from his neck wound. He could not see Rosnau. Instead, he took aim at the front passenger tire. He fired...watched as the hood of the truck began to sink, an inch, two, three.

A flash, a crack. Rosnau's shot jerked Pack's head backwards, shearing a patch of fur from the hood of his parka. Two inches lower and the top of his head would be gone.

Rosnau, certain he'd hit Pack, strained his neck around the front bumper. He could see the stump...no movement. Wait, he commanded himself. Then, he noticed the eerie glow. His hunting shack was on fire!

Inside were his jacket, rifles, ammunition, radio...the keys to his truck.

Yet, the fire would excrete the warmth he needed to survive this cold. His fingers were numb, toes like cubes of ice. Without mobility, even the heat might not help. He could feel the tingle on his face and shoulders—but standing for a long period had seriously impaired the circulation to his extremities.

One of them would have to take a daring initiative. If Pack was wounded, he might do something foolish, desperate. If not, Pack could be patient. Maybe doing nothing was playing into Pack's hand.

Rosnau calculated the distance between his truck and the south side of his burning cabin. Fifteen feet, five long strides. But, his feet were numb and, if he slipped...? Rosnau had to wait a while longer—wait for Carl to show up. Where was he? Perhaps, in a few minutes, it would be two against one. Would Carl be armed? He would see Moran's car parked somewhere out along the road. But, might he turn back if he did? No. Carl was in too deep to run. And Carl was too gutsy to run from a fight. Carl was a trump card in this standoff.

But, Rosnau considered, he couldn't base his decisions on what may or may not happen. Right now was all that counted. He and Pack—one on one! I was a mind-teasing game. Again he wondered, had his last shot been true? He hadn't heard a sound in nearly five minutes.

The fire raged. The skin on Rosnau's face was feeling uncomfortably hot, yet his hands and feet tingled from frostbite. "Where's your back up, Moran?"

Pack fired a reckless shot at the voice. He heard the bullet ricochet harmlessly off the hood of the truck.

Rosnau responded with a shot directly at the flash from Pack's pistol.

When Rosnau's shot split a large chunk from the rotted stump, Pack made a quick roll to the larger one to his right. From his new location he gained much better cover and improved his sight line. With the fire's light, he could now see the base of the far tire behind the truck. He would not waste another shot. Rosnau, he was certain, was less patient than himself. He waited, keeping his pistol trained on the truck.

Rosnau's feet were becoming increasingly numb. Carelessly, he shifted his position in order to get some circulation going.

Spotting the movement, Pack got a glimpse of Rosnau's leg under the front bumper. Having maintained a careful bead on the narrow space under the truck, Pack fired.

A scream pierced the still night.

Rosnau dropped to his knee as the pain shot through his splintered ankle. His revolver slipped into the snow as he instinctively clutched at the wound with both hands. Tears welled in his eyes at the excruciating throb. What would he do now? He thought of bleeding to death as he saw the blood pool around his foot. Despite the seriousness of his wound and the obvious immobility it presented, this was still a mind game. He must not panic. Rosnau forced a sinister laugh, "Bad shot, Moran. Your hands getting a little cold? You only grazed my boot."

Pack was certain Rosnau had been hit. Somehow, he must take advantage of the situation. He kept his eyes peeled for any movement, while maintaining a relaxed tension on the trigger with his ungloved finger. Anticipating another movement, he waited...said nothing.

The warm blood caused Rosnau's fingers to tingle. He tucked his shoulders under the wheel well of the truck. His revolver lay buried in snow an arm's length away.

Pack saw the hand move, then the arm. Rosnau was reaching for something in the snow behind the truck.

Pack fired at the movement...missed!

Rosnau pulled his hand back at the sharp retort, saw the puff of snow only an inch from his wrist. "Son-of-a-bitch!" he cursed.

56/ "IT'S ALL OVER, ROSNAU!"

Down the narrow road, the beam of headlamps flickered through the trees. Rosnau had a sudden surge of hope. Carl! Surely his friend had seen Pack's vehicle, and would see the flames from the shack in moments. His friend would know that something had gone awry. Then, the beam disappeared. Yes! Carl would park his car and approach on foot.

Rosnau would wait a few minutes before warning Carl of Pack's position. Or...? A crazy thought flashed in his mind—so crazy it seemed almost logical! Why hadn't he thought of it before? Could he possibly pin the Zench murder on Wicklund? Wicklund wasn't the sharpest knife in the drawer. If...if, he were able to kill Wicklund before...?

Desperate, Rosnau shouted. "You saw the lights. That's the man you're looking for, Moran. Not me. It's Wicklund, I swear to God! I was going to arrest him myself...tonight. That's why I came out here to his hunting shack. Believe me. It's Wicklund—he's crazy, you know. Hates niggers."

Pack recognized bald fear in Rosnau's voice. Could it be Wicklund out there? Pack was certain that Lawrence and Porter had the barman in their custody by now. But, what if something went wrong? He'd let Rosnau do the talking and not give away his position. He kept his left flank in the corner of his eye.

"Carl!" Rosnau shouted.

Pack glanced down the road; saw a furtive movement in the bushes. Someone was in woods...maybe fifty yards away—on Pack's side of the property. The snapping of the fire distorted Pack's ability to hear much of anything behind or to his left. Adrenalin rushed through his veins. Now, he would have to try to keep an eye on Rosnau as well as try to spot whomever might be circling around his position. He shifted himself in the snow...from flat on his stomach to his right shoulder.

"It's Wicklund, Pack! Moving in behind you right now. I can see him. We've got to work together on this, Pack. Rosnau was using Moran's first name now. "Pack, we're both cops for crissakes. He's going to get you in the fuckin' back." Rosnau needed a diversion of only two seconds to retrieve his firearm from the snow. He reached out, felt his numb fingers close around the barrel of his revolver. His ploy had worked!

Rosnau felt a surge of confidence. Now there were two legitimate targets out there. He was going to save his ass at any cost—even if he had to kill two people.

Pack heard the rustle of branches. Instinctively, he rolled over onto his back. His shift in position left him more vulnerable—both from Rosnau and behind. His sudden movement drew an errant shot from Rosnau—his fifth! Rosnau had missed him by several feet this time. His adversary must be hurt. Still, Pack was pinned down. For the first time, he felt the cold grip of fear. He sensed the person in the woods was close to his position.

A rustle of branches! Just a few feet away. Pack trained his gun... Then, he heard his name whispered..."Pack!"

Buoyed with new hope, Pack called in Rosnau's direction. "Your so-called friend, Carl is here, Rosnau. He says you're bluffing—trying to frame him for something you did." Pack paused. He let a long moment pass. "Come on out, Rosnau. I know you're wounded. What do you say to the three of us talking this over? I'll put my gun away. It's still not too late get to the bottom of this."

Rosnau had the sinking feeling of black defeat. It wasn't Carl out there. Pack wasn't fooling—he had backup coming. Now what? Maybe he couldn't get Pack, but he'd never allow Pack to get him. Life in Stillwater prison was not an option for him. His decision was made. He had to run—albeit, on one good leg. If he could drag himself into the dark stand of trees behind him, and somehow crawl through the underbrush to one of two cars up the road, maybe? He had to try. Rosnau began to crawl away from the shield of the truck into the shadowed forest. His movement did not draw any fire.

Slowly, he negotiated the first ten yards—then ten more. Within minutes he was well beyond the blazing shack and at the edge of a familiar clearing. He knew the property much better than his pursuers. A hundred yards...his lower leg throbbed, but with newfound hope the pain was becoming more tolerable. His wide arc took him a quarter of a mile—every step brought him closer to the county road. He stopped periodically to listen. Maybe he wasn't being followed! Maybe his escape had gone unnoticed.

Pack had a gut feeling that Rosnau had moved from his position behind the truck unseen. But, if he was wrong? Pack took a risk—kicking out his leg to see if the sudden movement brought fire. It didn't. Pack got up on one knee for the first time since diving into the snow at Rosnau's first shots long minutes before. He waited, staring ahead.

Nothing happened. If Rosnau were still behind the truck, Pack would be dead by now. "I'm going after him," he called over his shoulder to the man lurking somewhere behind him. "Keep an eye on the road."

Pack darted to his left, away from the blaze, to where he could charge in behind the truck. Seconds later he saw the dark bloodstains in the snow and the crawling tracks leading into the woods. "Damn!" Pack cursed out loud. Hunching down, he pursued—Rosnau had the advantage of several minutes but couldn't get too far away with a wound as serious as the blood loss indicated.

When Rosnau saw Pack's frame through the trees he wanted to chance another shot. But his antagonist was out of range. The entry road was only yards away. He crawled behind a tree. When Pack got a little closer he would risk one of his remaining three rounds. The woods were dark and his hands had lost most of their feeling.

When Pack was stepping between two tall pines, Rosnau took quick aim, pulled the trigger. "Fuck!" he mumbled loud enough to hear. Another bad decision. But, he couldn't wait here. His last measure of strength was slipping away. Turning his back to Pack, he dragged headlong toward the road. It was a desperate attempt—but the only thing left to do.

From the edge of the road, Rosnau saw someone lurking behind the car. He straightened his arms in front to him, lined his eyes on the barrel sight, and forced every last ounce of concentration on his next shot. If it was Wicklund, and he held little hope that it might be, there might still be a glimmer of hope. If it were Porter, or any of Pack's friends—then, he'd have a final satisfaction of taking someone down before he killed himself. His next to the last shot must be true! With the crack from his revolver the form dropped out of his vision.

"I'm hit...Pack!"

Rosnau recognized the voice. His fate was sealed in that instant. Now, he would use his last bullet. The barrel was still hot, burning his lips as he put it into his mouth.

Pack lunged, pressing his full weight on top of Rosnau, pinning the man into the bank of snow. With a swing of his forearm he knocked the pistol away—but, not before a blaze shot from the barrel, past his ear. Rosnau struggled to wrest Pack's pistol from his hand but the younger man was too strong. "It's all over, Rosnau," Pack shouted in hoarse voice. "You're under arrest for the murder of Jerry Zench."

Their eyes locked for an instant. Then, Rosnau gave Pack a twisted smile. The vanquished cop blinked hard on his tears. "All over? That's what you might think, Moran. I'll decide when it's all over—nobody else."

57/ A MORAN FAMILY CHRISTMAS

Without incident, Carl Wicklund allowed Chief Lawrence to take him in. Within an hour of his arrest, the brawny ex-football star related the sordid details of the Zench castration and lynching to Damon Porter. The conspiracy of four was much as the detective had imagined.

Unable to reach Pack on the police radio, Kevin left the Androy lounge to find his son. As he drove past the Rosnau house, he noticed tire prints in the driveway. Pack was not in his assigned surveillance position down the street. Without a second thought, he headed south on Highway 73. Within minutes, the radio he had borrowed from Lawrence came on. Wicklund's confession confirmed Kevin's instinct.

Half an hour later, Kevin spotted the old pickup truck blocking Rosnau's road. Taking the unlocked truck out of gear, he used his Cadillac to push the vehicle off to the side. Near the end of the narrow road, he saw the burning cabin, parked his car, and approached. Kevin spotted Rosnau hiding behind his truck and made an immediate assumption as to where Pack might be located.

~

"Dad...are you okay?" Pack hollered. Dragging the subdued suspect out of the ditch and cuffing him to the Cadillac door, he raced around the back of the car. Pack saw his father lying in the snow holding his right shoulder.

"I'm going to be fine, Pack," Kevin grimaced in pain. "I don't think it got the bone."

Pack huddled over his father, "You're bleeding pretty badly, Dad—I've got to call for an ambulance. I've got a radio in Grampa's truck." Offering Kevin his revolver, he said, "Keep an eye on Rosnau—I'll be back in a minute."

Kevin smiled, "Keep it yourself. Help's on the way, Pack. I had a radio along, too. Lawrence knows where to find us. He and Porter will be here any minute."

Kevin had no more than uttered his assurance when the headlamps of two police vehicles came into sight.

~

Christmas Eve was idyllic. Soft flakes of snow danced in the unseasonably mild air creating a fresh, white blanket across the Northland. Blessed Sacrament Church was filled to capacity for the traditional Midnight Mass. The concluding hymn, Silent Night, had never seemed more appropriate than it did on that Tuesday in Hibbing, Minnesota.

Maddie and Pack sat together near the front of the spacious church. Seated on either side of the couple, and occupying the entire long pew were Kevin and Angela Moran, Rick Bourgoyne and Maury Loiselle, Maribec and Steven Moran, Becca and Marco Zoretek. After Mass, all of them would spend the night on Maple Hill and celebrate Christmas together.

Perhaps more than anybody else, Pack was excited about the planned opening of gifts the following morning. He had spent two hours wrapping his gift for Maddie. The challenging project began with the diamond engagement ring and a package of Spearmint gum. With his mother's help, he made the ring fit into the thin foil-lined package by cutting five sticks of gum in half and refilling the Wrigley's tube. He began with a small box, then a larger one...and, another. When he was finished there were nine boxes.

"That's cruel, Patrick!" Angie scolded her son teasingly. "That poor girl will be totally stressed by the time she gets to her ring." Then she laughed out loud. 'But, it's going to be fun."

And it was fun! Each of them, in their own way, enjoyed that morning more than any other they had shared in months. At Maddie's insistence (after finally unwrapping her ring), Pack got down on one knee and reenacted his earlier proposal. His performance delighted everyone.

Maddie's gift to her beloved was equally creative and captivating. Tucked inside a lovely Donegal hand-knit Irish sweater was an envelope. Maddie had known for months that Pack was not a Californian at heart. Their time apart had been hard on both of them. When Pack opened the envelope he had to swallow hard on the emotions the papers evoked. Attached to a note that read 'You warm my heart more than all the sunshine in California' was the lease termination document.

That afternoon Pack and Maddie announced their plans for a June wedding. The surprise proved doubly amusing. Maddie and her mother had talked secretly about wedding plans. While seated about the Moran Christmas tree, Maury took Rick's hand and gave him a kiss. "This is not the way it's supposed to be," she announced. "But my man is not nearly the romantic that Patrick has proven himself to be." Getting down on one knee, Maury popped her question, "Will you take me to be your wife, Rick...and marry me in June...in the same ceremony as my lovely daughter?"

The verbose 'Radio Man' was speechless.

Two weddings were placed on everybody's calendar for June of 1957.

58/ 1957 AND BEYOND

The rivers of our lives move in an unabated course across the landscape, finding occasional pools of calm water, and rushes of white-capped current, toward an ultimate conclusion. A wise man once observed that we cannot see the same river from one moment to the next. Time changes everything under the heavens.

The next year, and those immediately following, would deliver a great measure of happiness and fulfillment for most of those at the Christmas table in the Maple Hill dining room that day. Most, but not all.

Pack would be promoted to Lieutenant in January. With the retirement of Don Lawrence two years later, Patrick Anthony Claude Moran would become the youngest Police Chief in the history of the Hibbing force.

Madeline Loiselle Moran would resume her teaching duties at the Cobb Cook Elementary School under a new Principal in September. Before the completion of her school term, however, Maddie would be granted a maternity leave of absence.

Kevin Moran would sell his beloved Androy Hotel to an investment consortium headed by local businessman, Dutch Webber, and begin his semi-retirement at fifty. His life would remain full with *pro bono* legal work and promotion of the Hibbing Community Foundation. And, each year he would award a full-ride scholarship to a deserving student-athlete in memory of Jerry Zench.

Angela Zoretek Moran would win the 1957 National Humanities Board award for her painting titled 'Snowbound'. The following year she would host an art exposition in Hibbing. The event would bring acclaimed art critics from as far away as Boston and San Francisco.

Steven Moran would be named to the 'All Minnesota' state band in his senior year-1959. His high school friend, Bobby, would leave Hibbing after graduation, change his name, and gain a significant reputation for himself in the music business.

Maureen Loiselle Bourgoyne would take over her father's vast radio network requiring her to spend several days each week in Duluth. Two years later, she would be featured on the cover of *Twin Cities Magazine's* 'Minnesota's Most Successful Women'.

Sean McDougal would finally accomplish his 'Ninth Step' of the AA program while attending the marriage of his former wife in June. And, he would remain sober for the remaining thirty-two years of his life.

Damon Porter would move from Minneapolis to the Iron Range following the death of his wife from cancer. The detective would become the Security Director for the Erie taconite plant in Hoyt Lakes. Five years later he would retire and move permanently to Hibbing and become Lester Bowman's replacement on the Police Commission.

Deward Bartz would be given the first full-time, permanent job in his life. 'Sweep' would clear off tables and wash dishes and help the Sportsmen's Cafe waitresses for the next eighteen years.

~

The new year would not be without tragedy and heartbreak for others.

Gary and Nora Zench would sell their Hibbing home and move to St. Paul where Gary would become the assistant manager at the prestigious Lowrey Hotel. Daughter Naomi, however, would not flourish in the heterogeneous urban environment and would drop out of Humbolt High School during her senior year.

Rick Bourgoyne would quit his job at KHNG after a serious dispute with his new wife and take a News Director position with a St. Cloud radio station. His divorce from Maury would become finalized shortly before Christmas two years later.

Becca Kaner Zoretek would miss the June weddings. In May, the lovely and beloved doctor, would walk the staircase and join her husband Tony in heaven.

Marco Zoretek, having suffered his secret since junior high school, would resign his teaching position at Hibbing High School. His remaining years would be shared with Roland, a concert pianist with the St. Paul Symphony Orchestra.

Maribec Moran would limp through life. A freakish fall from a tree limb occurred while focusing her camera upon a nest of black-capped chickadees behind her brother's house. Metal pins would hold her compound-fractured left leg together in three places.

~

Leonard Rosnau would hang himself in a Hibbing jail cell just down the hallway from the office he had occupied for so many years. His defiant boast to Pack on that frigid December night..."I'll decide when it's all over!" was, indeed, his final misguided decision.

Randy Tobin, Dave Dahlberg, and Carl Wicklund would be given life sentences at the Stillwater State Penitentiary. Each man would be paroled seventeen years later and move on to other places to live.

JR Roberts would be the primary prosecution witness during the '57 trials, and would receive a five-year suspended sentence. In years to come, the contrite young lab technician would prove himself to be a worthy citizen in his native community.

And, the *hurt* of Hibbing's racial homicide would heal in time. As with all human tragedies, memories fade with the advent of other more compelling and timely events. On the fourth anniversary of the Jerry Zench disappearance, however, the Hibbing City Council proclaimed a day in the young man's honor and had a bronze plaque embedded on the concrete stairway of Bennett Park's grandstand. The tribute read simply:

> *We will never forget. In memory of an athlete: Jerry Zench (1931-1956).*

EPILOGUE

I left Hibbing two days following Leonard Rosnau's arrest. Before departing my Androy Hotel 'home away from home' of the past four months, I made a final visit to Kevin Moran's office down the corridor. I wanted to thank him for his gracious hospitality. His wounded arm was in a sling and he winced whenever he moved, but as usual, Kevin appeared to be in the best of spirits. "Be sure to send me an autographed copy of your book when you're finished," he said with an engaging smile.

While we were talking, Pack entered the room. Although we had casually met casually a few times before, I could not say that I had come to know the young police officer very well. As I regarded his bandaged neck, I wondered how I might portray him in this story. Oddly, the two words that came most easily to mind were *enigmatic* and *remote*. Neither word seemed to contain the stuff most befitting a story's protagonist.

I extended my sincere congratulations. "What you did was very courageous. The community owes you a debt of gratitude."

Pack's expression suggested a smile about to happen. It didn't. Instead, his intelligent eyes moved from mine to the paper-stuffed leather case resting in my lap. *"There are no heroes in that story,"* he said in a flat tone. "Only losers. Everybody lost something precious over these past few months."

I nodded at the profundity of his insight. Perhaps, that feeling of loss was the key I had been searching for while contemplating this story's epilogue.

Pack looked beyond his father and me toward the window. Gazing into the gray December afternoon beyond the glass for a long and deeply reflective moment he said nothing. Returning his eyes to me he finally found the few words to express what he most wanted me to understand, "Like so many others...I lost a measure of hope and my sense of innocence."

Those last words have haunted the telling of this story.